Praise for
CHEYEN...

WICK...

"Blistering sex and riveti...
continues building toward its climax."
—*Romantic Times BOOKreviews* (4 stars)

"Has an even blend of action and romance, and most of the characters from earlier novels make an appearance. An exciting paranormal tale; don't miss it."
—*Romance Reviews Today*

"Cheyenne McCray shows the best work between good and evil in *Wicked Magic*. The characters are molded perfectly...sure to delight and captivate with each turn of the page." —*Night Owl Romance*

"A sinfully engaging read." —*A Romance Review*

SEDUCED BY MAGIC

"Blistering passion and erotic sensuality are major McCray hallmarks, in addition to a deft and exciting storyline. This magical series continues to develop its increasing cast of characters and complex plotline; the result is erotic paranormal romance liberally laced with adventure and thrills."
—*Romantic Times BOOKreviews* (4½ stars Top Pick)

"The slices of humor, the glimpses of the characters' world through fantastic descriptions, not to mention fascinating characters, landed this book on . . . [the] keeper shelf."
—*Romance Divas*

"Witches, drool-worthy warriors, and hot passion that will have readers reaching for a cool drink. Cheyenne McCray has created a fantastic and magical world where both the hero and heroine are strong and are willing to fight the darkness that threatens their worlds." —*A Romance Review*

MORE . . .

FORBIDDEN MAGIC

"McCray will thrill and entrance you!"
—Sabrina Jeffries, *New York Times* bestselling author

"A yummy hot-fudge sundae of a book!"
—MaryJanice Davidson, *New York Times* bestselling author

"Wildly erotic and dangerously sensual, this explosive para-normal thriller sizzles. McCray erupts on the scene with one of the sexiest stories of the year. Her darkly dramatic world is one readers won't mind visiting again . . . McCray knows how to make a reader sweat—either from spine-tingling suspense or soul-singeing sex. . . ."
—*Romantic Times BOOKreviews*

"McCray's paranormal masterpiece is not for the fainthearted. The battle between good and evil is brought to the reader in vivid and riveting detail to the point where the reader is drawn into the pages of this bewitching and seductive fantasy that delivers plenty of action-packed sequences and arousing love scenes."
—*Rendezvous*

"*Forbidden Magic* is a spellbinding, sexy, superbly written dark fantasy. I couldn't put it down, and you won't want to either . . . Longtime fans and newbies alike will be enchanted and swept away by this enduring tale of courage, love, passion, and magic."
—*A Romance Review*

"If one were going to make a comparison to Cheyenne McCray with another writer of the supernatural/sensuality genre, it would have to be Laurell K. Hamilton . . . *Forbidden Magic* definitely puts McCray in the same league as Hamilton. The book is a very sexy work . . ."
—*Shelf Life*

"Cheyenne McCray's *Forbidden Magic* is an intoxicating blend of luscious eroticism and spine-tingling action that will have you squirming on the edge of your seat."
—Angela Knight, *USA Today* bestselling author

DARK MAGIC

Cheyenne McCray

St. Martin's Paperbacks

DARK MAGIC

Copyright © 2008 by Cheyenne McCray.
Excerpt from *Zack* copyright © 2008 by Cheyenne McCray.

For information address St. Martin's Press, 175 Fifth Avenue, New York, NY 10010.

ISBN: 0-312-94959-6
EAN: 978-0-312-94959-4

Printed in the United States of America

St. Martin's Paperbacks edition / November 2008

St. Martin's Paperbacks are published by St. Martin's Press, 175 Fifth Avenue, New York, NY 10010.

10 9 8 7 6 5 4 3 2 1

To Kathryn Falk

ACKNOWLEDGMENTS

I want to thank the most important people of all—my readers. You are the reason I write and I hope you find escape and enjoyment in my books.

I can't thank Anna Windsor enough for all things Magic and for being with me from the very beginning. Anna, you *are* magic.

Patrice Michelle, Tee O'Fallon, and Cassie Ryan, much thanks goes to all of you for joining me along the way.

My editor, Monique Patterson, and my agent, Nancy Yost—an author couldn't be more fortunate than to have you both in her cheering section.

Thank you, Lorelei Kerns, for your support of Brenda Novak's 4th annual online Auction for Diabetes Research.

Much appreciation to the pair of Marines who spoke with me, taught me what a high-and-tight is, and, more importantly, provided great information—which of course I twisted and twisted to use in my own wicked way. Forgive me, guys, but a girl's gotta have some fun.

Many thanks to Dewayne Tully, the civilian component of the San Francisco Police Department Office of Public Affairs. I appreciate your help in finding information I needed. Told you I would blow San Francisco all to hell.

Special thanks to Justin Watt of justinsomnia.org who gave me a little extra advice on San Francisco when I tracked him down on the Internet. And surprisingly didn't run when I started telling him about Demons, warrior Fae, and modern-day witches in his city.

To my parents who taught me right from wrong, and about quality—doing the best in everything we do. Never shortchanging the customer, or in my case the reader.

Thank you to everyone in my adopted city of San Francisco for putting up with my very liberal use of "artistic license." I may have destroyed your city in my books, but I did it with love.

DARK
MAGIC

CHAPTER ONE

San Francisco

JAKE MACGREGOR TIGHTENED his grip on his Glock as he eased through the shadows, the midnight broken only in patches where moonlight squeezed its way through the clouds. The closest streetlight's glow didn't touch him.

Moist air chilled his face and his hands, but adrenaline and his raid suit kept the rest of his body warm.

Members of his reconnaissance team fanned out beside him in front of homes on each side of their target, slipping by cars parked in front of the garage-level entrances on Kearny. Several officers from the Paranormal Special Forces that he captained comprised half his team. The other half—

Magical beings.

The PSF officers, gray magic D'Anu witches, D'Danann warriors, and Dark Elves now called themselves the Unified Otherworlds Alliance. Or just the Alliance.

The only witch missing was Cassia, who had vanished to Otherworld after the last big battle against the dark magic and chaos threatening San Francisco. His gut tightened every time he thought of Cassia. She was such a mystery . . . a mystery he wanted to solve.

Jake blinked. Why was he thinking about her now? He wasn't even sure he could trust the witch after her past deceptions.

Six D'Danann warriors had unfurled their powerful wings to circle the target home, and the fire escape in the back, from above. Once they took to the sky, the warriors became invisible to human sight, including Jake's. The rest of the Alliance flanked him on the ground or guarded the back door and the gate to the minuscule alleyway.

A sense of déjà vu swept over Jake as they crept up to the historic home. Months ago, he'd been on a similar mission, preparing to raid an older apartment building. At that time, the only magical being who had accompanied the PSF had been Silver Ashcroft, one of the D'Anu witches.

That was the night Jake first realized someone was practicing dark magic at a whole new level in his city. That night everything changed—and not for the better.

This time they prepared to enter a well-kept home in a nice San Francisco neighborhood near Union and Kearny. With space at a premium in the densely populated but relatively small city, the house was like most homes—squeezed between similar three-story houses.

The houses were packed along a typical steep incline, which wasn't exactly optimum for a raid. But at the same time it would be difficult for anyone inside to escape—the only ways out were the front door and the three levels of upstairs windows. What could hardly be deemed an alleyway in the back had a locked gate for an exit—the only possible rear egress.

On this stretch of the street, residents normally kept the sidewalks and the fronts of their homes in good condition, and any bushes and trees well maintained. In light of the hell the city had been through recently, Jake wasn't surprised the neighborhood didn't look so perfect anymore.

All those months ago, they had been searching for Darkwolf at that apartment building. They were searching for him now, too.

Years ago, white witch Kevin Richards had picked up Balor's stone eye on the shores of Ireland. From that moment on, the man who was now known as Darkwolf had become a dark god's pawn.

Only now, the warlock had obtained the dark god's magic and his goddess wife's magic, powers so great that it was nearly incomprehensible. With the magic of two gods, how powerful had Darkwolf become?

That's what they had to find out.

A flash of lightning followed by a rumble of thunder

rolled through what had been a slightly foggy but cloudless night. Wind kicked up, bringing with it the sudden smell of rain.

And something else. Something musty and bitter. Like wet laundry soured from sitting too long.

Jake glanced at the sky. The clouds swirled overhead—almost as if a funnel cloud were gathering. Which was impossible considering they were in San Francisco.

Something was off, not right about that storm, and his skin grew tight.

Just like it had in that small Middle Eastern village . . .

Maybe he was overreacting. He turned his attention back to the house and the mission. Soft yellow light spilled through uncovered windows on the first floor above the garage. Jake crept up the three steps to the entrance and peered through the vertical six-inch-wide pane to the right of the door. No curtain obstructed his view.

He frowned. No movement, no activity. And if this was Darkwolf's base of operations, why would the home be lit up and the windows not covered?

Keeping his voice low, Jake spoke into the microphone attached to his raid suit. "Everyone in position?"

He counted the number of affirmatives as they came into his earpiece. Only eighteen of his men and women answered, which didn't include the magical beings. Mentally he ran through the voices of his team. Marks and Taylor hadn't answered.

Jake called to the two PSF officers who were part of the team covering the rear of the house. "Marks. Taylor. Are you in position?"

No response.

"Negative visual contact," came Ricker's low tone.

A prickling sensation rolled up Jake's spine as gut instinct took hold.

Either their information was wrong—or someone had leaked their plans.

He paused one moment as the realization sunk in.

This wasn't the warlock's headquarters.

It's a trap.

The slaughter of the men in his US Marine Force Recon squad outside that Afghani village flashed through his mind. He'd led them into a dark-magic trap, something he'd never been able to forgive himself for.

No fucking way. He couldn't let it happen again.

"Get your asses out of here," Jake growled in his microphone as he scanned the street behind him. "It's a setup!"

He turned and scanned the area. No sign of an attack. No one on the street but the Alliance.

But it wasn't right. Something wasn't right.

His heart nearly exploded when he caught the smell of dark magic. Evil magic.

Not again. Not again. Not again.

Another flash of lightning cracked the sky as Jake moved away from the house. Thunder growled, so loud it seemed to surround them. Wind blasted them and rain rushed down in a sudden torrent.

Water funnels spouted from the rain.

Water funnels.

A mass of them.

They barreled straight for the house and the members of his team.

"Oh, my goddess," one of the witches shouted—Rhiannon. "They're going to attack. Those funnels or whatever's inside them."

"Fuck!" someone cried out, followed by an "Oh, shit," from another voice, and then more shouts and screams.

Jake's pulse jacked as one of the funnels reached him. It came to an abrupt stop. Water hit Jake in the face with a hard slap. A naked being appeared—from inside the funnel. Some kind of creature that changed from water into the form of a man.

Water that had surrounded the being sprayed in all directions, then splashed to the concrete with the rest of the rain.

The naked being drove a dagger toward Jake's throat, above his Kevlar vest.

Jake ducked to the side but the blade sliced his right biceps, below his Marine tattoo, close to a healing wound. Pain seared his arm.

At the same time the assailant struck, Jake had raised his Glock and aimed for one of the two points usually good to bring down a supernatural asshole—the heart.

The creature twisted into a funnel before Jake got off a shot. He sighted a spot where the thing's head used to be, but he didn't see so much as the outline of a skull.

What the—

He didn't have time to think as the funnel moved around him in a circle. Jake's pulse raced as wind and rain continued to pummel him. It was difficult to maintain firm footing on the street's steep incline.

His officers, witches, and other magical beings fought the funnel-creatures. Witch-magic blazed and sparked, illuminating the night in eerie flashes. Gunshots cut the air along with screams, shouts, battle cries.

Jake crouched just in time when the funnel came to a stop and water splashed him hard. The naked being struck out again with its dagger. Moonlight gleamed off an almost crystal-like blade as it missed Jake.

He squeezed the Glock's trigger, his shot ringing through the night, mingling with all of the other sounds.

His bullet hit home. The being dropped—and solidified into the form of a flesh-and-blood male. Red blossomed above his heart, over a large tattoo on his chest, the pounding rain turning the blood pink.

A flicker of surprise sparked in Jake. These assholes didn't turn to silt and vanish like all of the other screwed-up things the Alliance had been fighting the past several months.

It had only taken a second for the man to go down. Jake's skin crawled and he whirled to see two more water funnels barreling down on him.

The funnels stopped simultaneously and two hard splashes hit Jake, almost knocking him on his ass. He swept out his leg, bringing one creature down as he shot at the other. The second being had already twisted into a funnel and the bullet went straight through the water.

Jake jerked his gun back to the being he had downed. It was getting to its feet, but Jake shot the creature in the heart before it could transform. The other funnel stopped behind Jake.

Instinctively, Jake dropped and rolled onto his back while keeping his gun clear. He shot the man point-blank in his forehead, blowing the back of his head off.

In one glance, Jake saw the devastation to his team and some of the funnel-beings—or whatever they were—as the battle raged. Dead bodies littered the street while gunshots still echoed. The night lit up with glittering magic as the witches attempted to use their magic ropes and spellfire. They protected themselves with spellshields when they failed.

Heads of funnel-beings rolled down the street. Invisible Fae warriors swung swords to decapitate the creatures when a funnel stopped.

Rain poured and wind blasted them as another funnel barreled Jake's way.

The funnel-beings seemed to be feeding off the water and the wind to transform into spouts. What would happen if they were cut off from their source of power?

As Jake prepared for the next funnel, he shouted at the witch closest to him. "Copper. Throw a spellshield around one of the funnels. Trap it!"

Without looking at Jake, Copper flung her glittering magic around one of the funnels headed toward her. Immediately it came to a stop and a *man* collapsed to the ground, contained by the shield.

Copper called out to the other witches, but Jake barely heard her voice through the wind, rain, and thunder as a funnel reached him. Jake feinted to his left as the being became visible, then Jake dogged to the right and shot the bastard in the chest.

The storm ceased as suddenly as it had started.

Dark clouds rolled away, allowing moonlight to spill from the sky.

Jake's breath came hard and heavy as he swung his gaze

around to see three naked men—beings—contained by witch spellshields while bodies of other men littered the street and sidewalk. No more water funnels.

A sick feeling clenched his gut as he saw how many of his officers were down. A quick count told him eleven of his PSF team remained on their feet, not counting the five in the back if they'd been attacked.

Shit. He couldn't see all of the witches. He jogged up to Copper as he scanned the street. "The D'Anu," he said as he reached her. "I don't see Alyssa or Mackenzie."

"There's Alyssa." Copper pointed toward a dark corner of the street. They both glanced up and down the street. "Mackenzie—there she is," Copper said with obvious relief at the same time Jake caught sight of her near King Garran.

"Thank God," Jake said as he nodded to Copper. The seven witches were still alive, although it looked like Mackenzie and Rhiannon were bleeding some. Thank God, too, that Cassia wasn't here and hurt.

All six D'Danann warriors materialized on the ground, gripping their swords as they studied the massacre with grim expressions. Garran, the king of the Dark Elves—the Drow—moved beside the D'Danann with two of his men. An equally fierce look hardened the king's battle-worn features.

Lieutenant Fredrickson hurried around from the back and stopped at the corner. "Got three officers down in the alley, including Marks and Taylor," Fredrickson yelled from his position.

"Fuck!" Jake glanced at one of their SWAT trucks. "Lyons," he shouted to one of the med techs. "Follow Fredrickson with your kit."

Fury coursing through him, Jake kicked the body of a dead funnel-being next to him.

He stared at the creature for a moment. They definitely looked human when dead. Each of the beings had a tattoo on its chest, over its heart. If Jake wasn't mistaken it was an inverted pentagram. The sign of a dark warlock.

One of the downed officers close to him groaned and

moved. Jake ran to her, his boots slapping the wet asphalt. Lieutenant Landers gave another groan and tried to get up, but Jake gently pushed down on her shoulder.

"Don't move, Landers," he ordered in a gruff voice.

Blood seeped from a gash across her throat. A quick inspection told him the cut hadn't been deep enough to kill her as long as they got her medical attention ASAP. He pressed his hand to the wound as he glanced at one of his officers who already had out pads and gauze from a med kit that had been in the back of one of their raid vehicles.

Landers's blood coated Jake's hand as he wrapped the cotton and gauze around her throat, just snugly enough to stem the flow. "Kicked some ass, didn't we?" Jake said as he secured the gauze, and she gave a faint smile.

He kept talking to her, keeping her awake until the paramedics arrived. Sirens wailed and Jake knew the paramedics and law enforcement would be there within two minutes.

His gaze roved the scene again. His gut churned and anger burned his chest at the sight of all of his injured and murdered officers. The seven witches continued to imprison the three men they'd captured within separate spellshields.

Fury burned through Jake's mind, so fierce, so intense, that he wanted to eliminate the beings within those shields.

He shook his head, trying to throw the violent thoughts from his mind. He was an officer of the law. The beings were no longer armed or able to fight. They would be taken into custody, questioned, and imprisoned. With the entire city in chaos due to the current state of affairs—and the loss of most of the heads of state and local military, government, and law enforcement—these funnel-things certainly weren't going anywhere for a long time.

"Get them into the truck," Jake shouted to the witches and Otherworld warriors. "Before the cavalry arrives."

Last thing he needed was to argue with SFPD over who had jurisdiction and explain that this was a paranormal crime before they could take the prisoners away. The Alliance would incarcerate the beings in special cells back at HQ. Contain-ments bound by powerful spells that wouldn't allow those inside to use their own magic.

The SWAT truck drove away with the witches and their prisoners as flashing blue and red lights crested the hill. Sirens silenced as the vehicles pulled up to the scene.

Jake glanced at the spot where the Drow and the D'Danann warriors had been standing. They had vanished into the night.

Normally citizens would've been out of their homes to gape at the scene once the gunshots stopped. But these weren't normal times and the city was under martial law enforced by the National Guard.

Furious heat washed over Jake, and he scrubbed his face with his palm as flashes of Afghanistan strobed through his mind.

Fuck, fuck, fuck.

Again. The magnitude of what had happened nearly slammed him to the ground as if the row of houses had come down on him.

He'd led his officers into a trap.

It didn't matter that the mission was something the Alliance had approved and organized. When the Alliance's recon passed on the info about Darkwolf's supposed headquarters, it had been Jake who'd pushed for the Alliance to go on the offensive rather than wait for Darkwolf to attack.

In seconds Jake was surrounded by paramedics and law enforcement officers. Military vehicles also rolled up the street.

Once he made it clear that this was a paranormal crime, Jake would have command. But first he had to follow goddamned protocol.

It happened again. Again.

Jake forced back the pain and anger like he had ever since that day, and immersed himself in picking up the pieces.

IT WAS CLOSE TO FOUR A.M. when Jake made it back to the warehouse. Dried blood streaked his hands and clothing, and likely his face. Paramedics had cleansed and bandaged his wounded arm but it hurt like a sonofabitch. When the witches got a hold of him, they'd no doubt use their magic and potions to ease the pain and help it heal faster.

At this moment he welcomed the pain. He deserved it.

When he entered HQ, he was still wet from the rain, and so tired he wanted to drop and sleep for at least a week. This war wasn't allowing anyone to get much rest.

Jake didn't let his exhaustion show as he walked toward the command center where he expected the leaders of each faction of the Alliance to be waiting for him.

He wasn't disappointed. Lieutenant Fredrickson had made it back to the warehouse before Jake and stood in the command center. He looked like he'd been to hell and back, his forearm bandaged, a cut over his left eye, blood streaking his face and arms, and his clothes still damp.

The fact that Lieutenant Landers was missing created a sharp pain in Jake's gut, but she'd be all right once the wound to her throat healed. In the meantime he'd have to find someone to replace her for the strategy sessions.

Like he had ever since that day two years ago, Jake forced back his feelings and erected an emotional distance from those he worked with.

The three D'Danann warrior leaders and three of the D'Anu witches looked as if they'd had showers and changed into clean clothing while Jake and his officers had been at the crime scene. But the witches' eyes were rimmed with red, with dark circles beneath. Lack of sleep was getting to them, too.

The Drow king and his men weren't around, likely because they had to get to ground before daylight. Sunlight toasted Dark Elves.

Jake jerked his thumb toward the enclosure covering the spelled jail cells. "Did you interrogate the bastards?"

"We thought we should wait for you." Rhiannon elbowed her husband, the scarred, hulking D'Danann warrior next to her, as he growled. She looked up at him with a frown. "Keir wants to kill them all."

Jake gave Keir a look that said, "You and me both, bro."

Out loud Jake said, "Yeah, I need to be in on this." He

rubbed his temples as he fought back a headache due to the lack of sleep. "Let's get to it." He glanced in the direction of the cells before looking back at the group. "Hawk and Copper, you come with me. The rest of you wait. It'd be too crowded with all of us."

Keir gave another low growl, and Rhiannon elbowed him again. Jake turned and headed toward the cells. He didn't care if they all agreed with his choices or not. Screw that. He wasn't in the mood to argue.

Solid, soundproof walls divided cells that had spelled metal bars in the front. The same sour smell that had been thick in the air during the battle, like a pile of wet laundry that had been sitting for days, hit him as soon as he walked into the room housing the "inmates."

In the first cell, a naked man—if he was a man—had his eyes closed and had curled into fetal position on the twin-sized bed. If Jake wasn't mistaken, the man was sucking his thumb. He couldn't be more than twenty-five and had shaggy black hair to his shoulders. His skin was so pale, almost transparent, that it was like looking through a cloudy block of ice that had started to melt.

Jake frowned as he assessed the "man." Jake was pretty sure the powerful warlock, Darkwolf, was behind the attack and using these men—beings—to do it. The inverted pentagram tattooed on their chests was a sign that Jake was likely right.

"They all had daggers," Copper said as she came up beside Jake, "made of *ice*, if you can believe it. The weapons melted before we even got these guys into the SWAT truck."

"We know spellshields stop them." Jake's mind churned over the night's events. "But that wouldn't be practical in any major attack."

"True. We don't have enough witches." Copper looked up at him with her cinnamon-colored eyes. "Unless we can come up with some other way to do it, there's no way our Coven could contain large numbers. Janis Arrowsmith and the white magic D'Anu Coven would likely refuse to help as usual. If someone could even find Janis."

Hawk nodded. "Perhaps we can experiment on these captives."

Copper glared at him. "Excuse me, but that would be entirely inhumane. You can't use prisoners like laboratory rats." She shuddered. "Experimenting on animals is another topic I won't get into right now."

Jake handed his Glock and a dagger to a guard just outside the cells, following standard protocol. No one in the cell would be armed with anything the prisoner could use against them if he attacked. Of course, they had Copper and her magic, which made for a fine "secret weapon."

He nodded to Hawk, who reluctantly handed his sword and a dagger to the other guard at the entrance leading to the cells.

"Let's start with talking to this guy." Jake glanced down at Copper. "Ready?"

She nodded as her fingers crackled with magic. The moment Jake unlocked the door and opened it, she had a spell-shield in place that moved with them and would make sure the prisoner didn't escape. When the three of them were inside the cell, Copper dropped her shield.

Jake crouched beside the bed. "Time to have a little chat."

The man didn't open his eyes, but his mouth worked as he sucked his thumb.

"You and your buddies did a number on my guys tonight." Jake's tone took on a hard edge as his muscles clenched and his body heated with anger. "You're going to give me some answers."

"Maybe he's in shock," Copper said.

Hawk stepped past her. "Then we will deal with him in another fashion."

"Hawk—" Copper started.

But the D'Danann warrior had already gripped the man's shoulders with his large hands and raised the guy upright. The man's eyelids popped open and the fiery intensity in his ice blue gaze made Jake frown.

He stood and faced the man. Hawk's jaw clenched as he kept his hold.

"Was Darkwolf behind the attack?" Jake fisted his hands at his sides.

When the guy didn't answer, Hawk shook him like a floppy rag doll.

"You won't hurt me." The man's voice came out in a high-pitched squeak as he kept his gaze on Jake. "You're a pussy cop."

"*I* am no cop and have no such reservations." Hawk growled and the man winced as Hawk visibly tightened his hold.

Pain shot through Jake's wounded biceps as he clenched his fist tighter. "After what you and your buddies did tonight, think I give a crap about one worthless sonofabitch like you?"

Copper's tension radiated behind him. He hoped she'd keep her mouth shut.

Instead, she pushed her way between Hawk and Jake. She wore an expression that he'd seen her blood sister, Silver, wear—on the times Silver had gone on raids with Jake. Using her magic, Silver would force Darkwolf's warlocks to spill all they knew. That was deep gray magic, and Jake had never seen Copper use magic so close to bordering on dark.

Gray fog rolled from around Copper and it wrapped its tendrils around the man. His eyes widened and he started to thrash in Hawk's grip. In moments, when the gray fog virtually shrouded the man's body, he slumped and his eyes glazed, the brightness dimming.

"Start from the beginning." Copper spoke in a low, demanding tone that Jake hadn't heard from her before—it was almost eerie. "You'll tell us everything you know."

As if reciting from a book, the man began to reel off information.

Interesting, useful information. Disturbing information.

Jake, Copper, and Hawk continued to the next cells. They were forced to use the same techniques with the two additional men, who refused to speak without Copper's gray magic influence.

By the time Copper, Hawk, and Jake finished, rearmed themselves, and headed back to join the others at the command center, Jake's head spun. He tried to grasp and work through what lay ahead of them.

"Darkwolf's gathering followers really fast," Copper said when they were together with the two witches and the two D'Danann warriors who'd been waiting. Copper looked beyond exhausted, probably from using her gray magic. "He's telling them they've got to prepare for the next Armageddon."

"Color me surprised," Rhiannon said, her arms folded across her chest. A red line streaked one of her forearms, the cut looking as if it was healing rapidly, no doubt due to witch magic.

"He recruits murderers, thieves. Anyone weak-minded enough to turn to his side." Hawk gripped the hilt of his sword in one fist.

"Darkwolf named them Stormcutters," Copper said. "And they're led by several men Darkwolf calls Blades."

"How did he manage to do that water-funnel-and-storm thing?" Rhiannon furrowed her brows. "And create those *Stormcutters*?"

"Balor was a god of the sea." Hawk looked to each man and woman. "Now that Darkwolf controls all of Balor's powers, along with the dark goddess's, and by using his own warlock dark magic, he is able to draw water from the ocean and other sources. His powers allow him to create storms and manipulate human form into water and back."

"They can't carry anything with them or wear clothes." Copper yanked on her long braid as if agitated. "That's why they're all naked."

"Also why their daggers are made of ice." Jake drew in a deep breath. "Darkwolf has to be relatively close to make everything happen. The storms, the funnels, the Stormcutters, the daggers."

Copper nodded. "He also manipulates the Stormcutters' minds."

"As you have seen, they each bear an inverted pentagram on their chests." Hawk braced his hands on the strategy table. "But it is more than a mere tattoo."

"Somehow it allows Darkwolf to keep track of all of his

puppets." Jake rubbed his temples again, trying to relieve his headache. "The tattoo supposedly burns when he calls for them."

"I wonder just how many minds he can control at one time?" Rhiannon said.

Jake gave a frustrated growl deep in his throat. "That last Stormcutter gave me the impression that it's a piece of cake for Darkwolf to control thousands of those guys. No knowing just how many that means. Right now it could be ten, twenty, thirty thousand?" Jake shook his head. "Apparently, from what the Stormcutters said, we were lucky and only got a taste. Probably just a warning."

"Thousands?" Rhiannon said quietly. "He's trying to amass thousands of these people, turn them into water funnels, and fight us?"

"That last Stormcutter looked like he was really into all this bull." Jake was finding it hard to believe the man's words, even as he told the others. "Darkwolf plans to control a million according to this guy."

Everyone was silent, as if trying to digest what Jake had said, and those who hadn't been in on the interrogations had stunned expressions.

"If that's the case, with as few of us as there are, it'll be like going into a typhoon in a rowboat." In an unconscious movement, Rhiannon rubbed the scars on her cheek. "The PSF, Drow, D'Danann, D'Anu—there's only around seven hundred of us. What can we do against thousands? Much less—" She shook her head like she was trying to get the thoughts out of her mind. "Can't even go there."

"We have to find more help." Silver looked to each person in the room with an almost pleading expression. "The National Guard has their hands full enforcing martial law. Where's the military? I know the overt war with the demons and Darkwolf has only happened over a period of a few weeks, but shouldn't we have more help by now?"

"The war overseas has the military spread thin." Jake sighed with exhaustion. "And big troop movements, even stateside, take time to organize and deploy. Add that to the

fact the demons wiped out all of California's highest levels
of government, the top military brass, and the wealthiest and
most influential people in the state."

His eyes burned from too many nights with little sleep and
he blinked. "Top it off with no one anywhere really understanding what we've been dealing with. A goddess and god
for Christ's sake. Now a warlock-god?"

Jake's eyesight grew even more bleary. He wasn't going to
be worth crap if he was up much longer. "I don't know about
all of you, but I've got to get a couple of hours of shut-eye.
We can get on this after we rest."

Jake didn't wait for anyone to agree and took off to his
temporary room in the warehouse.

Despite his exhaustion, he was automatically going
through weapons schematics in his mind. Shit. Not only did
he need to come up with something to kill a duo-god warlock, but now he had to wipe out men in water funnels.

Christ.

He reached his room, which was bare save for his clothing, some gear, a table with his laptop, and printed-out
weapons schematics. Jake stumbled inside and shut the door.
All he cared about now was sleep.

He passed out the moment his face hit the mattress.

CHAPTER TWO

Otherworld

FOUR CENTURIES.

Four centuries of waiting, biding her time, obeying the rules . . . and now the day had come.

Cassia ducked as Daire swung the *shirre*, a fighting pole, then immediately raised her own, blocking his next strike. Her physical strength had increased along with her magic, and she barely felt the blow vibrate from the *shirre* along her arms.

The burn in her chest, her constant concern about the wars waged and to be fought in the San Francisco Otherworld, added to her strength while she maneuvered the *shirre*. Urgency to get back to the city, to rejoin the Alliance, gave her more intensity to fight Daire, to match him with every thrust and parry.

Dear Anu, but she had to return to the Alliance as soon as her ascension was complete. The Great Guardian had provided no news of the war lately, which was strange, so Cassia wasn't certain what she would be going back to.

Cassia whirled and ducked as the powerful Elvin male swung his *shirre* at her, and it whistled over her head, skimming her hair. No mercy—that was why Daire was the best instructor of all the Light Elves.

Her thoughts spun in time with her movements. How were her Coven sisters? The D'Danann? The Drow? The PSF?

. . . And Jake?

In an impossibly fast movement, Daire whipped his pole around hers and she almost lost her grip. All thoughts of Jake vanished.

She managed to keep her hold on her *shirre* and performed a backflip, her two-piece body-hugging training suit allowing her to move fluidly. She landed solidly on her bare feet in the soft grass with her knees bent.

Cassia twirled her pole horizontally from her right hand to the left before spinning it vertically and going for Daire's midsection.

She anticipated his block and spun the *shirre* in the opposite direction. The pole landed solidly against his side and he made a sound of surprise. Her movements were a blur as she swept his feet out from under him with the *shirre* before he could react. In a blink she had him flat on his back with her straddling his large, bare chest and her pole against his throat.

The corner of Daire's mouth quirked. "So the student has overcome the teacher."

Cassia grinned. "Finally," she said, then shouted as he flipped her off of him.

Suddenly he was on top of her, his large body pressing hers to the ground. He had pinned her wrists over her head with his *shirre*, and her cropped training tunic rode up so that a breeze brushed the star birthmark around her belly button.

Dear Anu, he was fast and strong. But over the centuries he'd outmaneuvered her too many times to count. He was the best *shirre* and hand-to-hand combat instructor amongst all of the Light Elves, a master almost impossible to beat. The fact she'd even pinned him down for a few seconds was cause for celebration.

But as she looked up at his green eyes, her smile faded. He stared at her with such intensity, before his gaze settled on her lips.

She swallowed, becoming very aware of his bare chest against her breasts, his lean hips between her thighs. A small gasp escaped her as he pressed his erection into her belly, a hard rod through the thin material of his skintight training breeches. His warm, earthy, male scent invaded her senses.

This had never happened before. He had never crossed the line between instructor and student.

"Daire." Swirling sensations tingled in her belly. She had a hard time forcing any words out as she felt his warm breath against her lips. "What—"

"Long I have waited for you to reach your ascension." His gaze met hers again and the look in his eyes was more than desire. He kept her wrists pinned over her head using one hand and his *shirre* as he brought his other hand to her face and cupped her cheek. "Long I have desired you, Cassiandra."

Cassia's usual calm centeredness evaporated as tingles raced through her from head to toe. Tingles of awareness, even a thrill at being looked at like this by a man who wanted her in a sexual way.

At the same time, panic rose up within her like spiraling butterflies trying to escape her chest. A male had never expressed such blatant sexual desire for her before. It had always been forbidden—

Daire smiled. His white-blond hair trailed over her cheek as he brushed his lips over hers.

For the briefest flash of thought, Cassia imagined the dark-haired human cop, Jake Macgregor, between her thighs, and his mouth covering hers. His stubble would be coarse against her fair skin, his kiss hard and filled with need.

Her eyes widened and she gasped. Jake . . . why was she thinking of the human? Why now, when she was about to receive her first kiss? From an Elvin man revered amongst her kind, a man she had known from the time she had begun training with the *shirre* and in other hand-to-hand combat exercises, centuries ago?

Daire raised his head without kissing her, and she didn't know whether to be relieved or disappointed. He studied her for the longest of moments, his expression now serious. "After your ascension, you will be mine, Cassiandra. As it was always meant to be."

He pushed himself up, releasing her wrists from beneath his *shirre*. Stunned and speechless, she let him take her hand and draw her to her feet. His grip was strong, his palm smooth, his fingers long as they wrapped around hers. She felt like she might tip over, the way her head was spinning.

Daire brushed a few blades of grass from her hair before lowering his head and moving his mouth to her ear. "Tonight," he whispered before drawing back, giving her one last smile, and heading toward the Elvin city.

Kael, Cassia's white wolf familiar, bounded out of the forest with a low growl. *"What is wrong, mistress?"* he asked in her mind as he trotted up to her.

"Nothing," Cassia replied to Kael in her thoughts, then shook her head. *"Everything."*

Kael eased to her side and she slipped her fingers into his thick, white fur. He was large for a wolf, his shoulder blades as high as her waist. *"Did Daire injure you? I have always said he is too rough in your training."*

"No. He is never too rough." Cassia watched Daire walk away as she gripped Kael's fur in her fingers. *"You are always far too protective."*

Kael gave the wolf equivalent of a *"Humph."*

Daire moved so fluidly. He was perfection. A broad, muscular chest that led to narrow hips and strong thighs that had just been between hers. Long, white-blond hair that reached his shoulder blades, spilling over smooth, golden skin. Leaf green eyes and elegant but very masculine features. All a woman would want in a mate.

Her lips parted. To complete her transition she was to be intimate with an Elvin male. She'd never experienced sex—as the soon to be only female Guardian, it had been forbidden to do so before her time.

That the Great Guardian had apparently selected Daire to take Cassia through her transition tonight had caught her by surprise. She hadn't known what to expect, who would be chosen for her. Knowing now that it was Daire who would be inside her was comforting . . . yet not.

She clenched her fingers tighter in Kael's fur as she tipped her head back and looked at the clear, blue sky before closing her eyes. Images of Jake filled her mind. The San Francisco cop was handsome in a hard, rugged way. He equaled Daire in height, well over six feet, but Jake looked more powerful physically, even though it was doubtful he could best an immortal like Daire. She knew from observation that

Jake would never back away from a challenge and would not go down easily.

Images of Jake thrusting inside her, his hard, naked body melded with hers, made her knees weak.

The tingle of her magic sharpened right before she felt it shoot away from her.

A tree branch cracked, its loud snap echoing through the forest. *Bless it.* She had to gain control over her magic or the Dryads would be coming after her for damaging their trees.

Cassia looked in the direction Daire had been walking. Her cheeks burned and she brought her fingers to her mouth. No male could have been picked who could be more appealing to her among the Elves than Daire.

But only one man filled her thoughts now. *Jake.* She had always been drawn to him, even though she had kept an emotional and physical distance as she had with all males. It had become such an automatic thing—to separate herself from men, as she was forbidden to be intimate with one.

But now she felt a sense of freedom she'd never experienced before. She could lie with as many men as she chose to.

The idea held merit.

But not truth. She wouldn't choose to have sex with just any man.

Likely, Daire would lay claim to her and she would be expected to take him as a mate. She shook her head. He might be the one to take her through her transition, but that didn't mean he could claim her . . . or her heart.

CASSIA'S BELLY CHURNED as she stood upon a dais in her chambers, surrounded by handmaidens preparing her for the ceremony. She felt so light-headed she was certain she was going to pass out.

Where was the calmness, the centeredness that had been a part of her for so long that she couldn't begin to think of losing control?

Peaceful. Serene. The calm in the center of a storm. That

was what she was known to be by the members of her Coven and the Alliance.

Or rather what she was thought to be.

Right now she was the storm, far from being calm. As if to prove the point, a burst of gold magic shot from her fingers and a vase exploded across her bedroom. Two handmaidens close to the vase squealed in surprise. Pottery crashed to the floor and flower stems and blooms scattered across the polished wood.

"My apologies," Cassia said, feeling a little sheepish and frustrated at the same time, tension making her shoulders ache. She couldn't let her growing magic get out of control like that again.

She had just finished bathing in an orchid-scented bath, followed by the royal handmaidens rubbing rich oils of the same scent onto her skin.

Kael sat on his haunches off to the side, watching with what appeared to be a wolflike frown. *"Why can I not accompany you after your ascension ceremony?"* he said in her mind.

Cassia's cheeks heated as she thought about what was to happen after the ceremony and she bit her lower lip. *"Daire and I will leave . . . alone."*

Kael gave a low growl and another one of the handmaidens jumped.

Mistress Jaya glared at Kael. "Why you allow that beast to follow you around is quite beyond my understanding."

Kael gave a mental growl that only Cassia could hear.

Elves, Light or Dark, did not have familiars. The Elves thought of Kael as a trained protector, like humans had guard dogs. No one was aware that Kael was actually a familiar that Cassia could communicate with via her thoughts, nor did they realize he had strong magic of his own.

When Cassiandra was born, Kael came to Cassia's mother and communicated via mind-speak that he was to be the princess's familiar. Her mother was the only other being who could communicate with Kael telepathically—when Kael chose to do so.

Cassia's mother had accepted Kael as she did all things she believed to be preordained—as if she had expected him. And she probably had.

The handmaidens continued to fuss with her dress and clucked their tongues in disapproval when she shifted on the dais she stood upon.

"Jaya, please stop calling him a beast." Cassia looked into the Elder's dark blue eyes. "He is my familiar. And my friend."

Kael gave a sound of approval in Cassia's mind and looked somewhat appeased.

Cassia's hands trembled as she smoothed her palms down the fine material of her filmy white gown. When touched, the highly prized fabric felt like rippling water beneath her fingertips.

"Princess Cassiandra—be still, please." One of the royal hairdressers patted Cassia's hair before weaving in more strands of rare aquamarine diamonds the same shade as Cassia's eyes.

Her throat tightened and her skin tingled. She had been waiting centuries for this day. How could she be *nervous*?

Well, for one, she had no idea what she was about to face. The Great Guardian performed an ascension ceremony only once every thousand years, and the whole thing was far too secretive for Cassia's tastes.

Not to mention she was the Great Guardian's only daughter. The Guardian had borne all males until Cassia, four hundred and twenty-five years ago.

With her usual cryptic responses and mysterious air, the Great Guardian hadn't filled Cassia in on every detail. She hadn't explained why it was so important to complete Cassia's transition with a male of worth as soon as possible.

Among the Light Elves, descendants of the Great Guardian, the most powerful of their kind, were not allowed to reach their full potential until they reached four centuries and twenty-five years of age. Like her brothers before her, as she waited, Cassia had been placed in an Otherworld to guide and serve where and when needed—where Halfling Elvin children lived.

In her case, she had been sent to the Earth Otherworld, where she served the D'Anu witches, descendants of the Ancient Druids—four hundred years today. She had traveled from one Coven on Earth to the next, as the witches aged and she did not. She had assumed the identity of a bumbling apprentice witch in most cases.

When the Guardian visioned that Cassia was to go to the San Francisco Otherworld, to serve yet another Coven, Cassia had again taken on the identity meant to keep attention from her.

In the San Francisco Coven, however, she had revealed a part of herself too soon—that she was more than she appeared to be. But she was nearly at her age of ascension, and some of the changes in her could no longer be disguised anyway.

Just thinking about her friends in the Alliance made Cassia realize how badly she needed to get back to the San Francisco Otherworld and aid in whatever manner she could. Once her ascension was complete, she would be able to assist them in ways no one would have anticipated.

Cassia felt more bonded with her current Coven sisters and the Alliance than any other group of people she had served. The fighters in the Alliance were incredibly fierce, and they faced such overwhelming odds.

Dear Anu, what are they dealing with at this very moment?
I can't help them right now, so it does no good to worry.
She raised her chin. *Tomorrow or the next day I will return.*

Cassia sucked in a deep breath as another royal assistant tugged and arranged the fabric so that it draped perfectly from the aquamarine diamond broach on Cassia's right shoulder and across her breasts. The material then dropped to reveal her left shoulder, the curve of her breast, and down to her waist until the white fabric reached another large aquamarine diamond pendant. The material would part along her left leg when she walked, baring it to her hip, and her back was not covered.

The cool breeze sifted through the trees outside the palace window and brushed her bared skin. She shivered more from the fact that she was nervous than the chill. Soon she would be in front of a group of Elders, royalty, and others held in high regard among the Light Elves. It was a rare, sacred ceremony that few were allowed to attend.

Cassia almost groaned aloud at the thought of so many people being at her ceremony. Her cheeks heated like they had earlier when Daire had almost kissed her.

She had to squeeze her eyes shut when an image of Jake replaced Daire's face. She forced both images away before opening her eyes again.

What would they call it on Earth? A crush? No that was too juvenile. Perhaps an infatuation? All she knew was that she desired Jake so much that she couldn't stop thinking about him.

Don't want for what you can't have, Cassia.

Concentrate on the ceremony.

Accept that Daire will take you through your transition and likely be your life mate.

Cassia had not yet been born when her brother Nik's ceremony took place a millennium ago. Of Cassia's siblings, Nik was closest in age. Considering the Guardian had been alive countless millennia, even bearing one child every thousand years, she had many sons. Nik was the only brother she was remotely close to, and even then she barely knew him.

Of course double standards applied even in Otherworld, and her brothers had not had to remain virgins before their ceremonies.

Another zap of magic almost escaped her. She had always hated the fact that men were not kept to the same rules as women. And being the only female descendant of the Great Guardian, those around her had been even more protective and watchful.

"It is time." Kellyn, a red-haired Elvin maiden who was Cassia's dearest friend, took Cassia's hand and helped her down the steps from the short dais. Kael moved to Cassia's other side, and she stroked his pure white fur. Kellyn gave a deep nod before leading Cassia through the palace in the trees, Kael remaining at Cassia's side.

The polished wood was smooth and familiar beneath Cassia's bare feet as she walked beside her friend. Neither spoke, and even Kael was quiet in her mind. It was as if they both knew Cassia couldn't find words to say anything at all at the moment.

Cassia's skin tingled as a sense of the surreal made her feel as if she were outside her body, watching as she passed high arched windows with vines and flowers twisting through them.

They entered a great room with several Elvin women prepared to guide Cassia through her ascension. She had the strong urge to turn and run as her chest and belly squirmed.

Instead, she continued, her head raised high. She was the daughter of the most powerful being in the Elvin world, and she would present herself as such.

The Elvin females drifted to stand on either side of Cassia, their blue robes swirling around their bare feet. Kael refused to budge from Cassia's side.

The deafening silence made Cassia want to shout to break it. She reached deep for her calming center and held onto all the peace within that she had spent centuries cultivating.

But the wild strength of her growing magic was becoming harder to contain, and she had to fight to make it behave.

When four women lined up—two to either side of Cassia—they took a step back so that Cassia and Kael would lead them. Kellyn bowed to Cassia before slipping away and leaving her alone at the head of her attendants.

Despite herself, Cassia trembled as she walked slowly from the great room, through the archway, and into the gentle sunlight.

She stopped at the top of the many stairs leading from the palace to a courtyard. Stretched out in front of her was what seemed like a vast number of Elvin faces, but there were probably fifty at most. The orchid- and grass-scented breeze tugged at the material of her gown, pushing it aside at the slit and baring her leg to her thigh.

A slow murmur rolled through the crowd when she appeared and she swallowed hard.

Cassia kept her chin raised, but Daire caught her eye as he stood at the base of the steps. He was glorious, handsome beyond belief, in a robe as green as his eyes, his white-blond hair gleaming in the sunlight.

"Kael, you must go now," she said in her thoughts as she glanced down at the wolf.

Kael gave the slightest of nods, then silently padded down the steps and moved to the side of the crowd.

Complete silence filled the courtyard beneath the tree palace. Cassia's heart tripped as if it had tumbled down the expanse of stairs before her. She felt the Great Guardian's presence and caught her pure wildflower scent the moment her mother appeared.

Cassia tried to still her trembling as she turned to her right and faced her mother. She was so beautiful it almost hurt to look upon her. Her hair, even blonder than Daire's, tumbled to her feet, and her white gown flowed like liquid down her body. She had known countless millennia, yet her appearance was youthful, flawless. But her blue eyes . . . her eyes showed wisdom that Cassia couldn't begin to fathom. Wisdom born of time immemorial.

The Guardian's presence was awesome, even to Cassia. She knelt and lowered her head, as did every other Elvin man and woman who surrounded them.

"Rise, my daughter." The Guardian's voice rang clear and true. "Today is for you."

When Cassia straightened and looked into her mother's eyes, the Guardian smiled, sending joy to Cassia's very core.

"All, rise," the Great Guardian said, and Cassia was aware of everyone obeying without hesitation.

The Guardian was known by no other name, except "Mother" to her biological children. Cassia often wondered if the Guardian had ever had another name.

When the Guardian reached for Cassia's shoulders, Cassia started to shake so hard she was afraid her knees would give out. But when her mother's hands rested on her upper arms, calm and peace flooded Cassia's being. She stopped trembling and her belly no longer clenched. The magic that had been pinging wildly inside her slowed and Cassia contained it with ease.

"It is time for you to receive your birthright." The Guardian's voice softened and she spoke so low that only Cassia could hear. "You will feel great pain, pain beyond anything you have known."

Cassia's eyes widened and a knot formed in her belly. She hadn't known about the pain part. The ceremony was so Anu-blessed buried in mystery. And it was probably different for her than it had been for her brothers.

Double standards, my—

The Guardian studied Cassia. "Once you have received your powers, your transition will not be complete until you have lain with a male of pure Elvin blood."

Jake's face, his muscular body, and everything honorable about him flashed behind Cassia's eyes and she had to shove the thoughts aside.

As if she had seen the images in Cassia's mind, the Guardian narrowed her gaze. "An *Elvin* male *of pure blood.* Until you have mated, your powers will be strong, but the transition will not be complete."

"Yes, My Lady," Cassia whispered.

"There is something important you must know, Cassiandra." The Guardian's eyes penetrated Cassia to her very magical core. "You have no choice but to complete the transition. The magic growing inside you shall become vast and uncontrollable—and you will not survive without a male to guide you through the transition."

Cassia nearly stopped breathing and heat rushed through her in a violent wave. She would *die*?

The Guardian gripped Cassia's upper arms tighter. "The fates of Otherworlds depend on your ascension, on you taking my place. You will train over the next six centuries before you will rule for millennia after millennia as I have. Until it is time for you to bear a daughter to take your place."

Cassia couldn't find the words to respond as her world spun enough to make her dizzy enough to tip right off the stairs.

Her mother's eyes darkened so much the blue almost appeared black. "Prepare yourself for what will come now in your ascension ceremony," the Guardian said. "You must not cry out, struggle, or lose consciousness. You must not show your pain in any way. If you do, you will not ascend. You will never have another opportunity."

Oh, goddess. Cassia hadn't known about any of this. Why couldn't she have at least been prepared beforehand? To be left in such darkness about things so important was beyond not right.

But, then, the Guardian had not been known for giving anyone all of the information they required. Her and her damned mysteries!

"Do you understand what you must do at this moment, Cassiandra?" the Guardian said in a harsher tone.

"Yes, My Lady," Cassia managed to squeeze out of her throat as her heart pounded hard enough to hurt.

The Great Guardian didn't smile. Her body began radiating a golden glow. Soft at first. But the light soon grew so bright Cassia could barely keep from wincing or closing her eyes. In moments she could no longer see the Guardian.

Cassia tried to relax by focusing on her calm center. She had almost succeeded when pain blasted her body and she was encompassed by pure white light.

She barely held back a scream. The pain was so intense it felt like her flesh was being shredded from her bones. She could visualize it peeling away, charring until only her skeleton remained.

Dear Anu, help me!

Surely it was the goddess who answered her prayers to help her find the inner strength to keep her face a mask of what she hoped looked like perfect calm. Still she wanted to cry, let tears flood her cheeks. She wanted to writhe on the wood floor and beg the Guardian to stop.

In the back of her mind, she knew Kael felt her anguish and wanted to come to her, to lend her some magical comfort, but instinctively knew that he could not.

Cassia focused on her own face, her cheeks, her eyes, her

lips. As pain dug through her, tearing her inside out, she blocked as much of it as she could by continuing to concentrate on keeping her face a mask.

Then, along with the pain, a burst of power rocketed through her. Power that fought against the agony.

Power surging. Awakening.

Like a Phoenix reborn from ashes. The magic within her grew from what now seemed inconsequential compared to the all-consuming power that rose so high inside her she knew she would rise as a Phoenix does.

The pain left, swiftly and suddenly.

In its place the magic, the power, healed her, made her whole again. Every nerve ending tingled and her hair prickled on her scalp. Right now it was as if she could fly if she tried. She felt high, ready to soar through the cloudless sky.

Cassia's mask remained and the Guardian let her hands drop away from Cassia's upper arms.

The Guardian's smile was brilliant.

Cassia managed to move her stiff lips enough to return her mother's smile, but she didn't feel it in her heart.

"Great power is now yours." Again the Guardian's eyes darkened. "As long as you do as I have instructed and lie with an Elvin male of pure blood within fifteen days' time."

Fifteen days, fifteen days, fifteen days, chanted Cassia's mind.

The Great Guardian turned and faced the crowd that Cassia had all but forgotten. Cassia maintained her mask, knowing that was what her mother wanted.

"Cassiandra has completed the first phase of her transition." The Guardian's voice rang like bells breaking the silence. "Within fifteen days' time, following one more great and dangerous trial, she will ascend to the position of Guardian within the House of Guardians."

Applause broke out, loud enough for Cassia to wish for human earmuffs. When the noise died down, she looked up at her mother, who gestured down the stairs. Cassia followed the motion of the Guardian's hand and her gaze met Daire's.

Heat flushed her entire body. Heat of embarrassment, of fear, of doubt . . . and even the heat of arousal.

"Go. Now." The Guardian's voice was firm, as if she knew a strong resistance to going to Daire squeezed Cassia's body.

She cast a final look to her mother, then faced forward and took one shaky step after another toward Daire.

Her destiny?

It wasn't right.

Something isn't right.

But still she let Daire take her hand when she reached him. His grip was large, warm, and comforting. Her eyes met his—eyes that seemed to hold more than desire, but love, too.

Yes, she cared for Daire. As a mentor, a friend. But could she be his lover? His mate?

The crowd parted as Daire led her out of the courtyard, down a path, and through the trees.

Behind her Kael's disapproval reached out to her, but thankfully he did not follow.

Along the path orchids bloomed in the trees in brilliant shades of red, orange, yellow, and pink. The very rare blue orchid was not to be seen. The colors blurred the farther they walked from the throng and the more nervous Cassia became.

Daire squeezed her hand and she looked up at him. "Are you fearful, my sweet?"

His term of endearment set her back a moment before she said, "I—I don't know." Was it fear she felt?

As a future female Guardian awaiting her ascension, she had never been allowed to enter an unmated male's house. Despite her centuries of existence, she only had a vague idea where he lived in the large City of the Light Elves and had never been to his home.

Eventually they reached a fine residence. An Elvin servant opened the door and bowed, and closed it behind them once they walked inside.

Everything within Cassia twisted and squirmed. For the second time that afternoon, she wanted to turn and run. Run far away. It didn't matter where, just away from—from everything happening today.

Daire led her through a beautiful home filled with fine Elvin paintings, sculptures, furniture, vines, and flowers. They stepped onto one of the incredibly beautiful floor rugs that felt so soft to her feet that she wanted to lie down and snuggle on it—by herself.

But she continued allowing Daire to guide her through his home until they reached a door that swung silently open. It closed just as quietly when they were inside the room.

Cassia's heart pounded and everything twisted tighter inside her as Daire brought her around to face him at the foot of a large bed. Cool air stirred in the room, stroking the skin that was not covered by her dress. The material fluttered, just like the flutter in her belly.

"You are so beautiful, Cassiandra." Daire reached up and fingered a lock of hair on her forehead. His voice was firm, deep, unwavering. "I have waited for this moment for what seems an eternity."

No words would come to Cassia as Daire let his hand slip away from her face. He stepped back and unfastened the belt to his robe at the same time.

He eased the robe from his shoulders and let it slide to the floor, exposing every naked inch of him.

CHAPTER THREE

San Francisco

WHEN JAKE WOKE, SUN STREAMED in from overhead sky-lights, and he had to shield his eyes for a moment with the back of his hand until his eyes adjusted to the brightness. He checked his watch and cursed. He'd slept till noon, a full six hours, instead of his usual four.

His biceps ached from the double wounds from the Drow arrow a few weeks ago, and now the whatever-the-hell-it-was Stormcutter's dagger. And his head felt like someone had taken a sledgehammer to it.

After a quick hot shower and changing into a pair of well-worn blue jeans and a blue T-shirt, Jake headed toward the kitchen. His stomach rumbled, probably ticked he hadn't made it to breakfast. He walked out of the hallway into the central area of the warehouse.

"Captain Macgregor." PSF Officer Lorelei Kerns greeted Jake with a nod. Officer Kerns gave Jake a curious look. "A civilian is here to see you. She's in the kitchen."

"Thanks." Jake didn't let his surprise show as he nodded in return and headed toward the warehouse's kitchen. If the woman was in that room, she wasn't military, law enforcement, or government. She would have to be a civilian like Kerns had said. Jake had a pretty good idea who the woman in the kitchen was even though he didn't have a clue how she'd found him.

The ever-present buzz of voices, along with sounds of sawing and hammering, pounded at his temples, and the familiar smells of sawdust and old crude-oil splatters made his headache worse. The once empty warehouse was still a work in progress as the Alliance converted it into a fully functioning HQ.

When Jake reached the door to the kitchen, he pushed it open and delicious smells of fresh-baked cornbread immediately hit him, followed by what smelled like beef stew.

As he'd expected, Kat DeLuca sat at the large table, along with five of the eight D'Anu witches. He was keenly aware of Cassia's absence. She'd left so mysteriously after the battle that ended up with a dark goddess destroyed and demons sent back to Underworld, a sort of hell in Otherworld.

"Great investigating reporter's instincts, Kat," Jake said as the door swung shut behind him and he came to a stop next to her chair.

"The best." The beautiful woman only winced a little from her injuries, courtesy of a demon from the last battle, as she stood and reached up to brush her lips over Jake's. Her familiar exotic scent, like green tea and ginger, swept over him. "You haven't been to see me since I checked out of the hospital."

When she drew back, he noticed the looks of surprise on most of the witches' faces.

"Since when did you have a girlfriend?" Rhiannon said with a grin and her usual directness. "Mr. Too-aloof-for-words."

Kat arched an eyebrow, but Jake ignored the question. He'd never been inclined to discuss his personal life, and he wasn't about to start. Hell, he'd never been inclined to have much of a personal life, come to think of it.

But, yeah, he'd always had a woman waiting in the wings. And that was different. That was sex. Not personal at all.

With Kat, they'd enjoyed each other's company, but he'd never planned to take it beyond that, and he didn't think she ever had, either.

"While you're here I'll give you a little tour." Very little. Jake gestured to the door. Whatever reason Kat was here, he wasn't interested in discussing it in front of the other women.

Kat gave the sexy smile that usually set his insides on fire, but didn't even light a spark now. Maybe it was his irritation at her locating the HQ. He'd deliberately kept her in the dark as much as anyone else outside the Alliance.

He held the door open for her, feeling the curious stares of the women they left behind in the kitchen. He noticed Kat wore looser clothing than she normally did, likely to keep pressure off the stitched-up furrows in her side where a demon had dug its claws into her once perfect olive skin.

When they were alone—as much as they could be in the middle of a warehouse buzzing with activity—Kat studied him with a thoughtful expression. "You're angry that I found you."

Jake pinched the bridge of his nose before he looked at Kat again. "How did you locate our HQ?"

"Like you said, I'm a good investigative reporter." She cocked her head and sunlight pouring in through the skylights gleamed on her short dark hair. "You should have told me everything, Jake."

"You know I couldn't." He ground his teeth. "I warned you to stay in your home."

"And you know that no way I'd do that, regardless of the situation." This time anger sparked in her gaze. "But I would have been better prepared."

"I'm sorry." He took her by the shoulders. "I was under orders. And you're the press, baby."

She jerked away and looked at his freshly bandaged arm. "What happened?"

Jake shrugged. "Nothing."

"There's more going on now that you're not telling me." Kat propped her hands on her hips. "This madness isn't over yet, is it," she said as a statement, not a question.

Jake remained quiet for a long moment. "If I told you what to stay away from, you'd head straight for it. The best way I can protect you is to give you as little information as possible."

Kat clenched her jaw. "That's not fair."

"I don't want you to get hurt." Jake heaved out a sigh. "Damnit, Kat. You need to stay in your home. Especially now."

"You're not going to budge on this, are you," she stated in a flat tone.

He shook his head. "No."

She took a step back, but stopped just as she started to turn. "You never did answer the question I asked you before that—that insanity on the wharf. What kind of relationship do we have? We've been dating for a year—although the last six months I wouldn't call dating."

Jake had been running on adrenaline and exhaustion for so long that he wasn't clear on anything right now. It was definitely not the time to have this conversation. Feelings. Emotions.

Where are we going? Do we have something special? Something real?

He'd rather be beaten.

But he knew Kat deserved something. He'd given her all he could—even if it wasn't much. For that, he was sorry, and sorrier still he'd never find the words to explain the hollow, cold space inside him that just didn't connect.

Too much damage.

He knew lots of guys like that from the service. He could be their Special Forces Recon squad leader.

Only my squad got dead, didn't they?

Shoving away the bitter thoughts, Jake moved toward Kat, cupped her cheeks in his hands, leaned down, and gave her a soft but brief kiss. When he raised his head she looked at him with eyes that held questions he couldn't answer.

"A threat's still out there that's possibly even worse." He rubbed her chin with his thumb. "Stay inside. Stay safe."

Kat looked at him a long moment before she backed away from his touch. "I'll only wait so long, Jake."

Before he could respond, she turned and walked to a side door of the warehouse, and let herself out.

Why was he feeling so surprised?

It always went like this, didn't it? Real women, good women, *normal* women—they could only stick around so long, trying to love a straw man.

Jake cursed under his breath and strode toward the kitchen to get something to eat. After that he'd head to the park for a little solitude and a hard workout to burn off some of the frustration gripping his mind and body.

AIR STIRRED BLADES OF GRASS in one of Golden Gate Park's meadows as Jake went through his jujitsu exercises. He kept his breathing deep and even, his movements smooth and fluid.

Rather than being in his whites, he had stayed in his T-shirt and jeans, and remained armed. These days he didn't go anywhere without his gun and dagger. He probably should follow his own orders and have at least another officer with him, or stay and pump weights in the gym at HQ.

But, Christ, he was sick of feeling hemmed in and he just needed fresh air, space, and time alone.

A prickling sensation crept up the back of Jake's neck.

Blood pounded in his ears. His heart rate spiked.

Someone or something was coming at him from behind.

He dropped to the ground and rolled to the left. The warmth of the assailant's body brushed Jake's as the man attacked. Jake smelled the man's sweat at the same time.

The large man cursed as he missed and slammed his shoulder against the grass. But he never stopped his momentum. At the same time he rolled to Jake's right, the man smoothly and effortlessly got to his feet.

A man Jake recognized.

What the hell?

Jake didn't have a second for any more thought. He already stood, one foot solidly on the ground, the knee of his other leg drawn to his side. The moment the man got to his feet, Jake put power into driving his leg out and ramming his foot into his attacker's solar plexus.

The man grunted as air whooshed from his lungs, but he'd brought his hands up in time to grab Jake's foot. He twisted it hard to his right.

Jake flipped in the same direction as the motion, keeping his body moving fluidly. He wrenched his foot from the man's grasp. He again landed in the grass, his Glock digging into his hip as he hit the ground. Pain exploded in his injured biceps.

The assailant dove for Jake. The man's weight crushed against Jake's sternum and he couldn't breathe.

Before the man pinned him to the ground, Jake whipped his dagger from the holster on his belt. The blade met the assailant's throat. One movement and steel would bury itself in his jugular.

The man glared at Jake before he grinned, eased off Jake, and stood. "How's it going?"

"Sonofabitch." Pain shot through Jake's injured arm as he shoved the dagger into its sheath before pushing himself to his feet, still keeping an eye on his old friend. "Bourne, you're a real lucky man."

David Bourne laughed and rubbed his hand over his high-and-tight haircut. "So that's how you greet your Marine buddy, Captain Macgregor?"

Seeing Bourne brought back rushes of memories. Good ones, for once. Jake had served in the US Marine Corps for eight years after getting his bachelor's degree at San Francisco State University. He'd trained with Bourne for six months at Quantico, Virginia, in the Officer Candidates Course, and they'd both served in the MEU out of Camp Pendleton.

Over his years of service, during special recon missions, Jake had commanded his squad and dealt with some weird paranormal shit. After he'd led his men into the dark magic trap, he'd decided to leave the service to head the San Francisco Paranormal Special Forces.

He couldn't take back the past, but he could do all he damn well could for the future.

Every muscle in Jake's body tensed when he thought about last night.

Another failure. More good men and women dead.

Above his wounded biceps, Jake rubbed the eagle, globe, and anchor insignia tattoo on his upper right arm.

Jake pushed away the feelings, the failures eating away at

his gut. "These days it's dangerous to be pulling stunts like that," he said.

Bourne shrugged. "I had ya."

As he brushed grass off his T-shirt and jeans, Jake shook his head. "I'm the one who almost gave you a second smile."

"Could have taken you out but let you have it easy."

"Uh-huh."

Bourne hooked his thumbs through his jeans belt loops as he looked around the meadow where Jake had been going through his exercises. "Hard to believe there's a war going on in this city, peaceful as *this* place is, Bull."

When they were at Quantico, Bourne had given Jake the nickname "Bull" for his bullheadedness, and it had stuck throughout Jake's years of service.

Jake had retaliated by pinning the nick "Speed" on Bourne for his ability to get any woman into bed every time they'd been given leave.

"Believe it, Colonel Bourne." Jake scooped up a towel from where he'd left it on the grass and wiped sweat from his forehead. The chill San Francisco air was already cooling his body down from the workout. "Things are so screwed that for all I know you could be on the other side."

"Definitely fucked up." Bourne's green eyes met Jake's and his expression grew serious.

"'Bout time you were shipped in to get in the middle of this." Jake tossed his towel over his shoulder and began walking toward a tree-lined path, Bourne falling in step beside him.

"Brigadier General Christian's orders." Bourne's demeanor changed from casual to that of a highly trained military officer. Bourne commanded an elite unit of the US Marines out of Camp Pendleton, the Fifteenth Marine Expeditionary Unit, MEU.

"With the Marines being spread thin due to the war in the Middle East, getting our shit together for this magnitude of a threat, in such a short amount of time, hasn't been easy," Bourne added.

"I figured." Jake glanced at the sky and the thickening clouds. "It's all come down pretty fast since that stadium full of people were slaughtered. But the military—slow as Christmas."

"The whole country's losing it over this—whatever this is—now that it's common knowledge," Bourne continued. "And now that nobody's lying about *terrorist* attacks anymore. What happened in that stadium—"

"You don't know the half of it, Speed," Jake said as they reached his black sports car. A military jeep was parked behind him.

Bourne gave him a sharp look. "We've got three ships, twenty-two hundred Marines, and a crapload of major equipment."

"More than we have." Jake felt a measure of relief that at least some reinforcements were at their disposal. "I just hope that's enough."

"Must be worse that we thought." Bourne shook his head. "If that's the case, after we do some reconnaissance, they'll send in the MEB, seventeen thousand strong. Even with what's going on in the Middle East, we'll be able to pull that together." Bourne flexed his muscles. "Should be more than enough."

"Let's hope to God you're right."

"You can't be serious, man."

"I wish I wasn't."

The entire time they'd walked to the vehicles, Jake remained entirely aware of Bourne and every movement the man made. After all that had been going down in San Francisco, what Jake had said earlier to his old buddy had been true—no one could afford to completely trust anyone.

It wasn't until the last three to four weeks that it had hit the fan on a public, large-scale basis. What had been going down over the past few months escalated in the last few weeks from an unknown, practically invisible threat to a full-fledged paranormal war. With the destruction of the dark goddess, officials had thought the threat was over, but they weren't even close to being right.

"We've heard all the bullshit from the bureaucrats." Bourne leaned his back against Jake's car. "Not to mention every high-placed official in this city has vanished, from the mayor to a senator. And some of the wealthiest, most influential people in San Francisco. The world even." The tenseness in Bourne's body was obvious in the flex in his muscles. "Give it to me straight."

Jake snorted. "You probably won't believe it."

"I've seen the news footage." Bourne's stare was intense. "Our unit has reviewed the coverage over and over since we deployed, and we've been briefed—as much as they can tell us." He shook his head. "Looked like some sci-fi flick. A bitch with wings, monsters ripping throats and gutting civilians, then all of the monsters and bitch disappearing . . . this is some tripped-up mess we're supposed to believe."

"What you saw was real." Jake settled his hip against his car door and casually rested one hand on his duty belt, near his Glock. "We'd been fighting those sonsofbitches since Halloween, but managed to keep it under wraps for a few months until the winged bitch—a freaking goddess from a place called Underworld—started killing masses several weeks ago. In broad daylight."

"What's been handed down to us is that she was destroyed. Saw it on the tapes." Bourne shifted against the car. "Some think she'll be back."

"Fortunately we're positive she's history." Jake rubbed his temples. "Now the problem is a warlock named Darkwolf who somehow absorbed that goddess's powers and magic, along with the power of another god."

"God, goddess, warlock, magic, powers." Bourne gave a humorless laugh. "A little too much to swallow."

Jake wiped his sweaty face again with the end of the towel. "I wish."

Bourne's expression showed he was assessing the situation. "What's with this warlock?"

"Some heavy shit went down last night . . ." Jake shook his head. "I'll fill you in later. Things aren't looking too good right now." Jake pushed himself away from the car and studied Bourne. "How'd you find me?"

"I've got high-level security clearance on this one, Bull." Bourne uncrossed his arms and hooked his thumbs in the belt loops of his jeans again. "The higher-ups told me to find you and your Paranormal Special Forces team at that warehouse on the pier that you and a bunch of freaks commandeered to use as your HQ."

Jake's scalp prickled and he scowled at Bourne. "Those *freaks* are damned good in a fight and have saved all our lives more than once. Watch what you say or you might just find yourself on the receiving end of their 'talents.'" He clicked the remote and unlocked his car. "I'm surprised they'd give you my location."

"The chicks who called themselves something like Deeanoo witches checked me out." Bourne smirked. "One 'witch' named Rhiannon had a vision that I'd be covering your ass in some mess or another."

"D'Anu witches," Jake said. "They'll probably be bailing *your* ass out."

With a grin, the powerful Marine shoved his hand into his back pocket and pulled out his own keys. "Whatever you say."

Jake's muscles tensed, automatically wanting to defend every odd being on the team that was going to take down the warlock, Darkwolf.

Instead, Jake relaxed and the corner of his mouth curved in an amused smile. The team didn't need his defense—once Bourne saw the witches, D'Danann warriors, Dark Elves, and Jake's own PSF officers in action, Bourne would be choking on every ounce of skepticism.

The sudden smell of rain and a gust of wind sent a chill down Jake's spine. He looked up at the swirling black clouds directly above them. The early evening light vanished and everything around them darkened.

A musty, bitter odor filled the air.

Jake's heart jackhammered as he glanced at his friend. "We need to get the fuck out of here."

"What the hell's going on?" Bourne shouted, just as rain began pouring in sheets and plastering their clothes to their bodies.

A water funnel appeared. Then another.

"No time to explain." Jake drew his Glock and gripped it with both hands as he aimed it at one of the funnels barreling down on him. He had to shout to be heard over the growing wind and thunder. "When they come to a stop a man will be on you with a blade. Shoot to kill."

"What the—" Bourne started before the sound of a gunshot echoed through the park.

At least twenty more funnels appeared, surrounding them, and Jake's heart thundered harder than the vibrations from the storm. Water splashed his face hard as the first funnel came to a stop and a Stormcutter slashed at his face with an ice dagger.

Jake was ready and popped him in the head with one shot. Bourne was at Jake's back, cursing, the sound of his own gun muffled in the fierceness of the storm. Jake jammed his foot against one man's thigh, shoving him away at the same time he took out another Stormcutter.

Every time one of the funnels came to a halt, water splashed Jake's eyes, impairing his vision. But he continued to battle with a vengeance. He clenched his jaws as he fought with his elbows, his fists, his legs. Bourne continued to fire and shout, letting Jake know he was still alive.

Just as he was about to shoot a Stormcutter, another one appeared.

He shoved a dagger into Jake's gut.

Excruciating pain ripped through Jake as the Stormcutter buried the ice blade deep. A shout of agony tore from Jake's throat.

The Stormcutter cried out with triumph as he drove Jake to the ground with the power of his thrust.

Nearly blind with pain and weakness as blood gushed from his body, Jake still managed to get off one more shot, and blew out the bastard's brains.

Jake got off a few more shots before another Stormcutter

buried a second dagger below Jake's rib cage. His arms went slack, the gun too heavy to keep a grip on as blood bubbled up his throat. The gun slipped onto the grass. Rain pounded Jake as he looked through glazed eyes at the grinning faces of several naked men who now surrounded him.

One of the men stepped forward and stood over Jake, a dagger in his hand.

He drove the ice blade straight toward Jake's heart.

CHAPTER FOUR

Otherworld and San Francisco

"Jake!" Cassia screamed just as Daire reached for her shoulder broach to unpin her ascension dress.

Daire snatched his hand away as images of Jake dying almost blinded her.

"No! No, no, no." Her voice came out in sobs. She barely saw Daire, but managed to say, "I'm sorry," before she gathered the strength of her increased powers and entered the transference to cross the veil between Otherworlds.

Screams still tore at her mind as she flung herself through darkness and appeared next to Jake's body. Her feet hit wet grass and rain drenched her.

Naked, tattooed men surrounding Jake stumbled back in surprise when she appeared. One of them had been close to driving a dagger into Jake's chest.

Fury exploded within Cassia.

Fire filled her mind and heart, and flames flew from her fingertips. She shouted to the goddess as she spun in a circle, her arms outstretched as the fire blasted from her body.

Screams cut above sounds of rain and thunder as her fire burned the men and hit water funnels behind them. The water evaporated and fire engulfed each man that appeared. Their daggers melted. Smells of burned flesh and burned grass, along with something bitter and sour, filled the air as the men dropped to the ground, writhed, and turned to ash.

She wiped out every funnel-being using her Elvin magic. The only man she allowed to live was the one she instinctively knew had been fighting beside Jake. No remorse battled her consciousness for those she had killed. She was not a true gray magic D'Anu witch—those who would incapacitate but not kill. She was fully Elvin, and the Elves had no such compunctions when they fought.

One glance at the man beside Jake told Cassia the man would live.

But Jake was close to drawing his last breath.

Fear twisted her insides so hard it felt like her heart was being squeezed between two great boulders. Cassia dropped to her knees and cradled Jake's head and shoulders.

With a thought she transferred them both to Otherworld.

The transference seemed to last too long, a suffocating blackness that she'd never felt before, and Cassia wanted to shout.

She arrived on the warm wood floor in the palace in the trees, at an Elvin being's feet, the one being who could help her save Jake.

The Great Guardian.

"Please, Mother." Tears rolled down Cassia's face as she supported Jake in her arms and looked up at the Guardian. "He's not meant to die. He has purpose. He is needed for the battles ahead."

The Guardian knelt beside Jake and Cassia, and studied him as blood poured from his mouth and his chest heaved in hard jerks. His eyes opened and closed like he was trying to focus and as if it took tremendous effort to move his eyelids.

"You have feelings for this man, Cassiandra." The Guardian looked at Cassia. "But he is mortal. If he's near to death, we shouldn't interfere."

"Mother!" Cassia lowered Jake's head to the floor and ran her hands above Jake's body, her sparkling magic flowing in and out of him, telling her how extensive the damage was. Her head nearly spun at the magnitude of his injuries. "A lung, his intestines, spleen, and liver. This is beyond my skills."

"You know that with your ascension came power surpassing what you mastered before." The Guardian put her palms on Jake's bloody abdomen. "But it will take both of us to heal this human's wounds."

Cassia's breath came in heavy gasps and her heart

throbbed in her ears as she placed her hands over Jake's chest. Magic beyond magic flooded her veins, heat beyond heat.

He wheezed and coughed up more blood as he looked up at her with glazed blue eyes. Confusion, and something else she couldn't recognize, filled his gaze.

"I'll save you, Jake. I promise," she whispered without allowing her magic to be interrupted. "Mother and I both will."

"Cassia . . ." Her name died on his lips before he closed his eyes, and his body went slack.

Tears flooded Cassia's cheeks nonstop as she closed her own eyes and focused on his wounds. The ice daggers hadn't been poisoned, so at least they didn't have to be concerned about that.

With all her concentration, she focused on repairing every organ in his body. In her mind's eye, she watched as her sparkling magic combined with her mother's glowing powers. Organs and an artery began to knit themselves back together, stopping the loss of blood and allowing them to function as they should.

One by one, every organ, every part of Jake's body that had been ripped apart, was repaired.

Cassia began to feel light-headed from the drain on her body and magic. Her mind spun as she opened her eyes, and her focus wavered in and out. She continued using her own healing powers on Jake as she watched her mother. The Guardian's magic flowed strong and pure until Jake's skin had been sewn together, with only pink scars remaining.

The Guardian's features were impassive as she treated Jake's biceps on the right arm, below a tattoo. She erased those wounds as well, leaving only scars. "He will need time to completely heal and will require much rest."

Dazed and a little disoriented, Cassia looked up at her mother. "Why did you leave scars?"

"To remind him that he is mortal." The Guardian eased to her feet as gracefully as if water could flow upward. All of the blood that had been on her hands and robes vanished. "And to remind *you*, Cassiandra."

Cassia looked at Jake and brushed his dark, wet hair from his eyes, blood streaking his forehead from her fingertips. He looked peaceful yet exhausted, but no longer tortured with pain.

Blood coated her hands, her arms, and her once beautiful ascension dress. The rain-soaked dress clung to her skin and her hair hung in wet clumps. Her body numbed and shook as the power of her fear and anger began to subside. But the dizziness in her head increased.

Shock. She was going into shock.

"Ah, my child." The Guardian's voice seemed to come from far away and light pressure pushed against Cassia's head. "It is time for you to rest. Both of you."

Cassia slumped forward, her cheek settling on the blood-ied T-shirt that covered Jake's chest.

And felt nothing more.

CASSIA PACED BESIDE JAKE'S BED. He had been asleep much longer than she had expected. Her mother had told her that Jake would need more time to recover from the shock his body had taken, but it had been three days. The Guardian said he would need at least one more.

She studied Jake for a long moment, her heart pounding a little faster and the star birthmark beneath her navel tingling. The Elvin blanket only covered him from the waist down, baring his well-honed chest, carved biceps, and the eagle, globe, and anchor tattoo on his upper right arm. Through the thin blanket she could make out his muscular thighs, and—

Her cheeks burned. From the thickness and length of his erection beneath the soft material, it looked like he must be having a pretty good dream.

Time to change the channel, as Copper would say.

Jake had always reminded her of an Otherworld warrior—proud, fierce, powerful. He had strong, square, and hard masculine features with firm lips and stubble shading his jaws. When open, his eyes were a brilliant blue. But over the past months he'd had an incredible weariness in his gaze. As had nearly everyone in the Alliance.

Kael lay on the wooden floor, but his head was high, his ears alert, as he watched her pace. *"The human, Jake, will live, mistress. Why do you look so disturbed?"*

"I am not disturbed," Cassia said aloud as she glanced at Kael. She turned her gaze to Jake before meeting Kael's blue eyes again. "I just—" She rubbed her arms with her hands. "I don't—" She turned away from him. "Never mind."

Thankfully Kael didn't press her. She went to one of the tall, arched windows with ivy winding around the columns of the arches. Weather never changed in the Elvin city, so windowpanes were not necessary.

As she looked over the sunlit trees, she wondered if they were missing something special with no rain or storms in this enchanted place. Along with the occasionally sunshiny days, she had become used to fog, rain, and cold in San Francisco, and in some ways she missed it. Truthfully, she missed it a lot.

With a frown she shook her head. No, she missed what the city had been before the war with the demons. Now . . . nothing would ever be the same in the San Francisco Otherworld she had grown to love.

A hummingbird flitted nearby, drawing nectar from one of the red blooms that were much like hibiscus on earth. She braced her hand on the cool stone column as she leaned forward just in time to see Daire climb the steps leading to the entrance of the palace. Her throat grew dry. She hadn't seen Daire since she'd left him the night of her ascension ceremony.

Cassia glanced at Jake. His jaw was dark and rough with stubble, his brown hair ruffled on the white pillow. Even in sleep, he looked rugged, powerful.

Her breathing quickened before she looked out the window to see that Daire was no longer on the stairs. No doubt he had entered the palace.

Cassia did not want him to come to her in the same room where Jake was recuperating—she had a feeling Daire wouldn't be pleased to see her with the human. She slipped out of the room and Kael immediately trotted at her side.

Maybe she was being a coward, but she was grateful for her familiar's presence.

They moved down a short hallway and continued to the top of the staircase. Below, Daire looked up at her and she met his leaf green eyes. Her cheeks heated at the thought that the last time she had seen him he had been naked, prepared to lie with her.

"Cassiandra." His words came out soft but husky. "I would see you now."

Cassia sucked in her breath and centered herself. She had always taken care to keep her emotions in check, and now should be no different.

But her stomach still twisted as she walked down the smooth wooden steps. The bottom of her white robe brushed the tops of her feet and she gripped the finely carved wooden banister, probably harder than she normally would have.

Kael remained tight to her side. Daire glanced at the wolf, but said nothing.

When Cassia reached Daire, she looked at his eyes, trying to discern his emotions. He was so much taller she had to tilt her head back. He was beautiful with his perfect features, high cheekbones, and the blond hair that hung straight past his shoulders.

Shock made her rigid as he took her by the shoulders and lowered his mouth to hers. His kiss was smooth, soft, and he ran his tongue along the seam of her lips.

She didn't respond. She thought of Jake instead. What it would be like to kiss *him*. Confusion made her mind spin and her body tremble. Sparks crackled at her fingertips and in her belly, startling her.

From somewhere in the palace she heard something shatter.

Kael growled in Cassia's mind, and she mentally shushed him. Jealous males.

With an intent expression, Daire drew away. He raised his hand and brushed her cheek with his knuckles. "You chose a human over me the night of your ascension."

Cassia's eyes widened. "Jake would have died. I couldn't let that happen."

"Many humans die in their wars." He dropped his hand away. "You cannot save them all. What makes this one so important?"

Cassia struggled even more to center herself. "He is essential to this war. It was not his time to pass to Summerland."

"The gods make that decision." Daire's voice took on a hard edge. "It is not up to you."

Anger rose in Cassia, and she had an increasingly difficult time keeping her tone even. "The gods would not have given me a vision of his near death if they did not intend for me to save him. I am a Guardian ascending now, Daire. You should not forget that."

Daire studied her long and hard, and she met his gaze without blinking.

He straightened to his full height. "It is true. You have feelings for this human."

"I've known him for a long time." Cassia swallowed. "He has been part of our Alliance from the very beginning."

Daire shook his head. "It is more than that."

When Cassia didn't answer, he added, "Remember, it is an Elvin male of pure blood who you must mate with to complete your ascension. Or you will lose the new powers you have gained. And the fate of Otherworlds—"

"How could I forget?" she said quietly. "With you and the Great Guardian reminding me constantly, it is as if you believe I cannot think for myself."

"Twelve days remain." Daire bowed from his shoulders and straightened. "I will be waiting."

Cassia watched him as he turned and walked toward the palace doors. He glanced over his shoulder and their eyes met briefly before he strode through the doorway.

ADRENALINE PUMPED THROUGH JAKE as he and his team moved through the darkness and dry air along a mountain's rock wall near a small Afghan village. Everything had a green tinge to it through his night-vision goggles.

His men were virtually invisible in their black night-combat gear. He gripped his M-16 and motioned with a nod to Pacer to take the lead. Pacer's instincts were usually as right on as Jake's.

Where the team had deployed in the Bamiyan Valley, religious and artistic developments from the first to the thirteenth centuries were represented in the landscape and archaeological remains.

What his Marine paranormal special ops team searched for now didn't belong here. It didn't have anything to do with the natural order in this valley. In this country.

No, what they were looking for had to do with dark magic.

The darkest.

At one time, before they were destroyed by the Taliban, great Buddha statues had been carved into the solid sandstone walls Jake and his team now skimmed silently past. Caves had been hollowed out where entire monasteries had prayed and meditated.

Before.

Long before the evil they now searched for had tainted everything near this Afghani village and threatened to spread through the country like a virus.

Jake's breathing came a little faster as his ops team moved silently through the night toward one of the larger caves. Earlier their reconnaissance team had located the target of their raid—practitioners of such evil that the thought of what they performed was nearly crushing in itself.

Water flowed through a nearby canal, diverted from the Bamiyan River, giving the nearby Afghani villagers the water they needed to survive. To drink. To raise crops.

But if Jake and his special ops team failed—

Even that could end.

The sounds of the water blended with a few goats bleating in the night. The air stirred, brushing but not cooling the sweat on Jake's forearms.

Jake's whole being burned as he listened to constant sobs. The fact that magical healers and seers from around the world were being held as hostages and slaves by the black-magic cult was a constant fire beneath his skin. Hearing their soft pleas only increased his anger and determination.

His team would be in and out in minutes. They'd wipe out the cult and free the hostages.

And they'd do it now.

With a couple of hand signals, Jake had his men break up and move to either side of the cave's entrance.

The crying sounds abruptly stopped.

An odor bled from the mouth of the cave.

The stink of dark magic.

Like the stench of blood, and something bitter and acrid, like roof tar.

Hair prickled at Jake's nape. His heart rate spiked.

This is all wrong. Something's wrong.

Fuck.

Before Jake had time to pull his team back, Pacer stepped on a corner of the opening to the cave.

An explosion slammed into every man on Jake's team.

Pacer's body was ripped apart.

Jake's men were flung away from the cave, their flesh burning from their bones.

Excruciating pain tore through Jake as he was flung into the Afghani night.

JAKE WOKE WITH A JERK and barely held back a shout. Sweat coated his skin, he was breathing hard, and he felt as if he'd been running for miles.

It was completely dark. His hands shook as he brought them to his face and rubbed his eyes.

Shit. He hadn't had that dream in months. That *memory.*

Pain sliced his chest as the images of that night pounded at his head over and over.

The smell of magic rushed over him and he automatically reached for his Glock—which wasn't there.

At the same time he realized the scent now was of good magic, not black. The scent was fresh, like orchids and the smell of grass after a good rain.

"Jake," said a soft female voice that calmed him. Somehow that familiar voice caused his muscles to relax and his body went limp. "Sleep," she said, and he faded away.

GODDAMN, BUT HE HAD THE MOTHER of all headaches. Something pulled at the back of his mind, faint images and sounds, but he couldn't focus on it long enough to grasp whatever it was.

Jake brought his fingertips to his temples and rubbed them before dropping his hand to his side and opening his eyes.

His gaze wavered in and out as he tried to focus.

A blond woman. A smile. Fingers lightly brushing hair from his forehead.

"You're finally awake." Cassia's voice, soft, lilting. "I was beginning to wonder if you would sleep the week through."

Jake squinted and Cassia's face came more clearly into focus. She sat in a chair beside the bed and she looked like an angel. Sunlight shone through the strands of her golden hair so that she almost seemed to glow. Her turquoise-colored eyes studied him intently.

He glanced from her to see that he was in some kind of room with ivy crawling on the walls and through arches. The walls were a shade that wasn't white. Wasn't blue, wasn't green. Something different. Simple wooden furniture was tucked against walls and in corners. The bed had such a soft mattress that he could happily close his eyes and go back to sleep.

The scent of magic surrounded him.

Jake mentally shook his head. *What the hell?*

"Where am I?" His voice came out even, his tone controlled. "What's going on?"

Cassia continued to look at him in that same calm, mysterious way that had always driven him crazy with the desire to shake her. Or kiss her.

She gestured toward the windows, where he could see tree leaves glittering in the sunlight. "You are in the City of the Light Elves, in Otherworld."

He blinked. No way had he heard that. "I'm *where*?"

"Otherworld." She rested her hands in her lap. "You don't remember anything?"

Jake squinted, and didn't have to reach far for memories of the attack in the park. He winced at the images and flinched as he remembered sensations of daggers stabbing him in his gut and chest. Another man had been driving a dagger toward his heart—

A female voice cut through the mayhem. Fire. Fire surrounding them. Crackling. Smells of burned hair and flesh, and that horrible musty, sour smell.

He brought his hand to his chest to find he was naked beneath the covers. He felt rough skin, like scars. Scars where the wounds would have been. "I should be dead."

"You weren't meant to die." For the first time Cassia looked a little rattled. "I couldn't let you."

Jake scooted up in bed, the covers falling to his lap and baring his chest. He looked down at the thick pink scars and brought his hand up to touch them. He felt no pain except for the memory of the agony of the daggers driving into his flesh, piercing deep inside his body.

An odd sensation stirred in his gut as he returned his gaze to hers. "You saved me?"

"The Great Guardian and I, yes." Cassia maintained that calm expression that still made him want to grab her and rattle her. Maybe kissing her would do just that.

Instead, he squeezed his eyes shut and pinched the bridge of his nose before looking at her again. More memories, these more vague, came to him—rain, thunder, pain, and Cassia cradling him in her lap before he was thrown into a spiraling sensation followed by complete blackness.

"But you came for me," he said with no doubt in his mind. "Not the Great Guardian."

Cassia didn't say anything.

Why did she come for him?

"What happened to the rest of those Stormcutters?" Jake asked as he thought about the fire circling them and the smells.

"Those funnel-beings?" She cleared her throat. "I eliminated them."

"You killed the bastards?" Jake stared at her. "Gray witches *never* kill."

"I am not a gray witch," she said, her voice quieting.

"What—" Jake began, but she cut him off by holding up one graceful, delicate hand.

"You need to sleep now, Jake."

She started to stand, but he stopped her when he reached for one of her hands and squeezed. Currents of electricity shot through him. The same currents he'd felt every time Cassia had touched him in the past.

" 'Thank you' doesn't seem like enough," he said as she squeezed his hand back.

"I'm happy you're going to be okay." She smiled such a radiant smile that his heart beat faster.

Shit. Why did he want to draw her onto his lap and hold her? Hell, he didn't even trust her. She'd deceived the D'Anu witches in the past—she could still be deceiving them with everything she did or said. She'd just admitted to not being a gray witch.

So what *was* she?

There'd be time to sort all of that out later. Right now other questions had to be asked and answered.

Jake cleared his throat and released her hand. "How long have I been out?"

"Three days."

"No fu—friggin' way." Jake started to climb out of bed but Cassia put her palm against his chest and frowned.

Tingles radiated from her hand, straight to his cock, which decided to harden so much his balls ached. Jake gave another mental curse. He glanced down to make sure the covers hid that little fact.

Cassia was surprisingly strong as she braced her palm on his skin and kept him from getting up. "We repaired your internal organs, but they have needed the time to heal completely. Nothing can do that but rest."

His whole body jumped like a live wire, and not just from her touch, but from the need to get back to work. He had a lot to do to make his city safe again. Too much to do. He couldn't stay in bed. God only knew what was going on back in San Francisco.

As Cassia removed her hand from his chest, Jake clenched his fists. "How is the man who was with me at the park? How is everyone else in the Alliance? Have there been any more battles with Darkwolf and those Stormcutters?"

"Rhiannon sent word that David Bourne is fine. His wounds were simple for the D'Anu to heal." She leaned away from Jake and straightened in her chair. "I've let them know you are all right, too."

When he eased back in his chair he got a good look at her for the first time. White robes parted at the slender column of her throat, separating far enough down that her cleavage was exposed, showing the gentle curves of her breasts. His mouth watered and his cock ached. He adjusted the covers to better hide his erection and mentally willed it down.

A stab of guilt hit him in the chest, in the same place as one of his new scars. *Christ.* Cassia turned him on big-time, but he had no business having thoughts of taking her down to the mattress, sliding between her thighs, and being inside of her.

He should be thinking about Kat. He should be thinking about getting back to San Francisco and making sure she was okay—and that she wasn't getting herself killed by trying to cover news stories involving the insanity in the city.

Jake looked over Cassia's left shoulder to avoid her eyes and sucked in a deep breath. The fact that she wasn't even *human* should be enough to squelch any other erotic thoughts about him and this beautiful half-Elvin woman.

Or was she half Elvin? She wasn't a gray witch—so was she even a witch at all? She could be half dragon, or a friggin' shapeshifting eggplant. What did he really know about Cassia?

Nothing but the fact that he'd seen her in battle with the D'Anu witches and watched her become the person all of the witches turned to for help and guidance. She had gone from pretending to be an inept apprentice witch to their leader.

That, and she baked one hell of a mean cinnamon roll.

"Another battle has been fought." Cassia's voice jerked his attention back to her. She held her hands in her lap again, her expression calm. "Casualties on both sides."

The word *casualties* hit home, and any lustful thoughts and odd feelings he'd had vanished in a snap.

Fury rode him at the news of members of the Alliance dying. This time he did manage to sit up in bed and swing his legs over the side, but kept the blanket over his lap. Her calm expression made him grit his teeth. "Who?"

"I don't know." Cassia sighed. "But the leaders of the Alliance are certain there's a leak. A traitor." She shook her head, her long, blond hair swinging with the movement. "Every time the Alliance goes on a mission, Darkwolf knows and attacks."

Jake let out a string of curse words and slammed his fists against the mattress to either side of him. "I've got to get back."

"One more day." She studied him intently. "You need one more day to heal enough to be safe outside the protections and energies of the Light Elves."

"Bullshit," he growled.

Cassia stood and looked so calm that this time Jake did get up. He grabbed her by her shoulders. He didn't care that the covers that had been covering him fell away, leaving him naked.

He knocked that calm expression right off her face as she glanced down at his body before looking up at him when he shook her. He stared directly into her eyes. "You will take me home, *now*."

She jerked out of his grip, but her cheeks flushed pink. An angry glint lit her eyes that he'd never seen before. Good. Her shell needed to be cracked.

As a matter of fact, that shell needed to be cracked a lot more.

Jake caught her delicate face in his palms, spearing her silken hair with his fingers at the same time. Without pausing to think about it, he brought his mouth to hers and kissed her so hard and fierce she gasped. He took advantage of her parted lips and forced his tongue into her mouth, exploring her, letting her know he was in control of this moment.

He heard a loud smashing sound, like something fragile had crashed to the floor.

It felt as if sparks were igniting in his belly.

Cassia grasped him by his upper arms and clung to him, her fingers digging into his bare biceps. She remained stiff and unmoving. But he didn't stop his exploration of her mouth, tasting her, teasing her, provoking her to return his kiss.

And then she finally fell into the moment, taking everything he gave. She made soft little moans that sent zinging sensations straight to his cock as she kissed him back. Her kisses were tentative, almost like she didn't know what she was doing. Innocent, pure. As if she had never been kissed before.

God, she was sweet.

He heard a cracking sound behind him as she moaned louder and leaned into him. Her hands moved from his biceps, over his shoulders, until she linked her fingers behind his neck.

As he slid his hands to her waist, he brought her tight against his naked body and his huge erection, and she gasped again. This time he heard a much louder cracking noise behind him. Was Cassia doing that?

Who cared? He resisted the urge to part her robe and see exactly what she was wearing beneath it—if anything.

He kissed her again, letting all the frustration and anger turn into passion and desire.

Something itched at the back of his mind. He shouldn't be doing this.

Why? God, why?

He'd wanted Cassia for a while. Maybe since the day he first saw her out of her goofy-witch-apprentice disguise. He just hadn't admitted to himself, until now, how badly he wanted her.

She tasted so, so sweet. Of honey and desire.

The knocking at his brain grew louder as reality hit him.

He jerked his head back, breaking the kiss. He could barely catch his breath as Cassia looked up at him with a dazed expression.

Kat. He'd been dating Kat for a year.

He was an idiot for kissing Cassia.

He couldn't do this, couldn't cheat on Kat. If he was going to let anything happen between him and Cassia, he'd have to break off his relationship with Kat first.

Why was he even thinking about breaking up with Kat and becoming involved with Cassia? Just because right now she was sending his hormones into major overdrive?

Shapeshifting eggplant . . . remember? You don't even know what she is, much less who.

But, God, he'd wanted Cassia for so long. He didn't need his cop instincts to tell him she wasn't exactly what she'd made herself out to be. But then, who was?

Everyone had secrets. Even he did.

The memory of his failure in seeing that dark magic trap coming dug at his gut like a jagged dagger. They'd been set up by an Afghani leader who happened to be a warlock as powerful as Darkwolf had been before this thing with Darkwolf's double god powers.

Jake sucked in a deep lungful of air as Cassia pulled out of his arms and stepped back. It was as if an incredible spell had embraced them and now shattered, the shards scattering across the room along with his lust.

And whatever had broken while he'd been kissing her.

The expression on her face—he'd never seen her look like that. Her eyes wide and filled with confusion, desire, and maybe a little fear? Her usually smooth hair was wild where he'd slid his fingers into it, her normally fair cheeks had a high blush to them, and her lips were reddened and swollen from his kiss. She took another step away from him, clearly dazed.

Jake almost smirked. Perfect, calm, serene Cassia had just had the wind blasted out of her sails.

He mentally sighed.

Reeled himself back in like a veteran cop hauling an eager rookie back in line.

Down, boy.

Okay, he was a shit. He really needed to apologize. First to Cassia for acting like an ass, then to Kat for kissing another woman while he was still supposed to be dating her.

He tried to get closer to Cassia again, but the sudden change in her expression stopped him cold. The look on her face shimmered from vulnerable to a dangerous fury he had never imagined she possessed.

Streams of gold magic flew from one of her hands and the light zipped across the room. A crack split the air like a shot and a wooden table collapsed.

Oh, crap.

All thoughts of shapeshifting eggplants left his head and he wondered if she was going to toast his nuts like Rhiannon had done to Keir when she'd met the D'Danann warrior.

Only maybe Cassia would fry Jake's right off. He almost crossed his legs at the thought.

But then all signs of Cassia's magic faded. She took a deep breath. Her expression shifted back to that vulnerable look she'd been wearing before.

Jake's heart melted faster than one of those Stormcutter's ice daggers on hot asphalt. He wanted to hold her, reassure her. His emotions twisted so quickly that he'd never felt more confused in his life. In fact he'd never felt so much of anything, period. Not since Afghanistan.

A low growl came from the doorway and Jake jerked his gaze from Cassia's to see Kael, Cassia's huge white wolf familiar. Hair prickled along Jake's nape. If Cassia didn't fry his nuts, her wolf might just eat them.

Jake drew his attention from Kael back to Cassia and opened his mouth to apologize.

Before Jake could get a single word out, Cassia turned and fled.

CHAPTER FIVE

San Francisco

DARKWOLF SHOVED HIS HANDS IN THE POCKETS of his black Armani slacks as he stood on the pitcher's mound in the San Francisco Giants' stadium. Fog hung low overhead and the moisture in the air caused his black silk shirt to stick to his skin. Now that he had the power of two gods, he was a little over seven feet tall, even more buff than he'd been before, and he was forced to "shop" at big and tall men's departments.

Or rather he took what he wanted. He didn't pay for anything.

Darkwolf's growing army of Stormcutters surrounded him. They stood in disorganized groups, but Darkwolf and his Blades, his leaders, would soon have them in shape. As the men weren't on a raid, they wore pants and shoes. Darkwolf didn't allow the men to wear shirts and cover their inverted pentagram tattoo. He used the tattoo to control them, to call them when they were needed.

Elizabeth stood next to Darkwolf, her arms crossed beneath her extraordinary breasts, as she surveyed the "troops." She cocked her head to the side and looked up at him with her vivid blue eyes. "Amazing what you have accomplished in a mere week."

His reaction to the beautiful woman was almost always immediate. His cock hardened and he wanted to take her now. Maybe in the locker rooms.

No, better back at their penthouse where they could be alone. He wasn't into sharing her anymore, and he wanted to make sure they didn't end up with any voyeurs.

She was so gorgeous, so perfect . . . he could almost, almost, forget she was a Fomorii Demon Queen named Junga. He held back a grimace at the thought of the hideous, hulking, blue demon she was inside the beautiful human shell.

Darkwolf dragged his attention away from Elizabeth and focused on his Blades as they approached to report the results of last night's raid. With his incredible powers, Darkwolf had gifted each man with the ability to "create" Stormcutters.

"We eliminated nine more members of the Alliance," Ryder said after he assumed a military stance. "We beat the crap out of them last night."

"Our casualties?" Darkwolf asked as he looked to each of the twelve men he had recruited from various branches of the military to lead the Stormcutters against the Alliance.

"The Alliance killed twenty-two Stormcutters." Butch kept his expression neutral as he spoke.

Darkwolf's ten other leaders remained silent as they maintained their military stances.

He mentally shrugged. Insignificant, meaningless losses compared to the impact he and his Stormcutters were making on the D'Anu, D'Danann, Drow, and the worthless Paranormal Special Forces.

Thanks to his little traitor, who continued to give him all the information he needed to bring down the relatively small Alliance.

However, Darkwolf kept his face stone cold. "I expect better results after our next venture. And fewer casualties."

"Yes, *sir*," each man echoed.

Gods bless the military.

"We've got the other one hundred and eighty recruits to get started on." Turk nodded to a group of chained men behind Darkwolf.

Darkwolf appraised the men. A ragged group as usual— that would soon be among the most powerful beings in all of San Francisco, once his mark was upon them and they had received his gift of Stormcutter powers. Right now some appeared angry, rebellious, furious, where others looked like they'd wet their pants if Darkwolf said "boo."

That would change, in just moments.

Darkwolf nodded to Butch, Turk, Ryder, Zane, and Joe, five of his Blades.

At once the Blades organized the men into five groups. Butch started by forcing the men in his line to strip off their shirts. When they were naked from the waist up, Butch placed his hand over the first man's heart.

Immediately the man screamed, his face twisted in complete and absolute agony.

Butch started to glow. Power flowed from him. Black, thick, oily. A dark cloud encompassed the two men as the new Stormcutter continued to scream and scream.

When Butch drew his hand back, an inverted pentagram tattoo had been burned into the flesh over the man's heart.

The new Stormcutter's knees gave out and he crumpled to the ground.

"Get up, pussy!" Butch drove his military boot into the man's side.

The Stormcutter cried out again, rolled to his side, and got to his knees before forcing himself to his feet. His eyes took on a vacant look as Butch removed his cuffs and chains, and directed him to stand with the other Stormcutters, who were as silent and as animated as automatons.

They had no expressions. Like the life had been sucked out of them.

Darkwolf did smile this time. These men belonged to him. These men would put an end to the Alliance and eliminate every D'Danann and Drow warrior, every PSF officer, and every D'Anu witch.

At the last thought, Darkwolf felt like his chest had been crushed, the air squeezed from his lungs. Even Silver Ashcroft. Even she had to be killed.

Darkwolf took a deep breath, drawing air back into his lungs. His infatuation with the D'Anu witch was over. He didn't give a damn what happened to her.

If only that were true.

Darkwolf ground his teeth and let the screams of the new

recruits fade into the background. He grasped Elizabeth's hand and looked down at her.

She gave him one of the sexy smiles that made him so hard he thought he'd come in his pants. She always did that to him.

"I know what you want," she murmured.

He grinned. "That's no surprise."

"But maybe I have a surprise for *you* this time." Elizabeth gave him a secretive smile and his balls drew up so tight he almost gasped.

"I'm out of here," Darkwolf said to his leaders in his deep, resounding voice. "You handle these guys." He looked down at Elizabeth and said under his breath, "And I'll handle you."

She laughed. "You wish," she said just before they vanished into the transference and he took them back to the penthouse.

CHAPTER SIX

San Francisco

FOR SO LONG, I'VE BEEN SICK of all this self-righteousness. This Alliance and every member of it.

But now I can laugh. The Alliance can't figure out how the warlock-god knows their plans. How he finds and destroys them at every turn.

I wonder how long it'll take them to figure it out. If they ever do.

Unlike anyone here, Darkwolf has already lived up to his promises. He has strengthened me more than anyone in the Alliance could imagine. With every bit of information I give him, the great warlock-god feeds me, fills me, giving me power I've never had.

Just the thought of Darkwolf turns me on so much my pussy aches. I need to find the PSF cop who fucks me whenever I'm in the mood. He's promised to keep our "relationship" a secret. As long as he does, I'll let him live.

I have to make sure my familiar is not around. Good, he must be out. He knows of my sexual relationship with the cop, but I've made it clear it's none of his business.

Sometimes my familiar seems suspicious of me, possibly sensing the darkness, but I hope not. One day I'll have to kill him. Killing him might be the hardest of any life I'll be forced to take.

I will miss him.

Focus, damn it. The glamour's important.

I love how it feels when I become invisible to humans. I love this part, slipping through the warehouse, naughty and unseen. It's a thrill.

And there's Fredrickson working in the ammunition room near the PSF command. No one else is around.

So much for the glamour.

It's gone before I even close the door behind me.

And lock it.

Fredrickson sees me and grins.

I give him my sweetest smile and point to the locked door.

"Mmmm, babe," *Fredrickson murmurs when he reaches me.* "Here for a good—"

I silence him by clutching his cock through his jeans and squeezing. Hard.

His eyes practically roll back in his head and he grasps my breasts in his hands. My core is already clenching, knowing I'll have his cock inside me soon.

My T-shirt goes first as his eager hands paw against me, then my jeans, underwear, shoes, and socks. I unbutton and unzip his jeans and push them down just enough to release his erection. He has a nice-sized cock, and I don't want to wait for him anymore.

Fredrickson knows I like it when he keeps his clothes on and I'm naked. He knows I like it rough in every way.

I give a soft gasp as he shoves me up against one of the walls. Immediately I wrap my legs around his waist and he drives himself inside me.

To keep from crying out at his deep penetration I have to grind my teeth. He fucks me hard and fast, his jeans abrading the insides of my thighs as he thrusts. The unfinished wood wall scrapes my bare back as he drives in and out so powerfully.

I cling to him, digging my nails into his shoulders as he leans down and bites my nipples, making me want to scream even more from the pleasure of the pain.

As always, I imagine it's Darkwolf taking me. He'll be much bigger, I'm sure, but for now Fredrickson will do.

It's so hard not to make any noise, and I let Fredrickson know I want it even harder when I buck my hips and bring him deeper inside me as he thrusts.

My climax approaches. I use my magic to make the pleasure even more intense for us both.

The moment my orgasm hits, I bite his shoulder through

his T-shirt to keep from crying out. Fredrickson drives into me more. He's good. He knows what I want. I like it when he's rough and makes me come first, then makes me come again before he climaxes.

His teeth sink into one of my breasts and I have to bite his shoulder harder as I come again.

This time his body jerks and throbs, and I feel his hot come inside me. That makes my climax all the more intense, and I urge him on by thrusting my hips and clawing his back. He likes pain, too.

If I didn't have to worry about anyone finding us, I'd make him lick my pussy now and take me again. He'd do anything for me, and I take full advantage of him.

Without giving him time to say anything, I push him away and slip on my clothes. He adjusts his now flaccid cock, fastens his jeans, and tucks in his shirt. He looks like he wants to talk, but I shake my head and slip out the door.

I need more information about the Alliance's plans, and I'll use him tonight. Right now I needed to use him for sex.

I pull another glamour and slip around where Alliance members rarely go.

My pussy still spasms as I think about Darkwolf. If only I could go to him now. Serve at his side. Serve him in any way he chose to use me.

But no. Darkwolf needs me here, where I can continue to deceive those who have chosen to overlook me.

Chosen to overlook me like the stupid, psycho nuns who raised me before I found my calling as a Pagan.

The batshit crazy nuns thought I was dull. They thought I was nothing special. But I'm smarter than anyone imagines.

Try to find me.

Guess who I am.

I dare you.

CHAPTER SEVEN

Otherworld

JAKE SCOWLED AS CASSIA VANISHED. He felt like kicking something or punching one of the walls. What had he been thinking, kissing her?

But damned if it hadn't felt right. Even if he had reservations about her, it had still felt right.

No matter where he stood with Cassia, he was going to have to break it off with Kat. Kissing another woman while he'd been dating Kat exclusively was unfair.

Jake began looking for his clothing. He was freaking naked in *Otherworld*, and that witch—or Elvin woman, possibly eggplant-headed shapeshifter—was his only ticket back home. And he'd just pissed her off.

He glanced at the wooden table that was not much more than kindling now and he winced. The bed frame was cracked, too. To say messing with Cassia in any way might be dangerous was probably a huge understatement.

Still looking for his clothes, Jake checked the chairs and unbroken tables, then went for a nice trunk off in one corner of the room. The mosaic design on the lid was incredible, and he usually wasn't one to care about what furniture looked like. This one had an arch with a couple standing beneath, their palms touching as they stared at each other.

Ah, hell. Mushy crap.

Jake raised the top of the trunk and, to his relief, found his clothes, cleaner than they'd ever been, from his jeans and shoes to his socks and jockey shorts. The Stormcutters had probably eighty-sixed his T-shirt, but he found a royal blue shirt in the trunk in his size, made of soft brushed cloth. His shoulder holster, dagger, and cell phone were there, but his Glock was missing. He remembered dropping the Glock, and everything else must have been on his belt.

His arm twinged where he'd been stabbed just below the tattoo as he tugged on the clothing, and his chest ached. The fact he'd survived was a friggin' miracle.

No, not a miracle.

A mystery.

Cassia had come for him—somehow she had known. What did that mean?

Nothing. He was just a lucky sonofabitch.

After he finished dressing and cramming his feet into his workout shoes, he strapped on his empty holster and clipped the cell phone and dagger onto his jeans. The cell phone not because he thought he could make a friggin' phone call here, but purely because he expected to go home soon, no matter what Cassia said. He'd have to obtain another handgun at HQ.

He skipped tying the strings to the neckline of the shirt and set out the doorway to find Cassia. He had to get home and she was going to send him back now.

The moment he stepped through the archway, he nearly ran into a gorgeous redhead.

She bowed before looking at him with gray eyes that reminded him of a misty sky. "I am Kellyn, Princess Cassiandra's friend. She asked me to look after you."

Princess?

"Ditched me, in other words." Jake shook his head from frustration and curiosity. "Take me to Cassia."

Kellyn didn't have the same calm-in-the-center-of-a-storm presence that Cassia had always maintained in San Francisco. Instead, she looked flustered, a high blush rising in her cheeks. "The Princess is currently occupied."

He managed to be civil in that he didn't bite Kellyn's head off. "When will she be available?"

"I am uncertain." Kellyn gestured down a long hallway with a heck of a lot of carvings on the wooden walls. The wooden floor shone so brightly it reflected the sunshine gleaming through arched windows. "Would you like to see the City of the Light Elves?"

Jake wanted to say, "Hell, no. I don't have time for this crap," but figured that if he went along with it, he might find Cassia. "Lead the way."

Kellyn moved so silently beside him as they walked down the hallway that it was almost eerie. She was only about eight inches shorter than his six-six, graceful, with her long red hair tucked behind delicately pointed ears. He wondered why Cassia's ears weren't pointed.

"We're up in the trees?" he asked as he glanced out windows while they moved down steps in an expansive hall.

"Many trees." Kellyn moved silently toward a pair of wooden doors to their left. "The palace is in the trees, as are many members of the royal court. Other Light Elves live in homes beneath the canopy."

Due to his countless years as a cop, Jake automatically catalogued everything. Exits, vantage points, if the area was vulnerable to attack, and even potential weapons if he needed something in a fight—like the decorative spears on the walls or shards of a vase if he had to break one.

Kiss Cassia again and he might not need a weapon.

When they reached the double doors, they opened as silently as Kellyn walked. Two armed Elvin guards stood on the other side of the entrance, but neither moved, and Jake figured Kellyn had used magic to spring the doors.

The walk down the steps from the tree palace was a head trip. A massive staircase led down to paths that split in several directions. Likely invisible to most humans, Elvin guards perched in trees wearing clothing that blended in so well Jake wouldn't have been aware of them if it wasn't for his strong cop and former special ops instincts and training. No doubt being around magical beings for so long now aided his "sixth sense."

While continuing his mental surveillance, Jake listened intently as Kellyn explained how the city functioned, while also pointing out its beauty.

They walked by other Elvin men and women, who looked at him like he was the last thing they wanted to see in their precious city. It caused heat to burn behind his ribs.

He'd never felt so much outright prejudice since he was in school.

Being the kid on the wrong side of the tracks in South San Francisco, from a family of alcoholics and drug addicts, hadn't exactly put him on the fast track to popularity. Not that he'd cared what anyone thought of his family. He sure hadn't given a damn about his screwed-up father, mother, and one of his uncles.

Yeah, good ol' Uncle Gary. Now there was a fine, upstanding citizen. Real good about bringing on the dope and booze, and keeping his folks stoned.

Jake had one relative who'd been good to him. Uncle Frank was the man who'd willed Jake the apartment building in the Haight Ashbury District. The D'Danann, D'Anu, and PSF had used the building for their HQ before the warehouse.

Kellyn rattled on, a nervous sound in her soprano voice, but Jake barely heard her, he was so lost in thought.

When he graduated high school, after he turned eighteen, he joined the Marines and turned his back on that life. He'd lived and breathed being a Marine.

Then—he didn't want to go there again. For years his dreams had been haunted by what had happened.

Yeah, that pretty much smashed everything to shit.

The other part of the reason that he'd left the Corps, though, was to return to San Francisco and be close to his mother. When he'd come back, she'd been ill with emphysema caused by forty hard years of smoking. She'd passed on a few years after he returned. But he'd made peace with her and himself before she died.

His father was dead from liver disease due to alcoholism when Jake was still in the Corps. After he joined the Marines, he never saw his father again. He'd had a hard time coming to terms with himself over not resolving their differences.

Family was family, right?

Jake snorted and Kellyn glanced up at him with a confused expression.

He ignored her as he took in the beauty of the City of the Light Elves and felt the soft warmth of sunshine on his skin.

Jake never did hear whatever became of Uncle Gary, and he honestly didn't give a crap.

While Jake strolled down a path with Kellyn, he didn't bother to acknowledge any of the pure discrimination in the eyes of the men and women they passed. He simply continued listening to Kellyn talk while he studied the landscape.

Jake came to a full stop.

Cassia. On a small patch of grass, surrounded by wildflowers beneath the leafy canopy of trees.

Kissing an Elvin man.

Kellyn's voice became nothing but babbling as he stared at Cassia and the man.

Jake's insides flamed and his ears burned as fury rose up inside him. A jealous green monster clawed his gut and he clenched his fists at the same time he clenched his jaws.

". . . to lead Princess Cassiandra through her transition." Kellyn's last words penetrated the haze that had overtaken his mind.

"What?" He tore his gaze from Cassia and the man to look at Kellyn.

She looked flustered again, and he realized his voice had come out in a growl.

Kellyn's throat worked as she swallowed and said, "Daire is to mate with Cassiandra to take her through her transition so that she can fully ascend into her powers."

Cassia's mate, seared his mind as he looked at her.

Of course a woman that beautiful would have men interested in her, he thought, even as heat expanded throughout his entire being. In San Francisco he'd never seen her with a man—it had never occurred to him that she could be attached.

Jealousy and frustration warred within him, and irrational thoughts pounded at his head.

Mine, mine, mine.

She pulled away from the kiss.

Her eyes widened and her face reddened when she moved her gaze from the man and saw Jake.

CASSIA'S HEAD WAS GOING to explode from embarrassment as she looked at Jake. Wasn't she having the day.

First, Daire gave her a light kiss this morning. Then Jake had completely tipped Otherworld, her entire being, with a *real* kiss. And now Daire had just snagged her and forced another one on her. Only she hadn't wanted his like she had wanted Jake's.

Goddess!

A part of her wondered if Daire had been able to taste Jake on her lips, but she snapped herself away from that thought.

Then embarrassment rolled into anger that flared up within her like Dragon flame. How dare these—these *males* kiss her without even asking! As if it was their due!

Jake strode toward them with a fiery spark in his eyes and fury on his strong features, and Cassia straightened to her full height. Which wasn't much compared to Daire and Jake, who each were at least a foot taller than her. Cassia was short for an Elvin female, but she knew she more than made up for it in spirit. And magic.

Kellyn tagged along behind Jake, trying to keep up as they wended their way along the stone path. Tree branches slapped Jake in the face when he strayed from the path. Kellyn looked bewildered by the actions of the human male.

Jake reached her and Daire. He looked so angry that a large vein stood out on his neck, and she swore she heard his heartbeat.

"You and I need to talk, Cassia," Jake said to her, but his blue eyes were on Daire. "Alone."

"Say what you will here." Daire raised his chin as he crossed his arms over his chest. "There is no secret-keeping between me and my mate."

Cassia's jaw dropped as she swung her gaze to Daire, who

looked like he could spit fire as he glared at Jake. She raised her voice, "I am—"

"This is *private*," Jake growled, taking a step closer to Daire.

"I am not—" Cassia continued, trying to be heard over their voices.

Daire also took a step closer, until he and Jake were inches from each other. "Nothing is too private for you to say to my mate in front of me."

"I am not your mate!" Cassia screamed at Daire in a voice so powerful it didn't sound like her own. Brilliant white sparkles emanated from her in a powerful wave that forced both men to stumble back a couple of steps.

Cassia's magic burst from her in a wild, uncontrollable wave and a nearby oak burst into flame. Smells of smoke and burning leaves filled the small clearing.

Elves stopped whatever they were doing and stared at Cassia.

Kellyn hurried to use her magic to put out the tree flames. Another Elvin woman helped her.

The Dryads are going to be furious with me.

Cassia would deal with that later.

Both men stopped shouting, looked at the tree, and cut their gazes back to her.

Jake stared at her as if she'd grown into an underground Troll.

Shock and concern coursed over Daire's features.

Kellyn looked terrified, her eyes wide and her lips parted as she finished dousing the burning tree with her magic.

Cassia's face felt flushed and sweaty.

Serene, calm—screw it.

"I. Am. Not. Your. Mate," she told Daire as she shook with anger and sparks flew from her fingers, elbows, and shoulders.

She turned to Jake, who winced when one of her sparks skimmed his cheek. "And *you*. You I will talk to when I am good and ready. Not before."

Silence met her ears as she stormed away toward the

palace, not caring that she stepped on a wildflower and knocked a leaf from a tree with her flying sparks.

To the Underworlds with both of them!

How many times had Jake stared at the back of a retreating woman over the past few days?

Jake shook his head and turned to look at the Elvin guy named Daire. "So much for either of us having a word with her," Jake said, losing some of his steam.

Daire gave a slow nod, his arms still folded across his chest. "You must return home, human."

Jake just stared at the man. "What's your hurry?"

"Princess Cassiandra must go through her transition." Daire narrowed his brows. "She visioned your near-death, entered the transference, and left before we could begin the process."

Daire's voice grew deeper, and his words came out low and hard. "You must leave now so that I can mate with Cassiandra and finish taking her through her ascension. The balance of all Otherworlds depends on her attaining her full power. She is too valuable to—" His expression shifted to one of mild disdain. "To waste."

The anger that had been inside Jake before Cassia left returned in a cold wave. Thoughts of Daire taking Cassia to bed made his head ache and an ice block lodge in his chest. "I'll leave when it's time," was all he managed to get out before he turned away from the man and looked at Kellyn, who stood by the smoking tree. She had a black smudge on her cheek and the smell of burned wood canceled out the scent of wildflowers.

His skin crawled at the thought of turning his back on an enemy, but his gut told him Daire wasn't the type to literally stab a man in his back.

"Take me to the palace," Jake said in a growl to Kellyn. He sucked in his breath and evened out his tone. "Please."

Kellyn glanced from Daire to Jake and bowed. "Of course."

If Jake had thought the Dark Elves were not to be trusted,

he saw the Light Elves in a whole new way. He'd take the
Drow any day after getting a taste of these guys.

The walk to the palace went by a lot faster. Kellyn remained silent and didn't pause to show him any of the sights.
Instead, they made a beeline for the palace. Jake ignored
the distaste in several Light Elves' eyes as he strode beside
Kellyn.

"I want to see Cassia," he said to Kellyn as soon as the
double doors shut behind them and they were in the huge
great room.

Kellyn gave a stiff bow, firm resolve replacing her uncer-
tainty. "I will see if Princess Cassiandra is taking visitors."

He ground his teeth, but tried to keep a polite expression.
"Thank you."

Kellyn bowed and walked up the staircase. Jake followed,
but she had vanished by the time he reached the landing.

A moment later he thought he heard the muffled sound of
shattering glass.

He pinched the bridge of his nose with his thumb and
forefinger before raising his head and letting out a slow exhale. He recognized one hallway Kellyn had escorted him
through. Rather than waiting around for God knew how
long, he headed down the hallway, to the room he'd woken
in this morning.

Christ, but he had to get back to the Alliance and work on
how to end this war.

He rubbed his face with his palm as he went over the
numbers in his mind again. Including reserves, the beefed-up
PSF Department now had nine hundred officers—however,
it was three shifts of three hundred cops working at any one
time. The SFPD was doing what it could with its manpower,
but unfortunately the numbers weren't even close to being
enough.

Police officers from precincts around the entire Bay Area
had poured into San Francisco, but there were other things
they had to deal with, so Jake's team worked with officers in
the SFPD for the paranormal activities.

Add the D'Anu, Drow, and D'Danann—the Alliance was

barely seven hundred strong. The Drow made up most of the Otherworldly fighters but could only join them at night, which totally screwed the Alliance during the day.

Bourne had mentioned over two thousand Marines were battle-ready, so that gave them almost three thousand to fight Darkwolf. At night.

If Darkwolf's captive men were right, that number wouldn't be close to enough. Considering he had the power of two gods, it wouldn't be entirely surprising if Darkwolf had enough power to create a massive number of Stormcutters.

Jake gritted his teeth as he reached his room. He stopped in the doorway, and clenched the door frame with his fingers and shook his head.

One thing, though, was that the ideas for the weapon he'd been designing on his laptop were becoming more and more cohesive. He churned the ideas over and over in his thoughts.

He needed to get back to San Francisco and help the Alliance bring down Darkwolf before it was too late.

CASSIA DIDN'T KNOW WHETHER to laugh or cry or explode something else in her room. What used to be her favorite porcelain sculpture of an entwined couple was now nothing but powder covering the wood floor and her robes. She had already reduced a chair to kindling and balls of wool stuffing.

The Dryads were so not going to be happy with her.

Cassia's arms shook and she clutched one of the tall bedposts of her canopied bed in an attempt to gain control over herself. The finest embroiderers in the city had created designs of colorful leaves and flowers on the canopy fringes and the blanket covering the bed. Her gaze followed one of the vines on the cloth as she thought about Jake.

He had either been furious at her for not taking her home, or he'd been jealous. The way he'd been staring at Daire when he was speaking, rather than looking at her, gave Cassia the feeling that maybe Jake *had* been jealous.

Cassia took deep breaths as she lit all the candles in her chamber with a thought. Scents of vanilla and cinnamon filled the room as the candles began flickering and dancing in the slight breeze coming in through her window arches.

She could have cleaned the room with one sweep of magic, but she left the mess as a reminder to herself.

Get a hold of yourself, Cassia.

She moved away from the bed to the center of the large room and stepped into a circle inlaid on the smooth wooden floor. Fortunately the powder hadn't reached this far across the room.

Black Elvin runes of peace, serenity, and tranquility made up the circle around her. Beneath her feet was a colorful mosaic of an Otherworld fire orchid.

Cassia closed her eyes. She raised her arms from her sides and stretched then out, moving at an unhurried pace, taking deep inhalations and consciously slowing her racing heart. When her arms were even with her shoulders, she turned her palms up, facing skyward.

She reached deep inside herself, to the very center of her soul, for every bit of calm and serenity she could muster.

"Anu, please grant me the strength to maintain my true self." She inhaled the vanilla and cinnamon scents that helped her relax.

"Since my ascension day I have felt conflicting emotions battling inside me, and I have released them." Cassia swallowed. "I have experienced embarrassment, fear, concern, anxiety, terror, fury, and even . . . passion. I wish to banish these strong emotions and return to dealing with all situations as I had before."

Silence met her ears and her magical core.

"The Alliance in Otherworld needs *that* Cassia." She opened her eyes. "As I was. Stable. Soothing. Measured and, at all times, controlled."

No response. Not even a flicker from a single candle flame.

Cassia blinked back tears as she looked into the semidarkness of her chamber. Her voice came out in a hoarse whisper. "I don't want to change. My friends, the Alliance—all Otherworlds—need me as I have been." She thought about the spitfire of a child she had been before she began to emulate her mother. "No one would benefit from the unruly little demon I once was.

"I can't afford to fall apart." Cassia touched her finger to her cheek, blotting out a tear as she willed Anu to listen.

"Cassiandra."

Cassia whirled in the circle to face the doorway and the Great Guardian in all her radiance. "Mother."

"Return the human to the Earth Otherworld." The Guardian's features looked unusually cool rather than serene, as normal. "You, however, must remain here long enough to complete your transition."

Heat flushed over Cassia at thoughts of Daire, Jake, and her transition.

"Unless you act within this critical window"—the Guardian spread out her hands as if to emphasize what she said—"you will pass on to Summerland." Her expression darkened. "It is not a fate I would wish on anyone, especially not my own heir."

Cassia's stomach sank with every word her mother spoke.

"Remember," the Guardian continued, "as you well know, to *not* complete your transition will affect the balance of all Otherworlds."

Cassia had the urge to scream, but she managed to keep her voice somewhat controlled. "That's not fair. To put the weight of Otherworlds on me."

The Guardian gave a delicate shrug. "It is who you are. Why you were brought into this world."

Cassia sucked in a deep breath. *This is too much!*

Before she could stop herself, Cassia said, "Why must an Elvin male of pure blood take me through my transition?"

The Guardian raised her brows and her expression darkened further. "You are not thinking of lying with that human male, are you?"

Cassia felt like she was on fire from embarrassment. "N—no."

The Guardian focused intensely on Cassia. "Going through the transition is a powerful and frightening thing.

Only an Elvin male trained and prepared to guide you through this time is acceptable."

When Cassia opened her mouth to speak, the Guardian cut her off by raising her hand. "This is how it must be. Do not think to do otherwise."

Cassia lowered her gaze. "Yes, Mother."

"Then you will stay until your transition is complete."

"First I need to check that my Coven, my friends, in San Francisco are safe," Cassia said as she met her mother's eyes again. "And I must see if I might help the Alliance find the traitor betraying them to the warlock-god."

The Guardian simply studied her for a moment. "You must make your own decisions. I cannot choose for you, or instruct you otherwise—no matter how much I would like to do so. However, as Great Guardian, I must warn you. Do not tarry long. You will run out of time."

A ripple in the air and the Guardian was gone.

Cassia wanted to stomp her foot like a child. She wanted to explode everything in her room and scream.

The force of the emotions made her head spin, and she left the circle. She walked through the white powder still on the floor and sat on her bed. With a sigh, she absently traced a flower pattern on her blanket, then looked out the windows and watched darkness descend. The candles in her room glowed brighter as they filled the room with light.

What did this loss of control mean for her, for the Earth Otherworld, and for the battle to stop Darkwolf and restore balance across all Otherworlds?

And what did all of this mean—for her and Jake?

CHAPTER EIGHT

Otherworld

As IF SHE WOULD GIVE Jake Macgregor the satisfaction of going to him when he demanded it.

It was now the morning following the day of kisses and explosions. She was still making him wait. When she was good and ready she would return to his chamber and take them back to San Francisco.

She moved to one of the arches surrounding her room and sunlight warmed her face as she looked out at the beautiful world of the Light Elves. Tree leaves winked in the breeze. Streaks of red, blue, orange, yellow, pink, and white wildflowers swathed the city. Rich scents of flowers, grass, and the ever-present perfume of spring met her senses.

So perfect.

She bit her lower lip. Maybe too perfect.

Jake would probably be more than angry that she hadn't gone to him, but he could go to Underworld and live with the Fomorii for all she cared. Along with Daire.

Daire's mate. *Right.*

She turned back to face her room. She had already used her magic to clean up the porcelain powder of the sculpture, the scraps of wood, and the wool stuffing, and vanished them to nothingness.

It was time to return to the San Francisco Otherworld. She would dress as she usually did since they were at war. No skirts or dresses or robes. Jeans and T-shirts, and when they went to battle, body armor provided by the PSF.

Now that she was allowed to utilize her training with the *shirre* and hand-to-hand combat, and her magic was magnified, she knew she'd be even more of an asset to the Alliance.

After Cassia slipped into a pair of jeans, she pulled her

blond hair out of the collar of her T-shirt and let her hair fall past her shoulders. Her hair had grown quickly since she'd neared her ascension, and during the past few months her looks had gradually returned to her normal self.

Almost.

If she didn't gain control over herself, she would drop more of her illusion and her ears would curve up into their natural points.

Likely the others in her Coven would be surprised at the changes that did show in her appearance once she returned to San Francisco.

Along with changes in her attitude.

Fierce emotions, of anger and the fear of losing control of those emotions, made her body shake. She needed to seek solace. To know that this was temporary, not permanent.

Cassia moved from the window to the circle of runes and covered her face with her palms. She could have control over her emotions again so that she remained in a state of near serenity—most of the time.

Right?

She lowered her hands as no response from the goddess filled her. No tingling in her body, no warmth of the deity's presence as Cassia would feel if Anu had answered her confusion and pain.

Maybe that was an answer unto itself.

Figure it out your blessed self.

Well, so be it.

Cassia battled a surge of rage and had to rein in another burst of wild magic. She lowered her head as she left the circle to grab a pair of clean human socks from a chest. She tugged them on before she jerked on her jogging shoes.

For good measure, she kicked the trunk. Hard.

Pain shot through her big toe and she bit her lower lip to keep from crying out.

"You are acting strangely," Kael said in her mind, and she glanced at the doorway to see the white wolf had entered her chamber.

"Whatever," Cassia grumbled aloud. She'd been on Earth

for so long that she had picked up colloquialisms of the times easily over the past couple of centuries. When she returned to Otherworld, however, her language tended to slip back into the formality of the Elves.

"Tell me." Kael neared her and, instead of touching his head like she normally would, she crossed her arms over her chest and ground her teeth.

Another male thinking to make demands on her.

Okay, something was seriously wrong, with her thoughts running along this vein. How could she be mad at Kael?

Cassia closed her eyes and took deep breaths, again trying to find her calm center. It eluded her, evaded her with every attempt, and she wanted to scream and scream and scream.

She opened her eyes and glared out the window. She didn't like this. None of this. These extreme emotions were foreign, unwanted. Her head ached, her body tensed, tingles prickled her skin, and sparks snapped at her fingertips.

No. *No, no, no, no.* She did *not* want this.

Like she had a choice, though.

Cassia felt like her brain was about to melt.

"Cassiandra?" Kael cocked his large head to the side. *"Something has changed. Greatly."*

She wanted to laugh and say, "No kidding," but instead she said, "I'll explain on the way to Jake's room."

The wolf listened intently as she grumbled to him in her thoughts about the emotions bombarding her so hard she had difficulty controlling them.

Kael actually sounded relieved when he said, *"Finally."*

Cassia came to a full stop in the hallway just outside Jake's room. "Excuse me?" she said aloud as she stared at the wolf.

Kael gave the equivalent of a wolflike shrug. *"I have known you since you were born, Cassiandra. For over four centuries I have watched you bury your emotions as you emulated the Great Guardian."* He studied her with serious blue eyes. *"Do you not remember the adventures we had when you were a youngling? Before we left for the Earth Otherworld?"*

Cassia rubbed her fingers over her forehead. She needed

some lavender oil to ease the tension in her body and lessen her headache. "This isn't right."

"What's not right?" came Jake's voice and she snapped her attention to the doorway of his room.

For a moment she couldn't respond as she looked at him, let alone breathe. He was incredible. From his dark hair to his blue eyes to his firm lips that knew how to kiss so well.

The rest of him was just as spectacular. The sleeveless tunic he wore displayed his powerful biceps better than his T-shirts normally did, and the soft blue material stretched taut over his well-developed chest. Thanks to having seen him naked yesterday, she knew his entire body down to his calves was all sinew and muscle, raw power that she wanted to take for her own.

Desire stormed through Cassia like gale-force winds as her eyes met his. Images raced through her mind—of her bringing him down using her fighting skills and straddling his chest before kissing him.

He was so physically powerful and skilled, though— would her skills be enough of a match for him?

The corner of Jake's mouth curved as if he could read her thoughts and crooked his finger. "Come here, Princess."

Cassia's eyes widened but she obeyed, almost blindly following as he stepped back into his chamber and closed the door behind them, shutting Kael out.

The wolf made a disgruntled sound in Cassia's mind before letting her know he'd stay right outside the door until it was time for them to leave.

Cassia stopped in front of Jake and tilted her head up, her entire body shivering as they locked gazes. He was so close she felt his warmth, caught his spicy masculine scent, which made her belly feel like the gale-force winds had turned into a hurricane.

Jake brushed her cheek with his knuckles, then slid his fingers through her hair, causing her to shiver. "You grow more beautiful every day, Cassia."

She swallowed, not able to get any words out and trying not to melt against him at his sensual touch.

He lowered his head so that his mouth was close to hers, so close she was certain he was going to kiss her. Goddess.

Oh, how she wanted him to kiss her.

But, at the last second, he moved his face into her hair and inhaled.

"I'm sorry," he said as he nuzzled her hair, then drew away with an apologetic expression on his handsome features.

"Why?" She brought her hand to his chest and an electrifying sensation sizzled between them as she settled her palm over the soft cloth covering his heart.

She let her hand drop away as Jake sighed and stepped back. "I shouldn't have kissed you before. I shouldn't be this close to kissing you again."

"Why not?" Cassia asked again, before she could stop herself.

His gaze turned stormy. "For starters, you have someone you're supposed to 'mate' with."

She gave him an equally hard look. "Like I said, I'm not Daire's mate. He was chosen by the Great Guardian to—to—" She swallowed hard and now her cheeks burned. "Take me through my transition to complete my ascension."

"Ascension, transition . . ." Jake took her by the shoulders, drawing her closer to him. "I'm not getting any of this."

Cassia wanted to fall into his arms and wrap herself around him. Envelop herself in his embrace and his spicy, masculine scent and never let go. But she couldn't. Why she'd even allowed this brief, intimate encounter—she had lost her mind. These rampant emotions played havoc with her senses and released her potent desires.

"I am a daughter of the Great Guardian," she finally said in one breath. "Like all Elves, I stopped aging on my twenty-fifth birthday. As she did with my brothers before me, the Guardian sent me to an Otherworld. To the Earth Otherworld. For four centuries."

"You're kidding me." Jake tightened his hold on her upper arms, a stunned expression on his face. "You're over *four hundred* years old?" he asked with total disbelief in his voice.

"I first came to Earth toward the beginning of the 1600s."

Cassia straightened her shoulders, missing his touch. "I served my time before my ascension by watching over Elvin Halflings and others with Elvin blood, like Silver, Copper, and Rhiannon.

"My responsibility," she continued, "was to do so without revealing myself as a full-blooded Elvin being, to use my wit and determination, sharpen my intuition, understanding, and fighting skills. I traveled from D'Anu Coven to Coven as the witches aged and I did not."

"Christ." Jake released her and pushed his hand through his hair, ruffling it. She wanted to reach up and brush the strands into place, just to touch him. "So that's why you disguised yourself. You've been faking it all along."

"Oh, no. Never faking it." His words punched her gut even though she tried not to show it. "I serve Anu as much as any D'Anu witch does.

"But being months from my ascension," she continued, "I found it more and more difficult to hide my appearance and nature."

Jake sucked in his breath and let it out in a loud rush. "Okay. Let's say I manage to let that all sink in. What's with the ascension and transition?"

"On my four hundred and twenty-fifth birthday, four days ago, I ascended as I came into most of my powers." She stared at Jake. "I am far more powerful now than I have ever been. More so than most Elves."

He held her gaze as he scowled. "And this transition that guy Daire is supposed to take you through . . . ?"

"Sexual energy is one of the most potent forms of magic that exists." Cassia's whole body heated, and certainly her face turned as red as the setting sun. "It can be very dangerous for the male paired with a Guardian ascending."

She went on in one long rush, "I learned on my ascension day that Daire had been prepared by the Great Guardian to guide me through this transition, because . . . because an untrained male could die from the power released by my first mating."

"First mating?" Jake's jaw dropped. "You're a virgin?"

Cassia looked away from him and out one of the arched windows. Heat swept her from the roots of her hair to her toes. "Yes," she whispered. "As the daughter of the Great Guardian and a Guardian ascending, it was forbidden for me to have sexual relations." She turned back to him, trying to get her embarrassment under control. "And, as I have said, my first mating will be highly dangerous to the male."

"Jeez, Cassia." Jake dragged his fingers through his hair again. "A virgin."

She spoke in a hoarse voice. "I have no choice but to mate with an Elvin male of pure blood within a certain window of time, or I will not ascend into my full powers, or my Guardianship." A ball of emotion formed in her throat at the magnitude of what her choices meant. "And I am told the balance between Otherworlds could be tipped if I don't complete the task."

And I will die, she added silently in her mind, the thought terrifying and surreal.

"What a freaking guilt trip they've put you on." Jake turned his back to her for a moment before whirling to face her. "Why an Elvin man of pure blood? Why can't some other type of male be trained?" His features hardened as he glanced out the window, then to her again. "More of that prejudice I experienced when Kellyn took me for a little stroll?"

Cassia frowned. "No . . . I believe it is because only an Elvin male of pure stock has magic strong enough to protect himself, to survive my transition."

"Uh-huh." Jake started to look pissed. "I'll just bet."

"Why do you care so much?" Cassia whispered, tingles of hope rising within her. Did Jake actually care for her? "What does it matter to you?"

"Ah, hell." He rubbed his temples before looking at her and nearing her again. "I'd hoped you and I—that we might get to know each other better. A lot better."

Cassia's whole body went up in flames. "You did?"

He nodded. "Still do."

Shock coursed through her as he drew her into his embrace and brought her head to his shoulder. She wrapped her arms around him, relaxing into his strength. Her mind spun with the thought that he did want her, that he was attracted to her like she was to him.

She wanted Jake and no one but him. The thought of lying with any other man caused tears to burn at the backs of her eyes.

For a long moment he just held her before he said, "But screwing with your powers, with the balance of Other-worlds . . . that's pretty heavy." He let out a low sigh. "I imagine that means Otherworld will always be your home."

Cassia couldn't answer him. Over the years she had thought ascending was what she desired more than anything in any of the Otherworlds. Right now she didn't know what she wanted. But she had responsibilities, regardless.

She managed to keep her eyes dry before stepping out of his embrace. "Your question regarding my ascension and transition was the first you asked. What else do you have to say?"

"I, uh . . ." Jake suddenly looked uncomfortable, like his clothes were too tight. "I've been dating another woman for the past year. I shouldn't have kissed you until—"

Fury caused her to shake. This time brilliant light shot from her, filling the room. The entire bed crashed to the floor and feathers spurted into the air.

Cassia balled her hand into a fist. She punched Jake in the jaw so hard his face snapped to the side and her knuckles stung. "I can't believe you kissed me while you're dating another woman!"

He rubbed his jaw as he turned back to her. "There's no excuse."

"You're goddess-blessed right there isn't." She sucked in her breath and worked to calm herself down as she thought she heard more wood splinter. She made the anger lessen until it just simmered beneath the surface. "I shouldn't have let you, knowing I am to go to Daire. I'm not promised to him, as in marriage—or a committed relationship like yours—but he *will* take me through the transition."

"Cassia," Jake said softly. "When we get back I'll—"

A flash of a vision hit Cassia so hard she stumbled and

Jake caught her by the shoulders. She barely saw him as images fired through her brain.

Rain pounding on Union Square in front of the St. Francis Hotel with such power she could barely see. Lightning split the sky and thunder slammed into her mind.

Funnels whipped out of the storm. Countless funnels racing across the square.

Stormcutters!

They closed in on members of the Alliance. Many funnels stopped and the Stormcutters drew ice daggers.

Slaughter.

Cassia almost screamed as she saw blood splatter and people drop to the ground. Bodies littering the grass and concrete. Members of the Alliance and Stormcutters, too.

"We have to go back. *Now*." Cassia gripped Jake's arms as she said the words out loud to him, and in her mind to Kael.

Kael used his magic to open the bedroom door and rushed to Cassia's side. She gripped the fur on his neck.

She didn't give either male a chance to respond as she took them through the transference to the Earth Otherworld.

CHAPTER NINE

San Francisco

JAKE, CASSIA, AND KAEL ARRIVED on a marble landing, just above a set of stairs, under cover and out of the storm. Cassia released Jake and stepped away. His blood ran hot and charged through him as he tried to orient himself.

Sheets of rain, along with thick gray fog, obscured his vision. Shouts and screams arrowed through the rain and fog, along with sounds of weapons firing and the crack of thunder. Through the fog Jake saw varying colored sparks of witch magic.

Bitter, musty smells told him the Stormcutters were there, too, in the fog and rain.

In a quick scan, Jake saw that Cassia had transported them directly to the right side of a hotel entrance with three sets of blue-carpeted stairs leading down to the sidewalk. The St. Francis Hotel in Union Square.

Jake focused on the direction the noise came from. On the other side of Powell Street, in the middle of the Union Square piazza, around the monument crowned with the goddess Victory.

He reached for his Glock. Damnit! Not there—it had been left in that meadow. Instead he drew his dagger as he turned to speak to Cassia and Kael—

Cassia and her wolf both vanished.

In the next moment brilliant light exploded in the center of Union Square, cutting through rain and fog and glinting on the sharp metal of his jagged-edged dagger.

Cassia.

Somehow he knew she was responsible for what was happening in the center of the square. Even though he'd been close to unconsciousness, he knew she'd done something similar when she saved him in Golden Gate Park.

Kael's howl echoed through the storm.

Jake started to take the first step down the right staircase, ready to charge forward, into the middle of the battle.

Something to his left caught his eye and he pulled back just in time.

His heart tripped.

Darkwolf. With Elizabeth-Junga at his side.

The warlock-god stood just above another blue-carpeted staircase, this one on the opposite side of the hotel entrance, directly across from Jake. Elizabeth watched the battle with an amused expression.

Jake wanted to knock that smug look right off the demon-woman's face and kill the murdering bitch. Almost as badly as he wanted to eliminate Darkwolf.

The thick tan-and-white marble columns between Jake and the duo, along with the fact that Darkwolf was obviously focused on the battle, were probably the only reasons Jake, Cassia, and Kael hadn't been noticed.

Thank God.

Jake stayed hidden behind the smooth marble column closest to him. He gripped his dagger tighter in his fist and set his jaw. Every primal urge within Jake urged him to charge the seven-foot-tall warlock-god, take him down, and drive the dagger into the asshole's heart.

"I'm going to kill that sonofabitch." Jake's rumbled words were lost in the intensity of the storm.

"What the fuck?" Darkwolf shouted over the noise as he raised his hands, staring at the brilliant white light.

"The Elvin witch," Junga shouted back.

Fury twisted Darkwolf's features as he shielded his eyes with his hand. Like Jake, Darkwolf flinched from the nearly blinding white light exploding in the square.

Explosion after explosion after explosion.

Darkwolf tipped his face up and howled as he raised his hands. More swirling black and gray foglike magic emanated from Darkwolf's palms. Faster and faster it fed the storm with what looked like a shitload of his power. Lightning shattered the sky and more thunder rumbled over the noise in the square.

Jake's heart hammered harder and sweat broke out on his forehead. The black fog grew so thick in the square that he could no longer see anything beyond the hotel steps. Not even the rain.

The Alliance was fighting blind.

CASSIA'S INTUITION HAD TOLD her where to transport Jake before she entered the battle. As soon as they arrived at the hotel, she released her grip on Jake and transferred herself and Kael into the center of the battle.

At first the rain pounded down so powerfully that she couldn't see. It only took a moment to get a grasp on the situation. The Alliance was down to a handful of witches and PSF officers, and a fair-sized group of Marines. The few D'Danann fought from the air, beheading men who appeared out of the water funnels.

Cassia's stomach wanted to revolt at the sight of so many bodies littering the piazza, and from the coppery smell of blood and the sour smell the Stormcutters gave off.

Heated fury boiled through her like white, liquid fire.

A funnel spun directly toward her. In a split second, Cassia judged how many Stormcutters she could take down without hurting anyone else that might be in the way.

Just as the first one reached her, she crouched and released the white fire of her magic. "Eat this!"

The fire blasted into the first Stormcutter, evaporating the water and destroying the man within, charring him to ash. She took out five more Stormcutters in one large explosion.

From the corner of her eye she saw those around her cut their attention to her briefly before going back to battle. Like her, they didn't have time to think about anything beyond the next foe they had to face. But they all still had shocked expressions, especially her Coven sisters.

"I will tear these creatures to pieces," Kael growled in Cassia's mind.

Kael howled before lunging for a Stormcutter who had appeared. The wolf clamped his jaws around the man's jugular and ripped his throat out. The man dropped and Kael went after the next Stormcutter that appeared. More blood spattered Kael's white coat as he took down another man.

Cassia searched around her with a quick sweep of her gaze that brushed over every spark of magic that erupted from each witch.

Alyssa. Over there, Mackenzie. Silver beside Copper. Hannah fighting near Sydney and Rhiannon.

She counted all seven D'Anu witches in a split second. The witches had captured about twenty naked Stormcutters within magical shields, the men within them obviously unable to function once they were cut off from the storm.

Excellent thinking.

The shielded men were scattered all around the witches.

It had to be wearing her Coven sisters down to be forced to maintain so many shields.

"To your right," Keir shouted to another D'Danann as they fought from the air alongside other winged Fae warriors.

The D'Danann whom Keir had shouted to whirled in midair and sliced the head from a Stormcutter's shoulders.

A few D'Danann dove for the shielded men. The witches let up on the shields a flash before the winged Fae warriors beheaded the Stormcutters. A measure of relief allowed Cassia to not worry so much about the witches' powers. As long as they had help, they could continue to contain Stormcutters within shield bubbles.

Cassia continued to fight, her powers almost automatic as she assessed the battle.

Thank the goddess Marines are here. The Marines were putting up a good fight, but it twisted her gut to see the bodies of so many slumped on the square.

Only a dozen or more PSF officers in raid gear battled with guns, knives, and the specially designed demon Tasers they'd used on the Fomorii before the demons had been sent back to Underworld.

"Manning—coming hard from your left," Fredrickson cried over the storm at the same time he took aim at a Stormcutter's heart.

Too many of the PSF officers were down, wounded or dead. Without the benefit of magic it was far more difficult for them to battle and survive.

Cassia crouched and aimed for another group of funnels coming toward a line of PSF officers. Cassia let the force of her magic and her anger fire through her like a blowtorch, and she ripped apart eight more Stormcutters.

Not enough.

Anger fueling her, making her stronger, Cassia worked her way through the melee, taking out Stormcutter after Stormcutter, with explosion after explosion of her white fire. The charred ashes of the Stormcutters quickly soaked into the grass or washed away from the concrete parts of the piazza with the force of the rain.

The air began to grow thicker with rain and fog.

Goddess bless!

Cassia couldn't see but a few feet in front of her anymore and could only eliminate a Stormcutter or two at a time without endangering any members of the Alliance.

More screams, shrieks, and cries rent the air. Who were the cries coming from? *Dear Anu, let it be the Stormcutters.*

Cassia had fired at two more funnels when a chill scrabbled up her spine. She whirled to see a Stormcutter driving his dagger straight for her.

Oh, goddess.

No time for magic. Instead Cassia dropped to her knees, clasped her fists together, and swung at the back of the man's knees. He collapsed, giving Cassia enough time to use her magic to toast the goddessforsaken bastard.

She didn't take time to savor any of her victories. She turned to take out two more Stormcutters coming at her from the front.

"Princess!" Kael cried in her mind, and she saw a third closing in on her side, fast.

She ducked before all three Stormcutters converged on her.

Kael wrapped his jaws around one man's neck and snapped it.

Cassia rolled to the side, onto her knees, and let loose a blast of fire that toasted the other two men.

"Thank you!" Cassia shouted to Kael, but he was already downing another Stormcutter.

The storm made everything almost too dark to see, and her heart pounded like crazy. She created a ball of spellfire with her magic, and she caught flashes of magic spheres floating in the fog.

Cassia's own spellfire ball was far more brilliant. It settled above her shoulder, allowing her to see enough to burn each Stormcutter that came near her to a crisp. The force of her fire kept most of the rain from actually reaching her.

But she couldn't see any of the other members of the Alliance anymore. It was too chaotic, too frightening.

Shots, screams. Kael's haunting howls after a round of kills.

Just as she killed another Stormcutter, she found herself circled by at least ten of them. As if they had come just for her.

Well, bring it on.

As the men dove for her, Cassia transferred just outside the circle of men.

She released her magic in a blinding flash of white followed by an enormous explosion as she obliterated the Stormcutters.

As the warlock-god darkened the sky, Jake weighed his options.

His body vibrated with fury at what Darkwolf was doing to the members of the Alliance. His PSF team and the Marines were taking the brunt of the battle because they didn't have magic on their side like the witches, D'Danann, and Drow.

Damn, but the Drow couldn't be out now because, no matter how dark the warlock-god had made it, the moment he let up on the storm the sun would be out and, even if it was foggy, would be enough to fry the Drow. There was no question that the Dark Elves had to stay below ground during the day.

Jake looked at the warlock-god. He couldn't charge Darkwolf and tackle him because the warlock was too magically powerful. It might take only a flick of Darkwolf's finger and Jake could be dead.

I've got to take the bastard down.

And I've got to do it now.

Jake squeezed the hilt of the weapon in his hand. He looked around the column at Darkwolf before he glanced at the dagger.

Focus. He clenched his jaws and relaxed the muscles in his right arm the best he could.

He tossed the dagger in his hand so that he held it by the blade. He raised the weapon just over his head and aimed for Darkwolf's heart.

Jake flicked his wrist

The dagger somersaulted through the air.

Slow motion.

The knife flipped over and over and over—

The blade buried itself in the vicinity of Darkwolf's heart.

Take that, sonofabitch.

Darkwolf shouted and dropped to his knees.

Confusion seemed to cloud his thoughts as he looked down at the dagger and blood began soaking his T-shirt.

The storm and fog began to clear.

Jake didn't give the warlock-god a chance to react. He bolted the few steps from behind his column to where Darkwolf knelt. Jake launched himself at Darkwolf, tackling him and flinging them both down the stairs.

Pain splintered Jake's head when his skull struck one of the marble steps as they rolled down the short flight. Jake landed on top, and straddled Darkwolf's massive chest. The dagger had apparently been knocked out when they tumbled down the stairs.

The warlock-god had nearly a foot on Jake's six-six and

Jake knew he was in for a hell of a fight—if Darkwolf didn't kill him with his magic.

Instinct and years of special ops training kicked in and Jake rammed his right fist into the wound over Darkwolf's heart. He followed immediately with an uppercut to Darkwolf's nose.

Blood spurted onto Darkwolf's face. He looked dazed with pain, yet furious at the same time.

A purple wave of magic slammed into Jake. He shouted as the force flung him into the street, several feet away.

Shit.

Jake hit the pavement and rolled aside. He rushed to his feet.

Another wave of purple magic rammed him and tossed him into the air.

He landed on his back and slid several feet as air whooshed from his lungs.

Jake struggled to catch his breath as he pushed himself up and started toward Darkwolf again.

The warlock-god had gone limp. Maybe he was down for the count.

Jake sprinted back toward Darkwolf, but came up short.

Elizabeth-Junga crouched at the bottom of the stairs next to Darkwolf—and she started shifting into her demon form.

Her hands developed into long blue claws, and her mouth filled with needlelike teeth that she bared as she started the transformation.

Elizabeth-Junga halted as Darkwolf grabbed her still human-looking ankle.

"No." Darkwolf's face had paled and blood rushed from the gaping hole in his chest. "We . . . must . . . go . . ." he said, his voice starting to fade.

Oh, hell no.

Jake caught sight of his dagger lying on the sidewalk. He sprinted toward it, scooped it up, and whirled on Darkwolf.

In a shimmer of purple magic, the warlock-god and the demon-woman vanished.

Jake jammed the bloody dagger into its sheath on his jeans. "Goddamn. Shit. Fuck."

He turned to face the massacre on the Union Square piazza and his stomach burned.

A strange feeling overcame Jake. For a moment he couldn't move as the emotion slammed into him from somewhere ahead.

Hatred. Pure hatred.

So much malice was in the wave of emotion that it made Jake's skin crawl and he almost stumbled from the power of it.

Where the hell is that coming from?

His heart pounded and a steady beat banged the inside of his skull where he'd struck it on the steps. His body ached from being tossed around by Darkwolf's magic.

He shook off the feelings of hatred bombarding him, ignored the pain, and jogged toward the slaughter.

Bodies littered the square.

Naked Stormcutters and uniformed PSF cops, as well as Marines, were down. Some injured. Many dead.

At least a unit of the Marines had joined the Alliance.

Thank God.

Two D'Danann swords lay on the concrete. Since the Fae warriors turned into sparkles when they died, for all Jake knew those swords could belong to dead D'Danann.

The D'Anu witches—

There. By the monument. Five, six, seven—

Cassia? Where's Cassia?

Sirens shrieked as what looked like a hundred law enforcement vehicles surround the square. News vans with satellite dishes screeched into the closest parking spaces they could find. The news crews hurried to break out their equipment and cameras before police could cordon off anything.

"Shit," Jake growled. "Just what we need."

The Coven of thirteen white magic D'Anu witches appeared from nowhere on one end of the piazza. The white witches always seemed to know when they were needed.

Cassia's gray magic Coven had once been a part of them, but the eight witches in Cassia's Coven had been banished for using gray magic.

He narrowed his gaze at Janis Arrowsmith, who walked with the twelve other witches to do their healing thing. Apparently she was back after disappearing following the last battle. If it hadn't been for that old woman's interference one time, the war could have ended weeks ago.

Jake turned away from the white witches and jogged through the square toward the monument where the gray witches had gathered. He dodged bodies and weapons. Anger burned through him at every familiar dead face of his officers.

Along the way he saw David Bourne and they gave a quick nod to each other as they took care of business. Jake was relieved to see his buddy alive, but had no time for any kind of reunion right now.

Fear crawled up his throat as he saw a blond woman sprawled on the concrete.

Shit! Cassia?

He doubled his steps, his heart hurting from the force of its pounding.

As Jake neared the body, relief poured through him. Not Cassia, but a woman Marine who was stirring. The Marine wasn't dead.

Jake checked to see how bad her injuries were. A slash across her belly, but not too deep. "Over here!" he shouted to one of the med-techs.

He got to his feet as the tech arrived, and looked up to see Kael bounding across the piazza toward the witches. He howled as he ran.

Cassia stepped away from the witches, knelt, and hugged Kael the moment he reached them.

Jake almost stopped breathing. Cassia stood and spotted him hurrying toward her.

The moment Jake reached Cassia he grabbed her, hauled her into his embrace, and held her tight to his chest. She wrapped her arms around his neck and laid her cheek on his heart, which was beating hard enough to come out of his rib cage.

He wanted to kiss Cassia so badly to assure himself she was all right. But holding her in his arms as tightly as he could would have to do. For now.

When he drew away, he tried to brush a smudge of mud and smoke away from her cheek, but only managed to smear it more. "I should know better than to worry about you, Princess."

She smacked him on the arm. "Shhh. Don't call me that," she whispered as her Coven sisters approached. But her expression let him know she'd been just as worried about him.

Jake leaned down and murmured in her ear. "You'll always be Princess to me."

Cassia pulled back, her cheeks red as her gaze met his. Sparks snapped at her fingertips. He heard a cracking sound and hoped she hadn't just broken the piazza's monument. Her turquoise eyes were lovely, as well as her battle-worn clothes and wild hair.

"You know the drill." He brushed hair from her face. "Do your vanishing thing with the other witches. I've got to do my cop thing."

"I'll see you back at headquarters." She backed up before turning away to join her Coven sisters.

They all had surprised expressions as they glanced from Cassia to Jake and back to her. Cassia looked over her shoulder at him once, and gave him a little smile before turning away.

In a voice loud enough for Jake to hear over the craziness in the square, Cassia said to the other witches, "Join hands."

Cassia and Rhiannon gripped Kael's fur as he stood between them. The witches looked at Cassia with confusion, but did what she asked them to. As soon as everyone had joined hands, they disappeared.

A flash and they were gone.

Jake closed his eyes for a moment, wishing Cassia had transferred herself and the other witches to Otherworld to protect them from the horrors they now faced. But he knew she'd taken them back to HQ just like she'd said she would. These women fought with everything they had and they never gave up.

Never.

And he admired every one of them.

With a deep sigh, he readied himself to face the onslaught of military and law enforcement.

God, will this never end?

Jake turned around.

And almost groaned out loud.

Kat DeLuca stood behind him, her arms crossed over her chest, her beautiful features tight and angry. She gripped her reporter's microphone in her hand. A large number boldly stood out within a white circle near the top of the microphone to show that she reported for Channel 17. The cameraman was behind Kat, his back to her as he filmed bodies scattered across Union Square.

"What was that about, Jake?" Kat's biting tone cut over the sounds of chaos in the square as she marched up to Jake so that they were a few inches apart. "Don't tell me that woman's just a *friend.*"

Jake's stomach sank. Crap. He didn't want to end it with Kat this way. He'd planned to get together with her tomorrow and tell her everything as he broke up with her. Gently.

Not like this. He hadn't wanted to hurt her.

Ah, hell. He took a few steps closer to Kat. "I planned to tell—"

Kat drew herself up and clenched one hand around the microphone, and the other into a fist. She slammed her fist against the same spot on his jaw where Cassia had punched him earlier.

Damn, these women hit hard.

Between the two of them and the beating his head had just taken from the fight with Darkwolf, he was practically seeing stars.

He rubbed his jaw and sighed as she took a step back. He imagined he could see smoke from her anger drifting off her casual blouse and slacks. Like Cassia and her sparks.

There was so much more he wanted to say, but nothing he did would make anything right between them. This wasn't a "let's be friends" kind of moment.

All he could say was, "I'm sorry."

"Go to hell, Jake Macgregor." She gave him a piercing glare with her dark eyes. Her short black hair swung around her face as she turned and met up with her cameramen.

Christ. No, it wasn't the way he'd wanted to end it with Kat.

He heaved a frustrated sigh. At least it was done. Now he could go to Cassia and—

And what?

Where could he and Cassia go with a relationship? A Guardian ascending, life-threatening sex . . .

Jake looked over his shoulder to where the witches had disappeared.

He thought about Cassia and how he'd just seen her. Her hair and clothes drenched, smears of mud and smoke on her face and hands.

Beautiful.

The pain in his chest at the thought of letting her go was like someone had taken his own jagged dagger and stabbed him in the heart instead of nailing Darkwolf.

Not going to happen.

I'm not letting Cassia go. Somehow we'll work this out.

No matter how complicated it might turn out to be.

CHAPTER TEN

·

PAIN RIPPED THROUGH DARKWOLF's chest as he transferred himself and Elizabeth from Union Square to their penthouse suite. He landed facedown on the carpet with a hard thump. He still gripped Elizabeth's ankle, but released her as she stumbled and fell beside him.

"Darkwolf!" Panic edged Elizabeth's voice as she moved onto her knees and rolled him onto his back with her inhuman strength. "Dear gods," she whispered. Tears on her cheeks mingled with moisture from the rain.

Tears. From a demon-woman.

If he wasn't in so much pain he might wonder over that a little more.

Darkwolf jerked with the next bout of pain as a seizure grabbed hold of him. It caused him to convulse and obliterated his thoughts.

Blood rushed from the hole in Darkwolf's chest and Elizabeth braced her palm over it, applying pressure. "You can heal." Her voice sounded hoarse, maybe from trying to hold back from crying anymore. "He didn't take your heart out. You can heal."

Darkwolf didn't remember ever feeling so exhausted. He closed his eyes, wanting to slip away from the excruciating pain into darkness and sleep . . .

"Stay with me." Elizabeth's shout brought his attention to her as he snapped his eyelids open. Tears still rolled down her cheeks, but she now had a fierce expression on her face. "Concentrate on healing. This wound is bad. You must use your magic."

Darkwolf groaned and brought his hand up to hers, over

the hole above his heart. Blood coated their fingers as the thick fluid pumped out.

He imagined the wound sealing. Willed it. Healing the tissues above his stone-encased heart. The healing magic felt hot. Harsh. Infinite.

If not for stealing the god Balor's powers, Darkwolf would have died a fast death from the cop's blade. But thanks to the god's stone totem that Darkwolf had absorbed inside his chest, his heart was well protected.

Darkwolf looked into Elizabeth's beautiful blue eyes. Once she had demonstrated to him how easily an opponent could rip out his heart if he wasn't always on guard. She'd shown him he wasn't as invincible as he liked to think. And what had happened tonight proved it even more.

But he had the power of two gods.

It would be nearly impossible to kill him.

Nearly.

Next time he'd be more than ready for Jake Macgregor. The cop had been a thorn in Darkwolf's side since the early days, when Darkwolf had recruited warlocks to bring the demons and the god, Balor, to San Francisco.

What seemed like a lifetime ago.

And the fucking bastard, Macgregor, had almost killed Elizabeth when he shot her.

Darkwolf growled, and pain almost made him growl again. Macgregor should have been dead after the surprise Darkwolf had planned in Golden Gate Park, thanks to his little traitor.

But his informant had let him know afterward that one of the D'Anu witches, the half-Elvin one, had saved the cop.

More agonizing pain bound Darkwolf's chest and he shouted and writhed as his body healed itself. He hadn't realized the process would hurt like hell.

"You will live." Elizabeth brushed her lips over his cheek. "I will not let you die."

The warmth and tenderness she exhibited nearly shocked him speechless. He had felt the same kind of warmth for her when she almost died thanks to that bastard Macgregor, but Elizabeth had never shown those emotions to Darkwolf.

Shit. He *really* didn't want to analyze his feelings. They didn't make any sense. Elizabeth was a demon in a human's shell, so he shouldn't feel anything for her. Except to make sure she served him in whatever way he chose to use her.

Use her . . . The words mocked his thoughts, and he forced them away as he looked up at Elizabeth and met her eyes again.

Pain still squeezed his chest and they were both covered in his blood. He'd half expected his blood to be black now that the powers of both the dark goddess and god ran inside him.

But his blood was red. Perhaps it was the warlock-human side of him. The weak side.

Thoughts of being weak in any way made him clench his teeth. He needed to get up and prove to himself that he was still strong, still powerful.

"Stay down." Elizabeth kept his shoulders pinned to the floor as he tried to sit up. "Wait a little longer to make sure you're all right."

He could have thrown her off with his superior powers, regardless of her demon strength, but he listened and looked up at her.

She was so beautiful. All that long, dark hair, full lips, blue, blue eyes. Elizabeth was once a powerful business-woman, a ball-busting bitch, before Junga stole Elizabeth's human shell. Now Elizabeth and Junga . . . they had become one to him. The demon had evolved into a woman he—he—

Darkwolf closed his eyes, then startled when Elizabeth pressed her soft lips to his. She kissed him gently, moving her lips over his mouth. Almost without thinking, he brought his bloody palms to her cheeks and held her face as he kissed her long, hard, deep.

The kiss stirred him in ways that he'd never been moved before. He and Elizabeth never kissed. They just fucked. But, this—this was . . . he couldn't find the words.

Elizabeth pulled away before he was ready and he opened his eyes. Despite the continual pain in his chest, his cock and balls ached, wanting to be inside her more than anything right now.

She gave him a soft smile as she looked along the length of him and back to his face. "Later. Now, you heal."

Elizabeth slipped down so that her head rested on his biceps and he cradled her close to his side. She wrapped her arm around his waist and snuggled up to him as if they weren't both covered with blood and he wasn't injured.

As if they were lovers. As if they cared about each other. For more than power. For more than sex.

God, gods, goddesses—whoever was out there now that he could pray to, call to, shout at—

No, forget thinking about anything at all.

He'd just enjoy the feel of Elizabeth's body next to his while he slept and healed.

CHAPTER ELEVEN

DARKWOLF COULD HAVE DIED TONIGHT.

Tonight.

My head hurts and my chest aches as the horrible scene replays in my mind. Over and over and over again. The blood. So much blood.

I felt so helpless as I caught a glimpse of Jake Macgregor nearly stealing Darkwolf's life. The moment Jake struck Darkwolf, my chest burned with such incredible fire, as if the cop had stabbed me *with the dagger. I fell on the concrete piazza from the force of the pain.*

With all of his powers, his magic, how could this have happened? How could Darkwolf be vulnerable in any way?

My muscles ache from shaking so hard. The nuns had made me feel helpless as I grew up. That I was a bad person because my mother had been Pagan, a direct descendant of the Ancient Druids. When she died I was forced into the orphanage. According to the nuns, sins stained my soul because of my mother and I had to repent.

But I got even.

Oh, how I got even.

Before I left, I used my emerging Pagan powers to make them hurt. Make them pay.

If only Sister Anne Marie had died when I used my magic to shove her out a second-story window. She fell into a crumpled heap, but she didn't die. The bitch didn't die.

None of them did. I was too young to have enough control over my powers.

Now, of course, is different. I have control. I have power.

Light stings my eyes as the storm fades, leaving the daylight sun shining again.

This whole thing would no doubt end if Darkwolf could attack the Alliance's headquarters. But the Alliance is completely protected against Darkwolf's storms and his Storm-cutters by the thick-walled building, designed to withstand the greatest earthquakes that have ever hit San Francisco.

If the warlock-god hadn't escaped with that demon-bitch, I would have gone after the cop myself to save Darkwolf. I would have blown Jake apart.

With one word, one action, I could have screwed everything up that has been so perfect. I could have been exposed.

No way. I'll see this through.

I was there at the beginning.

I'll be there at the end.

CHAPTER TWELVE

THE MOMENT THEY ARRIVED in the kitchen at the Alliance's HQ, all seven of the D'Anu witches dropped hands and stepped back from Cassia and Kael.

It was the first time in four centuries that Cassia didn't feel as one with her current Coven—as a D'Anu witch.

Because she wasn't a witch anymore. At least not in body, or in duties.

She was fully Elvin, a Guardian ascending.

And once the battle with Darkwolf ended, her task here would be complete and she would return to Otherworld.

Forever.

Thoughts of leaving these incredible women, whom she'd come to think of as her friends and Coven sisters, made her heart hurt.

Thoughts of leaving Jake made her want to weep.

The threat of tears made her eyes ache.

For a long moment it was her looking at them looking at her. Everyone was soaked. Their shoes smudged mud and grass on the kitchen floor while water dripping from their T-shirts and jeans ran into puddles. Kael had blood on his fur. The room's scents of spices and candles were almost overwhelmed by the smell of wet clothing, dirt, blood, smoke, and rain.

Cassia glanced from one friend to the next.

Silver's gray eyes studied Cassia as if in deep contemplation. She had her wet silvery-blond hair held back with a clasp and, as always, her silver snake bracelet wound its way up her wrist. Like the rest of the witches, she wore a black T-shirt under her Kevlar body armor, and also wore black jeans and running shoes. The Kevlar probably wouldn't fit much longer, considering Silver's pregnancy.

Rhiannon, Silver's best friend, focused her green gaze on Cassia. The demon scars on Rhiannon's cheek stood out more than normal against her fair skin as she gave an almost angry frown. Her chin-length hair hung in wet strands around her face and she wiped droplets from her cheeks with the back of her hand.

Tension in the air mounted as Rhiannon's Shadows stirred within her. The Shadows were part of Rhiannon's half-Drow heritage that only Cassia had knowledge of until fairly recently. Rhiannon's Shadows could be—and had been— deadly.

Copper, Silver's blood sister, tilted her head, her long copper-colored braid swinging to the side with the movement as she looked at Cassia, as if for the first time. Her honeybee familiar, Zephyr, buzzed around her head and landed on her ear. Copper had finally had her ankle cast removed from an injury obtained when the dark goddess had escaped Underworld.

Alyssa, as usual, looked a little shell-shocked, and even more so with her hair plastered to her head and water rolling down her face. The brunette witch had always been the nervous one of the bunch. Everyone in the Coven tended to mother her a little because she'd been more fragile than the rest. Despite her delicate appearance and almost shy personality, she was as talented a witch as any of the rest of them.

Hannah had her hands braced on her hips, her expression cool and calculating. Even soaked, Hannah looked elegant. The blond lock of hair swept across her forehead to join the dark hair that she'd pulled back with a clasp. Her gold armband glittered just below the sleeve of her T-shirt.

Sydney's chic glasses didn't hide her beautiful lavender eyes, which were both curious and assessing. As usual, she had spelled the glasses to be rain-repellant. Her cheekbones seemed even more pronounced as her damp hair was held high at the back of her head in a clip.

Out of everyone, the rough-edged, blond, blue-eyed, petite Mackenzie looked the angriest as she glared at Cassia. Mackenzie had been the most eager of their small Coven to embrace gray magic. Silver had been the first to cautiously use gray magic, and physically paid a price for it. Mackenzie had seemed almost to revere gray magic, like one might a treasure.

"You definitely have some explaining to do, Cassia." Silver rubbed her snake bracelet. It was something she did when she was nervous, uncomfortable—or pissed. "This time you're going to give it to us straight. Every blessed bit of it."

"Uh, yeah." Copper flipped her wet braid over her shoulder, a spark in her cinnamon eyes. "If we have to tie you to the chair, you're going to tell everything you've been hiding from us."

Cassia almost smiled. It would take all seven of them to bind her now that she had ascended into most of her powers. If they could even manage such a feat.

"Do you want to change into dry clothing first?" Cassia buried her fingers in Kael's wet fur. "Or would you prefer to get right to it?"

The witches glanced at one another, communicating with their expressions. Silver looked back at Cassia. "It's probably smart to get out of these wet things, and then meet here as soon as we're dressed. I have a feeling you have a lot to tell us, and we might as well be comfortable."

Cassia sighed. This wasn't going to be easy.

She headed off with the witches to the temporary rooms that had been erected in the huge warehouse. Most of the witches were married and shared their rooms with their husbands—Silver, Copper, Sydney, and Rhiannon had married D'Danann warriors. Hannah had married the King of the Dark Elves, and was now Queen.

So that left Cassia, Alyssa, and Mackenzie, who roomed together. Mackenzie pointedly ignored Cassia as they changed, and Alyssa remained quiet. When they all had finished dressing in clean, dry clothing, they headed back to the kitchen.

The witches were completely dry from their hair to their toes thanks to their magic. A couple of the witches spelled the kitchen floor clean and lit sandalwood incense and vanilla candles.

When they were seated at the table, everyone looked at Cassia. She shifted in her chair, feeling uncomfortable from the intensity of their stares.

Where is my serenity? My calm?

Even if Kael is right and that's not my true self, why can't I fake it like I have all these years?

"Because you have ascended," Kael said in her mind as he pushed the kitchen door open with his nose. It swung closed again when he was fully inside. *"You must face and acknowledge who you really are."*

"I don't like this, Kael."

"You do not have a choice."

On that happy note, Cassia cleared her throat and looked at the witches. "I'm going to tell you everything, and what I have to say will more than likely surprise you." She reached out to them with her senses, projecting the love she felt.

Something harsh, angry, and dark slapped her so hard her mind spun with it. She jerked her head up. She swept her gaze from one witch to the next.

Could it have been Rhiannon's Shadows? Mackenzie's anger? Hannah's disdain?

Cassia placed one of her palms on her belly, over her star birthmark. Her stomach twisted at the thought that someone—or maybe more than one someone—was so angry with her that their response was like a physical attack.

Silver covered one of Cassia's hands on the table and squeezed, offering an encouraging smile. "No matter what you have to say, we'll still love you."

"Thank you." Tears stung Cassia's eyes. She was getting so tired of all of this emotion. "In my heart," Cassia said as she addressed everyone, "you are my Coven sisters in every way, and among my dearest friends."

"But . . . ?" Rhiannon said as she stared at Cassia.

Cassia managed a little smile. "Like each of you, I serve

the goddess, but I am not a D'Anu witch." Shocked expressions met her words, but she continued. "I am fully Elvin."

She took a deep breath before she slowly let the air out to tell them what would likely be the greatest shock of all. "I am the daughter of the Great Guardian."

Silence. Complete and absolute silence.

If their expressions had been stunned before, it was nothing compared to how they were looking at her right this moment.

"Whoa." Copper held her hands up as she cut the silence. "Did you just say the Great Guardian is your *mother*?"

"Yes." Cassia gave a slight nod. "I am a Guardian ascending and will soon be a Guardian like my brothers." Cassia felt a little of the tension in her body slide away as Kael leaned his big body against her leg and hip, giving her some comfort. She didn't want to tell them the part about her actually taking the Great Guardian's place one day.

"I am four hundred and twenty-five years old," Cassia continued, "young for one of the Light Elves. I have spent my first four centuries here on this Earth Otherworld, watching over Elvin Halflings and serving Covens around the world since the early 1600s."

The witches were even more speechless as they stared at Cassia, some with open mouths or wide-eyed shock.

Silver broke another long silence. "I don't know what to say."

"I have reached the end of my service in this Otherworld." Cassia clenched her hands on the tabletop, her heart beating hard enough to hurt. "When this battle with Darkwolf is over, I will return to Otherworld and take my place as a Guardian."

"That's more than I think I can digest at one sitting," Hannah said in her cultured, controlled voice.

Through the walls came the usual busy sounds in the warehouse.

Absolute quiet reigned in the kitchen.

Copper cleared her throat. "Uh. Well." She glanced toward the fridge. "It's worked before."

Mackenzie frowned. "What has worked before?"

"Häagen-Dazs," Copper said with a look that said she also needed some time to think about what Cassia had just told them. Probably to distract herself from her emotions as well as the others. "Nothing like a sugar rush to wake up the mind."

For a moment everyone stayed in their seats, looking at each other.

Then, in what seemed like an attempt to break the stranglehold on them all, Rhiannon got up out of her chair. "Dibs · on the rest of the chocolate chocolate chip."

"No way." Copper pushed past Rhiannon. Copper was lighter on her feet again now that her ankle cast had been taken off. "It was my idea."

Cassia tried to smile at what seemed like normality as everyone claimed pints of ice cream that they'd hidden from the D'Danann warriors, who ate *everything* in sight. But things were far from normal.

Once all the women, with the exception of Cassia, had spoons in their hands and pints of everything from butter pecan to cookies and cream, Cassia continued her story. She explained how she hadn't been allowed to use her full powers or her combat training while in this Otherworld. She'd had to use only what magic the D'Anu witches could wield.

"That brings up what I think we really need to talk about." Silver rested one hand on her belly. She still carried the baby in tight and her pooch hadn't grown very big yet. "That fire. Those Stormcutters . . ."

"You killed them, Cassia." Copper stuffed her spoon into her chocolate chocolate chip and stopped eating. "D'Anu witches don't kill."

"That's true." Cassia reached down and stroked Kael for comfort. "But Elves have no such qualms."

The nearly constant silence that greeted her every secret was starting to get on her usually calm nerves.

"Point taken," Sydney said quietly. "But to see you do it— that was frightening."

"You sure kicked ass," Copper said, in another obvious attempt at lightening the mood.

"You saved countless lives." Silver pushed some of her hair over her shoulder, her hair now free-flowing down her back instead of in a clasp. "The D'Danann are Fae, and we haven't judged them for killing evil. The Dark Elves kill, and we've had no problem with that. I don't see why we can't accept your abilities and choices as well."

"I suppose." Rhiannon's pentagram earrings winked in the sunlight streaming from the warehouse's skylights. It had been dark during the battle because of the warlock-god's magic, but it was actually the middle of the day. "It's still hard to stomach."

"How do we know you're telling the truth?" Mistrust still simmered in Mackenzie's gaze. "You've lied to us all this time."

Cassia sighed. "I have nothing but my word and my magic. You saw the power I wielded during the battle. I also transported us all directly from Union Square to this very room, something no D'Anu witch can do. Even a full-blooded Elvin male or female could not perform that magic without going through a transference point. Only a Guardian ascending or a Guardian can."

"That certainly was a trip." Copper shook her head. "I thought traveling to Otherworld was rough, but what you did—I was sure I was going to lose my breakfast when we got here."

"No kidding," Sydney said, and Alyssa agreed with a nod.

"Well, no matter who or what you are, you're still one of us." Silver smiled. "You are our Coven sister."

Words of agreement came from everyone but Mackenzie, who remained stubbornly silent.

Despite Mackenzie, tension around the table eased considerably and Cassia's heart no longer felt so weary.

The witches questioned Cassia on everything from what a "Guardian ascending" meant to her life on Earth over the past four hundred years. Cassia told them everything she was allowed to, but left out the part about needing to go through her transition with an Elvin male to complete her ascension. Or dying if she didn't.

"That's all great," Rhiannon said as she polished off her cherry chocolate chip ice cream. "What I really want to know now is what's going on between you and Jake?"

Heat rushed to Cassia's face and she wished for her serenity more than ever.

"Yeah." Copper twirled the end of her braid. "You two looked pretty, uh, attached."

"Nothing." Cassia swallowed. "Besides, he does have a girlfriend."

"That's right." Rhiannon pointed her spoon at Copper. "Kat DeLuca from Channel 17 News, right?"

Copper nodded. "Uh-huh."

Tingles ran up and down Cassia's spine. She hadn't known who Jake's girlfriend was, and the thought of the beautiful dark-haired reporter in Jake's arms left her hot and flushed.

Rhiannon said, "We didn't know anything about her until she stopped by, the same morning the Stormcutters attacked Jake and you had to take him to Otherworld."

The fact Jake had seen Kat just before going to Otherworld and then kissed Cassia a few days later made angry sparks buzz in her stomach. The teakettle rattled on the stove and no fire was burning beneath it. A couple of the witches glanced at the teakettle but turned to continue their conversation with Cassia.

"Jake and I are just . . . friends." Cassia clenched her hand in Kael's fur, and he nosed her knee with his large head.

Rhiannon folded her arms on the table, leaned forward, and smirked. "That sure didn't look like a 'friend' moment to me."

"Whatever," Cassia said, borrowing one of Mackenzie's favorite phrases. "Believe what you will."

Copper and Rhiannon grinned at each other, and the rest of those around the table looked amused. Again, everyone except Mackenzie.

"Besides," Cassia added, straightening in her seat. "I would never have a relationship with a man who has a girlfriend."

"We know you wouldn't." Rhiannon looked serious for the first time since bringing up Jake. "But for all we know, he's going to break up with Kat."

Cassia tried to control the heat flowing through her body and let the tension slip away. "It is impossible for Jake and me to have a relationship. So we'll leave it at that."

"Oh, no you don't." Rhiannon shook her head, causing her chin-length hair to fly into her face. "You can't just say that and leave us hanging."

Cassia shrugged and refused to answer the barrage of questions that followed.

When she had a chance, she found a good excuse to change the subject. "We need to scry together to see what must be done next. Or what's going on." As she looked around the circle of witches she added, "Maybe we can pinpoint the Alliance's traitor."

"It can't be one of us. And definitely not the D'Danann." Silver swept her gaze at all of the witches and Cassia. "So it must be someone in the PSF."

Mackenzie scowled even more. "It could be one of the Drow."

Immediately both Rhiannon and Hannah glared at her. Garran was King of the Dark Elves and Rhiannon was his daughter. And now Hannah was Garran's Queen.

"Don't even go there," Hannah said in a low, measured, deadly tone. "The Drow aren't traitors."

"What's wrong with you, Mackenzie?" Rhiannon's green eyes sparked with anger. "You've been sullen and angry, and now you're pointing your perfect little finger at my and Hannah's people."

"They're not your people." Mackenzie returned their glares. "If I have to remind you, a faction of them betrayed us just a couple of weeks ago, before Hannah married Garran."

"That traitor was sentenced to death." The anger in Hannah's voice became stronger. "Every one of the remaining Dark Elves support and follow Garran."

"How do you know?" Mackenzie clenched her hands on the black laminate tabletop. "What makes you so sure?"

"Because Garran is my husband," Hannah said.

"And he is my father," Rhiannon added.

"You're both blind—" Mackenzie started.

"Stop." Cassia automatically took control of the situation, as she always did, although she'd never seen this kind of in-fighting with these witches. "Arguing won't do any good. Hopefully scrying, and a little sleuthing, will."

Mackenzie, Hannah, and Rhiannon continued to glare at each other, but stopped arguing.

"Why don't we get started?" Cassia released Kael's fur, pushed her chair back, and stood. "Let's gather our scrying tools."

Everyone nodded and, without saying anything else, got up and left the kitchen. Cassia stayed behind for a moment and stared at the door.

"What's happening to this Coven, Kael?" Cassia said aloud as her chest ached. "Did this all start with me? Is this my fault?"

"No, Princess." Kael butted her hand with his nose so that she'd pet his head, no doubt to give her comfort. *"Something is most certainly wrong. But what, I do not know."*

Cassia gave a slow nod. "An infection. There's an infection among us. I don't know where it started, or how, but we need to find the source and deal with it."

AFTER SEVERAL GRUELING HOURS at the scene of the battle, Jake headed to the warehouse HQ on the pier along the San Francisco Bay. The warehouse actually belonged to a cargo company, but the PSF, with the help of the National Guard, had commandeered it to use as a headquarters during all of this madness. Who knew how long the Alliance would need it.

Jake glanced at the palm trees that lined the Embarcadero as he neared the warehouse. The trees weren't native to San Francisco and had been shipped in when the Embarcadero Freeway was torn down and the Embarcadero rebuilt as a boulevard with a wide pedestrian promenade. Businesses and housing had flourished.

Now—every bit of life in the city had ground to a halt.

Jake's stomach growled. He was starving, and needed to sleep like there was no tomorrow.

And he had to see Cassia.

When he reached HQ, he parked the unmarked police car he'd borrowed between two of the PSF vehicles that looked like a cross between a tank and a Humvee. Multiple SWAT trucks and military vehicles took up whatever space was available along the warehouse that ran down a long pier.

The smell of brine rolled in with the early evening air off the bay, and Jake's gut clenched in a knee-jerk reaction. The demons they'd fought since Halloween had smelled like rotten fish. Thank God the Fomorii were history.

Jake nodded to the two Tuatha D'Danann guards at the entrance to the warehouse before he entered. More D'Danann guards positioned themselves on top of the building, but they kept their wings out so they wouldn't be seen by human eyes. Unfortunately, their wings didn't hide them from magical beings.

Kitchen. He had to get some food. And none of that crap that the D'Danann ate from Dagda's Cauldron of Plenty. The kinds of foods they served two millennia ago just didn't have the same appeal as good old twenty-first-century chow.

When Jake walked through the door to the kitchen, he came to a stop. Cassia stood there, staring at the door. She looked tired and upset. Immediately all he wanted to do was make her feel better.

God, she was beautiful. All that long blond hair, full breasts, slim shoulders, a small waist, and hips that flared gently. He remembered, when he had first come to know the D'Anu witches, that Cassia had always dressed to disguise her beauty with bulky clothing, short curls, and somehow she'd made her features look pretty average.

Even then he'd been attracted to her.

He met her gorgeous turquoise eyes for a moment before he strode over to her, grabbed her in his arms, and kissed her so hard it made his head spin.

Cassia matched him with a kiss as hungry as his, their tongues meeting as they explored each other, tasted each other. She smelled so good. Vanilla and spices and woman.

In a rough movement she pushed him away, her breathing

ragged, her gaze filled with desire. Then the desire faded and her eyes now glinted with anger. "How could you do that, Jake? Kiss me. You have a girlfriend."

"Not anymore." Jake slid his fingers into Cassia's hair and she gasped as he cupped the back of her head and drew her closer. "Kat and I had a talk at the square." He mentally winced at the thought of exactly how that conversation went. "We called it off."

Jake brought Cassia to him again for another wild kiss. He settled one hand on her hip as he held her to him. His cock hardened and she gave a soft moan as he pressed his erection tighter to her belly. He could swear she wove magic around them as powerful as his feelings had grown for her.

Pots and jars rattled near the stove.

With her Elvin strength, she jerked completely away again, this time stepping back, out of reach. Her lips were moist, red, desire in her eyes again. She held her palm to her chest as if trying to slow her breathing. "This . . . can't work. You know about the transition, the ascension, and everything else."

Jake flinched at the thought of Cassia being with another man and his gut burned. "There's got to be some way around this. We'll work it out, Princess. Somehow." He clenched and unclenched his hands. "Get me an audience with the Great Guardian. I'll talk to her and ask her to help me get you through your transition."

"You know there's no way to change things." She shook her head. "And I doubt the Guardian would even consider what you're proposing." Her features were so sad he wanted to scoop her up in his arms and never let her go. "You and me—I wish I could make things different. But there's too much at stake. Not least of all your life."

Jake reached for her. "Whatever it is, I'm up for the job. I'll do anything I have to."

"Would you?" she asked quietly, but not in a manner that said she was genuinely asking him. More that she was pointing out a few facts. "Let's say you survived the transition— would you give up your life here to go to Otherworld forever? With a woman who holds the balance of all the Otherworlds in her hands? To a place where the Light Elves are clearly prejudiced against humans?" She shook her head. "I would never subject you to a life like that."

Her words slapped him and he didn't know what to say.

The door slammed open behind them and Jake glanced over his shoulder to see Mackenzie and Alyssa walking through with their scrying tools. They looked at Jake and Cassia for a moment before seating themselves at the table.

"You need to go." Cassia turned and he watched as she retrieved a small, soft bag from one of the cabinets. Clicks came from the bag as she palmed it. The sounds reminded him of times when he was a kid getting out his bag of marbles to play with, and how the marbles had knocked against each other. When Cassia faced Jake again, she said, "We— the witches and I—need to scry now."

He gave her a hard, long look before he could get himself to leave the kitchen. His chest hurt and his head ached.

No. He and Cassia would work this out.

Although the idea was really crazy. She couldn't leave Otherworld and he wasn't about to leave his career in the PSF, as well as aiding in rebuilding his city once the Darkwolf nightmare was over.

He rubbed his short hair in a frustrated movement as he walked through the warehouse.

It wasn't until he reached his room that he remembered he hadn't grabbed anything to eat and had pretty much been kicked out of the kitchen so the witches could scry.

Food from Dagda's Cauldron of Plenty wasn't looking so bad at the moment. A few D'Danann tankards of ale might just dull the pain in his head and his heart.

For a while.

CHAPTER THIRTEEN

IT WASN'T LONG BEFORE all of the witches gathered around the table with their scrying tools. Cassia lit myrrh incense to aid meditation, and used a lion incense holder. Lions represented caring for those you love, with protection, authority, and ferocity.

Cassia clenched her bag of rune stones in her fist as she seated herself. Mackenzie brought her tarot cards; Hannah was ready with her black mirror and salt crystals; Silver had her cauldron filled with consecrated water; Sydney arranged three candles and her silver bowl of consecrated water; Alyssa had a slender yellow taper candle and a fox candleholder. Someone grabbed a box of matchsticks.

Cassia was surprised that Alyssa had picked yellow. One of the things it signified was the witch's waning self-assurance. But it was also good for divination. Interesting, too, that she had chosen a fox candleholder, when foxes were known for craftiness, cunning, and charm.

Copper's ability was dream-visions, so it depended on the situation whether or not she had dreamed of anything that pertained to what all of the witches were currently scrying about.

Rhiannon had the ability to vision the past, future, and present, but she couldn't always do it on call. Weeks ago her mind had been taken over by the dark goddess. It had been difficult for Rhiannon to readjust after she'd banished the goddess from her essence. Rhiannon had confided only in Cassia about her struggles.

Automatically, the witches looked to Cassia to set the scrying in motion, as they had turned to her more and more over the past months for guidance. But now a few of the witches' expressions changed—to curiosity on Copper's part, confusion from Alyssa, and mistrust from Mackenzie.

The urge to cry caused Cassia to swallow past a huge lump in her throat. These women had been her friends for so long. They had gone through so much together. Why did Cassia's coming forth with her story make such a difference?

Because I've lied to them all along.

Pretending that nothing had changed seemed like the best thing to do right now.

Cassia looked at Sydney, who sat on her right. "Why don't you start?"

"Sure." Sydney nodded and took the box of wooden matchsticks, struck one, and began lighting the three fat candles between her and the silver bowl of consecrated water. The smell of sulfur immediately met the myrrh scent of the incense. Scents of sandalwood, honeysuckle, and cedar soon mingled with the other smells.

"I chose brown for grounding and learning more about the here-and-now, and sandalwood-scented for spirituality," Sydney said as she lit the brown candle, then moved on to the next. "Dark blue for augmenting divination and spiritual journeys. Honeysuckle-scented for focus." When she lit the final candle, her jaw tensed. "Black to aid in determining the truth, and cedar-scented for bravery to do what we have to do." She looked up. "Find the traitor."

Tension immediately thickened around the table like the combined scents swirling together. First, Sydney tipped the brown candle and allowed the brown wax to create a design in the water. "A crab. The traitor is misdirecting us. No surprise there," she added before she dribbled dark blue wax into the bowl. "Raven. Definitely a warning." Then she muttered, "No kidding," before picking up the black candle. After she spilled its wax into the water she was quiet for a moment. "A chameleon. Our traitor is someone who easily transforms to whatever suits him or her."

Alyssa shook her head, looking more than concerned. She had always seemed traumatized every single time they divined, ever since Cassia had known her.

Copper nodded. "That's right along the lines of what I've been thinking."

"Time to move on." Hannah never minced words. She looked at her dragon-framed black mirror and held up an open vial of large salt crystals. She watched the patterns the crystals made in the air, and then studied the patterns that formed on the mirror.

Hannah took her time before raising her gaze and meeting Cassia's. "Whoever it is, it'll be the last person we expect."

Cassia couldn't help but feel uncomfortable beneath Hannah's stare. Did the witches think it was her? She hadn't even been around when Darkwolf's Stormcutter attacks started—although she now commanded power that would allow her to betray the D'Anu easily. Only time would prove that Cassia would never betray anyone in the Alliance, especially her Coven sisters—although it still hurt to be suspected in any way.

Cassia moved her gaze to Alyssa. "Ready?"

Alyssa nodded. A match made a snapping sound as she sparked it to life and lit the candle. Cassia sniffed the air. Grapefruit-scented? Since when did anyone use grapefruit after the war started? It was primarily used for battling the blues. Apparently Alyssa was having some problems coping.

As she studied the flame, Alyssa took a deep breath as if drawing the candle scent into her. Her voice shook as she spoke. "Battles. Betrayal . . . Murder." She swallowed, her throat visibly working. "Someone *very* close to us will be murdered."

Sydney sucked in her breath. Silver's and Mackenzie's eyes widened. Copper's jaw dropped. Hannah's expression didn't change.

Cassia's heart had been beating faster as each witch scried, but now it pounded hard enough to hurt. Murder. Someone *close* to them all.

Dear Goddess.

Mackenzie turned her attention to her tarot deck, shuffled, and began laying the cards out in a Celtic cross spread. "I just can't seem to get a handle on anything with my cards lately."

Mackenzie analyzed the spread a few moments longer. "Challenges and opposition, which is a big 'Duh.' Movement and communication in that there will be change and the traitor is relaying information somehow to Darkwolf." She looked up with a frustrated expression. "It's all so vague, other than stating the obvious." She scowled and gathered up her cards. "This is such bull."

Cassia tried not to let her concern over Mackenzie show. She'd never seen the witch act like this before, or have such problems divining.

Silver went next. Sometimes her visions would appear in foggy 3-D images above her pewter cauldron, and other times only she could see the divination on the surface of the water itself. Cassia was almost fearful what they would see if the images rose above the cauldron—what if they saw the traitor and it was one of the witches?

It can't be.

Cassia's stomach lurched sideways as Silver pushed her long silvery-blond hair over her shoulders, then stared into the water. "Everything's kind of wavy, unclear." Silver frowned and cocked her head. "I see two images. Someone kneeling with his or her head bowed. The other person standing and looking down at the kneeling person." She looked up. "I believe the person standing is Darkwolf. I think if I could see the face of the person kneeling, I'd know who the traitor is."

Alyssa visibly shuddered and Sydney bit her lower lip. Mackenzie stared at Silver with a blank expression, while Copper looked concerned, and Hannah had tilted her head and had an analytical look to her features. Rhiannon's lips were twisted, and Cassia sensed Rhiannon's Shadows were close to the surface, and that they were waiting to burst free, out of Rhiannon's control.

Next Rhiannon took her turn. She had everyone take hands and close their eyes as she closed her own. Cassia kept her lids open just enough to watch Rhiannon. Cassia felt Rhiannon's powerful ability to vision race through her. Cassia also felt the Shadows, and for some reason she wanted to cringe from their touch. She had never had that reaction before.

In a tortured voice, Rhiannon said, "Darkness . . . and then death. A horrible, horrible death." A tear rolled down her scarred cheek. "Someone close . . . very close . . . is going to die."

Cassia's soul chilled. What if it was one of her Coven sisters? What if it was Jake?

The thoughts made the chill stab her belly like icicles, cold and sharp.

"I am *so* getting the creeps," Copper said as they dropped hands. "Maybe we're all just too into this traitor thing." She leaned her chair back and rocked lightly on its back legs. "Or maybe not."

Copper shuttered her eyelids and a sense of darkness hovered over her. "I've been dreaming a lot lately of a vulture, meaning a predator is close." She gazed above them at the skylight, as if she didn't want to meet anyone's eyes. "We don't have to look too far to find our traitor. Not far at all."

Silence met Copper's announcement.

"But who?" Mackenzie finally said, appearing genuinely perplexed. "Someone on the command team? One of the D'Danann, Drow, or PSF officers?" When everyone in the room remained quiet, Mackenzie frowned. "I refuse to believe it could be one of us. Not one of our Coven sisters would betray us."

"Of course not." Silver looked horrified. "That's impossible."

All of the witches nodded in agreement as they glanced at each other across the table.

Cassia said nothing. She wasn't sure what she felt right then.

Instead she focused on her rune stones, drawing thirteen from the bag and casting them onto the table in the Elvin way. Elves with the power of divination read the runes that landed faceup.

Six showed their faces.

Hagalaz. Storms, stress, crisis.

Nauthiz. Test, ordeal.

Isa. Stillness, silence.

Ihwaz. Life and Death.

Elhaz. Danger. Communication.

Teiwaz. Victory. Truth.

Cassia closed her eyes for a moment and let the energy of the runes filter through her. This time the stones almost all gave off negative energy in the patterns they had landed in, and it caused her to shiver. But she had to sort it out.

She raised her eyelids, looked at the stones again, then to each of her sister witches. "We already know we're in the middle of a crisis, and the storms are a huge factor. Anu is putting us to a test and she will remain silent until all of this"—she waved her hand to encompass San Francisco—"is over.

"I'm simply being repetitious in that we already know there's danger everywhere around us." She lowered her voice. "But it's more so because of the traitor. The dark goddess stole the lives of many, many people, including members of the Alliance." She took a deep breath. "But because of the traitor, our inner circle is breached. I, too, see death."

Silver braced her elbows on the table in front of her cauldron and buried her face in her palms. Her shoulders jerked and Cassia's heart broke knowing her Coven sister was crying.

Hannah looked at the skylights, her face pale. Alyssa stared at her hands in her lap. Mackenzie shook her head, and Sydney bit her lower lip again.

"How could Anu desert us like this?" Copper looked angry, hurt, sad. An expression mirrored on Rhiannon's face.

"It's not right." Rhiannon banged her fist on the table, startling Silver into raising her head and everyone into looking at Rhiannon. "She can't forsake us like this."

"It's a trial." Cassia swept the stones into the bag, each one weighing the bag down as if it were a concrete brick. "The stones said something else, as well."

"What's that?" Copper focused on Cassia, her gaze steady.

"One side or the other will claim victory—sooner than we expect." Cassia slowly looked from Coven sister to Coven sister, looking for some sign. Something.

"We will learn the truth of who the traitor is." With a sinking feeling in her gut, Cassia added, "And it won't be long."

WHEN THE WITCHES SCRIED, everyone made sure to steer clear of the kitchen, including Jake. He grabbed a quick meal of mutton, vegetables, and fresh bread along with a tankard of ale from the Cauldron of Dagda before returning to his room.

The cauldron had fortunately been taken out of the kitchen and set on a table that was easily accessible to everyone in the Alliance. Jake wasn't crazy about mutton, but it was food, and that's what the cauldron had served up.

It was fascinating, really. A guy just reached into the cauldron and grabbed whatever met his hand. Like what the D'Danann called a trencher—a foot-long, six-inch-wide, carved-out wooden plate. It was usually full of some kind of meat as well as bread, and sometimes vegetables. Reach in again and there'd be a huge metal mug the warriors called a tankard, full of a gut-stomping ale.

With his stomach roaring with hunger from the smells of roasted meat and freshly baked bread, Jake scooted his chair up to the table in his room. He focused intently on his laptop as he ate and studied the weapon schematics.

When he was in the Marine Corps, after his men had been murdered in the Bamiyan Valley, Jake had dedicated himself to creating weapons to fight dark magic.

A goddamned walk in the park.

Right.

Jake tore off a chunk of mutton with his teeth and grimaced at the strong, gamey, almost greasy taste. His stomach was bitching too much to give a damn about the taste of anything right now, so he worked on eating the mutton while he studied the latest weapons schematics.

As far as what he'd been able to design up until this point, he'd managed to come up with the heart-seeking bullets that had done their share in fights against the Fomorii. Modifying existing Tasers into demon-Tasers had been another one of his brainstorms.

All along, he'd been working his ass off to create some kind of god-stopping weapon, too. He'd dead-ended at every turn, with every modification. He'd used a sophisticated computer simulation program to "demo" the weapons, and each design would fail spectacularly.

Jake washed down the mutton with some ale and tore off a hunk of bread.

He *knew* he was onto something with the laser device he was working on now. But in every damned scenario the weapon failed. He snorted. Failing was definitely an understatement. No metal or any other material known to man could handle the intensity of the laser without exploding into a million goddamned fragments.

Jake went still as a thought occurred to him.

No metal or any other material known to man.

Known to man.

D'Danann. Dark Elves. Maybe even Light Elves.

Could they have any materials strong enough to handle a laser like this?

Well, hell. It was worth a shot.

Jake wiped his fingers on his jeans before snapping his laptop shut, grabbing it under his arm, and heading out the door. His strides ate up the distance toward the command center.

"I need to meet with every head of the Alliance," Jake said the moment he spotted Hawk.

The D'Danann warrior gave a quick nod as if he recognized Jake's urgency. "I will get word to Keir and Tiernan."

Jake gripped his laptop as he jogged the short distance to the PSF's own strategy room. "Fredrickson," Jake called out, then nodded to another officer. "Hopper. Join me in the Alliance command center ASAP."

"Gotcha, Captain," Fredrickson said as he and Davies set aside what they'd been working on and headed out the door.

Jake followed them. *Hell, yeah.* David Bourne and two other Marines were entering the warehouse. Bourne had a couple of healing scratches on his face and three or four stitched-up cuts on his arms.

"Speed." Jake went up to the man and they shook hands. "Thanks for covering my back at the park."

"Damn, Bull." Bourne stared at Jake. "I still can't believe you're alive." With a shake of his head, Bourne continued. "That knife wound you took to the gut, shit, but you should be dead. And that chick with the fire show—you weren't kidding about these guys being useful in a fight."

"If there was time I'd tell you, 'I told you so,'" Jake said, holding back a grin. "Right now we've got some matters to discuss with the Alliance.

"Good to have you join us." Jake nodded to the other two Marines, who stood at attention, before he looked back at Bourne.

Bourne rubbed his close-cropped hair. "You know it won't be long till the FBI, CIA, and fuck knows who else will be in here, too."

"For now they're concentrating their efforts in other ways," Jake said. "Thank God. The last thing we need is any of the agencies sticking their noses in our business. We don't have the time or the manpower to deal with anyone who doesn't have a clue about what we're dealing with."

Jake shifted his laptop to his other arm and glanced up at the night-darkened skylights as he walked with Bourne and the two other Marines to the command center. The day had slipped by incredibly fast, so he wasn't surprised to see the Drow King, Garran, in the midst of the mix of most of the key Alliance players in the command center.

Body heat warmed the crowded command center. The room smelled of sweat, but also had the clean scent of good magic, as well as the earthy smell of the slightly darker magic of the Drow.

The Drow King Garran was in the room along with two of his most trusted warriors, Yale and Zyn. Garran's First in Command, Carden, always stayed in the Drow realm in case something happened to Garran. Smart move.

The King of the Dark Elves matched Jake in height, weight, and build, and had silvery-blue hair down to his shoulders. His skin tone was bluish-gray, and his eyes were an odd liquid silver. Like other Drow warriors, Garran wore a breastplate with chest straps, although as King his gear was jewel-encrusted. He had recently married Hannah, one of the D'Anu witches.

Bourne and his men did a double take when they caught sight of the Dark Elves. Jake introduced the Marines to the Drow as well as introducing them to the D'Danann warriors. As usual, Hawk, Tiernan, and Keir represented the D'Danann.

The D'Danann had conceded to wearing human T-shirts and jeans, but under long black coats that concealed their swords, daggers, and any number of other weapons.

The Drow used bows and arrows as well as swords and daggers. They were quick when it came to whipping those suckers out and shooting pewter arrows with diamond heads.

Jake rubbed his formerly wounded arm. He'd had a taste of one of those arrows. Not something he wanted a repeat of. He'd rather have been shot in his arm with a bullet.

Lieutenant Fredrickson stood beside Officer Jamie Hopper. She was an excellent choice to replace the injured Landers.

The only absentees from the command center were the witches who were doing their scrying thing. The three witch reps were normally Rhiannon, Copper, and Silver.

Jake and some of the others pulled up chairs around the huge, backlit, computerized map table while others remained standing.

Through a port on one edge of the table, Jake hooked up his laptop to the map table and brought up the weapon schematics he'd been working on.

Bourne whistled through his teeth. "If that's what I think it is, that's one kickass weapon you've got there."

Hawk leaned forward to study the design that was now expanded on the large map table. "What is this?"

Jake explained how the weapon worked, and the power behind what he was pretty sure could take out a duo-god.

"It creates a high-powered electromagnetic containment field," Jake said to Otherworld warriors, who looked confused. "The intensity of the field would be so great that it could completely obliterate even a god."

David Bourne was nodding as he obviously grasped the concept while Hawk asked, "Obliterate—that is not a word we are familiar with in Otherworld. What is your meaning?"

"My guess is that Captain Macgregor means forget about heads and hearts." Fredrickson shook his head with a slight grin. "Darkwolf will explode into pieces so tiny it'll take a microscope to find a particle of the sonofabitch."

The Otherworld warriors gave nods of approval, but Bourne frowned. "That's one kickass concept." He leaned his hip against the workstation that ran along one wall. "But with the amount of firepower you're talking about, you'd blow up yourself and everything within a hundred-foot radius. There's nothing on Earth that can handle that kind of firepower."

"Yeah, that's what I come up with, too." Jake moved his gaze from Bourne to the D'Danann and Drow. "That's where you guys come in."

Garran raised one eyebrow and the D'Danann warriors had puzzled expressions.

Jake stared at the Drow and D'Danann. "I'm willing to bet there's some kind of material in Otherworld that would help us manufacture this piece of weaponry."

"The Drow are masters of many metals." Garran's brows furrowed. "I do not believe the Dark or Light Elves, even the D'Danann, have such materials."

Jake's gut sank, but he wasn't about to give up hope.

"It is . . . possible"—Garran continued as if he was considering his thoughts carefully—"the Mystwalkers have what you need."

The D'Danann made sounds of unease and Keir scowled. "How, when most are slaves to the Shanai?"

"As you said, *most*." Garran studied Keir. "There is a faction of free Mystwalkers to which your own mother belongs."

"This is true," Keir said in a quieter voice. "And they are creating weapons to aid us in this battle. Perhaps it is the metal they use that you speak of?"

Garran nodded. "I have heard rumors at best. Few know where the free Mystwalkers reside. But it is there that the metal can be located."

The gut feeling that Jake sometimes got grabbed hold of him. "Then we need to see these Mystwalkers."

Garran met Jake's gaze. "You will need to speak with Cassia. I believe it is she who can help you."

That made perfect sense. As the daughter of the Great Guardian, Cassia probably knew damn near everything. And if she didn't, she could ask "Mother."

"Shit, if you can put that thing together," Bourne said, "you'll have one slick piece of hardware."

"I'll get with Cassia." Jake closed the laptop and the weapons schematic vanished from the backlit table, replaced by the satellite image of San Francisco that had been there before. "Now we need to get to other business."

The team members made sounds of agreement and Jake took the reins.

"First off," Jake said, "do we have any leads on the sono-fabitch who's selling us out to Darkwolf?"

"Could be daughterofabitch for all we know," Officer Hopper said, and several of the Alliance leaders looked at her and chuckled, but their voices were uneasy.

Hawk braced his left hand on the hilt of his sword. "The traitor must be someone close to the Alliance leadership." He looked to each member of the team. "One who knows of our plans in advance to have time to warn the warlock-god." He paused. "It could very well be one of us."

Jake broke the silence that followed Hawk's statement. "The traitor wouldn't necessarily need more than a few minutes' notice. All it would take is a quick cell phone call, and Darkwolf and his Stormcutter bastards would hit us in no time."

"That would mean it's someone in the PSF—or one of the witches." Fredrickson glanced at the D'Danann and Drow. "I don't think you guys have gotten that far into twenty-first-century tech yet. Although you do that mind-speak thing pretty well and can fly like hell." He nodded to the Marines. "And you're just now joining the team."

Hawk, Keir, and Tiernan glared at Fredrickson. "Not the witches," Hawk growled.

Jake had a hard time himself believing it could be one of the D'Anu. He looked at Fredrickson and Hopper. "One of ours?"

Fredrickson scrubbed his hand over his short red hair. "Hate to think so, but we've got to consider everyone."

The idea that it could be one of Jake's officers had his shoulders tensing so badly his head ached from the back of his skull to his temples.

Another thought occurred to him that sent a chill up his spine. A thought he refused to voice.

Cassia. Could it be her? She had the power and the opportunity. Not to mention she'd been missing, supposedly in Otherworld, since the dark goddess was destroyed and the demons sent back to Underworld.

Jake mentally shook his head, not wanting to even think along that route. *Then why did Cassia save your ass, Macgregor? To throw the Alliance off the scent?*

He sucked in his breath. *You're a bastard for even thinking the traitor could be Cassia.*

Out loud Jake said, "Here's my suggestion. We pick *one* rep from each faction of the Alliance." He rapped his knuckles on the lit-up map table. "If we have a single person from each faction who knows the plans, we'll be closer to eliminating leaks."

Jake met every wary gaze. "*No one* else will be allowed to know the plans until we deploy, and then only the leaders of the Alliance. The rest once we reach the destination." When he had looked at all the men and the two women present, he continued, "This doesn't mean we don't trust everyone here. It just cuts down on the chance of the info getting to Darkwolf."

"Agreed," Garran said in his deep voice.

Jake nodded to him, then Bourne, before he said, "Garran, of course, as Drow King will represent his people. Bourne since he's the head of the Marine contingent. Also myself, as I'm in charge of the whole show on the human side of things." Jake moved his gaze to the three proud D'Danann warriors. "You'll have to choose among yourselves. I'm not going there."

The warriors looked at each other, each obviously wanting to be the one. They were Alpha to the bone, three powerful leaders.

"Hawk," Keir finally said, with a slight nod to his half brother.

Hawk looked about as shocked as Jake felt. Keir and Hawk had been the worst of enemies since childhood. But Jake had to admit that the two had been getting along better for some reason since Keir's marriage to Rhiannon.

"I agree." Tiernan glanced at Hawk. "Hawk was here when it started, from the very beginning. He was the one chosen by the Great Guardian to warn the D'Anu."

Keir smirked. "Although he did cross over without waiting for permission from the Chieftains after petitioning them."

Hawk shrugged. "But you came."

"And you had to face the Chieftains, and almost could not return to claim your mate," Keir said.

"Hawk, Garran, and myself then." Jake cleared his throat. "What about the witches?"

"Not Silver." Hawk sounded as though he was grinding his teeth as he spoke. "My mate is with child."

"Hear you on that one." Jake shook his head. Too bad. Silver had also been there from the beginning, and had been the one who'd performed the ceremony that brought Hawk to San Francisco. She started it all—if it wasn't for her, this city and other parts of the world would probably be history.

Jake glanced in the direction of the kitchen, even though he couldn't see it through the command center's walls. "I think we'll have to let them decide."

"That settles it, then," Bourne said.

Jake held up his hand. "One more thing. You're going to get the whole story later, but—" He rapped his knuckles on the map table a few more times before he got it out. "Learned something over the past few days." A lot of somethings.

"What?" Hawk asked with a hint of hardness to his voice, as if he knew something he wasn't going to like was coming.

With a sigh, Jake said, "Cassia—she's not a D'Anu witch."

Those who knew Cassia looked at him in a sort of stunned silence.

"She's Elvin. Full." Jake's gaze moved from the Dark Elves to the D'Danann warriors who would "get" the significance of what he was about to say. "Cassia is the daughter of the Great Guardian."

If Jake had thought the room was silent before, he was mistaken. This time it was as if everyone had stopped breathing completely.

"By all the gods," Hawk said, breaking the stillness. "I cannot believe it to be true."

"Believe it." Jake shook his head, still having a hard time getting the thought to gel. "Saw for myself when I was in Otherworld. Cassia and her mother—the Great Guardian—saved my life.

"Also saw a whole lot of other things in the City of the Light Elves while I was there. Cassia's a Prin—" He cut himself off, remembering Cassia had asked him not to mention she was royalty. "A principle member of the Light Elves' Guardians, or something like that."

After everyone had a moment to digest that tidbit, Hawk said, "Very well. As daughter of the Great Guardian and because she is fully Elvin, Cassia should represent the Light Elves."

It was Jake's turn to be stunned. He hadn't thought Cassia would be asked to be on the elite team.

Jake pinched his eyes closed with his thumb and forefinger for a moment before he looked up and nodded. "Done."

Chapter Fourteen

Jake hit the showers and turned the water on as hot as it could go, trying to ease the tension of exhaustion and frustration, not to mention being generally pissed.

There was a lot to be frustrated and pissed about. Darkwolf. The traitor. Cassia and the ascending Guardian thing, or whatever it was.

Not to mention the niggling at the back of his mind that *she* could be the traitor.

He'd made bad decisions, trusting the wrong instincts, and that had led to the loss of lives. He couldn't let it happen again.

His gut lurched and he drew his emotions in tight. He hadn't let anyone in for years and he wasn't about to start now.

His entire body and mind felt suddenly numb. And tired.

Thoughts of Cassia kept trying to prod him but he forced them away.

The one potential bright spot was the possibility of the Mystwalkers Garran talked about. If they had the metal Jake needed to make the god-containg weapon, that would be good news.

Everything else, though, not good.

Jake toweled himself off in quick, angry strokes, but the steam in the room kept his skin dampened. The bathroom smelled of some kind of honey-oatmeal soap the witches had made, along with the scent of eucalyptus and bay leaves from the shampoo they'd made for the guys. When he was pretty much dry, Jake wrapped the towel around his hips, grabbed his dirty clothing and boots, and headed for his room.

Being PSF Captain had some perks. He had his own space.

Small, but he didn't give a crap about that. He was just glad he had a place to sit back alone and think.

God, he had so much to think about.

As he held the towel tight around his waist, he nodded to a couple of members of the Alliance that he passed.

Cassia rounded a corner from one of the other bathrooms.

She held her palm to her chest, stopping several feet away from him.

Jake's heart jumped. The numbness that had gripped him, from mind to body, suddenly melted away at the sight of her.

Make that one *definite* bright spot in all this mess.

Cassia.

Whatever other possible light there might be in the tunnel of darkness was something he couldn't quite place anymore.

Not while he was standing there, looking at Cassia, a hard lump rising in his throat.

Even though her hair was dry, likely from her magic, it was obvious she'd just taken a shower. She had wrapped herself in a robe that matched her turquoise eyes, and she held a bundle of her own clothing close to her waist.

Her long blond hair fell in a sheet of smooth silk. Her gaze drifted from his eyes, down his bare chest, to the towel slung around his hips. He gritted his teeth as his cock hardened and pushed against the towel when she looked down. When she returned her gaze to his, color rose in her cheeks.

"I need to talk to you." Jake's voice sounded rough, like the rumble of thunder.

Cassia seemed like she'd been holding her breath before she exhaled. "In the morning."

This couldn't wait. He shook his head. "Now." Another PSF officer and then one of the D'Danann shouldered past them in the hallway. "Somewhere private."

Cassia glanced around as if searching for a place to talk. He shifted his dirty clothing to one arm and took her by the elbow with his free hand. She looked up at him in surprise as he guided her down the hallway to his room.

"I don't think—" she started before he pushed her into the room and shut the door behind them.

The moment they were alone, Jake threw his shoes and clothing on the warehouse's concrete floor. The shoes made clomping noises as they hit. He grabbed Cassia's clothing from her arms and ditched it, too.

Jake didn't give her time to react. He crowded Cassia up against the wall and put his arms over her head, bracing his palms against the wood. She gasped when he pressed his rigid erection against her belly and he went in for the kiss.

God, she smelled good. Sunshine and vanilla. She tasted even better, a gut-tightening feminine flavor. He wondered what she would taste like between her thighs.

He kept it slow, nipping at her lower lip before running his tongue along the place he'd just bitten. Cassia moaned and slid her fingers up his abs to his chest, over the thick, pink scars from his Stormcutter wounds. She wrapped her arms around his neck, drawing his head down and kissing him in her sweet, hesitant way. Just like the virgin she was.

A four-hundred-year-old virgin. Now if that wasn't a head trip, he didn't know what was.

Jake was afraid to move his hands from the wall because the urges rising in him made him feel like a predator, ready to push off her robe and take her down to the mats he slept on.

Cassia made soft little moans that vibrated through him and made his cock so hard he thought it was going to knock his towel right off.

With a gasp she placed her palms on his bare chest and pushed him just enough that he raised his head. He still held his mouth a fraction from hers, prepared to not give an inch—he wasn't about to let her out of his room until they'd talked about . . . things.

"Jake. We've got to stop," she whispered as he moved his lips along her cheek to her earlobe and dipped his tongue into her ear. She gasped again and moved her palms over the expanse of his chest like she couldn't stop herself. "We've been through this before."

"And we're going to go through it again," he murmured close to her ear, "until we find some kind of solution."

Cassia shuddered with obvious desire as he moved his mouth to her neck and she clenched his shoulders.

Jake moved his hands from the wall and grasped her waist, nearly mindless with more than lust. More than desire. More than need. "I want you so bad, Cassia, it hurts."

Her breasts rose and fell with her rapid breaths as he eased his lips down to the V of the robe she wore. "C—can't."

"Can." Jake brought one hand from her waist to push aside her satin robe, revealing one of her breasts. Before she could protest, he sucked her nipple into his mouth.

Cassia let her head fall back against the wall and closed her eyes while still gripping his shoulders. Sparks of magic flickered from her body, driving him on.

Something fell to the floor nearby with a loud thump, followed by a clatter. Sounded like his heavy-duty flashlight had fallen off one of the crates and rolled across the floor.

Barely conscious of what he was doing, he shoved the material away from her other breast and moved his mouth to that nipple. He pinched and pulled the nipple he'd just suckled while licking and drawing the other one into his mouth.

More thumps.

"So goddamned good." A primitive growl rose up in his throat as he raised his head and looked down at her face, which was still tipped back, her eyes closed. "Cassia," he said, and her eyes fluttered open.

Christ, he loved the look of desire in her eyes, the way he had reddened her mouth with his lips and his stubble, as well as the high flush on her cheeks.

"Let me taste you." He brought his hand up to her mouth and ran his thumb over her moist lips. "Please."

Cassia look disoriented, like she was on another plane. "Taste me?"

"Yeah." Jake trailed his finger between her breasts, down to the tie keeping the rest of her robe closed. "Your p—" He barely caught himself. Cassia was not the kind of woman you talked dirty with, even if she'd been around a while.

She was so beautiful, so *pure*. "I want to taste you between your thighs."

A FLUSH ROSE UP IN CASSIA that made her head spin. She had always stayed away from males because she wasn't allowed to develop a relationship with one. And she certainly had never talked with other women about sexual acts. She had been on Earth since the seventeenth century, and ladies just didn't go there.

But Jake . . .

He had his fingers at her robe's tie, prepared to pull it apart. "I promise you'll love it. And I'll love tasting your juices."

Cassia's star birthmark tingled like mad as she grew wet between her thighs at his erotic suggestion. She barely kept herself from crossing her legs to hold back the rush of need.

"Bless it." She shook her head to clear it. "How many times am I going to have to tell you we can't do this?"

"As many as it takes to change the rules." Jake cupped her cheeks in his palms and she shivered at his touch. "I'm not giving up on you."

"But—"

"I'm not going to push you now." He kissed her forehead. "But I am going to talk with your mom."

"Mom?" Cassia couldn't help the laugh that escaped her. "I don't think anyone has called the Great Guardian 'Mom' since the dawn of time. My brothers and I call her Mother."

He smiled, then nuzzled her hair. "She needs to be told to lighten up."

"Jake!" Horrified, her eyes wide, Cassia drew away. "We never speak of the Great Guardian in that manner."

He winked. "Maybe somebody should."

His teasing and smiles were contagious, and Cassia actually found herself grinning. "It's not going to be me."

"I'm up for the job."

"Uh-huh." Cassia shook her head as she smiled. "Wait till you meet her."

Jake slipped his fingers into her hair and ran his fingers through the strands. "I knew you'd agree to take me to meet your mom."

Cassia opened her mouth. Shut it. Then she said, "Jake Macgregor, you just tricked me."

"Whatever it takes." He brushed his lips over hers. "I want you."

She sighed, a blissful feeling settling over her as she leaned into him. She wished he could hold her in his arms forever.

He raised his head. "So what's this about your brothers? Are you close to them?"

"Not really." Cassia shrugged. "The Guardian bears a child once a millennium." Cassia paused, and he knew what she had to say next was important. "I'm the only female child the Great Guardian has birthed."

"I bet that's got a lot to do with why so much is placed on your shoulders," he muttered.

"When we're twenty-five," Cassia continued, "we're sent away to an Otherworld for four hundred years. With the age difference, lack of time around one another, everyone busy with their mates and occupations—you can image there's not a lot of bonding time."

"Yet you do spend time with certain people of your race, like Kellyn." His expression darkened. "And Daire."

Cassia felt a strange thrill in her belly, knowing Jake cared about her enough to be jealous. "Daire was always just a friend to me." She couldn't stop herself from reaching up and rubbing her fingers along Jake's stubbled jaw. "He's been a teacher, a mentor." A now-becoming-familiar wave of heat flooded her. "It never occurred to me Daire would be chosen for my transition."

Jake's throat worked, his expression still dark. "What exactly does Daire mentor you in?"

"Fighting skills." She linked her fingers behind Jake's neck. "I've been training for centuries. I could take you down before you knew what was happening to you."

An amused expression crossed Jake's features. "Could you now . . ." he drawled.

In a split second Cassia hooked her leg around one of Jake's ankles, jerked hard, and pulled his feet out from under him. She knocked him flat on his back on his bed mats. With a triumphant grin, she straddled him.

Jake laughed and gripped her hips with both hands. "Princess, you can show me your fighting skills anytime."

This time *she* kissed *him*. She moaned as she took his lips with hers, and she squirmed at the feel of his bare chest, now between her bare thighs. Her naked sex pressed against his skin and she writhed at the heady feeling it gave her to have contact with a male in a way she never had before.

Her skin prickled and flecks like stardust flickered and expanded from her body. Several more thumps echoed throughout the room.

Jake rubbed her bottom through the satin as they kissed. He slowly inched the fabric up until his big palms kneaded her bare flesh. He pulled her bottom cheeks apart from each other and cool air brushed her anus and her sex.

The sensation was enough to make her shake inside.

She felt something coming. Something new. Major. Wonderful.

But . . .

Cassia jerked her head up. A bolt of magic shot from her body, sailed across the small room, and struck a pair of Jake's work boots.

As the boots smoldered and the smell of burning leather reached her, Jake snorted like he was holding back laughter. "I can see sex with you will definitely be dangerous."

He trailed his fingers down her chest from between her breasts to her belly button, then traced the star below. "A birthmark?" he murmured.

Cassia nodded. She found it too hard to breathe and answer him. Her magic sparked like small fireworks being set off around the room.

They kissed again, and he kept rubbing and massaging her buttocks in a way that made her feel so wet that she was afraid his chest would be slick from her juices. The tingling between her thighs grew intense and she was afraid she was going to melt something again.

Maybe Jake.

Before she had a chance to, Jake broke the kiss by moving his hands to either side of her face and stilling her. "I don't intend for another man to have you, Cassia. You know that, don't you." A statement, not a question.

"Jake—"

"Mom and I are going to have a little talk."

Cassia wanted to burst out laughing at the way he was referring to the Great Guardian, but the moment was a little too serious. "It's not going to do any—"

Jake brought her to him in a hard kiss before drawing away again. "I know you can't have a man inside you who doesn't know how to take you through your transition." Cassia's whole body heated so much she felt like her Otherworld's sun had swallowed her.

"But," he continued, his expression serious yet sexy all at once, "can you have an orgasm without going supernova?"

Cassia felt like she'd already become a billion times brighter with embarrassment. "I—I guess so. I've never had one, though."

"Princess." He moved his lips to her ear. "I'm going to show you what you've been missing."

A shiver trailed down Cassia's spine and twined with desire. A strange kind of fear wove itself through her, much like the sparks chasing one another around her and Jake. It was almost like they were waiting to—to attack.

She eased off Jake onto the mat, while grasping her robe so that she was completely covered. Her gaze slipped downward to the towel barely hanging onto his hips before she looked at him again.

"You're not ready yet." Jake rolled onto his side facing her, his head propped in his palm, his elbow on the mat. "I shouldn't have pushed you."

Cassia wrapped her arms around herself as she fought to reel in the magic that wanted to burst from her and melt something. Sparks still whirled around them. She saw her magic had already scattered his clothes, body armor, a flashlight, and his duty belt across the floor. Not to mention she'd toppled a couple of wooden crates in one corner, too. She had not only heard thumps and rattles, but the mess hadn't been there when Jake had dragged her into the room.

"I'm scared." Cassia turned her gaze back to him. "I don't know what to do. I don't know what could happen."

He reached up with his free hand and tugged one of her arms away from her chest so that he could clasp her fingers. "I should be moving a lot slower with you."

"This shouldn't be happening, knowing I may have to be with another man." The sparkles whirling around them began to settle on Cassia's shoulders and arms. "There's no guarantee that the Great Guardian will teach you how to take me through my transition." She squeezed his fingers back, sadness and longing flowing through her. "She emphasized that the male must be of pure Elvin blood."

Jake growled as he released her fingers and pushed himself to his feet. He barely caught the towel, keeping it from falling. She half wished it would slip off.

"Doesn't matter where a person goes," he said with a bite to his tone as he snatched up a pair of boxer shorts. "Discrimination, prejudice—it's always there."

Jake had his back to her as he whipped off the towel and tossed it aside. Her mouth watered. He had the nicest ass she'd ever seen. Not that she'd seen a lot, but still.

She tried to turn her focus back to what Jake was saying. "You're right," she said quietly. "Elves and Fae have long held animosity toward each other. Of course, Light Elves against Dark Elves as well." She sighed. "I never realized just how snobby my people are."

"It's more than snobbery." Jake had pulled on his boxers and turned back to look at her. "It's pure discrimination. There's enough of that sh—crap out there."

"Something more is bothering you." Cassia sat on the mat with her arms wrapped around her bent knees as she looked up at Jake. "Do you want to talk about it?"

His muscles flexed as rubbed his temples with his fingers. "Christ, no."

"Why not?" A kindling of anger flickered in her. "I've bared my soul. The most intimate things about me." Her voice rose and she lapsed into the more formal speech of the Elves. "I refuse to accept you standing before me and telling me you cannot share your past."

Jake opened his mouth, then clamped his teeth shut, holding back whatever it was he had been planning to say. "It's not important," he finally said.

She patted the mat beside her. "I'll determine whether or not it is."

Jake made a noise between frustration and anger. The mattress made a squishing noise as he plopped on the mat beside her. He braced one hand on the mat while he propped his other arm on one bent knee. "What do you want to know?"

"Why are you so bitter?" She spoke low and even. "This affects you beyond what you witnessed and experienced in the city of the Light Elves."

He ground his teeth. "I grew up being discriminated against. But it's nothing compared to what one hell of a lot of people go through. So I'm not whining about my past. Any kind of bigotry against any race, creed, color, nationality, religion—it just plain pisses me off."

"There's something more than that," Cassia said. "Tell me what *you* went through as a child." Cassia leaned forward, her arms still wrapped around her knees. "I want to know about the young Jake Macgregor."

He snorted, a sound of derision. "I doubt if you have anyone who lives 'on the wrong side of the tracks' in your precious city."

Cassia leaned back, the tone of his voice like a slap. "Pardon me?"

"I'm sorry I'm acting like such a bastard." Jake sucked in his breath. "My story's nothing special. My family was poor—primarily because my parents wasted every spare cent on drugs and alcohol." He shrugged. "I grew up as the shabby kid who didn't have money for decent clothes.

Jeans too short, holes in my shirts, whatever. So I was treated like crap by everyone and their mother, father, brother, and sister, too."

Cassia's chest hurt for that little Jake. "Look at who you turned out to be. An incredible, honest, upstanding man who commands legions."

"I don't know if I can agree with you on that point." Jake studied her. "I joined the Marines after high school. Each time I went on a recon I unleashed every bit of anger I had stored inside me. Anger against my parents. My uncle. The kids who treated me like crap when I was growing up." He rubbed his temples again with his fingers. "I was young and stupid when I enlisted, and I did a lot of things I'm not proud of.

"Like fucking up a mission big-time," he added under his breath.

Cassia rose up on her knees and smiled as she cupped Jake's face in her palms and rubbed them along his jaws. "Everyone does things they are not proud of. Everyone screws up. I have lived for over four centuries, Jake. I survived many years of mass hysteria against Pagans and through the persecution of countless witches."

Her throat hurt when she thought of all the people who had died during those years, and she had a hard time continuing. "Many of those murdered were my friends, and to this day I cannot forgive myself for not saving them all." She wanted to cry at the memories that had never faded. "I could only save a handful compared to how many we lost."

"Ah, honey." Jake took Cassia in his arms and held her close.

"I have lived through centuries of racism against so many different peoples and religions. The Irish, African-Americans, Chinese, and Native Americans. Pagans, Catholics, Protestants." Jake rocked her as she continued, "You are right. It is everywhere. And you do not know how many times I have wished for the power to wipe discrimination and racism from this Earth Otherworld. But even as a Guardian ascending, I cannot."

"I *am* a shit." Jake squeezed her tighter. "It never occurred to me that after living here for so long you'd have seen so much of the ugly side of life. That you lived through it."

Cassia drew away from Jake and drank in the depth of his blue eyes. "I don't say these things to make you feel badly. I tell you this because I want you to know I understand how it hurts to be discriminated against. The way my people treated you—it is inexcusable." She reached up and kissed him before easing back. "And the way you were treated as a child—also inexcusable."

He stared at the wall directly in front of him and didn't answer.

"You hold yourself away from everyone, Jake," Cassia said. "That's not good for you, for any person."

The main warehouse lights shut off for the night, with only strategic lights left glowing. Even in the near darkness Jake's handsome features made her heart flip.

He remained quiet and she gently touched his cheek to bring him to face her.

"You're a special lady." Jake took one of her hands and brought her to him, once again holding her tightly. He was changing the subject, but she knew his words were sincere. "And you're mine. Got that?"

More sadness crept through Cassia like a low-hanging fog. "I wish that could be true."

"We'll make it happen." Jake offered her a smile, and Cassia had to hold back a snort when he added, "I just need to talk to Mom."

Cassia couldn't help another laugh, but she stiffened as Jake drew her down to the mattress, both their heads on his pillow. He brought her to him so that her back rested against his muscular chest, his strong arm around her waist, her body molded against his.

His rigid erection pressed into her backside but Jake did nothing more than hold her. She had never felt so secure, so safe, so cared for. She had never felt so incredibly wonderful.

Jake nuzzled her hair. "Goodnight, Princess."

"Goodnight, Jake," she whispered. And for the first time in her life fell asleep in a man's arms.

CHAPTER FIFTEEN

THE MORNING FOLLOWING THE FIGHT in Union Square, Darkwolf woke, his body fully healed, but he still had a sharp pain in his chest. Probably to remind him what an arrogant fuckhead he'd been.

How could a mere human take him down like Macgregor had?

His back ached from sleeping on the carpet. It was plush, but it was still a floor.

And he had Elizabeth wrapped in his arms.

Damn.

He raised his head and stared down at her. In all these months that he'd known the demon-woman, dominating and controlling her in the bedroom with hardcore sex, they had never done anything as intimate as this. Just holding each other.

Darkwolf closed his eyes, shutting away the image of the beautiful woman sleeping in his arms.

She's not a woman. She's Fomorii.

No. She's a woman now.

Who can turn into a malformed blue demon with apelike arms and distorted, massive body, as well as claws and a mouthful of needle-sharp teeth?

Darkwolf tried to burn the images from his mind.

She's Elizabeth now. Junga is gone.

Junga is gone!

But he was fooling himself.

Did it matter?

Elizabeth shifted, and Darkwolf opened his eyes to see her smiling up at him like a woman looking at her lover. He couldn't help but respond to her smile. She was so incredibly beautiful.

Last night she had saved his life. She had gotten him through the almost deadly attack.

Even with his dried blood streaking her face, hands, and arms, she was gorgeous. Her clothing had stiffened in places, soaked with his blood. His own stiff clothing itched and he needed a shower. Both he and Elizabeth smelled like blood and sweat, and the carpet freshener made his nose itch.

He swallowed as he studied her stunning blue eyes. "I think we both need to clean up."

"Definitely." Her smile slipped away as she pushed herself to a sitting position and looked from her bloodied hands to his chest. "How do you feel?"

Darkwolf eased to his feet. "I'll live now." He extended his hand to her, drew her up, and brought her close enough to him that her breasts brushed his chest and his cock began to harden. "Thank you."

"For what?" Her expression appeared genuinely confused.

He squeezed her hand. "If it wasn't for you keeping me sane and awake, and pushing me to heal last night, I might have fallen asleep. And never have woken up."

"Oh." She gave a little shrug that had a hint of not being so casual. "You did the same for me."

When that bastard cop Jake Macgregor had shot her twice and one of the Dark Elves had nailed her with an arrow, how could he not have helped to save her?

Darkwolf's gut churned and prickles of heat slid over his skin. He'd almost lost Elizabeth the night the Alliance destroyed the dark goddess and Darkwolf had taken the goddess's powers.

It had almost killed Darkwolf when he thought Elizabeth was going to die. He'd never felt so much pain in his life. Like his heart was going to explode.

"Shower then." He kept his hold on her hand and led her to the sumptuous penthouse's bathroom.

His head nearly spun as they undressed each other. Usually

they only took off enough clothing to fuck, and they fucked hard and long. Multiple times.

Darkwolf tried to grab onto those same impulses and desires, but they weren't there. Instead he wanted to take it slow with her.

What was wrong with him?

He knew.

How could this happen? It was insane. He was out of his mind. The past several months had charred his brain and his senses.

If he hadn't started to soften toward her before he took over the dark god's and dark goddess's powers, he would blame it on having two gods' powers inside him. Evil gods.

But he couldn't blame it on that, could he.

For at least the hundredth time, Darkwolf pushed thoughts of his feelings aside. Temporary insanity. That's what it was. If he were still Kevin Richards, once a white witch before he'd been lured into dark magic, he would be repulsed by the demon-woman.

Don't think about it.

When they reached the bathroom, Darkwolf released Elizabeth's hand and turned the shower knobs in the huge walk-in shower area. He ran the water until it was perfectly warm before he returned to Elizabeth.

They slowly stripped out of their clothing. He helped her pull her T-shirt over her head and tossed it aside. With a groan, he palmed her nipples before pinching them lightly and causing her to draw in her breath.

He released her and she shimmied out of her jeans after kicking off her running shoes. He didn't like her to wear underwear, always wanting her to be ready for him to take her, so she never wore panties or a bra, or even socks.

She kept her eyes focused on him the entire time she removed her clothing. The dynamics between them had changed, and she felt it as much as he did. She didn't have to say it. He knew it by the look in her eyes and in her actions.

When they were both naked, Darkwolf led her so that they stood beneath the three shower heads and water rushed over them. Blood that had streaked their bodies circled the drain, coloring the water rust red before swirling away.

They remained silent as he washed her. He couldn't find any words. He'd known how to act, what to say and do, before this morning, but not now.

The hotel's passion fruit–scented shampoo and conditioner mingled with the steam and replaced smells of blood and sweat. Now that he was over seven feet tall, thanks to his new-found god powers, he had to lean down. Although she was tall for a woman in her human form, she felt so petite against him.

His cock hardened to its massive godlike proportions and he pressed it against her water-slick back while he washed and then put the conditioner on her hair, before rinsing it again. It was a surprisingly erotic experience, washing a woman's hair and body. She wiggled against his erection the entire time and he groaned.

Primal urges stormed through him and he wondered why he held back. Why he didn't just take her now.

He was too tall for her to be able to reach up and wash his hair, so he did it himself. Then she insisted on scrubbing his body with a washcloth, and he thought he'd climax when she slowly, deliberately washed the area around his cock and grinned up at him.

When it was her turn, Darkwolf held her under the shower heads and scrubbed the rest of the blood off her with a clean washcloth and passion fruit–scented shower gel. His erection brushed her soapy belly, then her back when he turned her around.

Desire continued to flare through him and it took everything he had to keep from throwing her against the shower wall and taking her now.

"I want you inside," Elizabeth said, echoing his thoughts. She braced her hands on the tiled wall, her back to him, the shower water still pounding down on both of them. "Inside me, Darkwolf."

A deep rumble rose high in his chest. He positioned his cock, grabbed her hips, and slammed his erection deep into her pussy.

Elizabeth gave a combination of a gasp and a cry like she always did now that his cock was so much thicker and longer. She'd told him how much she loved it when he took her hard and fast, yet the oddest feeling overcame him now—what if he was hurting her?

Darkwolf shook off the thought and slipped fully into the moment. Elizabeth moaned and met his thrusts as he took her. He started out slow, but soon couldn't control himself and drove into her harder and faster.

Mindless of anything but being inside of Elizabeth, he focused on her core, which gripped him as tightly as if he was taking her in the ass. Only better. Smoother. Silkier. Now he smelled the musk of her juices blending with the other scents in the shower.

Water pounded down on them as he bent over her back and palmed her breasts, loving the weight of them in his hands. Elizabeth moaned and thrashed, and when he plucked and pinched her nipples she came with a loud cry.

Her pussy contracted around his cock, making his balls draw up and his head spin with his oncoming orgasm. He slammed into her a few more times before stars sparked in his vision and he jerked against her ass.

His cock throbbed inside her core, his energy and semen spent inside of her.

"Dear gods, Elizabeth." He brought her up and turned her around before taking her mouth with his, claiming her in a way he never had before.

And almost said those three damned words.

Chapter Sixteen

"Yes, my lord." *With Hannah and Garran in the realm of the Dark Elves, their bedroom is perfect for my private discussions with the great warlock-god, though the lingering Drow scent of earth and moss turns my stomach.* "It will be a lot harder to let you know what the Alliance has planned ahead of time, but I'll find a way."

"I know you will." *His tone warms my chest. He puts so much faith in me—as he should.* "Even if it's at the last minute, when you arrive at your destination," *he continues,* "it'll take no time to transfer myself there and call the Blades and Stormcutters."

"You are brilliant, my lord." *Pride makes my skin prickle. I'm a part of the warlock-god's plans and future. When I first went to him, it was with some trepidation—even though I've always been attracted to the darkness—but now, nothing but joy. Nothing but the incredible power of dark magic.* "I am honored to serve you."

"And you serve me well." *He sounds a little amused, yet pleased.* "I trust you. I know you'll let me know the next time something goes down, the second you can."

I smile. "I'll be in contact with you soon."

"Be careful and watch out for yourself. We can't afford for you to get caught." *His tone darkens and the low sound makes me jump.* "I need you to the very end, when those bastards are finally out of my way."

"Of course, my lord." *Jittery sensations course my body, like I'm nervous. I don't know why.*

Darkwolf ends the conversation abruptly, without saying goodbye, and that makes me frown.

He must be in the middle of something important.

Otherwise, he would never be rude to me.

He needs me too much, especially after those last surprises.

Damn the Alliance! My body shakes with anger and the darkness stirs within me, wanting to get out. I grind my teeth, pick up a pillow, and fling it against the wall of the room. I want to throw something much harder, and fragile, like Hannah's scrying mirror, and let it shatter across the warehouse's concrete floor. But I don't want to be heard.

Can't be heard.

I school my expression, slip out of the bedroom, and move silently through the warehouse. A good fuck with Fredrickson will lessen my anger.

Silver's and Hawk's voices echo just around the corner. I scan the hall while pulling a glamour to make sure no humans can see me, then listen to Silver and Hawk's conversation.

"You can't even tell *me?*" *Silver sounds angry.* "I'm your wife, for the goddess's sake."

"*A thaisce,*" *Hawk says, making me want to puke as he uses his pet name for her,* "You know I cannot. Each faction of the Alliance chose one representative. It is a test. We must find some way of discovering the traitor."

Traitor. The word grates on my nerves.

I am a loyal follower of Darkwolf now. I'll do whatever it takes to see that he gains the position of power that will give him control over this city. Then I'll be among the few who will be his most trusted advisors. Not a Blade, no. But a much more important position.

Darkwolf will make San Francisco his own. A city that no one, no government, no military, will be able to conquer once he achieves his ultimate greatness.

The power Darkwolf wields—to this date he hasn't shown the magnitude of it.

"Jake made the decision." *Hawk continues speaking to Silver.* "I believe it to be an excellent move on the Alliance's behalf."

I scowl and clench my fists. My head aches from grinding

my teeth. Jake Macgregor's attack on Darkwolf, the cop's success in hurting the warlock-god—that was luck. An anomaly. It was nothing. And the Alliance is stupid to believe otherwise.

Darkwolf will be taking new and stronger measures to protect himself when he directs storms and his Stormcutters.

Just let that cop try to stab Darkwolf again.

Jake Macgregor will get a nasty surprise.

Silver grumbles something I can't hear and Hawk gives a gentle laugh. "I love you," *he says.*

Gag.

"Dear Anu, I wasn't only there from the beginning," *Silver says,* "I brought you here to fight this war. This whole mess would have been over before it started if I hadn't. We would be under the god and goddess's powers now."

Silver's voice has risen, filled with anger, and for a moment I imagine her pulling her stiletto daggers from her boots and flinging them at a wall.

Maybe I should get a dagger. It might come in handy.

I hear a sound like she's stomping her foot. "I should be allowed to be a part of it."

"You are." *His voice is gentle.* "More so than I wish as you carry my child. Our child."

Double gag.

Silver says, "How many times do I have to tell you I am not helpless and the baby will be fine?"

This conversation is a waste of time.

I turn to leave when something Hawk says makes me pause. "I will tell you this. Kirra and Sheridan," *he says, changing the subject and naming two female D'Danann warriors,* "believe they found Darkwolf's lair during their last search. But I can say no more."

Silver lets out a sigh loud enough for me to hear. "Well, that at least is good news."

Cold rushes over me like a swift breeze off the bay. Could the D'Danann really have found Darkwolf?

I doubt it. But I'll see what I can find out, just the same.

Hair at my nape prickles.

One of the D'Danann warriors is walking up behind me. I sense it. As Fae, they are deadly silent. But my senses are strong.

I casually turn and smile at one of the hulking male warriors, who can see through my glamour as all magical creatures can. He wears a black coat that covers all of his weapons. He nods in return as we pass each other.

Fool.

My mind churns as I head out to where all the action is, in the middle of the warehouse. Should I make myself "useful" and see what else I can learn? Or should I find Fredrickson and fuck it out of him? I can use my gray magic to draw whatever I want out of him if I choose to.

I scowl as I realize Fredrickson is not a part of the now limited inner circle of one person per race. But I know he will still be useful.

I pass the PSF's strategy area, a room much smaller than the Alliance's strategy and command center. It amuses me to see what the PSF tries to come up with to attempt to hurt Darkwolf and the Stormcutters. Sure, they take down a lot of the cutters, but cutters are pawns and there's more where they came from.

When I fight with the Alliance, no one notices how much I avoid the Stormcutters. For the most part the Stormcutters recognize me as Darkwolf's informant and spin away, so I'm not forced to do anything to them. But still, I have to trap some of them with my magic for "show."

What I really get a kick out of, though, are the times I manage to kill Alliance members here and there—and no one sees me.

If anyone does catch me, no matter who it is, I'll have no qualms about killing the person before they can say anything to me or anyone else. An instant death. Just another Alliance member out of the picture. No matter who it is.

The Alliance is hardly an itch beneath Darkwolf's collar. Soon, he'll control so many Stormcutters that they'll be unstoppable and the Alliance destroyed.

And even more importantly, as Darkwolf's army expands, his power, his incredible magic, grows and grows.

When he attains his army of at least a million, there will be no stopping him, no matter where he decides to go and what he chooses to control.

I can't wait.

CHAPTER SEVENTEEN

THE COMMAND CENTER SEEMED BIGGER as only one rep from each faction of the Alliance moved into the room to sit around the illuminated map table. Jake glanced up at the skylights. It was dark outside, which meant the Drow were out.

Sure enough, Garran strode through the doorway the moment Jake started to take his seat. The King looked around the room as if assessing the occupants and then firmly shut the newly installed door behind him.

"Are you certain we cannot be heard?" The gems on Garran's chest straps glittered as he eased into a seat at the map table.

Jake turned his folding metal chair around so that he straddled it, and rested his forearms on the back of the chair. The room smelled of freshly cut wood and some kind of plastic from the soundproofing materials. Not to mention that ever-present, undefinable scent of magic that always accompanied the magical beings, including the witches.

Jake pointed to the padding that had been put up around the walls. "The room's now almost totally soundproof. Once the ceiling is up, no worries."

"This feels so strange." Rhiannon folded both of her hands on the tabletop. "Just us."

Hawk represented the D'Danann warriors, Garran the Dark Elves, David Bourne the Marines, Jake the PSF, Rhiannon the D'Anu witches . . . and Cassia, the Light Elves.

The moment Jake's gaze met Cassia's beautiful turquoise eyes a strange sensation hit his gut like a weird electrical storm. He'd never felt the kinds of things with other women that he did with Cassia.

God, but he wanted her. He wanted to bury his nose in her

hair and breathe in the clean scent of her vanilla shampoo and bathing gel. Whatever it was he felt for her left him shaken and unsteady, like he couldn't stand right now if his life depended on it. And his cock was so hard he was glad the map table was close enough to hide his erection.

He cleared his throat and looked at David Bourne. "What do you have on the military front?"

"More brass is on its way and all branches are trying to get their crap together." Bourne tipped his chair back. "Since the demons wiped out most of the heads of the military here in San Francisco, that means the Coast Guard, Army, Reserves, Navy, and Marines have to draw elsewhere for leadership. The National Guard did a pretty good job of getting in here and getting things started, though.

"But hell, these guys really don't know what they're up against," Bourne continued, "and they don't know how to eliminate the threat. They're so goddamn clueless." He rubbed his hand over his high-and-tight haircut. "I'm trying to bring them up to speed, but they're having a hard time 'getting it.' Or believing it."

Bourne went on, "Everyone is scrambling to establish some kind of local government and a strong military presence. Only the Marines are here to back the National Guard, and ready to do some reconnaissance and fight these bastards."

"I can't shake the thought that it's going to take magic to fight magic." Rhiannon fiddled with her obsidian ring. "So let's say the military takes out Stormcutters, and maybe even the Blades. Darkwolf will just make more."

"When I brought him down with the knife, it proved he has vulnerabilities," Jake said. "If we do find the metal we need to make the god-laser we'll blow him to pieces—end of problem."

"The Great Guardian would probably say it would tip the balance in all the Otherworlds," Rhiannon said with a wry expression, and looked at Cassia. "No offense."

"You're actually very right." Cassia sighed. "I don't have to ask her. Darkwolf is now a product of a god and goddess from Underworld, as well as being from this Earth Other-world. We can't allow him to be killed. He must be removed in other ways."

"Shit," Jake growled, echoed by Bourne.

Rhiannon's jaw dropped. "I was only kidding!"

Cassia gave a not-so-casual shrug. "I need to go home and have a chat with M—the Guardian to get her word on it, but I'm pretty certain that's the case."

"Goddamn it. We were so close." Jake rubbed his hand hard over his head as frustration exploded through him.

"What the hell do you do to get rid of a duo-god if you can't vaporize the bastard?" Bourne asked with anger in his voice. "Ask him nicely to leave?"

"Wait." Jake held up one of his hands while he considered the situation and went over the weapon schematics in his mind. Maybe . . . *yes.* "I think I've got it." He looked at Cassia. "You have the power to send him to Underworld?"

Cassia's throat worked as she met his gaze. "If I don't now, I will within days."

Thoughts of Cassia's mating requirement clashed with his focus on the weapon, and he ground his teeth and took a deep breath.

"How will you get the power if you don't already have it?" Rhiannon asked.

Cassia swallowed again. "The power will result from my ascension to becoming a Guardian."

Before anyone could ask any more questions that would turn the knife harder in his gut, Jake said, "I think we can pull this off."

While everyone turned their complete attention to him, Jake continued. "I can back off on the obliteration part of the weapon. Instead, we'll contain him in the array long enough for you to do your thing."

"That would be perfect." Cassia nodded slowly. "Witch magic, and even my own magic, won't be able to contain him. But if you can hold him in one location and prevent him from blocking my energies, then I'll be able to use my power to send him to a place where he can do no harm."

Hawk narrowed his gaze. "Underworld."

Rhiannon frowned and held her hand to her cheek, trailing her fingers over the scars. "I don't know why, as horrible as he is, I can't imagine sending Darkwolf to *Underworld*."

"It is better than he deserves," Hawk said in a low growl.

Cassia tilted her head to the side. "There may be another place more suited to him."

"As long as he's out of here," Jake said. "I don't give a damn where he goes."

"What about the metal we need to make that weapon?" Bourne shifted his stance against the workstation. "Will those mist—uh, mist-beings give us what we need?"

"Mystwalkers," Hawk and Garran said at the same time.

Jake brought Cassia up to speed on the discussion about the metal needed for the now god-containing weapon.

"The Mystwalkers have been working on other weapons for us," Cassia said with a thoughtful expression. "If their metal will also work for the weapon you're trying to build, they might help."

Jake gripped the back of the chair he was straddling. "You'll take me to see them?"

"I will attempt to arrange an audience," Cassia said. "Few are allowed in the free Mystwalker sanctuary and I don't know that they'd consider bringing a human to their secluded location."

With a frown, Jake narrowed his eyes. "I hope to hell you can."

"I will do my best," Cassia said.

Jake pressed on to other matters. "Do you think the Light Elves would help us fight Darkwolf?" he asked Cassia as they continued to hold each other's gazes.

Garran snorted and said, "Self-righteous bastards—" Cassia frowned and Garran pushed his silvery-blue hair over his shoulder plate. "My apologies," Garran added as he met Cassia's gaze. "However the Light Eves have never shown a willingness to aid *any* people."

"All right, all right." Jake rolled his shoulders. "We get it. Ancient history."

Garran snorted again, but Cassia looked like she was struggling to gather her normally calm expression.

"Back to the Light Elves." Jake focused on Cassia again. "Think they'd help?"

Cassia frowned. "Truthfully, I don't think so."

"But it can't hurt to ask," Rhiannon said as she leaned closer to Cassia.

Cassia slowly nodded, concern etched on her beautiful features. "Darkwolf is amassing thousands of Stormcutters according to the prisoners who were *persuaded* to give us the information. He's planning on gathering tens of thousands. Who knows how many he's already brought together?"

"Thousands." Jake thumped the table. "With the Drow, D'Danann, D'Anu, and PSF, we have maybe nine hundred. A huge number of fighters in the Alliance are Drow, and they can only come out at night."

"At this moment the Marines can back you with twenty-two hundred of our finest," Bourne said.

Jake looked down at the satellite images on the map table before raising his head. "That makes about three thousand, counting the Drow."

"If that's not enough," Bourne said, "within thirty days we'll have fifteen thousand more on his doorstep."

"Providing we can find Darkwolf's doorstep," Rhiannon grumbled.

"We don't have thirty days," Cassia said quietly. "We'll be fortunate if we have two weeks."

"THAT IS THE WORST FRIGGIN' carnival ride," Jake muttered as they appeared in a meadow in Otherworld. "Christ. My head is spinning."

Cassia held back a smile—she felt nothing but a soft breeze on her cheeks when she took them through the veil. Jake was human, yet a warrior in every sense of the word.

Kael had stayed in San Francisco to keep an eye on things there. The wolf familiar had expressed his unease over Cassia having to leave for Otherworld. She had no choice, but at the same time, one of them needed to remain in San Francisco to help monitor the situation and to help fight.

Before she looked away from Jake, Cassia felt her mother's presence and caught the Great Guardian's scent of wildflowers and spring breezes.

As it had been ingrained in her from the time she was a child, Cassia bent on one knee and lowered her head.

Jake was still standing and she caught his hand, jerked it, and he got to his knees beside her.

"Lay down your weapon," she said through her teeth. She should have prepared him for the formalities and protocol one should follow when around the Guardian.

Jake drew his new Glock from its holster and placed it on the grass before the Great Guardian. The Guardian's flowing white gown brushed the tops of her feet, and her gleaming blond hair nearly reached the hem of her gown.

"You may rise and retrieve your weapon." The Guardian spoke in a musical voice, as always, but this time with a hint of amusement. "I must say I have never had any being place such a weapon before me."

Cassia stood with Jake as he reholstered his gun and relief flooded her at the Guardian's light smile.

The Guardian turned her gaze on Cassia. "We have much to discuss."

Her brilliant blue eyes then moved to Jake and the smile vanished. "And I sense strongly that you wish to speak with me about matters that are best discussed in private."

"I sure do." Jake's features were calm, but Cassia's stomach twisted.

Oh, goddess.

She knew he wanted to talk about the situation with Daire taking Cassia through her transition. Not to mention the Elvin prejudice against humans that was eating at him.

Now was *so* not a good time.

"Then we will talk." The Guardian gave a slight incline of her head toward Jake. "After you have completed your task with the Mystwalkers."

"This can't wait." Jake looked at Cassia, his gaze filled with fire and emotion.

Cassia widened her eyes and gave an almost imperceptible shake of her head. "Jake—"

"Very well." The Guardian's voice now carried an unfamiliar hint of frost that made Cassia shiver. "I believe I know what it is that you wish to speak to me about, but I want to hear it from you."

"Train me how to help Cassia with her transition." Jake kept his head up as he spoke. "I want to be the one who goes through it with her."

Cassia held back a groan. She wanted to slide through the blades of grass and into the earth. By the goddess, this was very much not the way to speak to the Great Guardian.

The Guardian regarded Jake with now icy blue eyes. "Cassia *must* mate with an Elvin male of pure blood. Only a fully vested magical male—of our species—has the strength to take her through the transition. Only he can be beside her to serve all Otherworlds."

Jake's jaw tensed and his gaze locked with Cassia's. She had the sudden urge to clap her hand over his mouth.

Too late.

He turned to face the Guardian again. "I know your kind is prejudiced against humans, but Cassia—"

"My kind?" The Guardian raised an eyebrow and the very air around them grew frosty.

Cassia shivered from the chill. Her heart beat faster and she wanted to kick Jake or stomp on his foot. Maybe elbow him.

Better yet, knock him upside the head. Too bad she didn't have her *shirre*.

"Light Elves." Jake studied the Guardian dead on. "When I was in the city of the Light Elves, pretty much everyone I passed by acted like I was dirt."

The Guardian certainly didn't look as calm as normal, and that shook Cassia up more than anything. "We will discuss this later," the Guardian said.

Cassia resisted closing her eyes, but prayed to Anu for Jake to shut his blessed mouth.

Unfortunately her prayer went unanswered.

"I care too much about Cassia to let another man have her." Jake took Cassia's now shaking hand and she wanted to crunch his bones in a death grip.

Didn't he see what he was doing? One did not "piss off" the Great Guardian. Ever.

Cassia swore she saw a light tinge of pink in the Guardian's cheeks, as if anger had actually risen up within her. "Your decisions in the past have led to the demise of others. Many others," the Guardian said, and shock pitched Cassia's stomach.

Jake's expression told her the Guardian had wounded him as if she had thrust a sword into his chest. He didn't respond, but he didn't break his gaze with the Guardian.

"Go to the Mystwalkers, then return to me." The Guardian waved her hand in the direction of the forest. "Then we will discuss this . . . situation."

The Guardian turned away and walked toward the forest. Cassia did clap her hand over Jake's mouth this time, before he could say anything else that would anger the Guardian.

When the Guardian vanished, Cassia took her hand away from Jake's mouth and clenched her hands at her sides. Sparks started flying across the meadow from her fists. A harsh wind kicked up and flung her hair around her face.

"I'm not going to cow down, Cassia." He took her by the shoulders, mindless of the fact that she was beginning to glow and might just blow the both of them up, and everything around them. "I won't be intimidated by anyone—especially about this. Let her turn me into a two-headed snake or whatever. I don't give a damn. She *will* hear me. She *will* grant my request. I care about you too much."

"You don't understand."

"Yes. I do." He gripped her shoulders tighter. "I'm not going down without a fight, and even then they'll have to kill me."

Cassia's magic zipped across the meadow and hit a rabbit in the butt, causing the poor creature to jump at least ten feet in the air before landing and bolting into the forest. "Kill you? That might just happen if you don't shut your mouth when you need to!"

The corners of his mouth curved. "I know how to shut you up."

She blinked. "Wha—"

Jake jerked her to him and took her mouth in a deep, possessive kiss. The kind of kiss that made her feel like she belonged to him and no one else.

A soft moan rose up in her throat as she returned his kiss. Every bit of anger, concern—absolutely everything vanished, melting away in a blur of color and emotion as his kiss took complete control of her.

She belonged to Jake. Heart, soul, mind, body . . .

Several trees shook hard enough that the rattle of branches and shaking tree leaves broke any semblance of quiet. Was that a Dryad grumbling?

Who cared?

Jake kissed her so thoroughly. His taste, his delicious scent, the feel of his warm, hard body as she wrapped her arms around his neck, made the world disappear.

More trees shook their branches. The magical sparks now circled them completely. Light flickered through her closed eyelids that she barely noticed. But she felt it, and harnessed it in a warm embrace.

Jake drew away and she opened her eyes. He looked down at her with a gaze so filled with emotion that it took her breath away. Was it too soon for love?

No, it wasn't. They'd known each other over six months. It wasn't too soon at all.

He started in a husky murmur, "Cassia, I—"

"Cassiandra!" This time the male voice saying her name didn't sound pleased at all and came from directly behind her. She turned in Jake's arms to see Daire, his *shirre* clenched tight in one fist and a furious expression on his handsome face she'd never seen before.

Jake drew her close but pushed her behind him as if to protect her. He said in a low, controlled, and most definitely possessive tone, "Cassia is mine."

CHAPTER EIGHTEEN

CASSIA'S HEART HIT HER RIB cage hard as she looked at Daire from behind Jake's shoulder. The whirlwind of sparks and golden light she had wrapped around Jake and herself dropped to the ground. Like a small flood of gold, the sparks flowed away and vanished as if sinking into the earth.

"Come here, Cassiandra." Daire rammed one end of the *shirre* into the earth beside his foot.

A wash of heat slammed into Cassia and she clenched her fists. "Who do you think you are to order me to do anything?"

Daire scowled. "We have much to discuss once I rid us of the human."

"I'm not going anywhere." Jake's voice came out in a low, steady, deadly tone as he gripped Cassia's shoulders. "And I'm definitely not handing the woman I love over to you."

Cassia went entirely still as her ears started to ring. Jake . . . loved her?

His body tensed as if he had startled himself by his own words.

Daire stalked toward them. His strides were smooth, fluid, and silent. The navy blue tunic and breeches he wore accented his broad shoulders, chest, and powerful thighs. His long white-blond hair flowed around his shoulders. There couldn't be a more flawless-looking man—and Cassia had no interest in him more than the friendship they had shared over the centuries.

No matter how beautiful Daire was, Cassia found everything about Jake more attractive. From his sexy, stubbled jaws to his carved biceps to the way his jeans hugged his long legs, he was delicious. Absolutely perfect.

Daire reached them, his expression so furious that Cassia

almost took a step back. "You are not worthy to touch a female so special and powerful, *human*."

FURY ROCKED JAKE so hard he couldn't have stopped himself if he tried.

"You sonofabitch." Jake took one step forward and slammed his fist into Daire's chin.

Daire's head snapped back, an instant expression of shock on his features.

Jake expected the element of surprise to be on his side, but the Elvin man reacted in a movement almost too fast to see.

Daire spun and brought up his leg, slamming it into Jake's liver.

Pain blasted through Jake as he dropped. He planted his left knee between Daire's legs and Jake wrapped both hands around Daire's thigh.

Jake had no doubt that down and dirty was the only way he was going to have a chance at fighting with a being who had trained for centuries.

He pressed his chest hard against the Elvin man's legs and pushed his head against the right side of Daire's ribs. With a loud grunt, Jake moved forward with his right leg and hooked his foot behind one of Daire's as he drove his shoulders forward against the man's thighs.

Daire was so goddamned strong, Jake barely managed to move forward and shove himself against the Elvin bastard's hips. Daire lost his balance and Jake took him to the ground.

Daire moved so fast Jake was barely aware of what happened next. Daire anchored his thighs around Jake's midsection and flipped him backward, over Daire's head.

Jake landed hard on his back with a another loud grunt, but he rolled to the side even as he hit the ground.

Before he could get to his feet, Daire was on top of him. Jake saw a flash of a furious expression through the long blond strands of Daire's hair.

Daire pinned Jake to the ground, his right hand against Jake's throat, cutting off his air supply.

Jake choked as he struggled for breath. He grabbed Daire's wrist and twisted it to release some of the pressure that was making him start to see black spots.

Without stopping, Jake raised his hips in a bridging motion and forced Daire to use one hand on the ground to keep himself balanced.

Jake pushed off one foot and rolled over onto his shoulder. When he and Daire hit the ground they both started to roll, each now trying to choke the other.

A loud crack sounded in Jake's ears.

The next thing he knew, a branch as thick around as a tree trunk slammed down on him and Daire. Pain ripped through Jake's shoulder and chest. The sudden weight of the branch forced Daire and Jake to lose their choke holds.

Still Jake and Daire tried to reach for each other to continue fighting, but neither could move. They struggled as they glared at each other, their arms pinned beneath the branch.

"You idiots!" Cassia was between them now, on the other side of the huge branch.

She gave Daire a furious look and started yelling something in a language that had to be Elvin. It was like French—it sounded beautiful, even though he knew she was telling Daire off.

Cassia turned her glare on Jake. "What in Anu's name do you think you're doing, and who the hell do you think you are, fighting like this? You're both a couple of underworld trolls and you'll be lucky if I don't leave this branch on top of you for a week."

Jake felt the heat of Cassia's anger like a punch of fire to his solar plexus. His anger at Daire faded as he looked up at Cassia's beautiful but furious features.

"My apologies, Cassiandra," Daire said before Jake could respond.

He scowled at Daire before he eased his expression when he looked back at Cassia. "I'm sorry," Jake said. "I shouldn't have started anything."

"You're blessed right you shouldn't have." Cassia still appeared livid as she flicked her fingers at the branch, and it suddenly wasn't as heavy. She braced her hands on her hips and continued glaring at them. "Now I have to apologize to the Dryads on top of everything else."

She spun and marched away, leaving Daire and Jake alone.

"She's something else," Jake said as he watched Cassia stomp into the forest.

"That she is."

Jake glanced at Daire, and then they both looked at the branch. "On three?"

Daire looked like he had swallowed something bitter and disgusting, but he nodded.

Jake counted off and, as one, they braced their hands on the wood and pushed it away. Daire's Elvin strength no doubt made it easier to move.

Fucker.

Smaller branches and twigs scraped Jake's face and hands as they thrust the big branch off of them.

When they finally got to their feet, Jake rubbed his palm over his head, knocking off leaves and grass, before wiping dirt and more crap off his jeans. Scratches from the branch stung his skin, and his throat ached from where Daire had tried to choke him. Not to mention that his side hurt like a sonofabitch where Daire had gotten him in the liver.

Daire looked unruffled and clean, and Jake had the instant desire to knock the shit out of him again.

Jake had no doubt, though, that Daire could have used some heavy-duty magic on him. If he had, Jake probably wouldn't be breathing right now.

"I CANNOT BELIEVE THOSE TWO," Cassia muttered to herself as she marched toward the Dryad Queen's tree. Sparks crackled at her fingertips, and she tried not to catch anything on fire. "Daire calling Jake unworthy and Jake punching Daire—" She ground her teeth as she repeated, "Idiots."

After apologizing profusely to the Queen and putting herself in debt to the Dryads, Cassia returned to the meadow where Daire and Jake were again glaring at each other. They probably hadn't stopped giving murderous looks since she left them.

"It doesn't matter what you feel for the Princess." Daire's words had a sharp bite as she reached the pair. "Cassiandra cannot mate with a weak human. Her future, our people's future, the Otherworlds' futures—all ride upon her shoulders, and her choice of a truly *powerful* male."

Her anger vanished as stark reality hit her. It was as if every bit of her fury and magic evaporated, and she was left as nothing but an empty shell.

Of course. There was no ignoring her destiny and the countless lives depending on her.

As all warmth in her body vanished, she was vaguely aware of Jake saying, "I don't buy that anyone's so-called 'destiny' can't be changed. No one's life is mapped out like a goddamn chart, with little boxes that get checked off when a marker is reached."

"Cassiandra's is." Daire's expression turned impossibly more arrogant. "From the time of her birth she has followed her preordained path prophesied by the Seers. Cassiandra must continue it until the completion of her destiny."

More cold flowed through Cassia's veins when Jake moved to stand inches from Daire.

Cassia glanced up at Jake's dark expression as he said, "So you're telling me nothing has happened with Cassia that wasn't on your 'chart?'"

She cut her gaze to Daire's. "Nothing," he said.

"You know that's not true." Cassia shook her head. "No one knew I'd be fighting a monumental battle in one of the Otherworlds."

"Yes. We did." Daire's voice quieted. "The outcome is unknown, but your path was to participate in an Otherworld war. Then to return home and ascend."

Chills rolled down Cassia's spine. "That's not true."

Daire nodded slowly. "It has always been so." He moved his attention to Jake. "You are simply a blight on her journey, as many others she has faced."

Jake's expression hardened even more and his blue eyes

darkened. His body was tensed, coiled, as if ready to take on Daire again. She'd seen this side of Jake when he had fought the demons from Underworld, but this was the first time she'd watched him in a one-on-one confrontation.

Before Jake could respond, Cassia moved between the two men. She tried to summon her magic for strength, but Daire's words had left her feeling drained and almost . . . hopeless.

"Jake and I have a task we must fulfill," Cassia said, almost unable to gain the strength to raise her voice much above a whisper. "When we return, we will discuss this."

"I will accompany you." Daire wasn't looking at her. He was staring at Jake. "I will not let you go alone with this human."

"His name is Jake." Cassia sighed. All the fight and spark had left her. Even the battles waged in an Otherworld were preordained. How could anything become of her and Jake if the Seers had not visioned the two of them, come together as one? "Jake and I will complete this task together," she continued. "It was given to us and us alone."

Daire opened his mouth to argue more, and she had no doubt Jake was about to say something, too. "You are forgetting your place, Daire," she said. "I am your Princess and a Guardian ascending, and you will argue with me no longer." To make it even clearer that she wasn't going to tolerate this anymore, Cassia added, "This discussion has ended," with a regal tilt to her head.

"Of course, Princess Cassiandra." Daire gave a stiff bow, his words stilted. He gave Jake a hard look before he walked to his *shirre*, jerked it out of the ground, strode into the forest, and vanished from sight.

For a moment she and Jake remained silent. When she looked up at him she saw him pinching the bridge of his nose, his eyes shut, as if he had a headache.

"I shouldn't have hit Daire," he said when he dropped his hand away from his face and looked at her. "But I'm not sorry."

She studied him for a long moment. "But I apologize for how my people have treated you." She rested her hand on one of his biceps. "The Great Guardian—she had no right to use something from your past to hurt you. And Daire—he shouldn't have spoken to you the way that he did."

"I can't let go of you, Cassia." He studied her with his deep blue eyes. "It's not in me to give up. I care about you too much."

She sighed again, wanting to cry instead. The words "preordained," "destiny," and "path" kept running through her mind. Along with the fact that Daire and her mother kept pointing out that entire Otherworlds depended on her ascension.

"It's time to get moving," she said when she couldn't take her thoughts or the silence between them any longer. "We need to meet with the Mystwalkers, then return to speak with the Great Guardian."

The next thing she knew she was wrapped in Jake's embrace. They held on to each other and now she did cry. Her tears wet his shirt, and he squeezed her tighter.

He rubbed one of his hands up and down her back in strokes that comforted her but at the same time made her want to cry harder.

Her mind kept turning over and over the fact that he had said he loved her.

It didn't matter that she loved him, too. Telling him would only make it harder on both of them. She should never have allowed it to get to this point.

She backed out of Jake's arms and avoided his eyes. "The Mystwalkers are waiting for us."

As Cassia started into the forest, Jake felt like he'd been stabbed in his chest by a Stormcutter. He'd gone and opened his heart and soul. He'd let Cassia in.

God, he didn't even know why he'd said it. He'd flung the words out before he stopped to think.

Jake tried to take back the thoughts and feelings, but he couldn't. It had felt too right to tell that Elvin bastard that Cassia was the woman he loved.

Because he did love her.

He watched Cassia for a moment as she walked away. He ached even more as he took in the gold of her hair in the afternoon sunlight, the T-shirt that hugged her delicate frame, the jeans that showed her every curve. She was so beautiful, but there had always been something about Cassia that had drawn him to her.

She paused and looked over her shoulder, and his gaze met the startling turquoise blue of her eyes. She looked so sad. So small and alone.

No way was he going to let her feel like there wasn't someone beside her who cared about her in every way a person could.

He jogged to catch up with her, then took her hand as they went deeper into the forest. Her hand was cold in his.

"Are you okay?" He squeezed her fingers, but she didn't look up at him and she didn't answer right away.

He noticed then how silently she moved through the forest. He probably alerted every being within two hundred yards of him with each step he took, the way branches and leaves crunched beneath his boots, and from the slap of bushes and tree branches against his now sore body. For Cassia, it was like the brush moved aside for her.

"I don't know if I'm okay with any of this," she finally said. "All these years I've prepared to ascend to my place as a Guardian. And now I'm supposed to mate with Daire." She looked away as a powerful shot of jealousy dug into his heart.

Jake had never faced the green-eyed monster before and he didn't like it one bit.

He had to take a good lungful of air before he could speak without sounding pissed off. "So this has been something that's been planned all along—Daire taking you through your transition?"

"Apparently." Cassia's brow wrinkled. "But I didn't find out until the day of my ascension." Her cheeks took on a blush pink enough that he could see it as they walked in the thick forest. "I was supposed to go through the transition that night, and I couldn't stop thinking that it should be—" She met his gaze. "You."

Jake took her by her arm, came to a full stop, and jerked her to him. "Even then, Cassia? You wanted me then?"

She tilted her chin to look up at him. "It will never come to anything, but I wanted—I wish it could be you."

"Christ." Jake crushed her in his arms, making her gasp. He breathed in her soft perfume of vanilla and woman, and the scent of magic, like cinnamon, that was distinctly her own. "There's got to be some way to work this out."

"How many times are we going to go over this? The sacrifices we would both have to make." She gave a deep sigh. "Frankly, I don't think either one of us can give up what we would have to in order to be together. We need to stop thinking about it."

"I refuse to accept that." His chest felt heavy, as if someone had parked a SWAT vehicle on top of him. "I don't believe for a minute we can't change our destinies. I don't even believe in destiny to begin with. Life is what we make of it."

"There's no changing this, Jake." Cassia rested her cheek against him. "I'm sorry."

"No." He mentally shoved at the weight he felt inside. "There's got to be some way."

Cassia pushed herself out of his arms and started walking again, and he followed. Twigs, dead leaves, and pinecones crunched beneath Jake's boots no matter how quiet he tried to be. The smells of pine and loam reminded him of backpacking in the Sierras with one of his academy buddies.

Only the scents here were richer, the air so much cleaner. Not to mention colors were crisper, brighter. And some were unusual—like trees clutching blue or purple leaves tightly to them like a miser gripping thousands of dollar bills in his fists.

"I suppose I should tell you a little about the Mystwalkers before we meet up with them." Cassia stepped on a log with Elvin grace. It was almost as if she floated above the ground and then over the log. And directly away from the subject of their relationship.

Smooth in every way, aren't you?

Jake grunted as a sharp crack echoed in the forest when he came up behind her and stepped on the same log.

"Mystwalkers are distant relations of the Elves." Cassia slipped past a bush before pausing and looking at the ground. "They are beings who can change from mist to human form and back." With a bemused expression, she picked up a pine-cone from the forest floor and examined it. The pinecone had an unusual sparkle to it. Like sunlight winking through the trees.

She continued, "But Mystwalkers have to stay away from salt water—as far as possible. If they are touched by salt wa-ter, they cannot hold their mist forms. They must be well cleansed in freshwater to be able to shift again."

Cassia again scrutinized the pinecone she held before she stopped and set it upright on a tree stump. Jake almost bumped into her before she went back to walking.

"That's a Faerie cone," she said, "and it shouldn't be on the ground."

Jake glanced at the cone, which winked with tiny lights as he strode by it.

Before he could ask her what a Faerie cone was, she went on talking. "Some believe Mystwalkers are rightfully slaves to the Shanai, a warrior race that is situated near a large ocean far from here."

"Are they?" Jake watched Cassia's hair swing above her sexy ass as she walked ahead of him. "Slaves?"

"That's been of some debate." Cassia glanced over her shoulder at him. "Many, many years ago the Shanai offered the Mystwalkers a trade. The Shanai would protect the mostly defenseless Mystwalkers from evil forces in exchange for the right to enjoy the Mystwalkers' legendary talents at lovemaking."

She pursed her lips before facing forward again. "It was an agreement the Mystwalkers entered into willingly. But when they are in sexual service, they are banded with a ring made from a special alloy that keeps them from taking their mist form. That's where the slavery debate comes in."

"What's to debate? If they're trapped, kept from leaving, they are slaves." Another branch slapped him in the face, stinging his cheek and nose. "They don't have a choice."

Cassia sighed, the only sound he heard from her as she slipped around more brush. "Again, that's been questioned more times than there are leaves on this tree." She pointed up into a huge tree. "The Mystwalkers made a commitment. The Shanai are holding them to it."

"Slaves," Jake scowled. "Plain and simple."

"A willing trade, Jake." Cassia scooped up a large dead leaf shaped like an oak leaf, only blue. "But a great faction that is not 'protected' by the Shanai would agree with you. They are free Mystwalkers. There aren't a lot of free Mystwalkers compared to how many serve the Shanai, but the faction is growing. And they aren't as defenseless as they once were." She added, "In fact, the free Mystwalkers can be dangerous, if provoked."

"No way are you going to convince me that these Mystwalkers are anything but slaves," Jake said in a growl.

Cassia turned and studied him as they both came to a stop. "There's something more to this for you, isn't there," she stated in a thoughtful, gentle tone. "You don't believe in slavery, for clear-cut reasons that I happen to agree with."

She brought her hand up and rested it on one of his arms as she continued, "But something happened. Something bad. And that bad thing is what you've been holding back from me." She paused. "It has something to do with what the Great Guardian said, doesn't it," she stated softly.

Jake shook out of her touch and strode past her, his jaw set, his insides on fire.

Cassia was instantly at his side and she snatched his wrist and brought him to a halt again. "You're going to tell me."

He closed his eyes and inhaled the clean scents of the forest. When he opened his eyes, the words came easier than he'd expected, like Cassia had used magic on him to draw the story out.

"When I served in the Marines in Afghanistan, I led a special recon squad." Jake followed Cassia's lead and sat on a relatively flat rock while she perched on a large fallen log. "We were responsible for ferreting out paranormal threats to our nation and theirs."

Cassia nodded in a way meant to encourage him as she said, "Over the years I've heard that such military activities take place all over the world."

Jake ran his hand over his stubbled jaws. "Yeah, well, I really screwed up with the recon squad I led."

Cassia didn't say anything, and the words just kept coming out.

"We discovered that a group of magical seers, healers, and practitioners from around the world had been brought to a small Afghani village in the Bamiyan Valley. They were being kept as slaves by a dark magic cult." He spoke in a low, rumbling voice. "The people the sect captured were more than prisoners. They were forced to serve as slaves.

"The dark magic cult," he continued, "used the seers to vision, scry, or use whatever other methods they could to spy on the US military." He shook his head. "Bastards threatened the seers by telling them if the seers didn't give correct information on US government intelligence, they would eliminate a healer or practitioner of their magical faith. They'd kill one person every time a seer failed in his or her vision."

Cassia studied him, her hands folded in her lap, a quiet, calm expression on her face.

He leaned forward and rested his forearms on his thighs as his thoughts continued back to that time. "During our recon, we discovered where one of these cults held their slaves. I was a cocky sonofabitch, and immediately organized my squad to go in and take out those bastards."

At the memories, Jake wanted to slam his fist on the rock he sat on, but figured a broken hand wasn't going to do him any good. "I got approval, and took my men in"—he ground his teeth before continuing—"and got them slaughtered."

Pain from the gut-wrenching memories closed off his throat, and tremors caused his hands to shake. The image of Pacer's body exploding seared his mind, along with images of the bodies of his men scattered around the cave entrance.

Familiar rage twined with the pain and he wanted nothing

more than to be back at the village, tearing every one of those black-magic practitioners into pieces. The tremors in his hands moved through his body, and he wanted to slam his fists into one of the trees over and over and over again until his knuckles bled, all the skin torn off from the power of his fury.

Instead, Jake looked up and wasn't sure how to read the expression on Cassia's face. Shock? Concern?

"It was a trap, and I led my men right into the middle of it." He turned his gaze from Cassia's again. A bitter taste was on his tongue and he spit it out onto the leaves on the side of the rock. "Half my squad was taken out." He stared at the ground as he shook his head. "We finally eliminated most of that cult, but not before they killed my men—and most of the seers and other slaves."

He looked back at Cassia and her eyes were closed, an expression of pain on her face. Definitely pain.

Jake couldn't believe he'd just completely spilled his guts. He'd never even talked with Bourne about what had happened during that mission.

Cassia opened her eyes and got up from the log she'd been sitting on. She knelt between his thighs and rested her head against his chest, wrapped her arms around his waist, and held onto him.

"You blame yourself for this so much that you haven't healed." She tipped her head back to look up at him. "That's why you keep such an emotional distance from everyone."

The expression on Cassia's features and the way she held him calmed the raging beast inside him, and the tremors in his body stopped.

"I guess I do avoid getting emotionally attached." Jake heaved a sigh as he reached up and stroked Cassia's hair with his fingers. "To anyone but you," he said in a low voice. She hugged him again, her face buried against his T-shirt. "I don't know how you got in, but you did." He squeezed her closer to him. "And I won't let anything get between us and keep us apart."

She didn't say anything for a long time, but he felt the warmth of her tears soak through his shirt to his chest. Why was she crying?

When she finally raised her head, she moved to her feet and took his hand in hers, drawing her up beside him. "You have to release the pain." She squeezed his fingers. "Stop taking blame for something that wasn't your fault. You did what you had to and made what you thought was the right decision."

"It was the wrong—"

She put the fingers of her free hand to his lips. "Stop. Think about what I said."

Jake kept his mouth clamped shut as they started walking through the forest again. He didn't know what the hell to think. Somehow she had calmed him enough that the painful memories slipped away and his focus narrowed in on her.

Right now he just knew that Cassia was an extraordinary woman and he didn't want to screw up with her. Yeah, she'd gotten inside him, and he knew he could never let her go.

Cassia brought them to a stop when they reached a small clearing shadowed by extraordinarily massive trees.

Jake was about to ask what would provoke the mist-beings, or whatever they were, when he realized the trees here were bigger around than two or three houses crammed along a San Francisco block. Maybe bigger. And damn they were tall. He craned his neck up to see as he walked. You could stack four of those houses on top of each other and still not reach the treetops.

Jake turned his attention to the clearing itself. A crystal blue pond took up the center, the pond surrounded by thick grass and wildflowers that made the air smell perfumed. A breeze skimmed the hair on his arms and caused small ripples on the surface of the pond.

Jake caught her hand and brought her around to face him. "How much farther?" he asked and took her other hand and squeezed.

"Right—"

A prickling sensation traveled up Jake's spine and he caught the distinct scent of magic.

He jerked his head up at the same time his right hand went to his holstered Glock.

CHAPTER NINETEEN

JAKE'S HEART PUMPED AS HE scanned the meadow. He didn't see anything but a thick mist gathering just feet from them, and he caught the strong smell of magic.

It hit him. *Mystwalkers*.

He was sensing their presence.

And scenting their magic.

Cassia touched his arm and he let his hand fall to his side, although he remained on guard.

A sense of curiosity and wonder raised goose bumps on his arms as he watched forms rise out of the heavy mist and solidify.

Three males. Four females. All wearing clothing so light it could have been mist, too. Around each of their necks was an engraved gold band about an inch wide.

Didn't Cassia say the Shanai enslaved Mystwalkers with rings, not collars?

None of these men and women wore rings.

With the exception of one woman, the Mystwalkers had long blond hair and gray-blue eyes. The other woman's hair fell just as long, but as dark as the rich dirt at their feet, and she had an intense green, green gaze. The dark-headed woman's had small braids to either side of her face and one thick braid down her back. Gold bands fastened the ends of the braids.

The four men were as broad-shouldered and about the same height as Jake, and the women were fine-boned and a little taller than Cassia.

Cassia gave a slight bow and the Mystwalkers did the same. Jake wasn't into bowing so he settled for a nod in their direction.

The dark-haired woman stepped forward and extended her hands to Cassia, and smiled. "You look well, Princess Cassiandra."

Cassia smiled in return as they took each other's hands and squeezed. "As do you." She turned to Jake. "Jake, I would like you to meet Alaia, leader of the Council of free Mystwalkers."

Jake gave the beautiful woman a slight nod. "Nice to meet you," he said, unable to think of anything more original.

"Alaia, this is Jake Macgregor . . . of the Earth Otherworld." Cassia and Alaia released hands. "He is a commander of his people and a leader of the Alliance."

A clean pure scent, like the light perfume of carnations, met Jake's senses as she took a step closer and studied him. Her guarded look told him she was wary and that she was analyzing him, dissecting him. As if she might be able to reach inside and pull out every thought and emotion he had.

Jake studied her as intently as she stared at him. Damned if he'd back down in a staring contest. He'd been a cop too long to break. Judging by her expression, the shrewd look in her eyes, and the way she carried herself, she was likely a strong leader. A good one? He'd have to do a little observation before he made that determination.

Finally Alaia gave him a slight nod and turned her attention to Cassia. "Come. We have prepared for your arrival." She glanced at Jake again. "However, the location of the free Mystwalkers is secret. Perhaps we should blindfold the human?" A teasing glint sparked in her eyes.

"Let's tie him up, too." Cassia laughed. "I think I'd enjoy that."

Jake couldn't help a grin as he looked down at Cassia. "You'd enjoy being tied up?"

Cassia flushed. "You. Not me."

"Uh-huh." He looked at Alaia. "Lead the way."

"Humans are not known for their stealth." The Mystwalker leader lowered her voice. "Truly, we must be cautious."

Jake figured they'd probably heard him coming a mile away while he and Cassia approached the meeting place.

"I'll go barefoot if you'd like me to," Jake said, half serious.

"That would help." Alaia surprised him with her stern reply as she gave a sharp nod. "You *must* be as quiet as possible."

Jake had the urge to salute, as if he was back in his military days.

"If not, we will be forced to use other methods to ensure your silence," Alaia added before turning away.

"I'm not sure I like the sound of that," he muttered as he jerked off his running shoes and socks, stuffing his socks into the shoes.

Cassia smiled again. "Oh, I do," she said before following Alaia.

"I'll just bet," he added in a grumble.

The rest of the Mystwalkers vanished as they shifted into nothing but thick mist that hovered close to the ground and moved ahead of them. Alaia remained in her physical form while they worked their way through the trees. Small stones and twigs dug into his bare feet as he walked and gripped his shoes in one hand.

Soon it was pretty obvious that, for the life of him, Jake couldn't be as silent as Cassia and Alaia. Every brush of a branch against his skin, or tiny snap of a twig, or slight crunch of a leaf beneath his feet echoed through the forest like he'd taken a ball-peen hammer to one of the trees.

Christ, but he'd never made so much noise in a forest back home. Granted, this forest was in a magical world and he wasn't magical anything.

Alaia stopped. Jake came up short behind her, and he winced as another leaf crunched beneath his foot. An expression of both frustration and determined resolution glittered in her gaze as she stared at Jake.

Oh, shit.

"Breacán." Alaia glanced at one spot in the mist, and a male form rose up from the ground.

Jake stood his ground and clenched his shoes in one fist. The hard look in Breacán's eyes caused Jake's spine to feel like a rodent had crawled up his back to his nape. "What the—" Jake started when Breacán reached out and touched his fingers to Jake's forehead.

A sensation like all his bones had vanished caught Jake off guard. He had no feeling in his body and felt like he'd been shot with an elephant-tranquilizer gun.

He dropped.

Breacán caught Jake under his arms and then the Mystwalker slung Jake over his shoulder. His shoes slipped from his fingers and thumped on the ground

"Sonofab—" Jake mumbled just as his face hit Breacán's back.

Lights out.

CASSIA WINCED AS JAKE FLOPPED against Breacán's shoulder before the Mystwalker began striding north again. Jake was going to be *so* angry—or pissed, as he would put it—when he came to.

She scooped up Jake's shoes, which still had his socks jammed in them. She had to smile at the sight of such a huge man as Jake being carried over another man's shoulder.

Jake hadn't made that much noise—not for a human—but this was the world of Fae and Elves, and they made no sounds as they traveled. Any being trying to pursue them would find it nearly impossible. It depended on the race, though. Elves and Fae were excellent trackers, but so were races like the Shanai.

The Shanai weren't evil—far from it. They were a tough race of men and women who tended to be black and white in their judgment. And in their judgment these Mystwalkers were violating an ironclad bargain, and should be held accountable—not to mention returned to sexual service.

"How is Geldian Princess?" Cassia asked Alaia in a voice too light for the wind to carry it.

Alaia froze for a moment before continuing to walk. "The Shanai captured her." A silent, but matter of fact statement filled with pain and bitterness. "Taken with Cerra."

"Your half sister, Cerra?" This time Cassia halted, her eyes wide and unbelieving. "Both kidnapped?"

Cassia caught up to Alaia as she pressed ahead. "Once we fulfill our promises to the Alliance, we will rescue Geldian Princess and Cerra, along with all of the other pleasure-slaves." Alaia's eyes sparked with fury. "We have enough free Mystwalkers now, and a plan—"

Still carrying Jake, Breacán disappeared in the forest ahead of them as Alaia shook her head. "It matters not at this time. Now is for the Earth Otherworld, and our brothers and sisters in the Alliance."

Cassia let the subject lie. But she bit the inside of her lip as concern for these people gripped her.

In addition, would the Mystwalkers expect the Alliance to go to war with the Shanai in return for this assistance?

Deep in her emerging Guardian's instincts, Cassia knew that couldn't happen. For a long, terrible moment, she could feel the balance of all the Otherworlds, delicate yet more powerful than any energy known, teetering across her shoulders.

The Mystwalkers would have to fight the Shanai on their own for the balance to be protected. Cassia couldn't explain how she knew that, beyond the firm sensation in her flesh and bones, and the weight of it.

As a woman and a warrior, she'd definitely want to help the Mystwalkers.

But as a Guardian . . .

Oh, Mother, how have you born such responsibility all these years?

In one long, terrible, and seemingly endless moment, Cassia felt the immensity of her own fate, of the responsibility of being the only daughter of the Great Guardian.

Unless her mother bore another female child—which, given her age, seemed unlikely—Cassia would one day take her mother's position, and regulate the ebb and flow of energies in all Otherworlds. She would be, essentially, the gate-keeper for all life everywhere, making certain the infinitely complex patterns needed to support that life remained firmly in place.

Everyone would adore her.

And hate her.

She thought about Jake's stubborn smile. His determination to be with her despite the odds, the dangers, and the forces aligned against them.

Her heart swelled, then faltered in the face of so much unwelcome reality.

How could a human ever understand the magnitude of her duties?

It wasn't fair of her to even let him entertain the fantasy.

IT WAS A FULL DAY before they neared the veiled Mystwalker refuge. Few knew of its existence, and a mere handful had ever been taken to the hidden location. As the Elvin Princess and a future Guardian, Cassia was one of the privileged few who had ever been allowed entrance.

Around bends and copses of trees they followed an invisible path until they reached a sheer rock wall. After a tight squeeze between a break in the wall and another wall was an indiscernible trail. It opened up to a beautiful flower-filled meadow. Beyond that a waterfall pounded into a pool and roared its welcome as crystal droplets winked in the air. The waterfall could not be heard on the outside of the enormous wall they had slipped around.

Alaia and Cassia walked across the meadow and reached the waterfall. Its thrumming roar vibrated through Cassia and its misty spray chilled her skin.

They caught up with Breacán, who still carried Jake, and followed the mist of the other five Mystwalkers. Cassia and Alaia remained close as they stepped behind the waterfall—

And entered another world.

The Mystwalker refuge never failed to take Cassia's breath away. Towering walls of pure crystal, with veins of a golden metal, soared above the sanctuary. The crystal reflected the vivid greens of the trees, grass, and other greenery. Reds, pinks, yellows, and oranges glittered on the crystal from the amazing splashes of wildflowers throughout the expanse of the refuge. Gardens stretched out with all manner of fruits and vegetables, and Mystwalkers toiled by planting and checking the irrigation.

A waterfall, different from the one they had just passed behind, flowed over one of the crystal cliffs and tumbled into a large pool. The Mystwalkers managed the water for irrigation as well as personal uses.

Cassia paused and waved to some of the Mystwalkers she recognized. They smiled and returned her greeting with enthusiasm.

For a moment, Cassia closed her eyes and drank in the sweet scents of angel blooms and lyria buds. The flowers gave off a perfume that combined to make a scent that was like roses, carnations, and orchids all swirled together on a teasing whirlwind of a breeze. She held out her arms, tipped her head back, and took another deep lungful of early evening air. Night tralls serenaded and crickets started their songs, the birds and insects making beautiful music together.

"Cassia." Alaia's voice held amusement as Cassia opened her eyes. "I believe if I allowed it you would stand in that very spot for the rest of the evening."

"You know me well." Cassia smiled and relaxed her arms as she looked at Alaia. "I love it here."

Alaia returned her smile. "Come, Princess." The Mystwalker leader turned away and headed toward one of the many wooden huts dispersed throughout the enclave.

They reached the beautiful little hut Cassia had stayed in before, the place where most of their infrequent visitors stayed. Alaia's people fashioned their huts from the glossy wood of siren trees. Cassia had always wondered what kind of bargain the Mystwalkers had to make with the Dryads to use wood from the rare trees, but had never questioned Alaia or her people.

"How many free Mystwalkers have you gathered?" Cassia asked.

Alaia didn't answer as she slipped inside, Cassia behind her. Breacán stood in the large three-room hut alone. Cassia figured Breacán had settled Jake on the mattress in the bedroom, as she didn't see him in the main room.

"Breacán," Alaia said to the large, blond Mystwalker. "You can wake the human now."

Cassia grimaced. *This should be good.*

Breacán disappeared into the back room again, and the next thing Cassia heard was Jake growling, "What the hell is going on?"

JAKE'S HEAD SPUN LIKE he'd turned into one of those funnel-bastards.

He managed to sit on the edge of the mattress he'd been tossed on. The mattress was about two feet thick, but lay flat on the floor instead of on a bed frame.

Jake looked up and really wanted to slug the amused expression off Breacán's face. He would've, too, if his bones would grow back in his legs. Right now, Jell-O City.

"Do you require anything?" the Mystwalker asked as he towered over Jake.

"Yeah." Jake rubbed his forehead with his fingers and squinted up at Breacán. "You. Me. Wrestling match. As soon as I don't feel like I already got the crap beat out of me."

Breacán laughed. "Perhaps you will get your wish, human."

"Jake," Cassia said from behind the man. "His name is Jake."

Breacán shrugged, the equivalent of a human saying "whatever." Jake would have ground his teeth if his head didn't hurt so friggin' much. It hurt just to talk, and he'd done about all the talking he was going to for now.

The Mystwalker left the room, leaving Cassia alone with Jake. She sat on the low mattress beside him, wrapped her arms around her knees, and said, "Sorry."

Jake grunted.

"If the Shanai find this place . . ." Cassia trailed off before she added, "It would be bad. Really bad."

He grunted again.

And wondered how he was getting out of here when it was time to go, because he sure didn't plan on playing the part of a side of beef slung over some man's shoulder.

"Alaia and Breacán left for the night." Cassia placed her palm on his thigh, warming his skin through his jeans with her touch. "They'll send dinner, and then we'll get some rest."

If he didn't feel so bad, he'd have told Cassia food wasn't what he wanted for dinner.

He wanted *her.*

Maybe for dessert.

"I know their delicacies will make you feel better." She squeezed his thigh. "Their food is wonderful, and has a way of making a person feel revitalized."

Jake managed a third grunt.

Delicacies. Yeah, right. He just needed some plain old grub and he'd be fine.

Cassia patted his thigh, then stood. Immediately he missed having her beside him, feeling her heat and smelling her soft vanilla-and-spices scent.

The Tilt-A-Whirl in Jake's head slowed enough that he didn't feel like upchucking when Cassia returned with a large tray of food. Instead, his stomach growled, telling him he'd survive.

"Thanks," he mumbled as Cassia set the tray on the mattress. She eased onto the bed so that she was on the other side of the tray from him.

He eyed the food with definite skepticism. Arranged on the tray were strange-looking orange and blue vegetable things, with some kind of itty-bitty croissant-wrapped meat pies. The smells were delicious despite the appearance of the food.

His stomach rumbled again as smells like roast chicken, vegetables, and cornbread rolled over him. But damned if he didn't catch the scent of magic, too.

"I'm not eating anything with magic in it," Jake said, despite the desperate growl in his stomach as he met Cassia's blue eyes.

She tilted her head. "It's food, Jake. Grown fresh, cooked or baked. Just like home only"—she glanced at the plates—"weird-looking."

"I smell magic," he said, finally dropping his hand from his temples and straightening. He felt like his bones were whole and his head wasn't spinning.

She looked at him with some confusion in her expression. "You . . . smell magic?"

"Yeah." Jake gestured to her. "You, the other Elves, Drow, Fae, witches—you all have a scent that's hard to pinpoint." He frowned. "Like some kind of exotic but earthy perfume mixed with sunshine. And it's light, like air."

He frowned more. "That doesn't really describe it, but hell if I know how to. It's barely noticeable, but I've always caught the scent around anyone with magic. Elves. D'Danann. D'Anu. Now Mystwalkers. The Drow, too, but theirs is a little different. Kind of darker, but not sickening like black magic."

"First time I've ever heard anyone say that." Cassia wore a "that's interesting, but odd" expression. "The food is naturally grown, though, and prepared in the cookhouse."

Jake's appetite got the better of him. He grabbed one of the tiny croissant-looking things, eyed it with suspicion, then popped it into his mouth.

He didn't think he'd eaten anything so incredibly delicious in his life. "Definitely magic," he grumbled in between bites of the vegetables, fruits, and pastries. "Nothing normal could taste this great," he added, and Cassia laughed.

He couldn't begin to explain the tastes. It was like eating food from another country, with exotic spices. Like Thai food with its liberal use of peanut sauce and coconut milk. Or Chinese potstickers and the assortment of dumplings at dim sum. Just different. Unusual. Unexpected.

The drink was like blackberry wine, with a hint of some kind of unusual spice.

When they finished eating, Jake helped Cassia take everything to the small kitchen part of the front room and they washed the wooden plates in water pumped from a spout. The water from that pump was actually warm. The other hand pump released cold water. Interesting.

He'd been feeling pretty exhausted after a long day of arguing with a "Great Guardian," getting in a fight with Daire, and trekking through the forest. And especially after being knocked out by some kind of magic that had made him feel loopy, like he'd had a major hangover.

But now he felt energized.

His cock hardened as he watched Cassia from behind. The gentle sway of her ass as she moved, all that golden-blond hair that tumbled almost to her small waist. He could just drag her jeans down and over her hips, bend her over, slide into her wetness . . .

Hold on Macgregor. Jake ground his teeth. *Virgin. Guardian ascending. Transition. Instant death. No sex.*

Not yet.

His cock wouldn't listen to a thing that shot through his mind.

Cassia turned, and he sucked in his breath when her gaze met his. She stood maybe five feet away, but a couple of steps in her direction and he'd have her in his arms.

His little head spoke and his big head took a vacation.

Cassia's eyes widened as he went to her, his gaze never breaking from hers. He caught her face in his hands and kissed her so hard it made his own mind spin like it had been earlier, and his knees wanted to give out again.

Sweet Jesus, he'd never tasted anything as good as Cassia. Never felt anything as powerfully as he did with her.

To hell with instant death.

She was his.

CHAPTER TWENTY

THE ENTIRE WORLD VANISHED.

Cassia fell under Jake's spell as he kissed her. His was a different kind of magic. A magic of seduction and desire that made her heart pound and her body vibrate with a need she had never experienced before.

Jake's palms rested on her backside and he drew her to him, molding her body to his so that his erection was rigid against her belly. Cassia slid her palms up his chest, every flex of his muscles causing more intense feelings to wash over her. She linked her fingers behind his neck and clung to him, and he took control of her mind, body, and soul.

He already had her heart.

No. We can't do this, can't . . .

It was only a kiss. Just a kiss.

What a kiss.

Jake dipped his tongue into her mouth and explored her so thoroughly she thought he would discover every secret she possessed. He tasted of blackberry wine, exotic spices, and male.

He alternately nipped at her lower lip and searched her mouth with the mysteries of the magic they could make together.

Cassia's liquid gold and stars sparkled around them before her magic wrapped them in an embrace as firm as Jake's arms around her. She felt caressed everywhere. Her skin hot, the place between her thighs wet, her body tingling with the twining sensations of Jake's kiss and her power.

Something shattered in the kitchen, but she couldn't get herself to drag her attention away from the moment.

This could go no farther than a kiss. But she felt as if she'd had too much wine. Dizzy and relaxed, yet tense and charged.

The wonder of the feelings Jake stirred within her made her want more. She had never experienced anything so precious as what they shared at this very moment.

Jake groaned and gripped her impossibly tighter as he moved his mouth from hers. He trailed kisses along her jaw-line to the curve of her neck, just below her ear. He inhaled audibly, as if drawing her scent into him, filling himself with her.

Catching her by complete surprise, Jake pushed her T-shirt up over her bare breasts. She'd never been able to get used to human bras, and without her shirt there was nothing to hide behind.

"God you're sweet, Cassia." Jake lowered his head, and she shivered and gasped when he skimmed his lips over first one, then the other nipple. "Like kissing silk." His warm breath flowed over one of the hard nubs as he spoke.

"Jake," she said in a pleading tone, but didn't really know what she was begging for. This couldn't go far.

She wouldn't let it get out of control. Just a little more touching, feeling, kissing.

A loud crack echoed through the room and a part of Cassia hoped she hadn't broken another table. The other part of her didn't care.

Cassia gripped Jake's shoulders and whimpered as he flicked his tongue over one nipple. Firecracker sensations sparked straight between her thighs. Her magic continued to whirl around them, intensifying everything they were feeling. She tried to rein it in a little but she had no control over it, like she had no control over her body's reactions to Jake's touch—his mouth, his hands.

Something hit the floor with a loud thump as her magic grew hotter.

A chair?

When he sucked her other nipple, she cried out and almost dropped straight to the floor.

This time a louder crack bit the air—a cupboard door?—and Cassia knew she should stop Jake.

Yes. She would stop him. Now.

In a minute.

Or two.

Jake scooped her up in his arms and held her tight to him as he strode from the main room to the bedroom. She placed her palm on his chest and looked up at him, her lips moist, the area around her mouth a little roughened from his stubble.

Her mind grew dizzy and her thoughts scattered as golden magic surrounded them as he carried her. The glow kept the darkness outside from pressing in.

"We shouldn't be doing this," he said as he set her on her feet in the bedroom.

"What?" Her foggy, confused mind couldn't process what he was saying as her gaze was drawn to what surrounded them.

Look at all the pretty sparkles.

Ooh, they're so gold and glittery.

Pretty, pretty sparkles.

Drunk. She had to be drunk.

On love and lust.

She dragged her attention from the glittery magic to Jake.

Forget the sparkles. Look at the gorgeous man in front of you with the dark blue eyes.

Such beautiful eyes.

Cassia sighed and smiled. Yes, definitely intoxicated with love for him.

Should she tell him now?

A tiny bit of reality tried to push its way into her mind.

If she allowed any of this to continue, it would only make it harder to leave him.

But couldn't they enjoy what time they could until she had to face her destiny?

"Jake." Her voice came out a breathless whisper on her lips. "I don't want to hurt you." *Or your heart.*

"We won't go too far." His voice was low, husky as he

pulled her T-shirt over her head and let it drop on the floor. Her magical glow made it easy to see in the otherwise darkened room. "I promise."

She shivered as he bared the top half of her body. Her nipples turned into hard nubs and more desire rushed through her.

Several thumps. A shutter banging against the window?

"I just want to touch you." He pushed her back on the mattress and unfastened her jeans. "And taste you," he murmured just as he zipped down her jeans, then sucked in his breath. He skimmed his fingers over her hairless mound, and she squirmed with want and need. "Your pussy—no hair. So ready for my mouth and tongue."

He was going to put his mouth on her?

That thought made her head spin a little more.

The room completely filled with gold sparkles. The scent of her musk twined with the scent of magic swirling around them.

Jake was right.

Magic did have a smell.

Why had she never noticed that before?

When Jake had completely removed her clothing, he took both of her hands and drew her onto her feet.

"I want to see what you look like." She ran her palms over his T-shirt as a nearby mirror rattled against a wall. "Please."

Jake jerked off his T-shirt and she noticed the scars from the Stormcutter blades. Her heart jerked at the thought of losing him.

She reached up and traced the tattoo on his upper arm. "What does this mean?" she asked as she ran her fingers lightly over the tattoo. "An eagle on top of what looks like Earth, with an anchor behind it."

"Eagle, globe, and anchor." Jake brought his fingers up to hers. "It's the US Marine Corps insignia. It symbolizes distant service under the American eagle. Service by land and sea to represent our nation's interests in every clime and place."

"Oh." Cassia's eyes met his. "I wondered. I didn't know you served in the military until we talked earlier."

"It's been a few years." He settled his hands on her hips and rubbed his erection against her, over her star birthmark, causing more crazy sensations to spiral through her.

"Princess," he said. "I know I can't take you the way I want to—yet—but I need to feel your hot little body against mine."

Cassia clenched her legs shut. His words made that ache between her thighs more intense.

His feet were still bare from his trek through the forest. "I'm going to take you as far as we can go," he said as he pushed down his jeans, and his erection jutted out toward her.

She caught her breath. The mirror rattled harder against the wood.

Almost without thought, she reached out, wrapped her fingers around his staff, and began exploring it with both hands, from the head of his erection to the large sac at its base.

He groaned and tried to pry her hands away, but she refused to budge. "No." She stared at his erection, fascinated. She'd never touched a man before, and had only seen one other naked man—briefly. "I need to see and feel you."

She eased to her knees so that her mouth was right in front of the head of his staff. "This is semen?" she asked as she smeared a drop of the pearly substance over the head of his erection. "What does it taste like?" she asked, just before she licked him.

THE MOMENT HER TONGUE SWIPED his cock, Jake thought his bones were dissolving, like he had felt when the Mystwalker had used magic on him. "Jesus Christ," was all he could get out as he slid his hands into Cassia's hair. "You've got to stop, Princess."

"Why?" Cassia asked, and his mind went blank as she slid her warm mouth over the head of his cock.

Jake gritted his teeth. Her golden magic swirled in the bedroom, but Jake knew it was the woman swiping her tongue across his erection who was going to drive him to his knees. "I want to get a taste of you." His breath came in harsh pants as if he'd been running a good mile. "I didn't plan—didn't intend—*Jesus.*"

Cassia had started sucking him. She closed her eyes, fondling his balls and licking and sucking his erection. When she stopped, he nearly cried.

"Your body is so tense." She looked up at him with her beautiful turquoise eyes. "You're shaking."

"Yeah." Jake tried to stop shaking and failed big-time. "Who'd have figured."

"What happens if I keep sucking?" she asked, her expression truly innocent.

"Did you like the taste of my semen?" He clenched and unclenched his hands in her hair. "A whole lot of it is going to go into your mouth if you keep it up."

She swiped her tongue up his cock and he wanted to shout. "Will it feel good to you?"

"Hell, yes," he said, and she took him in her mouth again.

Dear God. Every nerve ending seemed focused around his cock and balls. All sensation, all feeling, gathered in that one location. Sweat broke out on his skin as he tried to hold back a little longer.

Not happening.

His come spurted from his cock in a hot rush as he climaxed and his orgasm burst within him. His body rocked and sparks flickered in his head. He had to hold onto her hair to even keep standing. His mind drifted in circles like the golden magic swirling in the room.

Jake's cock gave a final jerk, and he pulled himself out of Cassia's mouth. Her tongue darted out to catch a drop of semen that had escaped onto her lower lip, and his cock spasmed one more time.

He didn't think he could breathe any longer. His muscles gave way and he fell to his knees in front of Cassia, brought her into his arms, and pressed her head to his sweaty chest.

"Thank you," he said in between trying to catch his breath. "That was—" *The best head of my life.* "—incredible."

"I'm glad." Cassia started kissing his chest. "You taste so good."

When he stopped breathing like he'd hit a home run and sprinted around all the bases at least half a dozen times, Jake forced Cassia onto the low mattress so that her back rested on the soft, filmy bed covering and her ass was at the edge of the bed. He hooked his arms under her knees and spread her beautiful pussy wide open.

THRILLS WENT THROUGH CASSIA, as if the golden sparkles drifting through the room were in her belly, too.

The mirror rattled harder.

A sensation of power rolled through her as Jake leaned close to her mound and folds, and took another audible inhalation.

"You smell musky and sweet." He pressed light kisses to her smooth mound. He looked up and met her eyes. She was feeling hotter and hotter from his words and his steamy gaze.

"Have you ever touched yourself?" He stroked her clit, and she jerked as a spasm of sensation washed over her.

"No," she whispered as she shook her head again. "It was forbidden."

The mirror dropped off the wall and shattered. The tinkling of shards scattering across the floor seemed to be in time with the winking sparks of her magic.

Stop. I've got to stop.

Just a minute. One more little minute.

I could hurt Jake. No more!

"I know I can't be inside you—yet," he said in a gravelly rumble before she could say a word. "But I want to taste you and give you your first orgasm. Now." He swiped his tongue from where her slit met her anus all the way to her mound, and she gasped and arched her back as sensations shot from her folds throughout her being. "Is that okay with you?"

"Ah . . ." She could barely think. Then her concern hit her again. "What if I hurt you?" she said as she slipped her fingers into his thick, dark hair. "What if having an orgasm does bring about the transition?" She swallowed. "What if it isn't something that will only happen if I have a male inside of me?"

"For a taste of you, Princess"—he looked at her from between her thighs—"I'm willing to take that chance."

She started to argue, but her words were nothing but a low wail as Jake dove into her folds with his tongue and mouth. He kept her legs spread wide and moved them so that her knees rested on his shoulders, and he now used his fingers and mouth to give her pleasure. Unbelievable pleasure.

Gold sparkles continued to swirl around them. They seemed stronger. More intense.

She wanted to scream. The whole room seemed to shake.

He slipped one finger inside her and she tensed. He paused before slowly sliding in and out of her wetness until she relaxed.

"If you aren't the tightest thing I've ever felt," he murmured as he pumped his finger in and out of her core, "I don't know what is." With his finger still inside her, he laved her folds in one long swipe of his tongue. "You're so tight I don't know if my cock's going to fit when I do take you."

The sensual promise in Jake's voice, and the vivid image of him sliding his thick erection into her, added to the firestorm growing inside of her. Not to mention the ever-increasing glitter and crackle of light from her magic.

Dear Anu. I'm going to melt the bed.

Warning sparks lit off in her mind as she realized she had no control of the magic swirling in ever-tightening circles around them.

"I don't want to hurt you," she got out in a hoarse whisper.

"You're not going to." He raised his head just long enough to say the words, then delved back into her folds.

What Jake was doing to her was like a hurricane. Wind, lightning, a battering feeling like moisture and debris stinging her skin as the magic sparks started flinging themselves at her and Jake.

Were their clothes spinning around the room? Was that Jake's shoes?

He didn't seem to notice the sparks, or anything that was flying near their heads, and Cassia was too far gone to get any more words out.

Gold and fire and lightning followed by the low rumble of

thunder in her ears dampened all sound. Her own moans and cries were as muffled as Jake's hungry groans.

Vaguely, from some distant part of her conscious being, she knew something was wrong. Desperately wrong.

No, it was so right.

Her. With Jake. Now.

It was right for Jake to be the one to teach her pleasure, to give her the most beautiful experience of her life.

Jake pumped his finger in and out of her core as he sucked the hard nub and licked her folds. Her skin prickled. More stars flung themselves at her. Now a hairbrush and perfume bottle joined their clothing in the dance around the room. Perspiration broke out over her entire body, making her slick with sweat.

Everything shifted. Turned upside down. Like someone moved the moon and stars, and galaxies collided.

She started vibrating. Distantly she heard her moans grow louder and louder until they became cries. One after another.

Something was going to happen. She was right there. The world was tilting. Tilting. Tilting.

White-hot light exploded from her entire being.

Cassia screamed from the power of the climax.

Somewhere she heard Jake shout. Felt him as the force of her orgasm and magic flung him across the room. She heard his body slam against the far wall, and a loud crack cut through the storm.

The magic! It roiled within her, burned her inside and out. She didn't know what to do as her body throbbed and bucked and burned.

It was exquisite. It was painful. It was beautiful. It was terrifying.

It was everything.

It was too much.

Tears rolled down her cheeks as she tried to rein in the power.

Somewhere—voices. Calming. Soothing.

Calling her back.

Bringing her home.

Letting her fade away until nothing was left but pure pleasure and exhaustion.

And the feeling that something so right had gone so terribly wrong.

CHAPTER TWENTY-ONE

SHE WAS ROCKING. LIKE A BOAT tossed on gentle swells in a vast ocean. Cool sea breezes, then warm sun, touched her skin. The smells, though . . . fresh, clean water, and orchids, roses, carnations . . . nothing like the salty ocean.

More rocking. Cassia snuggled into a blanket in the swaying boat. She was tired. So, so tired.

"Cassiandra!" The cold, hard voice jolted Cassia's mind as she opened her eyes and the Great Guardian appeared.

The Guardian was beautiful as she stood in the sun-drenched green meadow. Her white-blond hair gleamed in the sunlight as her hair tumbled straight to her bare toes like a silken cloak. Her delicate features were lovely, even as her brilliant blue eyes turned icy.

In an instant clouds obscured the sun and everything grew dark and dangerous-looking—including the Great Guardian.

"Mother?" Cassia mumbled as she tried to speak and focus on the image of the Guardian. "Why are you upset?" *In all my years, I have never seen the Great Guardian* angry. *What did I do?*

"You crossed me, Cassiandra." The Great Guardian bit out each word. "I gave you nonnegotiable instructions. I made it clear you are not to have sexual relations with the human." Her eyes seemed to glow in the growing darkness.

Cassia reached out for her mother's hand but the Great Guardian might as well have been a mile away. "I am sorry, Mother—"

The Guardian's robe stirred around her feet as a harsh gust of wind cut through the near darkness. "There can be no repairing what you have started."

"Started?" Cassia frowned as she dropped her hand back

into her lap. She suddenly realized she was sitting in the grass in a meadow. She was naked. Grass prickled beneath her bare buttocks, and cold air swirled around her and raised her hair from her shoulders. Her nipples tightened, painfully hard in the cold wind.

Heat flushed over her body from being naked in front of the Guardian, but it didn't chase away the chill in the darkened meadow. Cassia crossed her arms over her breasts and shifted so that her legs were folded to the side in such a way that her sex didn't show as much. "What do you mean, *started*? Did I not go through the transition with Jake?"

The Guardian gave a humorless laugh. "What you experienced was a mere spark of what will happen as you proceed." She had never seen her mother's face look so dark. "Your human would be dead now if he had entered you. He would have taken the full brunt of your magic with no way to channel it."

Cassia hugged herself tighter. "No. I can't hurt him. I won't hurt him."

The sky lightened and the wind lessened until it was a light breeze caressing her skin. The Guardian's expression softened. "If you care for this human, you must let him go."

Cassia's heart nearly stopped beating. "Isn't there some way? Some way at all that I can be with Jake? That he can be the one?"

The Great Guardian stilled, and it seemed as if everything around them froze as she studied Cassia. The Guardian's expression told Cassia nothing, and her own heart seemed to come to a stop.

"This human . . . he means that much to you?"

Cassia voiced the words she had been afraid to say to Jake. Now was the time for honesty above all else. "I love him, Mother."

A range of emotions passed over the Guardian's countenance. Cassia found herself bewildered and confused to see her mother show emotion at all. Cassia's entire body tingled, and she felt as if the roots of her hair stood on end.

Anger, disappointment, sadness, hopelessness . . .

Cassia wanted to cry. She didn't want her mother to feel the kind of pain that seemed to be surging through her. The Guardian was solid, strong, perfect.

Wasn't she?

She was the place through which the energy supporting the universe passed. Beyond-powerful energy. The Great Guardian's magic allowed her to see every one of the conditions that must exist for the greatest good for all life-forms to be maintained.

The Guardian worked to ensure those conditions, and her Guardian sons had done what they could to aid her.

But the Guardian's vision was so vast she couldn't possibly explain all that she saw. Cassia knew it was likely her mother was so used to silence and noninteraction that she no longer really knew how to explain herself thoroughly and not be cryptic. Cassia wasn't even close to that level yet because she wasn't very old—

But Cassia would see centuries, millennia pass.

And one day she, Cassiandra, Princess of the Light Elves would be . . . the Great Guardian.

The enormity of her future slammed into Cassia as if the tree palace had fallen and crashed upon her.

Her eyes filled with tears. She didn't ask for this, didn't want it. But how could she let her mother down? Allow her to continue to bear such incredible responsibility for millennia after millennia more?

Cassia bowed her head, a tear falling to land on a blade of grass, where it beaded before rolling down the blade.

"Cassiandra." The Guardian's voice had softened. When Cassia brought her gaze up to the Guardian's, her mother looked thoughtful yet pained at the same time. "When you come back to me from the Mystwalkers, I will offer your human two options."

Cassia blinked, not sure she was hearing right. The vastness of what lay before her made her mind, body, heart, and soul ache.

"What," Cassia said slowly, "do you mean by giving Jake choices?"

The Guardian paused again before continuing. "I will allow the human to take you through the transition if he chooses one of two options."

The devastation in Cassia's heart was still so great she wasn't sure what to think of this now. "What are the conditions?"

"Do not forewarn the human that I will do this thing for you." The Guardian's robe pressed against her slim form as another whirl of wind slapped Cassia's bare skin. "Do you understand? You must leave him free to make his own choices."

Even as she hugged herself tighter, every painful thought whirling through her, Cassia nodded. "Yes, Mother."

The Guardian gave Cassia one last long look before turning and vanishing.

Cassia collapsed on the grass and faded away.

"PRINCESS."

The soft voice tugged at her mind and she frowned. She didn't want to return to reality. The reality she must face seemed so dark, so heavy.

No. She wanted oblivion.

"Princess." The feminine voice was insistent now. "Wake, Cassiandra."

Oblivion.

"Wake." This time the woman spoke in a commanding tone. A force shook her. Hard. "You must come back to us or the human could die."

"Human?" Cassia mumbled.

"Jake," the woman growled. "Your human, Jake."

Cassia's lids sprung open as she came fully to her senses. "Jake!" His name rang like a bell as she called out. "Where is he?"

Alaia held Cassia like the Mystwalker had been cradling her while she had been unconscious. That was what had given her the sensation of rocking—Alaia holding her.

Cassia tried to sit up, but her head and neck felt like she was trapped in a stockade and unable to move.

"Careful." Alaia eased Cassia up in slow, slow move-

ments, despite the imaginary stockade, until Cassia sat up on
the floor mattress. Her legs curled under her, her knees to the
side. Cassia now wore a robe similar to the gauzy fabric of
Mystwalker clothing.

Her thoughts cleared, her mind crystallizing. Horror replaced confusion as she remembered blinding white light
and the sound of Jake slamming against the hard wooden
wall when her magic flung him away from her.

She cut her gaze to Alaia's as panic rose up inside like the
magic was trying to burst from her again. "Where is he?"

"We were afraid to move him." Alaia glanced to the left of
Cassia, and she swung her gaze in the direction Alaia looked.

Jake lay in a corner of the room, on his side, facing her,
his back to a wall. A huge crack, which had definitely not been
there before, was now in a beam seven feet above where Jake
had crumpled on top of fine, white powder that covered the
floor.

She'd blown up something porcelain again.

Who cared about that? Her heart pounded and she held
her hand to her chest. Jake. Jake was all that mattered.

A filmy Mystwalker blanket rested on his big body, to his
hips, and he was naked from the waist up. His skin was a
pale shade of yellow, the scars a horrible white instead of
pink, his breathing shallow, his body limp.

A woman knelt near his head, crushing herbs that smelled
of chamomile and mint in a mortar as she looked at Jake.

"We are not sure if he suffered internal damage," Alaia
was saying. "Our healers do not understand what has happened to him."

Cassia had knelt in the white powder by Jake's side before Alaia finished speaking. Heat seared Cassia's veins, her
entire body flushing so hot she thought her blood might boil.

Her healer instincts kicked in even as her heart pounded
so much harder it hurt. She still smelled her musk on Jake as
she raised her hands and moved her palms above him from
his head to his waist. The magic that she used to heal had always been more iridescent than any color, but now it was
like liquid gold mixed with stars.

At this moment she hated it because of what her new powers had done to Jake. But, at the same time, that enhanced
magic made it clear in her mind what was wrong with him
and how she could heal him.

Visions of the Great Guardian tried to force their way into
her thoughts but she shoved them back. Not now. *Not now!*

"An overload." Cassia closed her eyes and let the surges
of knowing rush through her. "Like some cases of being
struck by lightning. He might experience temporary paraly-
sis, numbness, tingling, and he will feel like his skin is burning." She swallowed hard and glanced at Alaia. "Did his
heart stop beating? Did he stop breathing?"

"Barely breathing, but not completely stopped, nor was
his heart, as far as we know." Alaia shook her head. "He was
just like this. His condition hasn't changed."

Cassia let her healing magic flow into Jake. His color
gradually changed from the horrible yellow shade to his normal tanned brown. "How long has it been?"

"Not long." Alaia knelt between Cassia and the woman
using a pestle to grind unfamiliar herbs into the mixture in
the mortar. "Perhaps twenty minutes? We heard you scream,
your human cry out, and then a loud cracking noise." She
glanced up at the wall above them, and Cassia saw again the
split wooden beam.

"Dear Anu, he's got to have the biggest egg on his head
known to any beings." Cassia concentrated her magic on
Jake's skull and mind as she moved her hands above his
head and closed her eyes.

"Definite bruising," she continued. "A lump the size of
Texas on the back of his head."

"Texas?" Alaia said, but Cassia ignored her and continued to examine Jake.

She let out a long exhale. "But his skull did not fracture."
She glanced up at the beam again. "He did more damage to
it than the beam did to him." She looked back at Jake. "I
think I can relieve some of his pain, but not all. He's going to
have the Underworld of headaches when he comes to."

Cassia ran her hands along Jake's body, drawing out

some of the electrical charges still playing havoc with his internal organs. It was a wonder he hadn't had a seizure.

The smell of herbs grew stronger, and Cassia opened her eyes to see the Mystwalker healer spreading a paste over Jake's forehead. "To ease the headaches when he wakes," the pretty woman said. Ringlets of flaxen hair fell around her shoulders, and she looked at Cassia with misty gray-blue eyes. The telltale eyes, hair, and pale skin of a Mystwalker made them easy to identify. No other being looked like a Mystwalker—there was something special about them. Something unique.

Cassia glanced at Alaia, the only exception she had ever known among the Mystwalkers. Dark hair, green eyes, and fair skin, about the same shade as the Light Elves', certainly not the pale, pale flesh that distinguished Mystwalkers. Alaia never spoke of her differences and Cassia didn't ask. It was far from polite to do so.

When Jake's breathing deepened, his tan had returned to its normal shade, and his body no longer crackled with as much electricity, Cassia gave a sigh of relief.

"Shall I spread the paste on the human's chest?" the healer asked, leaning forward as if to do so.

"I think he will be fine now." Cassia relaxed and smiled at the healer. "He is already resting more comfortably."

Alaia laid her hands on Jake's ankles over the covering. "It is safe to move him?"

Between the healer and Alaia, Cassia was not sure she liked any other woman's hands on Jake for any reason.

"Yes," Cassia said. "We should put him on the mattress so he can rest more comfortably." No doubt Jake wouldn't be too happy to learn that two women could lift his big body onto the bed, but she and Alaia did so with ease. Distant cousins of the Elves, Mystwalker men and women had inherited Elvin strength, and lifting any man—Fae, Elvin, or otherwise—was usually not a problem.

Cassia decided she'd keep that little bit of information to herself.

Chapter Twenty-two

"Abort!" Jake shouted as Pacer stepped onto the mouth of the cave.

An explosion erupted in the night.

Frozen, almost fried in the roiling fire, Jake watched Pacer disintegrate. Slow-motion. Vivid. Every detail sharply outlined in yellow-white flames and black smoke.

"No!" Jake's voice vanished in the booming sound of the blast as horror ripped through him.

The explosion slammed into each of Jake's men. In the orange glow, Jake watched as each was flung from beside the cave. Their flesh burned from their bones before they landed on the ground.

Jake started to shout out again, but the blast's power slammed into his own body and propelled him through the air, away from the fire.

As if leaving him alive to remind him of his failure—and to torture him for the rest of his life.

Jake shouted as he bolted upright in bed. Images of fire and flesh being ripped from bones were all he could see.

Sweat poured down his body and he could barely breathe as he slowly returned to reality.

A nightmare.

A memory.

Pain.

Jake rubbed his chest. He deserved the pain. The agony he went through every time he had that dream.

More agony pierced Jake's consciousness as pain splintered through his head.

He felt as if a Drow warrior had shot one of their diamond-headed arrows through his skull.

Jake collapsed onto the mattress so that he was flat on his back. He stared up at an open-beamed ceiling, gradually remembering where he was and what he was doing here.

Why the hell did his head hurt so bad?

Oh, yeah. Life-threatening sex. Giving Cassia an orgasm had just about killed him.

Jake put his hand to his forehead, planning to rub his temples, when he touched something slimy and wet.

What? Jake rubbed the slick substance as he opened his eyes and brought his hand in view. Thick greenish-white paste was on his fingers, which smelled like herbs the witches used back home.

Speaking of witches. He wiped the stuff on his sweaty, bare chest, figuring he could take a shower, or a bath at the least.

He pushed himself up on the mattress and looked around the room where he'd given Cassia her first orgasm. Right before her magic pitched him like a fucking baseball.

He winced and glanced up at the ceiling.

Yep. One of the wooden beams was cracked.

Good thing he had a hard head.

Hard-headed and bullheaded. That was him.

If this was what happened every time he made love to her, it would be a wonder if he survived their next time alone.

Had that been the transition? Was she through it? Jake wondered if that was all there was to it, and if they were on the home stretch. Or, when they actually made love, would it be worse? If he survived that, would it happen every time they made love?

And they would be making love.

If this hadn't been the transition they'd been warned about, and there was more, maybe worse, to come—he had to convince the Great Guardian to teach him how to do this without getting his skull fractured.

The polished deep gold wood of the room looked the

same—except for that crack in the beam. Unfortunately, not everything in the room had survived. A mirror lay shattered on the floor. The glass of the window had been blown out and the shutters hung cockeyed. White dust coated the floor like something had been ground into a fine powder. A chair had lost all of its legs and a cabinet lay on its side.

Whoa.

He gingerly touched the egg on the back of his head. Thing was as big as two fists side by side.

Yeah, it was a wonder he'd survived.

But, Christ, what an incredible moment that had been.

Jake eased off the mattress and spotted his jeans and T-shirt folded neatly on a long, narrow table against the wall that had managed to survive Cassia's orgasm. Next to his clothing lay his shoes, still stuffed with his socks.

Other than a killer headache, a little dizziness, and slight numbness—he couldn't feel the pads of his fingers or his toes—all in all he felt better than he'd expected.

What a woman.

On the polished wooden surface of the narrow table, a clean, dry cloth lay next to a pitcher and a water basin. His grandmother used to have one of those.

Before Jake put on his clothes, he poured water from the pitcher into the basin and then splashed the water onto his face. He splashed his face a few more times and rinsed the gooey crap off his forehead.

Some of that powder from the floor was on his body, too. He wet the cloth with clean water from the pitcher and washed his face and chest before draping the cloth over the basin.

He dressed, and his clothing looked, felt, and smelled freshly laundered, as if it'd hung on a clothesline in the wind and sunshine.

The nightmare wouldn't totally leave him and the pain of it clenched his chest. He was still numb from whatever Cassia's magic had done to him, and he felt like that ball-peen hammer was being slammed into his head instead of him slamming one into a tree. Jake left the cabin and entered the world of the free Mystwalkers.

That thought—free Mystwalkers as opposed to the ones who were kept as pleasure-slaves—gnawed at his gut.

Mellow sunshine warmed his skin as he walked away from the cabin. Thanks to the fact he'd been knocked out when he was hauled off to the sanctuary, he hadn't seen anything but the inside of the cabin.

Man, the place was incredible. Sheer crystal cliffs veined with gold stretched toward the sky, and a waterfall cut a loud path through jagged spears of crystal. Flowers in brilliant shades dotted the landscape. Small fields, about the size of a football field, of what might be vegetables, stretched out in one area of the sanctuary. Fruit trees, as well as trees with leaves of unusual colors, made the scenery bright and beautiful.

The sanctuary was even more beautiful than the City of the Light Elves, as far as Jake was concerned. But he figured he might be a little biased considering the Mystwalkers actually seemed friendly. Whatever they were doing—working in fields, caring for animals, or just passing by—the men and women here acknowledged Jake with a smile and a nod. A few Mystwalker children giggled and waved at him before dissolving into low-hanging mist and slipping away through the trees.

Jake had to smile. Cute kids.

Cassia caught him off guard, seemingly from nowhere, and flung her arms around his neck.

So much for my Spidey-senses.

He winced as the jarring movement rocked his skull, but didn't care. It just felt good to have her in his arms again. He only wished his fingers could feel her soft body as he stroked her arms.

"Jake," she said against his chest as he held her close to him. "I was so, so worried about you."

"I'm fine." He leaned back and managed a smile. "In fact, incredible."

Or it would be if only the haunting nightmare would leave him.

Cassia looked so worried it was adorable. "After what I did to you?"

He raised his hand and brushed her cheek with his knuckles. "I liked being your first."

With an indignant and almost angry expression, she let him go and braced her hands on her hips. "I almost killed you!"

"What a way to go." He grinned and she frowned, but he gripped her waist, brought her tighter against him, and kissed that frown right off her face.

Jake couldn't get enough of her kiss, the taste of her, which included a slight honey flavor, as if she'd just had something to drink that had honey in it. He felt her gold magic expand and start swirling around them.

He groaned as he kissed her, and remembered the way her lips had felt around his cock. The suction of her mouth, her soft little moans, and the way she stroked his balls. Christ, he could come right now.

A loud crack followed by a popping sound startled Jake, and something slimy pelted his skin.

Cassia broke their kiss as she moved her hands to his chest and pushed. He kept his grip on her waist, but raised his head to see her gold magic starting to wane. Next to them lay a wooden field tool snapped in half, probably the crack they'd heard. Beside the thing, a vegetable that looked like a purple pumpkin had exploded. Goo scattered across the ground and pasted Jakes and Cassia's clothing.

He turned his attention back to her. "I'll take that as a 'You really turn me on, Jake.'"

Cassia shoved harder at his touch, her expression turning confused, frustrated, sad even.

"What's wrong, Princess?" He took a lock of her hair and rubbed it between his fingers, enjoying the silk of it even as his concern for her rose.

Cassia closed her eyes then opened them. "What we did— it was a mistake. A really big one."

It was his turn to frown, but she continued, "Not only was it the wrong thing to do, but I was terrified for you. I was so afraid I had hurt you . . ." Her eyes looked a little misty and her voice grew softer. "Or worse."

Jake smiled, wanting to brush away her concern. "You could say sex with you is nothing short of explosive." He moved his mouth to her ear and murmured, "I can't wait to see what happens when I'm inside you."

Her cheeks reddened. "I *cannot* let anything like this happen again."

"Sure you will, only next time I'll wear a radiation suit and a football helmet," he said with a smile.

Cassia's expression was so sad that his smile faded almost instantly. He was going to make her tell him what was going on when Alaia and Breacán walked up.

Jake looked at Breacán. "Where's that wrestling ring?"

Breacán's expression was serious but he had a teasing light in his eyes. "When we finish our discussions, I will be happy to show you, human."

"You're on, Mystwalker," Jake replied, and Breacán gave a low nod, laughter now in his gaze.

Cassia glared from Breacán to Jake. "You are *not* fighting." She narrowed her gaze on Jake. "Again."

Jake knew these guys had superhuman strength, like the Elves, but he was spoiling for another fight and he wouldn't go down easy. He was a black belt in jujitsu and a highly trained Marine who'd served on countless high-risk recon missions.

After splitting a wooden beam with his head, he figured he got a few points, or an honorary Otherworld black belt, or something.

Cassia still glared at him as they walked with Breacán and Alaia along a path and around a couple of bends to a bunch of shaggy trees. They slipped behind the trees and entered the yawning mouth of an enormous cave in the crystal wall.

Torches came to life as they walked into the cave made of pure, clear, cut crystal. The torchlight glittered and refracted on the crystal and a guy couldn't help but be impressed.

The cave opened up even more into a small cavern. Here the crystals varied in colors, like different gems that glittered within the stalagmites pushing up from the floor and stalactites hanging from the ceiling. The veins of some kind of gold metal were thicker in here than they had appeared to be in the crystal walls.

"We did not complete our contribution to the war before the final battle with the dark goddess," Alaia said as she moved toward a pile of something gold that Jake couldn't make out. "We could not effectively produce the kinds of weapons required to destroy the demons and the dark goddess."

She continued, "Our seers made it clear you would need weapons effective in water, after you dealt with the dark goddess. That, of course, is where our specialty lies."

They reached the pile and Jake raised an eyebrow. Piles and piles of collars like the ones the Mystwalkers wore. "Collars?" he said.

Alaia had a regal tilt to her head as she looked at Jake. "Not everything is as it appears, human."

"Jake," Cassia grumbled for the hundredth time. "His name is Jake. Not 'human.' "

Alaia reached up and touched her collar. Jake raised his eyebrows. The collar unfolded into a gold-handled dagger with a glittering, jagged, silver blade. "This blade will slice through the bands the Shanai use to keep our people as pleasure slaves."

"And . . ." Jake said, inserting a good dose of skepticism in the word.

"Patience, human," she said with a deliberate look at Cassia, who clamped her mouth shut. Alaia put the handle of the dagger back up to her throat and it simply melded back into the shape of a collar with unusual runes that encircled her neck.

She picked up a collar from the huge mound on the cavern floor and pressed her thumb firmly against the metal. It, too, unfolded into a dagger. "We have daggers," Jake said. He winced as Cassia stomped on his foot, hard. Maybe he should shut his mouth.

"Ah, but your daggers are worthless against a water funnel." Alaia eyed him as she raised the weapon so that the light glinted off the blade. "With this blade, your warriors can kill a Stormcutter before the being takes human form."

Jake whistled. He sure hadn't expected that. "No kidding?"

By her frown and her narrowed gaze, the Mystwalker woman looked like she was starting to get irritated with him.

Breacán remained at her side and appeared amused, as if enjoying the exchange.

"Your people can wear the collars as we do." Alaia trailed her fingers over her own collar. "This shall also leave their hands free to carry other weapons if needed."

She pressed her thumb against the hilt and it folded back into a smooth collar. "It adjusts to the neck size of the wearer. A simple, deliberate touch and it instantly forms a weapon again." She demonstrated by touching it once more, and the collar smoothly formed a jagged dagger.

"That's incredible." Cassia leaned down and chose a collar from the enormous pile.

Jake grabbed one at the same time she did. They each touched their rune-engraved collar firmly. Both unfolded into daggers with thick, solid, hilts, with grips that wouldn't slip out of a person's or being's hand easily. He ran his finger along the blade and winced as the edge sliced a shallow cut in his forefinger and blood beaded on his skin.

"Niiice," he said as he looked back at Alaia. "So with these we can eliminate the funnels before they take human shape."

Her gaze was direct as always as she gave a "Yes," but by the inflection in her tone, she was likely thinking, "Isn't that what I've been saying, moron?"

"Impressive." Jake chose to ignore her attitude and stared at the cache with a whole new respect.

"However," Alaia started. Yup, a catch. There was always a catch. "It takes time to create these weapons because we must mine the metal from our caves. We have not the number of people needed to make greater numbers."

Alaia gracefully swept her arm out over the enormous pile of collars. "We have made perhaps five hundred in addition to what we ourselves wear."

Jake stroked his jaw as he considered what she had to say. "Darkwolf's supposedly gathering thousands of followers.

We've got three thousand, max, if we count the twenty-two hundred Marines and the Drow. Although if it's daytime, the Drow are stuck below ground."

"We will continue our work," she said. "But again, it takes us much time."

"This metal you use"—Jake gestured to the cavern walls and the thick gold veins—"the Drow and D'Danann think it may be strong enough to use to build a human weapon."

"Cassia sent word to our sentinels near the D'Danann village." Alaia looked at Breacán, who handed her what looked like a roll of parchment. "I believe this will tell you all you need to know about our metal."

Jake unfurled the parchment and stared in amazement at a graphic of one of the gold bars. The drawing was surrounded by moving numbers and symbols. Bit by bit, he realized what the numbers meant. The figure beside the little flame—that had to be the metal's melting point. And the tiny picture of the metal being bent—yes. Tensile strength. It *was* all he needed. He shifted his gaze to Alia.

"Incredible." His mind whirled ahead to putting the god-containment array into construction phase. He barely managed to remember a quick, "Thanks."

"May I see what it is you need the metal for?" Alaia asked.

Before Jake could dig in his back pocket, Cassia withdrew the folded weapon schematics from her own back pocket. She glanced at Jake. "I took it from you to make sure it wasn't ruined when your clothes were cleaned."

Cassia unfolded the paper. "This is a weapon that would be made from the humans' greatest technology." Cassia pointed to the parts of the weapon they needed the metal for. "However, the power they would manufacture would be too great for the materials that exist in the Earth Otherworld."

Breacán looked over Alaia's shoulder as she studied the paper while Cassia held it. Alaia's brow furrowed. "How odd. We have never seen anything like this."

Jake drew his Glock from his belt and held it in a safe position. "It's more or less a gun like this, but larger."

Breacán and Alaia studied the Glock with narrowed gazes. "Interesting, but very strange," Alaia said.

"What we need to build is even stranger yet." Jake holstered his gun. He explained how the weapon would confine Darkwolf so that Cassia could send him someplace where he couldn't hurt anyone.

"We don't know what all power he commands," Cassia said as she told Alaia and Breacán how Darkwolf had absorbed the magic of two gods on top of being an extraordinary warlock in his own right. "But he's dangerous and power hungry."

"Certainly not a welcome combination." Alaia looked at the weapon schematic with a perplexed expression. "Do you know how much of our metal you will require?"

"For now we'll make a single laser-containment gun," Jake said, "and see how the metal holds up. If it works, then we can look into making more of them." He gestured to the paper Alaia still held. "Right now this is all theory that I need to put into play and tweak as needed."

"I have spoken with the Council of free Mystwalkers." Alaia returned the schematics to Jake, who still held the parchment she had given him. "We have agreed to give you what metal we can."

"It is much appreciated," Cassia said with a slight bow from her shoulders, her features relaxing.

Jake breathed a sigh of relief. "We don't have a lot of time, though. We've got to leave now to get back before Darkwolf attacks again."

Alaia considered him for a moment. "I shall see what I can do."

"Thank you." Jake hoped to hell they could get out of there and back to San Francisco ASAP.

Jake saw Cassia clench the collar she'd been holding even tighter as she spoke. "Has the Council of free Mystwalkers made a determination as to sending a number of your people to aid us in our battle?"

"We can send one hundred at best." Alaia moved her head to glance at the pile of collars, the thin braid on each side of her face swinging a little with the movement. "There are not many free Mystwalkers, and the rest of our warriors must stay to guard our sanctuary."

"Thank you." Cassia's shoulders seemed less tense. "Your people will be valued beyond measure."

"I am certain we have an advantage that others of your Alliance do not." Confidence was in Alaia's tone as well as her posture. "Our powers grow when it storms, and our ability to fight will be even greater."

"Your one hundred are likely to equal five hundred of our other fighters." Cassia held out her hands and clasped both of Alaia's in hers. "The Mystwalkers are an important part of our Alliance now." She released Alaia's hands. "We would like one person to join our circle of leaders who represent each race at our command center."

"As long as you have freshwater available," Alaia said with no hesitation, "then I am able to stay with your people." She glanced at the Mystwalker male. "Breacán will take my place while I am gone."

Breacán gave a deep nod to Alaia. "As you will," he said.

Alaia returned her gaze to Cassia. "When it comes time for battle, I am certain you have the means to bring my people to the San Francisco Otherworld."

Cassia nodded. "As a Guardian ascending, I have the power to do so myself."

Alaia looked surprised. "It is already time for your ascension?"

"My ceremony was a few days ago." Cassia cleared her throat, and didn't look at Jake as her cheeks turned pink. "I will reach my position as a Guardian shortly."

"I cannot believe the years have passed so quickly." Alaia shook her head.

"Yes." Cassia's voice sounded hoarse before she changed the subject. "Jake and I must return to hold audience with the Great Guardian."

Jake blew out his breath in a hard rush as he looked at Cassia. "Do you think it's possible that your people, the Light Elves, will help, too?"

Her brows dipped as if she was deep in thought. "I'm not certain. I will need to speak with my mothe—the Great Guardian."

"Seems like we have a lot to talk with her about." Jake's voice softened as he glanced down at Cassia and saw her expression of concern.

"Yes," she said quietly. "I suppose we do."

CHAPTER TWENTY-THREE

"SONOFABITCH." JAKE RUBBED HIS FOREHEAD as he opened his eyes, and Cassia winced. She'd known he wouldn't be happy once Breacán woke him, and by the look on Jake's face she was dead on. He glared in the direction Breacán had vanished. "A few minutes. My fist in his face. That's all I wanted."

Cassia rolled her eyes as she gripped her Mystwalker collar. Men. "Breacán had to knock you out and carry you again. You're too noisy, Jake, and you know it. They can't take any chances. We're talking about the end of their way of life. The possibility of being captured and turned into slaves again. Would you wish for that?"

"No." Jake grumbled a little more, but got to his feet and scooped up his own collar, which had been beside him. He took a good look at their surroundings. They were at the same pond where Cassia and Jake first met up with the Mystwalkers, before being taken to their sanctuary. He hooked the collar to his belt, leaving his hands free.

When Jake's gaze returned to Cassia, his expression softened. "Sure you're all right?"

Cassia stared up at him, wanting him more than she'd wanted anything in her entire life. But she couldn't have him. She forced herself to nod.

"Bull." Jake pulled her into his embrace. At first she resisted. They couldn't do this. No intimacy of any kind.

But as she breathed in his clean, musky scent, she couldn't help but lean into him and let him hold her.

"Did you enjoy last night?" Jake asked, his chin resting on the top of her head.

She drew back a bit so she could meet his gaze. "If I had

enjoyed that any more than I did, you probably wouldn't be standing here with me."

A smile tipped the corner of his mouth. "A guy could take that a couple of ways."

"You know exactly how I meant it." She rested her head against his chest, wanting the comforting warmth and solidness of his body. This was not fair, not being allowed to have Jake. But then, was it fair for the Great Guardian to continue carrying her burden for eons longer? She let out a deep sigh. "It was the most amazing experience of my entire life—except for the fact you're lucky to be alive."

He caught a lock of her hair and twirled it around his finger as she raised her head to look at him. His expression turned serious. "How do you think this conversation is going to go with your mother?"

Cassia sighed and placed her palms on his chest. He felt so perfect beneath her hands, and she could feel his heart beating. "Depends on how much you piss her off."

Jake grimaced and tugged on her hair. "First meeting not so hot?"

"Ice-cold." She shook her head and rubbed her fingers over his pecs. "She's used to complete and absolute respect. She's earned it."

"Has she?" Jake said, and Cassia frowned. He let out a frustrated huff and released her lock of hair. "I'm sorry. Yeah, she's been around longer than dirt. Yeah, she's a know-it-all—I mean, knows everything. Yeah, she tries to help—in her annoying, cryptic way."

"Jake . . ." She raised her brows. "You *are* talking about my *mother*."

Jake's frown vanished and he gave her a grin like a little boy trying to get out of trouble. "Haven't you heard that son-in-laws aren't always crazy about their mothers-in-law?"

The thought of marrying Jake sent warmth through her, and she almost laughed as she tried to imagine the Great Guardian as a mother-in-law to a human.

Then the dream-vision came back to her and she remembered the Guardian saying she was going to give Jake two choices. A small well of hope rose within Cassia. What would they be? And would his choice allow her to be with Jake? Forever?

But then, she was immortal . . . and he would die one day. She would watch him age as she remained youthful.

The thought of Jake passing on to Summerland made her heart ache, and tears stung the backs of her eyes.

Live in the now, Cassia. Take everything a day at a time.

She wasn't so sure she could do that.

So she chose to ignore his statement. "Come on." She glanced at the sky. Unlike the City of the Light Elves, in the Fae woods rain wasn't unusual, and the promise of a thunderstorm charged the air. "We need to get back."

She almost smiled at the way leaves, twigs, and branches cracked under his shoes as they walked the distance toward the meeting place where the Guardian would be waiting. She glanced at a Dryad watching them from inside the wood of a tree, while at the same time they passed a group of Faeries hurrying to gather dandelion nectar before the storm hit.

Cassia knew that, as a human with not an ounce of magic in him, Jake didn't notice all of the Fae. Gnarled, knee-high Brownies peeked around tree trunks, looking at Jake's shoes as if wanting to devour them. She had to glare at the Brownies and flick a few sparks of magic at them to get the buggers to back off.

Pixies, with wings that looked too small to carry their chubby bodies, flew overhead, mischievous expressions on their round faces as they whispered to one another. No doubt trying to form a plan to tease the human.

When Jake wasn't looking, Cassia raised her finger and sent a stream of gold magic that zapped one of the Pixies in the butt. They scowled at her, then looked up at the sky as fat rain droplets started to splatter through the tree branches and plopped on their heads. They scooted away after darting scowls at Cassia, who just smiled.

She loved the smell of rain and an oncoming storm. In the clean, crisp air of her Otherworld it was even better than in the Earth Otherworld.

The thought of thunderstorms in San Francisco made her frown. Darkwolf with his Stormcutters and Blades, bringing with them the smells of laundry gone sour.

Jake took her free hand and she allowed it. She clenched the collar in her other fist and let thoughts of Darkwolf's storms fall away, and concentrated on the *now*. Living in the *now*. It felt so right being with him. Everything felt right—

Except what had happened last night.

Except for her foreordained future.

Except for Otherworlds counting on her.

Except for her vision of her mother.

Cassia sobered, her moment of happiness vanishing, and she swallowed. "I need to tell you something."

"Hmmm?" Jake glanced down at her with his devastatingly sexy smile.

"It's about . . . what happened. What we did together." She sucked in a lungful of air and let it out. "My mother came to me in a vision while I was unconscious."

Jake immediately tensed, and she felt it through their joined hands. He squeezed her fingers tighter as he asked, "What did she say?"

Bigger droplets of water splattered on Cassia's hair, and one hit her nose, scattering some water on her eyelids. She could have put up a shield to surround and protect them from the storm, but she had a feeling Jake leaned on the edge of having had too much magic, and she wanted some normalcy between them.

"She's never looked so angry, Jake." Cassia's heart took a serious nosedive to land in her stomach. "The Great Guardian is serene. Perfection. Not an angry being, ready to throttle her offspring."

Jake stayed silent, and she couldn't read his expression when she looked up at him.

"She told me what we did was wrong. That I could have killed both of us with my growing power." Cassia squeezed Jake's hand. "If you had entered me, it would have meant certain death for you." She glanced down at her feet before looking at him again. "And not by her hand. By my magic."

Jake looked straight ahead. Bless it, why didn't he answer? Rain came down harder, seeping through Cassia's hair to her skull, chilling her. She tugged at his hand, drawing him to a halt. "Say something."

He studied her for a moment before he replied, "She sounds like a mother who thinks she knows what's best for her daughter." He leaned in close and said in a low, deep voice, "But Mommy doesn't always know what's best, no matter how powerful she is."

"You don't get it." Cassia took her hand from his. "She is all powerful. If we push this, she could end your life." Tears stung at her eyes. "Please don't make her angry. I want her to see how worthy you are."

Jake's expression clouded. "So I'm unworthy? Because I'm a human male? Because I'm not *pureblood* Elvin stock?"

A tear rolled down Cassia's cheek, joining the raindrops steadily hitting her face, and she hoped he didn't know she was crying. "You know I don't feel that way."

He made a low growling sound in his throat. "But your mother and probably every other one of the Light Elves do feel that way."

"I—I don't know what to say." Cassia turned away from him and started walking again through the forest. At once he moved into step beside her. "But Mother did tell me we will have a discussion once we meet up with her again." Not mentioning the options the Guardian planned to give Jake.

He said with a hard edge to his voice, "I don't like these riddles and games."

Cassia could have jumped in to defend the Great Guardian again, but she didn't have the heart for it. "I don't want to talk about that anymore." She stared straight ahead. Now water dripped from tree branches, along with the rain that had already soaked her T-shirt and jeans. Even her socks and shoes were growing wet.

"I've shared a lot about me," Cassia added. "Very intimate things. But we hardly talk about you."

Jake still looked mad, with his face twisted into a scowl, but his features finally relaxed. "We already had the discussion about my childhood." His expression tensed again. "And my mistake in Afghanistan."

"Let's talk about other things. Like what did you do before you started working with witches and fighting demons?" She blinked water from her eyes, and shivered from the slight chill of the water drenching her. "Hobbies or something. You can't just eat, breathe, and survive on being a cop."

"Why not?" He gave her a teasing look before he went on. "You could say that before all this sh—crap happened with the demons, goddess, and Darkwolf, that I lived, breathed, and survived on being a diehard San Francisco Giants fan."

"I always liked the Boston Red Sox," Cassia said, with a grin when he gave her a look like she was some kind of traitor. "Hey, I lived in Salem, Massachusetts, for a good portion of my life."

He winked at her. "Guess I'll have to give you that."

"What else do you like to do?" she asked.

"Go hiking with a couple of my buddies who live out of state." Water splattered both of them when Jake pushed a branch aside and it swung back. "We've traveled around. Hiked in the Sierras, the Appalachian Trail, and other spots in the Smokies. Done a little rock climbing, too. Last time I went was to Beck's Tower at Castle Crags State Park—a couple of months before the demons showed up."

She managed a smile as she looked up at him. "Are you as noisy in your parks as you are now?"

His boyish grin made her belly flutter. "Compared to here I don't sound like an elephant walking on eggshells. So no, I manage to be quieter in my world."

"Rock climbing is something I've never done." She imagined herself rappelling down the surface of a sheer rock wall. "I think I would like to try that."

"Really?" Jake raised his eyebrows. "I never pegged you as the danger-seeking type."

"Ah, but you didn't peg me as old as I am, either."

His lips twisted into a wry smile. "Got me there."

"I think hang gliding and bungee jumping would be interesting, too." She nodded with resolution. "Parachuting always intrigued me, but ensconced in the life of a D'Anu witch and an Elvin Princess, I never thought to actually try it."

Jake laughed. Warm, genuine laughter. "A thrill seeker. I know I'm in love even more than I was before."

Cassia shot him a look, but all she felt was warmth and hope. Maybe they could work this out?

The Great Guardian had said "I will allow the human to take you through the transition if he chooses one of two options."

Should she dare to hope?

She was so blessed confused.

Cassia mentally shook her head. Right now she was *not* going to think of what her preplanned future was supposed to be, or whether or not things might work out with her and Jake.

Instead she was going to enjoy the moments for what they were.

They swung their clasped hands as they walked in the rain, Cassia grilling him on the types of rock climbing he did, what they'd have to do to get her started, how much fun she'd have "thrill seeking."

"Oh, and a helicopter. Never been in one of those." Cassia pictured herself in one of those military Blackhawks.

"Have you flown at all?" Jake asked. "Other than on a broomstick?"

"Witches do not fly on broomsticks." Cassia slugged his shoulder. "We take flights on airplanes, like any human does." She pursed her lips. "Although I do miss horses. I always loved them. Kael enjoyed our runs, too." She smiled when she thought of her wolf familiar. "I think not having the chance to run through the forest here in Otherworld was one of the reasons Kael wasn't crazy about staying in the city."

"I have a friend who owns a ranch." Jake squeezed her hand. "When this mess is over, we can head out there and he'll let you ride all the horses you want."

Cassia almost jumped up and down in delight. "I would

so love to do that. It's been at least fifty years since I've ridden one."

Jake chuckled. "Being with you will be one adventure after another."

Cassia sobered. *Not going to think about destiny. Preordained futures. Not going to, not going to.*

While she pretended she could have a future with Jake, she smiled and enjoyed the heavy rain soaking them both to the skin.

THE CLOSER THEY GOT TO THE PLACE where they were to meet the Great Guardian, the harder Jake's gut clenched.

He and Cassia were sopping wet when they stepped out of the forest, and into the sunshine.

Of course the Great Guardian was waiting for them.

Cassia immediately bowed and set the Mystwalker collar in front of her. Jake went down on one knee as she jerked him with her. He removed his Glock and placed it on the ground.

This time the old witch didn't tell them to stand right away. She made them wait.

Cassia kept his hand pressed with hers to the grass. But that didn't stop him from raising his head and looking the Guardian straight in her eyes.

An exasperated grumble came from Cassia, but Jake refused to break eye contact with her mother. The Great Guardian let them stay kneeling a moment longer before she finally said, "Rise."

About goddamn time.

The Great Guardian turned her gaze on Cassia as she picked up her collar and rose with Jake. He holstered his Glock.

"You have greatly disappointed me, daughter," the Guardian said in a voice as cold and brittle as icicles along the eaves of a porch after a snowfall.

Cassia didn't lower her head, but met her mother's gaze head-on.

That's my girl, Jake thought.

"Before we address other . . . concerns," Cassia said with

her chin high, "I must ask an important question. Will you allow the Light Elves to join the Alliance in the San Francisco Otherworld, to aid in their battles against the duo-god warlock, Darkwolf?"

The Great Guardian considered Cassia for a long moment. "This is for the Elvin Elders to decide. I will not sway their opinion."

Jake's throat ached as he held back a shout. The Guardian could damned well influence the Elders but she was choosing to sit back and watch the show.

Cassia gave a bow from her shoulders. "Thank you for taking this matter to the Elders," she said in a tight voice.

"Now we have other pressing matters to discuss," the Guardian said with ice in her voice. "Explain why you disobeyed me."

"I did not know what we did would trigger my transition." Cassia's voice sounded formal, but she clenched her fists at her sides, the only outward sign she was distressed. "I chose to be with Jake. And it is Jake who I want to take me through my transition."

The Guardian shook her head almost imperceptibly. "You have no idea, youngling, what you are facing."

Cassia's lips parted. "What do you mean?"

"You have only sparked your transition," the Guardian said. "That was naught but a small measure of what will happen when a male enters your body."

Cassia's cheeks flushed deep red as the Guardian looked at Jake and met his eyes. "No mere human can endure what will occur when you go through your full change."

Anger flared up in Jake, and he imagined it melting the ice between him and the Guardian. "Teach me. I'm willing to take the chance."

"Are you?" The Guardian's features became placid as she focused on Cassia in turn. "And you, Cassiandra. Are you willing to risk your human dying?"

"No," Cassia said, and Jake started to speak, but she continued. "I will not take that chance. But there must be a way Jake can take me through it without hurting him."

"I will allow you one of two options." The Guardian gave a regal tilt to her head. "Even then there will be choices and consequences."

"What?" Cassia sounded breathless, as if she couldn't wait to hear how they could get through this crazy mess. "What can we do?"

The Great Guardian focused on Jake. "Your first choice, human, is that you may accept a gift of magic from me. You will no longer be fully human, yet you will not be Elvin. You will have magic, which will perhaps be enough to survive mating with my daughter."

Her words hit him like stones in a windstorm. Magic? *Fucking magic?*

"The other option," she continued without pause, "is to have Daire present when you and this human go through the transition."

"Hell, no." Jake ground his teeth and fisted his hands. "No other man is going to be with Cassia and me. Ever."

"Then you accept the gift of magic?" the Guardian asked.

"No." Jake ignored the crestfallen look on Cassia's face. "I have no desire to have magic. I am who I am. You'll just have to give us another option."

The Guardian simply looked at him, expressionless. "You have made your choice."

And then the bitch vanished.

CHAPTER TWENTY-FOUR

THE AIR IS THICK AND STALE in the storage room I have slipped into so that I can "call" Darkwolf. The deep closet, crowded with mops and cleaning supplies, reeks of disinfectant and Pine-Sol.

Each time I talk to Darkwolf, I've tried to use different methods of communication. We've even used cell phones in the past, but now that's too dangerous. The Alliance has ways of tracking all types of phone calls to and from the Alliance headquarters.

Most of the time, the magic Darkwolf endowed me with allows me to see him clearly in a water-filled cauldron, or I can see him in a three-dimensional image above it. Like Silver does, only I can't vision like she can. This is more or less a magical telephone call.

Once again I have taken Silver's pewter cauldron from its storage place. For these few minutes she won't miss it, and I'll return the cauldron as soon as Darkwolf and I finish our discussion.

For some reason Darkwolf likes it when I use Silver's cauldron. When I do, his image is always stronger. I wonder if he's still infatuated with her. My skin crawls and heat burns up my neck to my scalp.

I go as deep as I can into the storage room and set the cauldron on a box of Styrofoam cups. "Darkwolf," I say as I close my eyes for a moment, pushing my thoughts out and searching for him.

It takes only a few moments and I sense his presence.

I open my eyes and smile at the three-dimensional image of Darkwolf rising above the cauldron. His image is per-

haps three feet high, but his presence is as powerful as if I were standing next to the seven-foot-tall warlock-god.

"You rang?" *he says with an amused smile. I like it when I catch him in a good mood.*

"I have news, my lord." *My own smile falters.* "Through Rhiannon's vision just a little while ago, we know the Myst-walkers of Otherworld have joined the Alliance. Worse yet, the Mystwalkers have created a weapon that can kill Storm-cutters before they even materialize."

Darkwolf scowls so harshly that for a moment I recoil, but then his expression relaxes. "No problem. I have created thousands of Stormcutters, and will continue to do so until our forces are tens of thousands strong."

A breath of relief eases through me. I don't like delivering bad news to him. He's taking this very well.

I rub my sweaty palms on my jeans. "The Mystwalkers will still be an asset to the Alliance. With their ability to turn into mist—"

A loud gasp behind me.

I whirl and catch my breath when I see Mackenzie standing just inside the doorway. One of the self-righteous D'Anu bitches.

How could I have forgotten to lock the door?

No matter. I know what I have to do.

"You?" *she whispers, and puts her hand over her mouth, her eyes wide with shock.*

Fury flushes my body with heat and power. The dark, dark power Darkwolf has given me.

Mackenzie starts to take a step back, but I whip out a strong rope of my enhanced magic, wrapping it around the doorknob and jerking the door shut. I seal it with a shield so she can't get out. The shield is strong enough to keep anyone from hearing what will happen.

"Dear Anu—" *Mackenzie starts to throw a shield up between us, but I'm too fast.*

My skin prickles with dark magic and I feel invincible as I fling another rope using my other hand.

I wrap the magic rope around her neck.

Mackenzie tries to scream, but I'm taking away her ability to even breathe.

"Bitch," *I growl as my gaze never leaves hers.* "You've always thought yourself better than me. Or anyone else for that matter." *Heat and power flush through me, along with triumph as she instinctively claws at the rope of magic.*

At once I see the realization that she can't remove my rope. Hope ebbs in her now bulging eyes as she makes a weak attempt to use her magic against me.

The small spellfire ball she releases lands short, dropping into a mop bucket, where it fizzles.

Mackenzie mouths, "Please," *as she begs for her life.*

She is an interesting shade of purple now. Her back hits the door as she crumples. The shield I cast behind her muffles the sound of her body striking the wood.

She puts up a good fight and doesn't die as fast as I expected her to. She thrashes on the floor.

I tighten my rope of dark magic.

The crack of bone echoes in the confined space.

Silence.

Mackenzie's entire body goes slack, her head twisted to the side at an odd angle.

When I turn back to the cauldron, to my surprise, Darkwolf hasn't left. He's been watching.

He nods and his smile broadens. "I didn't know you had it in you. I'd say you've more than proved yourself."

"I never really liked her, anyway." *I look at Mackenzie's body at the same time I draw back my magic, although I keep the door shut tight and my shield up. The moment I drop my shield the other witches will sense Mackenzie's murder.*

It already smells of death in the storeroom, and I wrinkle my nose before looking back at Darkwolf.

"Go on before you get caught." *His form starts to waver and I miss him already.* "I look forward to your next report," *he adds before his image disappears.*

"Yes, my lord . . ." *My voice trails as I scowl at Mackenzie's body. A total nuisance since I'll have to get out of here as fast as I can without being discovered. I glance at Silver's cauldron and consider it. I'll just leave it where it's at.*

A plan begins to form in my mind and a pleasant shiver skims over my body.

For all anyone will know, Mackenzie could have been murdered by Darkwolf when she was in contact with him. With the power of two gods and his own dark magic, he could do it easily. Somehow I'll make sure everyone thinks Mackenzie was the "traitor."

With a feeling of satisfaction warm in my belly, I use a quick spell to wipe any fingerprints or traces of my magic from the cauldron. I even cause the water to disappear to make sure none of Darkwolf's essence is detected—nothing they might use to discover me.

The moment I'm finished, I step over Mackenzie's slack body, ignoring her wide, terrified, bulging eyes. I wait before I drop my shield and use my enhanced senses to determine if anyone is close.

A D'Danann warrior walks by, followed by two PSF officers.

I hold my breath.

Finally the corridor is empty. The moment I release my shield, I pull a glamour. I practically bolt from the storage room after I quietly shut the door.

I hear Silver's anguished scream from across the warehouse.

Closer, Rhiannon shouts, "No!"

I curse under my breath as I rush from the hallway to my bedroom.

For just a moment, as I drop my glamour, I lean my back against the door and catch my breath.

Then I scream, too.

CHAPTER TWENTY-FIVE

CASSIA STARED AT WHERE HER MOTHER had been standing, a hopeless feeling washing over her. The Great Guardian wasn't going to help them beyond what she had offered.

And what she had offered wasn't acceptable.

Slowly Cassia turned her gaze from the now empty spot on the grass and met Jake's eyes. He had refused the Guardian's two choices—

Magic or Daire.

For a moment she didn't know what to do. What to think.

"I'm sorry, honey." Jake shook his head. "I can't do it that way. I won't have another man with us, and I'm not about to change who I am to suit your mother."

"I wouldn't want you to change." Cassia tried to smile but just couldn't do it. "And Daire . . . it was wrong of the Guardian to ask that of either one of us."

Jake looked at the place the Guardian had been standing. "That b—your mother—" He met Cassia's eyes again, his gaze hard. "I'm just not going to accept that there isn't another way to make things work with us."

Cassia clenched her teeth as tightly as she was clenching the Mystwalker collar in her fist. Even though she knew she should keep her distance, Cassia started to move toward Jake, needing to be closer to his warmth.

A vision hit her so hard she stumbled backward.

"No!" She screamed and almost doubled over from the pain of the image that burned into her mind.

Mackenzie sprawled on a floor, her head twisted at an odd angle. Eyes wide, frozen with terror and confusion.

"Cassia?" Jake grasped her upper arms, but she barely felt his touch or registered the concern in his voice.

"Mackenzie!" Cassia's insides wrenched even as her mind tried to reject what she knew was the truth. *"No!"*

Almost without thought, she brought her hands up, clenched Jake's wrists, and entered the transference.

The only other time she'd traveled through the veil between Otherworlds so fast was when Jake lay dying in her arms. On a subconscious level she knew wrenching a conscious Jake through the veil might make him ill, but she couldn't stop herself.

Their feet left grass and met the concrete floor of the warehouse in an instant. They arrived outside the circle of witches, who were sobbing and crowding around a woman who was sprawled on her back just outside one of the storage rooms. Shouts of D'Danann warriors came from various parts of the warehouse as they realized something was horribly wrong.

A sick sensation twisting her belly, Cassia released Jake and pushed her way between Hannah and Alyssa. Hannah had her arms wrapped around her belly as she rocked to and fro, and Alyssa shook and cried as she held Mackenzie's pale hand.

Cassia didn't need to look at Mackenzie to know she was dead.

Tears rolled down Cassia's face, pain ripping her heart and soul to shreds. She dropped the Mystwalker collar, which clattered on the concrete floor and rolled away.

Sharp odors of Pine-Sol and must seared her senses, overwhelming every other smell—

Except something black and horrible. Something that didn't belong.

Kael came from somewhere in the warehouse and pressed his big form against Cassia, lending her his strength.

She raised her hands above Mackenzie, and her magic flowed between her palms and her friend's body. She tried to send healing energy, even though she knew it was too late. If a spark of life had been inside the petite blond, Cassia could have whisked Mackenzie to Otherworld and begged the Great Guardian for help.

But not the slightest ember of life remained.

"Can you do anything?" Silver whispered in a sob.

Cassia managed to shake her head once as she let her power flow into Mackenzie's body, questing for answers.

Blackness met Cassia's magic.

It was so dark and powerful that pain hit her like a fist burying itself beneath her rib cage.

The strength of the dark magic flung her away from Mackenzie's body.

Cassia's back slammed against someone's legs. Jake's, she thought vaguely, as pain of another kind stabbed her chest like knives.

She cried out and fought the dizziness that overcame her from the dark magic and threatened to render her unconscious. Voices called to her as she pushed the spinning nothingness away and crawled on her hands and knees to Mackenzie's side.

"Dark magic," she managed to get out in a hoarse voice as she knelt and held her hands over Mackenzie's body again. As she pushed away the painful barrier of darkness, images assaulted Cassia of Mackenzie's death. "She—she was murdered with dark magic."

Gasps joined the sobs of the witches who surrounded Mackenzie. Cassia went deeper with her magic and she closed her eyes.

As she felt the magic ropes wrap around Mackenzie's throat, a choking sound squeezed from Cassia's chest, as if she was the one being strangled. She struggled to see through Mackenzie's eyes, but everything became a painful blur.

A dark figure. Two figures?

Cassia brought her hands to her throat as the choking sensation intensified so badly her own air passages were blocked.

Dark blotches appeared behind her eyelids as she fought for breath. Hands grasped her as she slumped to the floor.

Strong hands. Shaking her.

Light fading away leaving dark.

A deep male voice calling to her. A voice edged with panic.

A firm mouth met hers, forcing air into her lungs. Her body refused it. The mouth moved away. Pressure on her chest, then the mouth pressed against hers again.

Cassia coughed. She drew in another breath of air.

She blinked, dazed, as she looked up into Jake's frightened eyes.

Why was she on her back on the floor? Why was she struggling to breathe?

She jerked in another harsh breath before darkness shrouded her.

CASSIA DIDN'T WANT TO WAKE. Tears rolled down the sides of her face from the corners of her closed eyes as she slowly became aware of her surroundings.

She was lying on what felt like a thin mattress and a soft pillow beneath her head. The warm, strong hand gripping hers, the welcome body heat, and the masculine scent she loved, told her Jake sat on the floor at her side. Still, she couldn't open her eyes.

From the smells of sawdust and wood, combined with the witches' herbs and incenses, she knew she was in the warehouse.

It was eerily quiet. Enough so that she heard the soft whump of the ceiling fans and the almost indecipherable sound of whispering voices.

Pain weighted her down, kept her eyelids closed. Her head ached from crying and her throat hurt as if she had been strangled instead of Mackenzie.

Mackenzie.

"No," Cassia whispered, wishing it was a dream but knowing it wasn't. *"No."*

Callused fingertips brushed her forehead and she forced her eyes open to meet Jake's gaze. She saw so much love in his eyes that it hurt, and more tears rolled down her face.

"God, Cassia." Jake's voice sounded rough as he gathered her into his strong arms and held her tight in his embrace, and she closed her eyes again. "I'm so sorry."

For a long time she cried as Jake cradled her.

When the tears gradually ebbed, she gave a deep, shuddering breath and looked up at him again. He pressed his lips to her forehead and her heart ached with pain at the loss of one of her Coven sisters.

How she needed Jake right now, and the comfort of his arms.

It took some time before she could find the energy to sit up on her own. Jake seemed reluctant to release her as she pushed herself out of his arms so that she was fully on the mattress again.

"It doesn't seem real." She slowly looked around, her gaze traveling over what belongings Jake had in his room. Yesterday—was it only yesterday?—they'd picked up the mess she had made in here with her magic the night before they left for Otherworld.

She met his eyes again. "Tell me it's not real."

He sighed and scrubbed his hand over his face. His jaws were dark with stubble and his eyes showed how exhausted he was.

"My team did a complete investigation of the—the crime scene," Jake said with a heavy sigh. "Nothing. We didn't find a thing. Not even a fingerprint."

Cassia hadn't expected him to. From the power of the magic she'd felt, she was certain every trace of the murder and murderer had been wiped away.

The heaviness inside her was almost too much to bear.

Jake continued, "Silver, Rhiannon, all the rest—they tried to get some kind of magical vibes from where it happened, but they didn't come up with anything."

That didn't surprise Cassia either. What they were dealing with was evil. Evil that shouldn't exist where it did.

Amongst the D'Anu.

Anger, pain, fear, hurt, sadness—the emotions balled so tight inside Cassia that she suddenly felt like she would explode.

The walls began to shake, the door rattling in its frame as the feelings grew more intense.

Fierce and terrible anger threatened to rip out of her

chest. For a moment, her fury was so powerful that a vision of the warehouse decimated slammed into her.

A rumble grew as the entire building started to tremble, as if an earthquake shook the ground. She grabbed onto her magic with everything she had.

"Hold on, honey." Jake stroked her forehead. "It's not going to do anyone any good if you bring the whole place down on top of us."

Cassia nodded and struggled to find her calm center. The calm that had been so elusive since the start of her ascension. It took all she had, but she finally grasped a piece of it and let the calm blanket her anger and pain until the rumble of earth and the rattle of the building finally stopped.

"It's one of us." Cassia wiped the backs of her hands across her eyes that felt so swollen they hurt. When she could, she looked at Jake again. "It's one of *us*. The D'Anu." To Cassia it didn't matter that she wasn't really D'Anu. The witches were her family, a part of her, and she a part of them.

"The other D'Anu have been talking." Jake gave another tired sigh. "They think it's possible Mackenzie could have been the traitor—and that Darkwolf killed her somehow through their connection."

Cassia's scalp prickled as she stared at him. The thought pierced the haze in her brain, but she dismissed it at once.

She shook her head. "They're wrong."

"Silver's cauldron was in the storage room," Jake continued. "They think Mackenzie could have been using it to contact Darkwolf."

"One of them knows that isn't the truth." Cassia looked away from Jake's strong features and stared at a knothole on a plain wooden wall. "And as much as they don't want to believe it was Mackenzie, the others desperately refuse to accept that any of our remaining friends could be a murderer."

When Cassia brought her gaze back to Jake, she found him studying her. "Are you sure?" he asked.

"I have no doubt." She pushed her hair behind her ears and over her shoulders, the feel of it against her face and neck heavy and hot with sweat. "But who . . . my mind wants to reject every single one of the witches I consider."

Jake's expression switched to that of a seasoned cop. "Who do you think it is?"

"It's like slamming my head against a wall." The rage and other emotions churning inside Cassia had started to numb. She bent her knees and wrapped her arms around them as she started to rock on the mattress. "I see one image after another of my Coven sisters and it's as if I'm looking at a one-dimensional photograph."

Quiet descended between Cassia and Jake, matching the eerie silence of the warehouse.

"Mackenzie's familiar died," Jake said softly, and Cassia jerked her head up. "The ferret. Kael found him."

More blood seemed to drain from her body. "Merlin? How?"

"The D'Anu think it was the shock of Mackenzie's death," Jake said. "Kael took the witches to him after you passed out."

"Kael—" Cassia scrambled up and off the mattress. No one could speak to him or understand him but her. Maybe he knew the truth. Or something that would help her figure out who the traitorous bitch was. "I need to talk to him."

Jake frowned, a confused expression on his face as he got to his feet and stood beside her. "Talk?"

"Where is he?" She started toward the door, but swayed a little from her sudden movements.

"Careful." Jake caught her by her arm. "He's been waiting outside the door for you to wake. Like he's guarding the room."

"Kael," Cassia called to him in her thoughts as she stilled.

"Waiting for you, Princess," Kael responded clearly in her mind. *"How do you fare?"*

"We've got to talk." Cassia pulled free of Jake's grasp and started for the door. She didn't have time to discuss how she was feeling right this minute. *"I need your help to figure this out."*

"Of course." Kael was sitting on his haunches just outside the door as she pulled it open.

Cassia dropped to her knees and wrapped her arms around Kael's neck as she buried her face in his soft fur. Waves of magical comfort emanated from him, surrounding her for a moment like a cocoon that could block out all of the horrors of the world.

"I don't know what I would do without you," she whispered in her mind.

"You would go on, Princess," he said calmly, and Cassia fought back more tears at the thought of ever losing the closest friend she'd ever had.

She kept her face against his fur. *"How did Merlin die?"*

Kael gave a mental sigh. *"I am certain that the manner of his witch's murder was so horrific that it traveled through Mackenzie and Merlin's connection."* Kael paused. *"It appears as though he stopped breathing, as if he, too, was choked to death."*

A tear escaped, rolling down her cheek like a warm droplet of water down a cool windowpane. Chills ran through her body, yet her tears were hot.

"You stayed behind when Jake and I went to Otherworld," Cassia said. *"Did anything unusual happen?"*

She imagined Kael mentally frowning. *"I sensed nothing. Except . . . at times I felt such a powerful evil, such dark magic, that it felt as though the dark goddess herself was here. I attempted to search out this evil, but could never place it. The darkness was elusive."*

Cassia remained quiet for a moment before she spoke to him in her mind again. *"Did you follow any of the witches around during the day?"*

"No." Kael shook his big furry head. *"Do you wish me to now?"*

Again Cassia didn't speak as she churned the thought over in her mind. *"Yes,"* she finally said. *"I think we have no choice."*

Alyssa's owl familiar released his haunting hoot from somewhere in the warehouse. Chills traced Cassia's spine at the sound of Echo's cry.

Jake touched her shoulder and she looked up at him. She'd

all but forgotten he was there. "The others are waiting for you in the kitchen," he said.

The others. Dear goddess.

And one of them was a killer.

Cassia got to her feet, and Jake put his arm around her shoulders. Her steps were unsteady as he guided her through the hallways of the makeshift headquarters toward the kitchen.

She wanted to jerk out of his hold, turn around, and run back to the room and cry some more. Maybe forever.

At the same time she wanted to charge into the kitchen and know instantly who the murdering bitch was and—and—

Do what to her?

Kill her?

Put her in a human jail that might not hold her?

Banish her to some forgotten place in Otherworld?

Cassia's throat threatened to close off. Her steps grew heavier and heavier the closer she, Jake, and Kael got to the room where the remaining D'Anu waited.

When she pushed open the door of the kitchen, a burst of pain, shock, and anger slammed into her.

And darkness. The darkness was there. Right in the room. A living, breathing thing that filled the entire kitchen.

Cassia moved her gaze from one D'Anu witch to the next. Sydney had buried her face in her arms on the table. Her Doberman familiar, Chaos, rested his head on her thigh to comfort her.

Banshee, Hannah's falcon familiar, perched on Hannah's shoulder. He and Hannah stared at Cassia. Hannah's face was pale, but her gaze assessed Cassia as if she was considering Cassia as a suspect.

Alyssa looked blankly into space, her face white, her gaze unseeing. Echo sat on her shoulder and blinked his wide, golden eyes as he turned his head and looked at every person in the room, as if analyzing them. He even looked down at Alyssa.

Silver leaned against her blood sister, Copper, who had her arms wrapped around her. They both looked too shaken to move. Silver's python familiar, Polaris, wrapped himself around Silver's and Copper's ankles, as if comforting them both. Copper's bee familiar perched on her ear.

Rhiannon, the sixth remaining witch, stroked her cocoa-colored cat familiar, Spirit, who had curled himself in her lap. Rhiannon stared at Cassia in the same manner Hannah was, as if Cassia could be the murderer. Except in Rhiannon's case, her dark Shadows screamed to get out of her control. Cassia sensed that Rhiannon held them back by a mere thread.

Were Rhiannon's Shadows the darkness Cassia felt?

Cassia looked up at Jake, telling him with her gaze that she needed to be alone with her Coven sisters. He paused before giving a single nod and letting the kitchen door close behind her and Kael.

The feel of dark magic was so strong, so overwhelming. How could she have missed such evil? When they had scried before, she had sensed malice in the room, but not this.

No, this was residue of murder.

Everyone remained silent as Cassia slipped into a chair. Kael settled himself on his haunches at her side.

Instead of the power of their love, Cassia felt her Coven sisters holding their emotions tightly—and alone. They distanced themselves physically and emotionally as if each had cocooned herself in a bubble of protection.

Everyone except for Copper and Silver, who supported each other as only true sisters could.

Mackenzie's murder had shattered the Coven.

"I can't believe Mackenzie could have been the traitor." Silver raised her head from Copper's shoulder. Like almost everyone else at the table, Silver's eyes were rimmed with red from crying. "But one of us?" She refused to meet anyone's gaze. "How could any one of us be a traitor or a murderer?"

Sydney raised her head and removed her glasses to wipe tears from her eyes with the heels of her palms. "Darkwolf has used transference to get from one place to another." She coughed and cleared her throat as she settled her glasses back on her face. "Maybe he came here and—and—"

Cassia said nothing. Instead, she tried to read each and every one of the witches.

Nothing.

The room was still shadowed with dark magic, but Cassia couldn't tell where it came from. Who it came from.

What good was being a Guardian ascending if she couldn't read something that should be so simple?

"Sure, Darkwolf could have used the transference to get in here," Hannah said as she looked at Sydney. Out of all of the witches, Hannah managed to maintain a visible semblance of poise. "But it still doesn't make sense. Why would he kill someone who was feeding him information, if that's what she was doing? Even if she'd threatened to tell us, what would he care? He's a duo-god, for Anu's sake."

"We have only one option." Cassia broke her own silence and everyone looked at her. "We each work with one of the PSF as a partner, and no longer work together as a Coven."

Shocked expressions from every one of the witches met Cassia's gaze.

Cassia kept her voice as calm as possible. "This sisterhood is broken."

CHAPTER TWENTY-SIX

THE NEXT FEW DAYS were the hardest emotionally that Cassia had experienced since coming to the Earth Otherworld centuries ago.

Each witch had been paired with a PSF officer, even those D'Anu who were married to Otherworld husbands. The witches avoided one another, walking around with their PSF partners like ghosts of the women they had been. Mackenzie's death hung over them like the darkest of skies.

Even when they buried Mackenzie in one of the sacred places in Golden Gate Park, with her ferret familiar beside her, none of the witches spoke. Sadder yet, their familiars stayed away from one another, too.

Three days later, as morning sunshine threaded through the fog and into the skylights, Cassia lay on her side on Jake's mattress in his room. He wrapped his arm tight around her waist, his body pressed against her backside.

She had started sleeping with him—minus sex of any kind—since the day of the murder. She couldn't go back to the room she had shared with Mackenzie and Alyssa. Not only because of the pall Mackenzie's death had caused, but Cassia, too, was keeping her distance from any of the witches, and that included Alyssa.

Cassia frowned as she considered again the quiet witch who had always been the most timid member of the Coven, and Mackenzie's best friend. Cassia had thought of Alyssa as delicate, fragile. Yet Cassia had never discounted the strength within Alyssa that had served her well in every battle they had fought.

Could Alyssa be the murderer?

Cassia squeezed her eyes shut and settled more firmly against Jake, and he kissed the top of her head. Her mind constantly spun and ached as she asked the same question about every one of the witches countless times.

Who was the murderer? The traitor?

Why was the truth blocked from her?

It was apparently blocked from Kael, too, as he discovered nothing when he followed the witches and their familiars.

If Cassia returned to Otherworld, would the Great Guardian have the answers they needed?

"Something has to be done." Cassia opened her eyes and stared across the room at her chest of ceremonial items, which she had moved in from her old room. She traced every etching, every scar in the ancient wood with her gaze. "We can't go on like this."

"We'll find a way to draw Darkwolf out into the open." Jake squeezed her tighter. "We'll finish him like we've been planning in our strategy sessions."

Cassia sighed and rolled over in Jake's embrace so that they were lying face-to-face and she could look into his blue eyes. He smelled so warm and spicy and masculine.

She stroked Jake's stubbled jaw. She liked the roughness of the shadow of his beard beneath her fingertips. Elves didn't have facial or body hair. She found it incredibly sexy on Jake. "You don't think it will be that easy, do you?" she asked.

"No." Jake clenched his teeth and she felt it through her touch. "But he's not making any moves, and we've got to do something before he's created so many Stormcutters we'll never be able to bring him down."

Cassia's insides twisted and sickened as she wished desperately that nothing had changed in her Coven. Right now all of the gray-magic D'Anu witches could have been in the kitchen, together, scrying to find any answers to the many questions spread out before them.

"Are you sure the Mystwalkers are ready?" Jake asked as

he rubbed Cassia's upper arm. "That they'll send the metal, too, so that we can try out that weapon?

"I'm confident in Alaia and her people. I will be bringing her to join us along with the weapons." Cassia pushed herself onto her elbow so that she was looking down at Jake. "We established a strong mental connection and, when we're ready for the Mystwalkers to join us, I'll use my powers to bring them here as well."

Jake let her hand slip from his. "No one should know about them yet."

"I don't like the idea of such a powerful weapon being in the murderer's hands—she might manage to get it to Darkwolf, and he could figure out how to eliminate their threat." Cassia clenched her fists. "And there isn't a blessed thing we can do about it."

Cassia studied Jake. He looked tired like he did every morning after a restless night. Every now and then he would say something in his sleep, and Cassia knew he was having a nightmare about what had happened to his special ops team in Afghanistan.

"You dreamed again," she said as she stroked his jaw. "The same nightmare you have every night."

He looked surprised. "How do you know?"

"Your sleep is always troubled." She moved her fingers from his jaw into his soft hair. "You talk a little, shout some."

"Christ." He shut his eyes.

"Tell me about your dreams."

"Every night that op haunts me." Jake opened his eyes and his gaze was filled with pain. "But it's as much as I deserve for failing my men."

Cassia moved her hand to his shoulder and would have shaken him if he wasn't so big. "When are you going to accept the fact that it wasn't your fault?"

"Never." Jake's throat worked as he swallowed. "There's nothing that can take that pain away."

"You're a good man, Jake Macgregor." She moved closer to him and hugged him as close as she could. "If you'd known it was a trap, you would never have allowed them to get close to that place."

He said nothing, but held her just as tightly.

Jake's mind whirled with possibilities while he stood beside Cassia and Alaia as they looked at the pile of Mystwalker collars.

Without anyone else's knowledge, Cassia had used her increased powers to bring Alaia through the veil a few moments ago. Cassia had also transported the weapons from Otherworld into the large equipment room by the command center.

What Jake was more interested in, though, were the bars of the gold-colored metal that Alaia had brought with the collars.

He crouched and picked up one of the bars, and weighed it in his hand. "Not too heavy." The material felt rough in his hand, but according to the metal's properties, it would be as smooth as the Mystwalker collars when melted. "We'll have to find out if this is as durable as the Mystwalkers, Elves, and Fae seem to think it is."

"As far as it is known in Otherworld"—Alaia knelt beside Jake and picked up a bar—"there is no stronger metal. Few know of its existence, but the Mystwalkers are well versed in every other metal that has been discovered."

"The Drow, as well, believe there is nothing that can withstand what this metal is able to," Cassia said. "The Dark Elves' specialty lies in all materials mined in Otherworld, and I'm confident with their assessment."

"Excellent." Jake looked from Cassia to Alaia. "I'm going to take this to my team so we can melt it down as soon as possible and start making the parts for the weapon I designed."

Hopeful for the first time since they'd begun this fight with Darkwolf, Jake picked up the other two bars on the floor and Alaia handed the fourth one to him.

"Thanks for all you're doing for the Alliance and our fight against Darkwolf," he said to her.

She acknowledged him with a slight nod. "We hope our assistance will be enough to help you in your battles."

He blew out a breath. "It'll definitely help."

Jake stared at Hawk, finding it hard to believe the warrior's words. "Darkwolf has been keeping his army in the stadium all this time?" Jake asked.

"We are certain." Hawk moved his gaze to each representative of the Alliance who stood in the command center. "Silver scried the location and Copper dream-visioned the Stormcutters training and multiplying in the stadium. Copper and Silver are positive."

Damn bastards, Jake thought, *using the San Francisco Giants stadium.* He'd been a diehard Giant's fan since he could talk, and seeing the abuse the stadium had gone through at the hands of the dark goddess and now Darkwolf was enough to piss a fan off big-time.

Never mind all the other havoc they'd created.

Copper and Silver, being blood sisters, were the only two witches who had refused to stay apart. A measure of energy thrummed through Jake now that he'd heard what the sisters had scried. It looked like the Alliance finally might have a decent lead.

Rhiannon frowned. Despite the Coven being disbanded, she still served as a representative of the witches. "I haven't had any visions of the stadium."

"How did those sisters mark the place all of a sudden?" Bourne said as he leaned his hip against a console. "From what you guys tell me, none of the witches had been able to see a thing before."

"Silver and Copper believe the traitor used dark magic to hinder all of the witches' scrying sessions." Hawk braced one hand on his sword hilt, which looked a little odd strapped to the waistband his Levis. "Now that they scry apart from the other witches . . . there is nothing to block their divination powers."

Cassia nodded, her expression thoughtful. "I sensed something dark and filled with malice among the D'Anu when I first returned from Otherworld after my extended absence. But I couldn't place it."

She glanced briefly at Rhiannon before looking back at Bourne. Rhiannon narrowed her gaze.

"Now that I think about it," Cassia said, not meeting Rhiannon's, gaze again "I'm not surprised the traitor managed to skew the visions."

Jake cued up a map of San Francisco on the computerized map table and, with a few clicks on the keyboard, drew up a satellite image of the city. A few more clicks and he had the stadium filling the screen, and they could see each seat in the stands and every chalk line on the field.

"There's nothing here." Jake straightened as he studied the map. "He could have his army hidden inside the building itself. But when we've considered it before, the D'Danann scouts didn't find any signs of Darkwolf or his Stormcutters anywhere near the stadium."

"His god-powers." Cassia focused on the map table. "With the strength of two gods and his own dark magic, there's a good chance he's been shielding the entire stadium."

"I bet you're right." Jake braced his hands on the table as he swung his gaze to meet Cassia's. "Think that will keep us out?"

"It's difficult to say," she replied. "It might just be a masking spell, and once we're there we can break through his defenses."

"We need to flat out go after his ass." Bourne pushed away from the console he'd been leaning against and moved beside Jake. "It's not doing us any good standing around waiting for the bastard to do his thing and outnumber us before we can adjust our Jockey shorts."

Everyone in the room nodded or spoke their agreement, but Alaia remained quiet as she studied each one of the Alliance leaders. Jake had taken the metal she'd provided to his weapons team and they'd already gone to work on it.

"We have a little surprise in store for the Stormcutters, too." Jake nodded to Alaia, whom he had introduced when they first started the strategy session. "Alaia has brought with her some weapons that are going to be pretty damn useful in this fight."

Alaia explained how the weapons worked, and demonstrated with her own as she had in Otherworld. As they listened to her, Jake could feel the additional excitement rippling through the Alliance leaders.

"The metal we talked about"—Jake nodded to Alaia—"she and the other Mystwalkers were more than generous and brought us enough to make a prototype." He pulled the roll of parchment that Alaia had given him in Otherworld from his back pocket and spread it out on the map table.

Bourne and Fredrickson pored over the information.

"Damn," Bourne said as he looked from Alaia to Jake. "I think you've got something here."

"Now to make that weapon," Fredrickson said.

Hawk gripped the hilt of his sword tightly. "But now we go to this stadium and fight."

Adrenaline pumped through Jake's veins at the prospect of going one-on-one with Darkwolf again.

"Let's do it."

CHAPTER TWENTY-SEVEN

SAN FRANCISCO FELT LIKE A MASSIVE graveyard in the still night. Everything was eerily quiet and a shiver scoured Jake's spine.

It was as if the Alliance was nothing but shadows and dust as the growing task force came at the stadium from all directions.

Jake was beyond sick of screwing with all of this paranormal crap. This was *his* city, and hell if he was going to let Darkwolf win the war. The Alliance had taken out the goddess-bitch from Underworld, and one way or another, Darkwolf was going down, too.

They'd waited till night for their offensive move so that the Drow warriors could join their ranks. The Drow stood at strategic points where they could best use their bows and arrows to take down as many funnel-men as they could before the Dark Elves joined in the fight with their swords.

Twenty-two hundred Marines hunkered down, prepared to do their thing. The D'Danann were already positioned at the highest points of the stadium.

All of Jake's PSF officers were present, most of them wearing the Mystwalker collars.

Jake hoped to God all of the Alliance fighters would be enough.

His thoughts turned toward the D'Anu. Broken as they were, he wasn't sure how much good they'd do in the battle. He was more worried about them being hurt than anything. The witches also wore the Mystwalker collars, and their familiars were at their sides, though, even Silver's python.

The traitorous murdering bitch among the D'Anu . . . he wanted to know who she was before—

Before what?

Jake's blood ran thick and hot as he watched Cassia close her eyes. The collar around her neck glinted in the faint streetlight. Jake had refused to take one of the things, letting others use the limited supply. He was more comfortable with his Glock and his own dagger anyway.

Cassia's features took on an almost ethereal glow as she focused on bringing the Mystwalkers from Otherworld. She stood in a large open area in the middle of the stadium's Willie Mays Plaza, Kael beside her.

In the plaza there'd be enough space to bring in the hundred or so male and female Mystwalkers who would join the Alliance in the attack.

While he waited for Cassia to transport the Mystwalkers, Jake checked in with the commanding officers of every unit via his mic. According to the commanders, no sign of movement or acknowledgment of their presence came from Darkwolf's camp.

But Jake had no doubt the warlock-god knew they were here. The traitor would have made sure of that by now. One way or another, she'd have figured out a way to contact him.

Air began to shimmer around Cassia and low-hanging fog gathered in the plaza. In moments figures rose from the mist. It still made Jake's heart rate kick up a notch to see men and women appear out of nothing, even though he'd watched them do it in Otherworld.

When the mist vanished and the Mystwalker warriors stood in the street, Alaia stepped out of the Alliance's ranks and joined her people. She gave Cassia a nod, then did the same to Jake.

He returned Alaia's nod just as lightning split the sky and thunder boomed across the city.

Show's on.

Jake gave one long look at Cassia and tried to tell her with his gaze how much he loved her. If her answering expression was any indication, she was thinking and feeling the same thing.

He focused on the mission and spoke into his transmitter. "Green light," he said as he drew his Glock from its holster. "Don't wait for an order to shoot. Remember what's going to be coming your way and go after the bastards with everything you have as soon as they're on your asses."

The moment Jake gave the order, the Alliance descended on the stadium.

As planned, someone threw the stadium lights on.

More lightning fragmented the sky, with bellows of thunder close behind. Rain poured down fast, heavy, and sudden, like a million buckets of water sloshed over the Alliance nonstop.

If a man could wield that kind of power—it was no wonder Darkwolf had been so hard to find and destroy.

The Alliance warriors maintained their air of stealth as they moved through passageways. They'd figured Darkwolf would want them in the open where he could use his Stormcutters, so the Alliance commanders weren't too concerned about being attacked from behind. Still, each man and woman remained on guard as they flowed through the stadium's arteries.

When they burst onto the field, Jake's gut clenched at what waited for them, clearly seen in the stadium lights.

Thousands of water funnels.

Battle cries, shouts, and the sound of gunfire tore through the rain-soaked night. The sour stench of the Stormcutters slammed into his senses, obliterating every other smell.

Jake's heart stuttered as Cassia shoved her way to the front ranks of the Alliance and met the Stormcutters head on. Brilliant flames whirled around her as she released her magic. Funnels evaporated and fire incinerated the men inside them in an instant.

A moment's pride flashed through Jake, but then a funnel was nearly down his throat and he had to focus wholly on kicking some Stormcutter ass.

At the same time he needed to figure out where Darkwolf was and go after the sonofabitch. He didn't have his god-containment weapon yet, but, just maybe, he didn't need it.

SUCH INCREDIBLY POTENT MAGIC surged through Cassia that her body burned with it. Her hair and clothing felt like they would fall to ash from the strength of her powers.

"I will stay outside your fire," Kael said in her mind before he lunged at a Stormcutter, took him down, and tore into his throat. *"I cannot fight if I stay with you."*

Cassia went to work releasing another burst of fire. *"Take care."*

Fire ringed her, flaring outward and blasting funnels into nothing as she moved into the swirling, shouting, screaming insanity. If her magic stuttered even a moment, she knew the Stormcutters would be on her in seconds.

But that wasn't going to happen.

She was too strong, too powerful, with magic that had magnified with her ascension. Maybe she hadn't obtained her full abilities without going through the transition, but what she had gained made her feel nearly invincible. At least in this battle.

For the briefest of seconds her failure at identifying the traitor flashed through Cassia's mind, but she shoved thoughts of it away. Justice would come, sooner rather than later. Her powers told her that much.

The ring of fire that surrounded Cassia protected her enough that she could assess some of what was happening around her.

Where was Jake? Her heart pounded harder at the thought that he could be injured or dead, and she wanted to find him to make sure he was all right.

Jake will be okay. She blasted more Stormcutters. *He'll be okay.*

Rain pelted the Alliance, but most of what came toward Cassia evaporated before it reached her. Still, she had to concentrate to see through the downpour outside her circle of flames.

Fog curled around the bases of funnels as the mist wove its way over the muddy, grassy field. Intermittently, Myst-walkers rose from the mist. In fluid motions, they silently removed their collars and sliced through water funnels.

At once each of those funnels came to a stop, the water splashed onto the ground, and pale, bloodied, tattooed men crumpled to the sodden battlefield, their bodies often in pieces.

By the time the Stormcutters had dropped, the Mystwalk-ers had already returned to their mist forms and moved on to their next targets.

Cassia continued to force fire and heat from her body, eliminating Stormcutters while being careful not to hurt any-one from the Alliance. At times she was forced to jerk her flames back before they singed a PSF officer or a Marine.

Screams and shouts, along with the roar of battle cries, rose above the rumble of thunder. Cassia soon smelled blood and death that blended with the sour stench of the Stormcutters.

Her stomach churned and her heart ached for those of the Alliance whose bodies now littered the ground next to dead Stormcutters.

Anger fed her magic, and for a brief moment she thought she would lose control and obliterate everything and every-one near her. She fought to command her powers and won—barely.

Sparks of witches' magic erupted across the battlefield and a knot formed in Cassia's throat. Before, the witches had always worked in tandem, close to one another even when they paired up with a D'Danann warrior or PSF officer.

Now—

No. She couldn't pause to think about what had shredded the Coven's sisterhood and shattered it beyond repair.

Cassia's magic obliterated every Stormcutter that neared her. The power inside her magnified, growing stronger the more she used it.

Drow arrows cut swiftly and silently through the rain, the diamond heads exploding in the chests of every Stormcutter the arrows pierced.

Cassia spotted Hannah and Garran in the middle of the field. Banshee, her falcon, ripped out Stormcutter eyes and shredded their faces with his talons. Hannah was actually using gray magic in her spellfire to burn off the heads of the Stormcutters. With his sword, Garran took down every Stormcutter that Hannah missed.

D'Anu didn't kill, gray magic or no.

Hannah was, though, and from her expression it was without any reservations or regret.

The witches were no longer a Coven. There were no longer any Coven gray-magic guidelines.

Cassia shook off the queasy thoughts it gave her as she belted out more fire. Being Elvin, Cassia had no reservations about killing evil. It just seemed strange to see any of her former Coven sisters doing the same.

From the sky, D'Danann beheaded Stormcutters. The warriors' powerful wings held them safely above the water funnels.

Marines and PSF officers fought with courage and fortitude. On every man's and woman's face Cassia saw only fierce intensity to destroy their enemies.

But too many Marines and PSF officers were being killed, even using the Mystwalker collars. Funnel after funnel appeared, and Cassia's stomach sickened as she began to wonder if this entire battle was futile. If any of the Alliance would survive.

Cassia caught the eerie sounds of laughter—both male and female—that somehow reached her through thunder, gunfire, screams, and shouts on the battlefield.

Somewhere in the midst of the melee, the traitor was laughing.

And so was Darkwolf.

So much anger surged within Cassia that again she almost lost control of her flames. For several minutes she had to focus solely on eliminating Stormcutters around her. Long enough to rein in what could wreak devastation amongst the Alliance if she wasn't cautious.

It was so hard. Rage and horror balled tightly inside her

as she saw people she knew lying on the now bloody muck of the field. Dead, dying, or injured. Too many of them had fallen.

Cassia passed by Copper and Silver, who worked with their D'Danann husbands to kill Stormcutters. Silver's python moved faster than Cassia had ever seen him. He wrapped his long body around every Stormcutter that came close to Silver, and quickly squeezed the man until his bones snapped and crunched and the Stormcutter fell lifeless to the ground.

Copper's bee familiar was probably doing his bee-stinging thing, causing allergic reactions and holding up every Stormcutter he could. The rain was no doubt hard on Zephyr, but he had strong magic. He was not even close to being an ordinary honey bee.

Silver's husband, Hawk, and Copper's husband, Tiernan, both hovered nearby, their wings giving them power and strength to battle from above—and likely to snatch their lovers out of harm's way if need be.

On and on the Alliance fought the Stormcutters. The roar of battle and the stench that accompanied it added to the queasiness in Cassia's belly.

With determination, she worked her way through the mass of funnels, trying to get to the opposite side of the field where Darkwolf might be watching.

Oh, she knew he was watching. And enjoying.

Alyssa's familiar, Echo, gave loud hoots nearby, startling Cassia.

She slipped in a slick of mud and landed on her hands and knees next to three bodies. The force jarred her so much her teeth clacked together and she almost lost hold of her fire. She slipped as she tried to scramble to her feet. She dropped again, slid in the muck, and twisted onto her back.

Her concentration shattered and her ring of fire broke.

Funnels swarmed her so quickly that terror expanded in her chest and she thought her ribs would crack.

A circle of five Stormcutters came to a stop, and a surge of water splashed her face and body as men surrounded her.

Panic ripped through Cassia when her fire didn't answer her call. Still flat on her back, she only managed a fistful of flame and flung it at one of the Stormcutters.

Not enough!

The Stormcutter she hit with her ball of flame shouted and dropped, but the other four raised their ice daggers.

Cassia screamed and grabbed the collar from her neck as she tried to draw on her magic. She couldn't even transport out of the middle of the men.

Something dark and heavy, something completely evil, clung to her powers, keeping her magic out of reach.

With all her might, she sliced out with the dagger and took one of the men down at the knees before swiping the belly of another Stormcutter, causing his guts to spill from the gaping wound.

The other men drove their daggers toward her and she tried to summon her fire again, even as she felt the black power, Darkwolf's duo-god power, pressing her down.

Goddess! It can't end like this.

Gunfire exploded over her head.

Four rapid shots echoed in her ears as the two remaining Stormcutters dropped.

She jerked her gaze up and saw Jake in a protective stance above her. He grabbed her hand and helped her to her feet. He met her eyes only a fraction of a moment, as if to check to make sure she was all right, before he turned his attention to more Stormcutters whirling closer.

The torrent of rain nearly blinded her—she'd become accustomed to having the ring of fire evaporate most of what had poured on top of her.

Fire. I need my fire!

Cassia spotted Alyssa through the melee, and saw the witch using her ropes of magic to strangle Stormcutters. Even she had thrown out the book on do's and don'ts of gray-magic witches.

That awful darkness still clung to Cassia's magic as more Stormcutters came at her and Jake.

With all the power she had, she tried to fling the darkness

away. It stuck to her magic like a leech and began sucking it from her.

No!

Cassia struggled against the horrible pull. She used her Mystwalker blade and her centuries of hand-to-hand training to fight at the same time she called to her magic.

She more than called to it. She screamed at her powers to obey. She was a Guardian ascending, and her magic *would* do her bidding!

The intensity of her determination reeled in some of her magic. Fire burst from her fingertips.

Not enough! Not all of it.

Even as she gutted and beheaded more Stormcutters, she fought to bring her magic back inside her.

She jerked hard while pushing away the evilness that clung to her magic.

Cassia almost tumbled back as her magic slammed back into her, clean of dark magic.

A ring of fire circled her and Jake.

In her mind she thought she heard someone's shout of frustration and rage.

Cassia put the dagger's hilt near her throat and it formed a collar around her neck once again.

She glanced at Jake, who stood beside her, holding his weapon in a two-handed grip, his jaws tight and his expression fierce. He fired one bullet after another through her flames, taking out targets too far for her magic to reach without hurting one of the good guys along the way.

"Where do you think Darkwolf is?" Cassia sounded and felt winded as she spoke.

Jake glanced up at the luxury boxes. "Probably enjoying the show from the best seats in the house."

The sick feeling in Cassia's belly magnified as she saw the sheer number of water funnels between them and the luxury boxes.

She reached out with her enhanced senses. Now that she knew where to look, she had a better chance of locating Darkwolf.

"There!" she shouted to Jake as her senses touched Dark-wolf's black presence. "In the luxury box directly behind home plate."

Jake gave a sharp nod and moved with her as she used her fire to cut a path through the battle, toward Darkwolf.

While still keeping her fire in place, Cassia glanced around them.

Sydney came into view, her husband, Conlan, fighting by her side. Her Doberman, Chaos, ripped out throats or the genitals of every nearby Stormcutter who revealed himself.

Cassia and Jake continued to work their way through the madness. Rhiannon and her husband, Keir, backed each other not much farther ahead. Rhiannon had unleashed her Shadows, which were strangling and tearing apart Storm-cutters.

Strangling.

Cassia's thoughts bounced from Rhiannon to Alyssa, who were both using their powers to strangle opponents tonight.

No time to think about that.

A sea of Stormcutters continued to hammer the Alliance.

Cassia's chest ached as the truth hit her.

The Alliance was losing.

Hopelessness swirled through her like black water flowing down a rusted drainpipe. Not hopelessness for herself, but for all the beings in the Alliance. All the people of San Francisco.

Just as the magnitude started to crush her and grind her into the earth, the stadium rumbled.

A sudden shift in energy had Cassia jerking her attention toward left field. It seemed as though every member of the Alliance felt it, too. Even the Stormcutters slowed their spinning. It was almost as if the very ground tilted.

Bellows of rage—or confusion?—tore across the field, coming from the luxury boxes.

Darkwolf! What is he doing? Cassia's fire ring flickered as she looked from the location the bellows had come from and back to left field. *What's happening?*

She thought her head would explode from redoubled fear.

Was this a new foe they had to face when they were already devastated by losses? Were they doomed by a new threat?

A rumble rolled through the stadium.

Familiar war cries ripped through the air and Cassia's jaw dropped at the roar of the countless shouts.

It couldn't be.

But it had to be.

How?

Cassia's heart stuttered, then welled with hope again.

Her people had come.

They had come!

"What is it?" Jake was shouting, his voice thundering above all the yelling.

Through the rain she saw the gleam of polished Elvin bows. The glint of swords in the stadium lights.

It was. It really was!

The ranks charged toward the battle with the litheness and stealth only her people possessed.

"It's them," Cassia yelled back, joy fueling her fire, raising the flames around them. "The Light Elves have joined the battle!"

Chapter Twenty-eight

"That was almost too easy." Elizabeth moved closer to the luxury box's thick glass as she stared out at the battle. "I expected more from the Alliance than this pathetic resistance."

"So did I." Darkwolf looped his arm around Elizabeth's shoulders. Her passion fruit scent teased his senses as she leaned against him, her head on his muscular arm. "You're right," he said. "It's definitely been too easy."

He released her, moved away, and placed his palm to the cool glass. One man or woman after another dropped to the muddy ground, Alliance and Stormcutter alike.

He drummed his fingers against the window. His murdering traitor had told him at least three thousand members of the Alliance would meet his five thousand Stormcutters on the field.

Even though his creations outnumbered the Alliance's ranks, Darkwolf couldn't help but feel that something was off. "Don't get too comfortable yet," he murmured, to himself as much as Elizabeth.

She shrugged and leaned her hip against the window as she looked up at him. "I don't see why not. Look how much their numbers have dwindled. Our defense is far stronger."

He let the comment slide past as he analyzed the battle.

A part of him still clung to the hope that one witch, Silver Ashcroft, had remained unscathed. He scowled. His infatuation with her was long over.

Darkwolf studied the ring of fire that continued to move in the direction of the luxury box he and Elizabeth were in. For a moment he'd been able to hamper the Elvin witch's magic with his own, but she'd flung it away. He ground his teeth at the thought. He should have more power over her than that when her defenses were down.

No matter. Soon the Alliance would be destroyed.

A rumble jerked his attention to one end of the field.

Darkwolf shouted, the sound of his god-voice rolling out like thunder.

"Who are those people, those warriors?" Panic edged Elizabeth's tone. "Where did they come from?"

Darkwolf's heart thrummed as his god's senses told him exactly who they were. "Light Elves." He clenched his teeth. "From Otherworld."

"Look at the Stormcutters." Elizabeth took a step back from the glass. "They're dropping. Fast."

Hundreds of arrows hurtled through the night, across the battlefield, taking out one target after another. It seemed like the moment a funnel came to a stop and a Stormcutter appeared, an Elvin arrow pierced his chest.

Darkwolf had unleashed every Stormcutter he had on the Alliance, confident he could create more of the beings in the time it took human government and the military to get their shit together and retaliate.

In the meantime he and his Blades would convert at least a million men into deadly Stormcutters, whether the men did so willingly or not. Darkwolf had been sure that by the time the government and military came at him, he would have more than enough Stormcutters to repel any attack.

But right now he couldn't afford to lose all of his Stormcutters. Especially his Blades. It took a great deal of Darkwolf's magic to create the Blades, because he gave them the power to transform men into Stormcutters.

Elizabeth looked from the battlefield to Darkwolf. "What are you going to do?"

"The only thing we can." Darkwolf reeled in the storm and sent his remaining Stormcutters to the hiding place he had prepared in case they were discovered in the stadium.

"Retreat."

CHAPTER TWENTY-NINE

I GRIND MY TEETH AS THE STORM rolls *away, taking with it the remaining Stormcutters.*

Even though so many died, many of the Alliance members survived.

And the Light Elves. What the hell are they doing here? At least a thousand of them are on the field, helping those who are injured now that the Stormcutters are gone.

I relish the stench of death because it means Darkwolf and I are coming closer to our goal.

My hair's plastered to my head and cheeks, and my jeans and T-shirt are so soaked they stick to my body. Damn rain. My arms ache from fighting Stormcutters with the Mystwalker knife that is beyond effective against Darkwolf's creations.

No, D'Anu do not kill.

But thanks to my murdering Mackenzie, which resulted in the D'Anu's separation, each witch is a solitary practitioner. We now each have our own individual guidelines.

I hold back a smile as images of the other witches come to mind. They fought with ferocity and anger, using a combination of magic and the Mystwalker knife.

They aren't so untarnished now, are they?

I catch sight of Copper and Silver, but none of the others. Perhaps Darkwolf and I are lucky enough that the rest died on the battlefield.

No. There's Hannah with her disgusting Drow King husband.

I really hate that snotty rich bitch. Maybe I'll kill her next.

I turn my attention on the oh-so-perfect Silver Ashcroft, who is using her magic to heal a gouge in Copper's arm. She glances at me but quickly averts her gaze.

Better yet, Silver and her baby should die.

Yes.

I imagine Darkwolf's pleasure as I eliminate the other witches one by one. They'll be frantic wondering who'll die next, and how. Before anyone can catch me, I'll get out and let them wonder where I went.

Darkwolf gave me the ability to use the transference when we're ready. Our mental connection is strong, much stronger once I killed Mackenzie and embraced the dark magic that I used to commit the murder.

How he'll thank me for ridding us of more of the D'Anu.

The thought makes my clit ache and my nipples harden.

Who cares about death, about the stench of battle?

Darkwolf's going to fuck me.

I'll share in Darkwolf and his incredible powers. I'll rub people's faces in it, people who always thought I was weak and less-than.

That's all I can think about, all I care about.

His cock will be so long and thick, stretching me wide as I beg for more. I'll want him to take me over and over, as I've imagined countless times while I've waited for Darkwolf to come to his rightful power.

Maybe he'll take me from behind when I'm on my hands and knees. Or maybe he'll take me against a wall, hard and fast and satisfying. Better than Fredrickson or any other one of the PSF officers I have taken secretly. Some in their sleep without their knowledge.

Maybe I'll fuck a Marine or two while I wait to be with Darkwolf.

I need to get a grip. I'm shuddering like a school kid. At least nobody can see my erect nipples beneath my body armor, and I hope they don't notice the lust in my eyes.

For appearance's sake, I kneel beside a dying Marine as if I'm going to save him. I let my magic flow from my hands to his body and I know he's too weak to be a match for me. I glance around at the hundreds of people on the field and see no one looking, and again I hide a smile.

I touch the Mystwalker band around my throat and it

forms a dagger in an instant. The man's eyes meet mine a second before I stab him low, where no one can see. The blade pierces his kidneys.

A strangled sound comes from his throat. His eyes widen and he reaches for me.

So strong, these Marines.

I easily block his reach with an invisible barrier and I twist the dagger.

He coughs more blood before his body slackens and his head lolls to the side, his eyes wide and unseeing like Mackenzie's had been.

But her death was far more satisfying.

Dark magic fills me, stronger than ever before. The Marine's murder enhances my dark powers. I feed on it and know that not one of the other witches can stop me from helping Darkwolf achieve his goals. They don't even know I'm the one they're looking for.

Oh, they suspect me. But only as much as they suspect any other of the D'Anu.

Let them wonder. It only makes the game more fun.

CHAPTER THIRY

DAIRE CLENCHED HIS BOW and looked over the mass of bodies as he searched for Cassiandra with his gaze. The hollowness that had taken residence in his chest since her rejection expanded at the thought of her being one of the many dead scattered across the field.

I would have felt her death, would I not?

The loss of such a powerful presence would leave a greater hole in his heart and ache in his chest.

No, Cassiandra is here. Somewhere close.

Daire caught a whiff of something exotic over the stench of death. Something strangely enticing that did odd things to his senses. Like the scent of a sun goddess rose twined with myrrh and sweet woman's musk.

He followed the scent while at the same time searching for some sign of Cassiandra. Frustration caused his muscles to bunch and ache. Where was the Princess?

The exotic perfume strengthened as he skirted the dead and wounded until he reached the far end of the field.

Cassiandra's powerful presence hit him. Relief to know she was alive eased the hollowness in his chest.

There. On her knees, tending wounded with her magic.

The honeyed scent he had been following closed in on him, drawing his gaze. A woman approached him, her lips parted as she focused on his face.

Unlike Elvin females, her hair was short, but still she was one of the most beautiful women he had ever been in the presence of. The human's features were as exotic and enticing as her perfume. Her breasts swelled beneath her clothing, and her curves begged for his touch.

As she came closer, he noticed she held something in her

hand that had a human symbol on it he couldn't read. Despite the horrors and chaos surrounding them, he found it difficult to tear his gaze from her dark eyes and full lips. Somehow she had cast a spell on him that he couldn't break. Yet he sensed no magic in her of any kind. She was fully human.

In moments she was but two steps away from him. She cleared her throat. "Kat DeLuca, Channel 17 News," she said, and he let the smooth sound of her voice flow through his veins. "Why don't you tell me your name?" Her gaze drifted over his face before she met his eyes again. "And *what* you are?"

Surprise tickled his chest as he studied the woman who called herself Kat. How could she not recognize his kind?

"I am Elvin, of course." Daire realized he still gripped his bow in his fist. He slung it over his shoulder. "I am known as Daire."

"Daire." The way she said his name sent a swirl of need through his body. It was as if they were alone in another time, another realm. She raised the thing she held and brought it close to her mouth, and it was as if she was speaking to the black ball atop it. "That would explain the pointed ears. Where do you come from?"

"Otherworld," he replied when she put the ball in front of him before drawing it back.

He frowned as movement caught his attention.

A man stood behind Kat, wielding a black box on his shoulder. Daire saw his own reflection in a circle of glass on the box. His senses vibrated with the wrongness the thing projected. What the man carried needed to be destroyed. Immediately.

Daire's muscles tightened as he raised his hand and released invisible energy directly at the black box. His magic hit the thing with such force that it flew from the man's grip.

Daire's power flung the box against something high and hard, like gray stone only completely smooth. The impact shattered the box, the crash loud before its many parts scattered across the wet ground.

"What the—" the man started with fury in his voice.

But when Daire raised his palm again and faced it toward the man, his anger quickly turned to palpable fear. "Uh. Hey. No harm done." He turned and slipped in the mud before he fled from where Daire and Kat remained.

"So much for that." Kat tossed the thing she'd been holding onto the ground, where it landed with a thick splash in a slick of muck.

"What was that?" He glanced from the thing Kat had thrown over her shoulder back to her beautiful features.

"A microphone," she said almost absently as she looked past him. Her features paled as her gaze swept the battlefield. "Somehow all of this didn't seem real when I held the microphone with a cameraman standing behind me."

Kat brought her hand to her side and winced as she slid her palm down the material that covered her. "Even with these wounds as a reminder." A look of fear and pain flickered in her eyes as if she was remembering something terrible.

"Are you injured?" he asked, taking in her body from head to toe but seeing nothing that remotely appeared as if she'd been touched during the battle.

"This injury was from—" She shook her head. "If Jake hadn't been there to save me after that demon got to me, I'd be dead."

Heat curled in Daire's belly at the mention of the human's name. The human who was attempting to steal Cassiandra from him.

Daire cocked his head in thought. Somehow he had forgotten about the Princess in these few moments he had been enthralled with Kat.

Even though Daire did not like the human male, he felt a surge of gratefulness at the fact Jake had saved this woman's life.

An expression of hurt and sadness, if not a little anger, crossed Kat's face as she stared at the battlefield. "There's Jake, with the woman he left me for. A so-called witch."

Daire followed her gaze and saw Jake kneeling beside Princess Cassiandra, next to an injured human.

Oddly, the sight of Jake and Cassiandra together did not

bring the familiar pang to the hollowness in Daire's chest. Instead he found himself more aware of the human woman beside him.

"I should be helping instead of standing around watching and reporting all of this tragedy to people who don't have a clue." Kat sounded angry with herself, and he looked back at her. "I've been hiding behind that microphone ever since all of this—whatever it is—started.

"I thought I was helping by reporting everything that's been happening." She tilted her chin, and resolution filled her gaze and tightened her features. "But all I've really done is sensationalize these horrors that have been destroying our people and our city."

Daire had been so captivated by Kat that he, too, had failed to perform his duty.

He bowed low, and surprise lit her dark eyes as he rose.

"Come," he said. "We shall do what we can to aid your people."

CHAPTER THIRTY-ONE

CASSIA USED HER HEALING MAGIC on a Marine who had taken a Stormcutter dagger to one of his lungs. Thank the goddess his injuries weren't beyond what healing abilities she possessed.

When the Marine breathed easier, the hole in his lung repaired with her magic, Cassia looked up at Jake, who had stopped at her side. He had been tending other wounded with a human first aid kit the last time she had seen him.

In the stadium lights he appeared tired, frustrated, and angry from battle. But his expression softened when their gazes met.

Jake crouched beside Cassia. "Sure you're okay?"

"Not a scratch." With her magic and her eyes she scanned his mud- and blood-covered body, and she felt or saw nothing life-threatening. Shallow wounds at best.

"Cassiandra." The familiar male voice caused her to jerk her attention up to see Daire standing above her.

"Daire!" Such incredible gratitude welled inside her that tears stung her eyes. Despite the muck and blood covering her, she pushed herself up from where she knelt and flung herself against Daire. "Thank you for coming." She sniffled and rested her head against his chest. "You and our people saved countless lives."

He held her for a moment, and the familiar comfort of such a close friend embraced her.

She drew away and tilted her head up to look into the intensity of his green eyes.

"I petitioned the Elders when I visioned your need." He rubbed his hands up and down her arms, and studied her from head to toe as if making certain she had suffered no injuries. "To my great astonishment, they acquiesced the moment I asked it of them. As soon as our warriors had prepared for battle, the Great Guardian sent us to this San Francisco Otherworld. I think it was she who influenced the Elders."

Surprise tingled through Cassia. Had her mother truly helped, even though she had said she would not?

All that mattered now was that the Light Elves were here.

Cassia completely stepped out of Daire's grasp when she came to the full realization that Jake was at her side.

Jake's expression was hard, but he wiped muck off his hand onto his jeans and reached out to shake Daire's hand. "Thank you doesn't say enough," Jake said. "Showing up like you did—I don't think there would have been anything left of us if you hadn't."

Daire took Jake's hand and gave him a slight nod before they released each other's grip. "We have come to join your Alliance until this threat is eliminated."

Cassia let out a long exhale and silently offered her thanks to the goddess Anu. The Light Elves were staying—this wasn't a onetime shot.

Daire glanced across the field of bodies to where Light Elves tended to the wounded. "We are a thousand strong."

Cassia looked up at Jake. "The abilities and magic of the Light Elves are such that it is more like three thousand of them have joined us," she said.

Jake nodded. "They were pretty impressive."

She became aware of someone watching her and met the gaze of Jake's previous "girlfriend," who stood off to one side. Cassia's face burned due to the fact that she was the reason why Jake had broken up with Kat.

Kat DeLuca glanced from Cassia to Jake. "What can I do to help?"

Jake raised his brows. "You're not reporting for the news station?"

"No." Kat glanced at the devastation and back to Jake. "Right now there are more important things to do."

Jake gave Kat an expression of approval. "We can use all

the help we can get." He gestured to the field. "Let us know when you find someone who's injured so we can take care of them. We're running low, but more trucks with first aid supplies should be here any moment."

Kat nodded and turned away. Before he followed her, Daire said, "Many of my people can use healing magic on those we find who might still live."

"Healing magic?" Kat's voice drifted back as she moved across the field with Daire.

Cassia stared at the vast number of dead and wounded. It all looked surreal beneath the stadium's lights. A fist lodged in her throat and tears slipped down her cheeks. This city was being torn apart.

And so was she.

A FEW DAYS HAD PASSED since the massacre in the stadium, and the Alliance was no closer to figuring out where Darkwolf was now than they had been before.

Jake rubbed his forehead with his thumb and forefinger as he paced back and forth in the Alliance's command center. At the moment he was alone in the almost totally closed-in room. The door was open but the lights were off. The illuminated map table, various computers, and other equipment gave the place an eerie glow.

He clenched his fist in frustration as he brought his hand away from his face. The Alliance didn't even know how many Stormcutters Darkwolf had created. For all the Alliance knew, the warlock-god had thousands more that he'd kept hidden someplace else.

Darkwolf could have his army scattered in every city around the Bay area.

The anger burning in Jake's chest had never let up since that last battle.

Volunteers from the Red Cross, police, and fire and rescue had flowed in from all over the nation when the dark goddess mummified thousands and thousands of people just a few short weeks ago. Because that time the bodies had been nothing but withered husks, there had been no decomposition or disease. The bodies had been moved to one of the buildings in the city.

The volunteers and the National Guard had worked around the clock to identify the dead and to be certain people received burial or disposal in accordance with their religious beliefs. Even with the tremendous number of volunteers, they were still working on the beyond-daunting task.

Now, after the battle with Darkwolf, a "morgue" had been set up in one of the buildings with cold storage to prevent disease, and to process bodies quickly. More volunteers continued to flow into San Francisco, but with so many dead from the dark goddess's massacre, and now Darkwolf's, there weren't enough people to handle it all.

Speaking of not enough people—or beings—if those fifteen thousand Marines Bourne had promised didn't show up soon, things could go from bad to worse in a hurry. He hoped Darkwolf wasn't churning out an army that could match what they had coming after him.

But the god-stopping gun—Jake's weapons team was nearly finished. They were waiting for one difficult-to-obtain, highly dangerous material that Jake and his men were going to have to beg, borrow, or steal in order to get.

For the time being the Light Elves, Drow, and Mystwalkers had returned to their homes, until their commanders summoned them. Daire had stayed to represent the Light Elves in the Alliance, and Alaia remained for the Mystwalkers.

Due to the fact that Kat was human, and Daire had previously shown a clear dislike of humans, Jake found it amusing that Daire was spending so much time with her. She had begun dropping by HQ, minus her microphone and reporter's ID badge. To help or just to be with Daire, he wasn't sure. But one thing was sure—he was a lot happier with them hanging together than having Daire panting around Cassia. Maybe he'd given up on this whole having-sex-with-Cassia-transition thing.

Otherwise Jake just might have to kill the sonofabitch.

"Jake?" Cassia's voice brought him to a stop from pacing and he faced her.

She was so beautiful. A bright light in such dark times.

"Are you all right?" She moved toward him and his body tightened as he caught her sweet scent of vanilla, sunshine, and spices, which carried to him over the warehouse's now too familiar smells.

He didn't know how much longer he could take being with her but not *being* with her. He needed her in every way he could have her, in every sense of the word.

"Hell no, I'm not okay." His tone came out harsher than he'd intended, but he couldn't stop himself. "The whole world is falling apart." He scrubbed his hand over his face before looking at her again.

"And you—us . . ." He came close enough to her to grab her by her shoulders. "Christ, I can't even kiss you without you blowing shit up."

Cassia averted her gaze so that she was staring at the wall. "I don't know what's wrong with me." She looked miserable when her gaze met his again. "Why I let us get this close emotionally—I knew better."

"Hey." Jake's heart twisted as her words hit home and he softened his tone. The last thing he wanted was to chase her away. "I shouldn't be pushing it between us right now." He caught her under her chin with his finger, forcing her to look directly into his eyes. "We'll find a way to make it work."

Like usual she didn't respond, but she settled her face against his chest and let him hold her close.

"Take me to Otherworld." He rubbed his palm over her back, imagining the softness of her skin beneath his hand rather than the cotton of her T-shirt. "I want to talk with your mother again."

Cassia remained silent for a moment as he held her. "I don't know what good it would do," she finally said. "The Guardian . . . How can I explain her? She's as old as time, and revered above all others. Some believe she is a goddess in Elvin form."

Jake quirked his mouth into a grin and tugged at a lock of her hair. "Should I start calling you Goddess Cassia instead of Princess?"

"Don't you dare," she said, but his teasing coaxed a little smile from her.

"Well, goddess or not," he said, bringing a serious note back to their conversation. "I need to have a word with her."

"Maybe." Cassia wiggled out of his embrace and rubbed her arms with her palms as she looked up at him. "If you promise to stop making her angry."

With a frown he scrubbed his hand over his face a second time. "I can't be someone I'm not."

"I don't want you to change." She stopped running her palms up and down her arms and hugged herself. "I'm just asking you to maybe show a little tact?"

Jake glanced up at the newly built ceiling of the command center before meeting Cassia's gaze again. "Tact, huh?" She nodded and he smiled. "I guess I could try that this time around."

"You are the most tenacious human I have ever known." She moved close to him and tilted her head. The dim lights in the room added to her etherealness. "You don't take no for an answer do you."

"Now you're getting the picture." God, he had to kiss her. Just a little kiss. He caught her face in his hands and brought his mouth to hers so fast she didn't have a chance to do anything but gasp.

A moan rose up in her as she placed her palms on his chest. Sparks of magic traveled through his T-shirt from her touch, and he knew he shouldn't be playing with fire. Literally.

Just a taste.

She'd had tea with a hint of lemon, which danced with her unique flavor that he loved so much. He loved everything about her.

He dipped his tongue deeper into her mouth and felt her little moans straight to his toes.

Then he realized he actually was feeling her to his toes. Her magic ran up and down their bodies, a tingling fire that made his erection even harder. He wanted to take her down to the floor and slide his cock inside her, driving them both on until they'd climaxed at least six times.

No, better yet. He'd take her to his room and make slow love to her. She deserved to be treasured as she gave him her virginity.

Then he'd take her five more times.

His mind spun as he brought his hands to her hips and ground his erection against her belly. The fire surrounding his body grew more intense and he started to see sparks behind his closed eyelids.

Need to stop, Macgregor. He groaned and thought about taking his mouth from hers, but couldn't force himself to.

Just a little more.

Cassia seemed as lost as he was in their kiss. She made hungry, desperate sounds as she clenched her fists in his T-shirt.

Maybe they could do it. Maybe having sex with this woman wouldn't literally kill him.

The sound of something popping and crackling, and the smell of burning plastic and wiring hit him as well as a two by four might have.

They jerked away from each other as smoke spiraled from one of the computers, which also spit electrical sparks onto the concrete floor. The keyboard had been reduced to a bubbling mass of goo.

She winced as she glanced at the damage. "Oops."

He would have laughed if he didn't want her so bad. Instead he adjusted jeans that felt like they'd shrunk down two sizes around his cock.

"Yes." She looked weakened and breathless as she braced her hands on the map table behind her. "Let's go talk to Mother."

FEAR MADE CASSIA'S HEART POUND. She wasn't scared of the Great Guardian. Cassia was afraid the Guardian was right—there was no way to make things between her and Jake work.

Disappointment and hopelessness gripped her heart when she and Jake arrived in the meadow. The Guardian wasn't waiting for their arrival. Definitely not a good sign.

The seemingly all-powerful, all-knowing Guardian always arrived where any being needed to speak with her about something important. Or if the Guardian believed she needed to impart her wisdom.

And riddles.

Her mother had the irritating habit of speaking in riddles that bent one's brain trying to figure them out. In Cassia and Jake's case, the Guardian had been pretty straightforward.

Like, *"No way in all of the Underworlds am I going to allow you to be with this human. Or make it easy for you."*

Cassia sighed, and Jake squeezed her hand. "Where do we find your mother?"

"She usually finds us." She glanced up at him. "This doesn't look promising."

Jake gazed calmly around the meadow. "Guess we'll just have to deal with it and track her down."

How does one track down the Great Guardian?

She faced him and took his other hand so that she was holding both of them. "The palace is as good as any place to start," she said just before she used the transference to take them to the city of the Light Elves.

Jake groaned and swayed a little the moment they appeared in the sunshine-warmed city. "I hate when you do that."

Cassia smiled. "Come on, big man."

He shook his head as if to clear it. "After you, Princess."

She clasped Jake's hand in hers as if he might disappear any moment. The Great Guardian had the power to do exactly that, and right now Cassia wouldn't put it past her mother.

The palace in the trees was considered to be Cassia's true home, but after four hundred years in the Earth Otherworld it didn't feel like home. More like a place she went to when she wanted to visit what friends she had there, or to work on her physical and magical training.

Scents of roses, orchids, and rare flowers flowed over her in the balmy air. Elves they passed bowed in deference to her, but most refused to acknowledge Jake with their gazes.

Bigots.

Cassia felt out of place in her human black jeans and

T-shirt, but she needed to be prepared in case they had to return to the San Francisco Otherworld in a hurry.

Jake squeezed her hand, and she realized she'd been trembling. She glanced up at him and offered him a smile even though she didn't feel it. Her chest was too tight thinking about confronting her mother.

The stairs leading up to the palace entrance seemed to go on forever, as if the Guardian was making it more difficult to reach her.

When they finally passed through the enormous wooden doors into the hall, Cassia felt like she couldn't get enough into her lungs. Even though the place was enormous and airy, at that moment it stifled her.

As the guards shut the door behind them, Jake looked around the great hall. "Where do we find Mom?"

Cassia elbowed him in his side. "You're going to make this harder if you keep that up," she said under her breath. "Not that there's a chance in all the Underworlds that anything will be easy for us with the Great Guardian."

A pair of royal guards approached her and Jake, and she stiffened. She recognized the blond twins at once as her mother's personal guards. Not that the Guardian needed any. The presence of the men was more of a formality than anything else.

The guards carried no swords, daggers, or bows. They wielded such great magic that weapons were inconsequential.

Each man bowed to her. "Princess Cassiandra, the Great Guardian awaits you."

Cassia gave a regal nod to acknowledge the summons and followed the guards, still clenching Jake's hand so tightly that she might break his fingers if she didn't ease up. His nearness, the warmth of his body, and his male scent that she loved so much gave her strength.

The path to the Guardian's receiving room wound up to the height of the enormous trees. Flowers and vines curled around columns while yellow and red butterflies floated in and out of the great archways along the path.

She's going to roast us, slipped through Cassia's mind.

When they reached the topmost step, she and Jake stood on a wide landing that led into a vast open chamber devoid of any decoration, with the exception of the ivy and fire orchids climbing through the windows. Cassia had always imagined that if her mother had collected "treasure" over the countless millennia, the entire city of the Light Elves would be buried beneath it all.

The Great Guardian stood at the center of the room.

Sunlight spilled through the arched windows, caressing her and causing her floor-length blond hair to almost glitter. Her wildflower scent swirled around the chamber, a perfume that captivated the senses.

Until Cassia and Jake had asked to be together, she had never seen the Guardian as anything but calm. Like still water with the strongest of currents rushing beneath.

The Guardian's expression showed nothing, but the fact that she did not smile or appear serene made Cassia's heart stutter.

This was not a good idea. Definitely not smart. And with Jake's penchant for saying exactly what was on his mind, it was a double mistake to be here now.

Cassia tried to keep her own expression calm as she held Jake's hand and walked toward the Guardian. When they were a few feet from her, Cassia dropped to one knee with her head lowered.

Thankfully, Jake did the same, and laid his weapon at the Guardian's feet.

Maybe Jake could show a little tact and respect after all.

"Daughter." The Guardian's voice fell flatter than usual. "Human. You may rise."

A burst of anger sizzled inside Cassia's chest as she rose with Jake. From her side view she saw him clench his jaw, as if he was fighting to hold back words that would definitely make the Guardian angry.

But Cassia couldn't stop herself or keep all of the heat out of her voice as she said to her mother, "Jake. Not human. His name is Jake."

The Guardian let silence hang between them for a long moment. "You refused the choices I gave you when last we met. What brings you to me now?"

As if she doesn't know.

To her relief, Jake spoke in a calm, controlled tone. "There's got to be another option." He glanced at Cassia and his expression softened before he met the Guardian's gaze again. "This isn't about sex—that's not why I want to be with Cassia."

"Then what is required for her ascension should not be a problem for you to concern yourself with." The Guardian focused on Jake, her blue eyes glinting with the same sharpness as her words. "Once a male of pure Elvin blood guides her through her transition without your interference, she is free to experience intercourse with any male of her choosing."

Cassia's face burned hot and flames licked the inside of her chest. Sparks crackled at the ends of her hair even as she fought for control of her emotions.

Jake's face had completely reddened, anger obvious in the set of his jaw, the tenseness of his body.

"Cassia is *mine*," he said in a low growl as he released Cassia's hand and put his arm around her shoulders. "I love her, and there's no way she's going to be with another man."

Cassia's jaw dropped.

Jake had more or less just told the Great Guardian to go to hell.

Wind whipped through the room, spiraling around them so fiercely it was almost painful. Cassia's hair rose from her shoulders and across her face. She and Jake swayed from the force of the wind that plastered their clothing to their bodies.

The Guardian's clothing and hair didn't so much as move a fraction.

Dread anchored itself deep in Cassia's belly, but the anger in her heart overpowered it.

"Stop it!" Cassia moved out of Jake's embrace. She clenched her fists at her sides as she tried to take a step closer to her mother without teetering from the power of the wind that continued to blast her body. "I don't want to be with any other man," she shouted above the wail of the wind. "By the goddess, I love Jake and I will have no other!"

The wind stopped. Dazzling white light flooded the room, outshining even the Great Guardian's glow. The entire palace trembled as the trees embracing the palace shook and the ground rocked.

Almost unable to keep her balance, Cassia backed into Jake and hit his solid chest. He grasped her shoulders. Her heart raced as she blinked and tried to get used to the brilliance.

It felt as if some great being had entered the room. A tremendous presence that nearly overwhelmed Cassia.

Shock coursed through Cassia like the prickle of needles on her skin to see an equal measure of shock on the Great Guardian's face. Even the Guardian looked unnerved as she stared into the white light.

Having a hard time believing what she was seeing, Cassia's jaw dropped and her eyes widened.

Wind rushed through the room and Cassia could almost swear the sound of someone speaking was on the wind.

Then her mother's stunned expression gave way to one of resignation. The Great Guardian bowed her head in deference toward the light . . .

It hit Cassia.

The presence was Anu herself.

Cassia gasped and moved so that she could grab Jake's hand and she jerked them both to the floor in a kneeling position for yet another time. She kept her head bowed until the light faded, the palace and grounds stopped rocking, and the wind vanished.

After a moment's silence, Cassia rose and Jake got to his feet along with her. The Guardian turned and faced them again.

"What the *hell* was that?" Jake asked.

"*My* mother," the Guardian said under her breath.

Cassia thought Jake was going to burst out laughing and she elbowed him, hard. He kept his mouth shut.

The Guardian studied Cassia. Jake gripped her again with

his arm around her shoulders in a possessive, protective stance.

Her mother looked like she was having a hard time not glancing back to the window where Anu had made herself known.

"Apparently Anu believes you should be allowed to make these difficult choices of your own accord," the Guardian said, looking extremely miffed.

"If this human takes you through your transition," she continued, "you will face consequences when your time on the Earth Otherworld has come to an end." The Guardian's gaze held Cassia's, and Cassia couldn't have looked away if she tried. "These are choices born of your decision to be with this human in this most crucial time of your life."

"I accept," Cassia said with no doubts in her mind and heart.

Jake stiffened, his whole body taut against hers as he held his arm around her shoulders. "What is she going to have to deal with in this game you're playing?"

Shock bolted through Cassia at Jake's words and she jerked her head up to look at him.

Mother's going to kill him on the spot.

The Guardian didn't say anything. When Cassia snapped her attention back to the Guardian, Cassia saw her mother studying Jake. Silence fell so heavily Cassia felt as if the Guardian might create a hole in the floor for them to drop through.

The Guardian didn't move her gaze from Jake's as she said, "Daughter, it is you who will confront difficult consequences and choices when it is time to bring you home." She turned her head to stare at Cassia. "Do you wish to maintain your decision to go through your transition with this human?"

Jake looked like he was going to say something, and again Cassia dug her elbow hard into his gut.

"Yes," she said clearly.

"Then so be it." The Guardian raised one of her hands and opened it, palm up. A clear glass tube rested there, and it contained something that looked like black sludge.

"The contents of this vial will not change you in any way," she said to Jake, her tone icy. "You will remain fully human, without even a minuscule amount of magic in your body outside of the transition." She lowered her hand, but the tube continued to hover between them. "Take it if you wish to live."

Cassia's stomach churned and her heart beat faster as she stared at the vial. What was her mother doing?

"In addition," the Guardian said, "you will require instruction on how to take Cassiandra through her transition. I will summon Daire."

To Cassia she said, "At this time the only other stipulation I will place on this mating is that you must complete it here. Alone, but in your own chambers."

The Guardian gave Jake the hint of a humorless smile. "Better yet, one of the empty chambers where there is less opportunity for Cassiandra to 'blow shit up.'"

CHAPTER THIRTY-TWO

THE GREAT GUARDIAN VANISHED like sunlight shrouded by mist, leaving the chamber dark and unwelcome.

Cassia stared at the place her mother had been and swallowed back fear combined with excitement and relief.

"Talk about a mood killer." Jake squeezed Cassia tight, his arm still around her shoulders. With his free hand he reached for the tube hovering a foot away from him. He pocketed it, then brought Cassia completely into his arms. "So the old—the Guardian has been spying on us."

Cassia rested her head against his muscular chest. "I think it was more like you projecting your feelings for me. You want to be with me, but the possibility of being killed by sex is no doubt a little daunting."

The thought about what might lie in her future made Cassia's throat tighten. Would the potion really get Jake through the transition? What consequences would she face?

Jake sighed and rubbed his palm in a circular motion on her back. His warm hand caused a tingling sensation where he touched her through her T-shirt. "After all of that—Jesus, I don't want anything to happen to you."

"I want to be with you." Cassia swallowed. "I need this. I need *you.*"

"We don't have to have sex, honey." Jake kissed the top of her head. "I just don't want any other man to have you in any way. I love you too much."

"Someone has to take me through the transition." She looked up at him and felt the sting of tears behind her eyelids. "Terrible things will happen if I don't go through it. I choose you, Jake. I will only be with you."

He released her and rubbed his temples with his thumb and forefinger. "Maybe I *should* let Daire do it, but I can't."

When she took his free hand in hers, he moved his fingers away from his temples and caught her other hand in his. "Even when I was right there," Cassia said softly, "when I was supposed to go through the transition with Daire, I don't know that I could have. The only man I could think about was you."

Jake let out a harsh breath. "I can't do anything that will hurt you. The consequences—what the hell could they be?"

"It doesn't matter, Jake." Cassia held his eyes with hers as she added softly, "If I don't go through the transition within the next couple of days, I die."

He jerked his head up, an expression of shock on his face as he looked at her, as if he had lost the ability to speak.

"So no matter my choice," she said, trying to continue as she faced the stark reality, "there will be a consequence."

HOURS LATER, JAKE STILL TRIED to come to terms with this whole mate or die thing, and anger had burned continually in his gut. The heat only strengthened as he stood outside of Daire's home, his back to the door, not quite able to make himself face it and knock.

Jake and Cassia had spent the rest of the day holding hands and walking along a lot of the paths cutting through the City of the Light Elves. Even as Cassia showed him her home city, he remained almost blind to it. All he could think about was Cassia and what the Elves had done to her. Taken away her choices, giving her no options. What right did they have to do this to her?

When it was late afternoon, Jake and Cassia had arrived at Daire's front door. Cassia kissed Jake, and he swore electricity traveled to every nerve ending in his body. He'd heard a crackle and the smell of something burning before she drew away. He half expected the trees around them to be on fire, but it was only a spot on the grass that she rubbed out with one shoe. A tendril of smoke rose up from the place.

Now, even after she'd walked away, his lips tingled as if he still felt her mouth against his.

Despite the lack of any sound indicating Daire's door had opened behind Jake, he felt the other man's presence. Jake turned to see Daire, who gave a slight nod. He held his arm toward the doorway, indicating Jake should go into the home.

It was a nice place, Jake had to give Daire that. Vaulted ceilings, high arched windows, rich furnishings with blue-cushioned chairs and couches. Jake couldn't help but compare it to his own sadly neglected bachelor pad, which he'd never had a chance to take Cassia to. He wondered what she'd think of it.

Jake folded his arms across his chest and faced Daire. "Would you like to fill me in on a few things?" Jake asked, his whole body tense.

The door closed behind Daire with no sound and without Daire even touching it. He followed Jake into the room. When they came to a stop in the middle of the large space, Daire studied him almost long enough to piss Jake off.

"Regardless who the male is," Daire finally said, "Cassia must be taken through the transition or the force of her own powers will kill her."

Jake rubbed his temples before dropping his hand to his side. "You just said 'regardless who the male is.' Are you telling me it never had to be a full-blooded Elvin guy?"

"That was the Guardian's choosing." Daire's expression remained placid. "But the one who takes her through the transition must be a male who can survive the full power of Cassiandra's magic. As a human, you do not have that ability."

Jake dug into his pocket and pulled out the tube with the crap in it that looked like sludge. "Except with this."

Daire studied the tube for a long moment. "Interesting that the Guardian is allowing this mating." Jake repocketed the tube as Daire continued. "I have never known her to change her decisions once made."

Jake didn't bother sharing the fact that the Great Guardian's own mother apparently had had something to do with it. "Maybe she likes my winning personality," he said instead.

"Perhaps that is it." Daire gave a hint of a smile. "Although I find it most unlikely."

"No kidding." Jake sat on one of the hard-backed chairs that Daire motioned to. "Let's cut the bull," Jake said as Daire reclined in a nearby chair. "What kind of consequences are we dealing with after Cassia goes through this transition?"

"I do not know, now that the Great Guardian is displeased." Daire shook his head. "I have never seen her angry in all of my centuries."

"Guess Mom's not too happy with her daughter going for the guy across the tracks," Jake said. Daire raised his eyebrows, but Jake chose to continue his questions about the transition. "Just tell me if the Guardian is going to hurt Cassia in any way if we go through with this."

"Harm, no." Daire sighed. "Difficult choices, yes."

"What—" Jake started, but Daire held up his hand to stop him.

"It matters not any longer," Daire said. "I must instruct you in helping the Princess through her transition."

Jake leaned forward, his forearms braced on his thighs. "I'm listening."

"Sexual relations are among the most powerful of magics," Daire said. "When Cassiandra is aroused in any fashion, her magic will be almost uncontrollable until her sexual energy is leashed and takes her to the next level of her abilities.

"When a man enters her," he continued, "it will amplify the strength of her ascending powers. They will reach the same pinnacle, where they would have eventually taken over her mind and body. But with the right male to guide her through the transition, the magic can be harnessed and redirected."

Hair prickled at the nape of Jake's neck. "What you're getting at is, by taking care of this during sex she'll have the control she needs over that power instead of it taking control of her."

"That is so," Daire said with a slow nod.

Jake felt the pressure of the vial like a lead weight against his leg through his jeans pocket. "What do I have to do?"

"Begin slowly." Daire's eyes remained fixed on Jake. "The contents of the vial will allow you to absorb the flux of power that Cassiandra will radiate. You must hold that power within you and not allow it to flow into her until you both reach completion."

After everything Jake had been through over the last months, this was the strangest moment of his life. Completely surreal. "So this happens when she climaxes."

"You must reach orgasm at the same time. As your seed spills into her, so will her power. You will be feeding it back to her and she will be able to control it fully."

"Can she get pregnant?" Jake asked as the thought occurred to him.

Daire shook his head. "Only if she chooses to, but not during her transition. There is far too much of an exchange of magic to allow conception."

Jake scrubbed his hand over his face, thinking about the unreality of it all. Definitely something he'd never dreamed he'd ever go through. "Any words of wisdom?"

"You will need your strength, so eat well," Daire said. "Drink the contents of the vial when you are finished.

"Whatever happens, do not lose consciousness," he added with an intense expression. "If her magic remains within you, you both will die."

CASSIA'S HEART POUNDED AS SHE PACED the length of her chamber. What was Daire telling Jake? What would he have to go through? Would it be painful for him? Or pleasurable?

She prayed that whatever happened would not involve any kind of pain on his part.

Beneath one of the arched windows, the handmaidens had finished spreading out a small feast, along with a flagon of wine and two gold goblets. Despite rich smells of baked breads straight from the ovens, along with the delicious aromas of vegetables, puddings, and fresh fruits, she wasn't hungry. The thought of eating added to the churning in her stomach that increased more and more as she paced.

Jake should be here by now. Her white robes caressed her bare skin and swirled around her feet as she turned to walk back toward the door—

And there he was.

Cassia came to a complete stop and couldn't move as she met his blue eyes. She caught her breath as she took in all of him. From his short dark hair to his broad shoulders, to the perfection of the rest of his muscular body that a snug Elvin tunic and breeches accentuated. His hair was damp as if he had just bathed, and he was barefoot, too.

Jake's throat worked as he visibly swallowed. "Hey, Princess."

"Jake!" So much joy burst through every cell of Cassia's body that golden light filled her bedchamber. She ran to him and flung her arms around his neck.

He caught her by her waist and held her tight against him. A sensual smile curved his lips, and he brushed his mouth over hers in a soft, sweet kiss.

"I can hardly believe you're here." She drew away, and already sparks snapped in the air around them. "I love you so much."

He placed his forehead against hers. "You already know how I feel about you."

"Say it." Her entire body sizzled with magic just by being close to him. "I want to hear it again. And again."

"I love you." He kissed her and murmured against her lips, "Damn but I love you."

Cassia pressed her face against the soft fabric of his tunic and smiled as the warm, spicy male scent seemed to fill her every pore.

Jake gave a low laugh that she felt rumble in his chest. She tilted her head to look up at him. "I didn't think I could perform on demand." He moved his hands up her sides and caressed her upper arms. "But just being with you—God, you make me forget about everything but you."

"I know what you mean." Magic glowed around them, continuing to crackle like logs in a fire. "I don't care about anything but you." She sobered. "As long as you don't get hurt."

He tweaked a lock of her hair. "Your mother may not approve of me, but I don't think she'd kill me."

"You're right." Her smile turned into a wry grimace. "Although I had my doubts when we had our little 'talk' with her." Cassia shook her head. "I thought my mother would fry you after a couple of your comments. Especially the one about her playing some kind of game."

Jake winced. "Guess I got a little carried away."

"Uh-huh." Cassia glanced at the table laden with food. "Kellyn was sent to tell me that you needed to eat to build up your strength."

"Daire said the same thing." He studied the table. "I don't suppose there's a chance any of the food is poisoned?"

Cassia slipped her arms from around his neck, took one of his hands, and squeezed it. "She would have killed you already if she wanted you dead."

"That's reassuring."

She couldn't help smiling as she led him to where the handmaidens had positioned the chairs across the table from each other. Jake held out one of the chairs and assisted her. Rather than sitting on the other side of the table, he dragged his chair away, the chair's feet scraping the wood floor. He moved it near her and seated himself so that they were at the same corner, close enough to touch.

She could almost swear Jake's hand trembled a little as he poured wine from the flagon into her goblet, and then his, before he set the flagon back on the table. Her own hands definitely shook.

He raised his goblet and she did the same. Words neither of them spoke hung in the air as they touched their goblets together before they each took a drink of the wine. The berry-flavored sweetness flowed over her tongue and warmth traveled straight to her stomach.

After they set their goblets on the table, Jake picked up a piece of blue melon and brought it to her lips. His eyes held hers as she took the fruit into her mouth.

After she swallowed the melon she couldn't help a teasing grin. "I never pegged you, Jake Macgregor, as a romantic."

"Saw it in a movie once." He grinned back. "Some chick-flick."

She laughed. "Glad to see you're such a quick study."

"You have no idea." He fed her a blackberry this time, its tart sweetness even better because he slipped his forefinger into her mouth with it.

She sucked, but then he replaced his finger with his lips and tongue, sharing the taste of the blackberry.

Cassia found her appetite as she and Jake ate their meal. A constant swirl of golden magic surrounded them as her arousal magnified. Dampness grew between her thighs and it felt like many of the sparks traveled from her navel downward. Her nipples tightened and her breasts felt heavy and ached. Her skin glowed as if fire raced along her arms.

When he finished eating, he wiped his fingers on a napkin. "You have always been beautiful to me." He set the napkin on the table as he kept his gaze on her. "But now—you look like an angel. No, more like a goddess." He gave her a teasing smile. "Which you are, apparently, since Anu is your grandmother."

Heat flushed throughout Cassia's body, only making the swirl of magic around them more intense. It grew almost cloudy, and she could barely see the room through it anymore.

She cocked an eyebrow. "You thought I was beautiful even when I played the bumbling witch?"

"Yeah." He nodded, but his expression remained serious. "From the time we first met, I felt there was something different about you. I knew you had secrets and I was the one who was meant to find out exactly what they were."

Jake's words sent a spiraling sensation through her. He wasn't even touching her at this moment, and still the magic swelled and threatened to take her over.

For a moment she was puzzled when he reached into a pocket of his breeches. Then her stomach twisted as he brought out the glass vial the Great Guardian had given him. With an expression of distrust, he uncorked it.

Immediately the thick black substance absorbed the magic in the air. What had looked like sludge shimmered and turned into smooth, golden liquid. Jake met her gaze as he raised the vial to his lips, closed his eyes, and drained the contents.

Cassia's heart pounded in her throat as she watched him remain still for several seconds. When he finally opened his eyes he smiled at her. "It tasted like your scent, your perfume. As if your essence had been captured when I uncorked the vial."

"You are the romantic." A jittery sensation prickled her body even as she teased him. "Do you feel all right?" she asked as he set the vial on the table.

"Nothing's changed." His voice came out in a low rumble. "I want you as much as I ever have."

He stood, the legs of his chair scraping the floor again, only this time the chair almost toppled over. He caught it, then came around behind her and helped her move her chair back. Before she could stand, he held out his hand.

Her whole body vibrated as the gold light filled with snapping sparks obscured her entire bedchamber from sight. Something rattled and hit the floor with a loud crash.

So what?

She didn't care if they destroyed the entire room. The whole palace for that matter.

"Forget what your mother said." Jake gripped both of her hands. "Get us out of here where it's just you and me."

Cassia smiled. She knew exactly where to take them.

She squeezed his fingers and they entered the transference.

CHAPTER THIRTY-THREE

SHIFTING SAND BENEATH HIS BARE FEET was the first thing Jake felt, followed by a cool wind off the Pacific Ocean that stirred Cassia's hair around her face. From where they stood, he had a clear view of the Golden Gate Bridge and the lights glowing across the bay in the dark night.

Jake didn't feel the usual aftereffects of the transference, and the cold, salty air didn't bother him. Cassia's golden magic whirled around them, probably blocking out most of the chill.

For a moment they stood, their gazes locked, still gripping each other's hands. The glow of her magic made it easy to see her stunning beauty and the turquoise blue of her eyes. His body was so tight, so ready for her. He'd waited so long to be with her.

"I don't recognize this beach," Jake said over the sound of waves slapping the shore. "And I know this city backward and forward."

"This is a place sacred to the D'Anu." Cassia released one of his hands to reach up and trail her fingers along his jawline. Her touch tingled against his skin. "The D'Anu discovered it and used powerful magic to hide it from human sight long before the first settlers arrived."

Jake didn't care about hidden beaches, witches, Elves, or any other beings at that moment. All of his focus narrowed in on Cassia.

He caught her face in his hands and lowered his mouth to hers. The sweetness of her lips and her taste had nothing to do with the fruit or wine they'd had earlier. There was something so innately a part of Cassia that it was almost like she was a fine scotch that made him dizzy with longing and need.

Jake slid his hands from her face, down her slender throat to her shoulders. Her robe felt like silk beneath his fingertips and his erection hardened even more as he realized she was naked beneath all of that material. Soft, satiny skin he wanted to explore with his hands, his lips, his tongue.

Cassia's moan reverberated through him as they kissed and her hands moved over his body. Fire burned through him wherever she touched, and he knew it wasn't just her magic that sparked around them.

God, he needed to feel her, taste her. Everywhere. His cock strained and ached against the snug fabric of the Elvin clothing, even though it had more give than his jeans. He grasped her ass and brought her tightly to him so that he could press his cock against her belly.

At the same time he trailed his lips down her neck, flicking his tongue out and tasting the light sweetness of her skin as he inhaled her vanilla-and-spice scent. Cassia gasped and moaned as she tilted her head back and sank against him.

Jake groaned. From the moment he'd known he wanted her, he'd planned to take it slow. She deserved to experience all the pleasure he could give her the first time they made love.

Now that she was in his arms, such intense, primal need gripped him that he shook from it.

Slow down, Macgregor.

Jake drew in a harsh breath as he reached for her robe and pushed it off her shoulders. A burst of magic slammed into him as she let the robe slide down her arms. Sparks flew like fireworks all over the beach.

He reeled from the power of her arousal, but then his body absorbed it. Held it.

The potion was working.

But Christ. If her magic pummeled him whenever he touched her, he might be dead before he had a chance to sink his cock inside her.

The robe fell to the sand and Jake stared at her body, which glowed in the light of her magic.

"You—God, Cassia." Jake reached for her breasts and cupped them, her nipples hard as he stroked his thumbs over them. The moment he did, more magic flowed into him, heating his body through and cutting off the rest of what he was going to say.

"I want to do this now. To feel you inside me." Cassia moaned as she leaned into his touch. "I don't want to wait."

"We're taking it slow, honey." Jake met her lips with his as he pinched her nipples.

She was throwing off so much magic that raw power began to swirl inside him. He slid one hand down her flat belly to her mound. Her star birthmark tingled beneath his palm as he skimmed over it.

When he slipped his fingers into her wetness and heat, her next wave of energy made his legs tremble. Then he realized it wasn't him trembling—the ground was shaking.

He stroked her clit and she cried out, while rocks slid down the embankment, tumbling over one another until they made soft thuds in the sand.

If this kept up, neither one of them would live much longer.

"Let's take our time, honey." Jake tweaked one of her nipples as he slipped one of his fingers into her tight, wet—

His brain was about to melt. He wasn't going to be able to think much longer.

She clenched his shoulders with her hands, her grip so tight she'd probably leave imprints where her fingers were. "I don't know how much more of this I can take."

From the rumbling of the earth around them, Jake didn't know how much more *San Francisco* might be able to take. As for himself, he was on course for exploding on the spot.

Something inside his mind told him she wasn't giving off as much magic as she should be—despite the whole earthquake thing. He needed to draw more from her to be able to feed it back when it was time.

Jake released her and took a step out of her grip, and she gasped. Her chest rose and fell in the glow of her magic. "Please don't stop."

"Hold on." He pulled his shirt over his head and shoved down his pants, glad he didn't have to mess with briefs, or socks and shoes. He was naked and had her in his arms before she could say another word.

THE GALE OF MAGIC WHIRLING through Cassia made it difficult for her to breathe. She tried to tamp her powers so she wouldn't hurt Jake, but the more she wanted him the harder it became.

"Don't hold back," he murmured in her ear as he pressed his warm body against hers. "Let go. Just don't flatten the city or there won't be anything left to save."

Cassia would have laughed if there wasn't so much desire and need flaming through her that she was afraid she would burn them both to ash.

Jake kissed the line of her neck as his warm, callused palms cupped her breasts and he pinched her nipples with his rough fingers. Her body trembled and the ground trembled along with her.

Even his incredible male scent caused more desire to rush through her. She thought she heard a tree above the embankment crackle and smelled smoke twining with the scent of brine on the air. She barely had the presence of mind to snuff it out with her magic before she did set fire to everything around them.

"Jake, please." Moisture stung at her eyes and she felt like she really was going to explode. "I can't take this much longer. It's too much."

"You haven't let go of enough of your magic," he murmured as his mouth neared her breast. She wondered how he could know that, but no longer cared when his warm mouth possessed her nipple and he sucked.

It felt like he was sucking some of her magic through her nipples as he moved from one to the other. His skin now let off a golden glow that slowly intensified with every draw on her magic, with everything he did to her. His Marine tattoo seemed to glow even brighter than the rest of him.

He moved his mouth between her breasts and began to kiss his way to her belly over her star birthmark, nearing her mound. The closer he came to her wet folds, the more she shook, as did the ground. Just the memory of his mouth on her hard nub, when he gave her the first orgasm she'd ever had, sent more energy from her into him.

The amount of her power that he was absorbing—could he survive if she released too much magic?

He swiped his tongue along her slit and she cried out. As he tasted her folds and sucked on her hard nub, she tilted her head and shouted to the goddess. She didn't know when she'd slid her hands into his hair, but she gripped it in her fists and held on as she let out countless cries and whimpers from the incredible pleasure searing her body.

Tears rolled down her cheeks, the wet trails quickly drying in the cool wind. The pleasure in her body became so intense that she gave off more and more of her magic. Her legs barely had the strength to remain standing.

She was climbing and climbing. Blind now to anything but the pleasure of Jake's mouth and tongue.

And then it was too much.

A nearly blinding flash cut across the sky, and she realized it was her.

Cassia screamed as she hit a climax so powerful that her knees gave out and all of her magic left her in a rush she couldn't control.

Vaguely she was aware of Jake taking her down to the sand, then the feel of her silk robe beneath her back. Pulse after pulse of her orgasm continued, and her body jerked with every throb.

She struggled to breathe and focus as she looked up at him. He glowed so brightly it was like staring at a god. Maybe the sun god, Lugh, himself.

"Are you with me, honey?" His voice sounded hoarse, strained as he held himself above her. The hardness of his erection pressed against her folds as he settled between her thighs. "Are you all right?"

She found the strength to nod, the silk robe sliding under her head with the movement. The haziness in her mind cleared a little.

Jake glowed so much that he radiated strength and power. His body shook with it.

Then Cassia realized her magic was gone.

Completely gone.

When she had climaxed she had given Jake *everything* she had.

Fear crawled up her throat. She had never been without magic, without power infusing every cell of her body. For a moment she thought she would never get it back and she couldn't keep tears from rolling down the sides of her face from the fear.

No magic? How could she live without it?

She was helpless now. Completely vulnerable.

Jake kissed her tears away, flicking out his tongue and taking her tears inside him like he had taken her magic.

A flash of what it would feel like to never have magic again made her heart pound low in her throat.

"Are you ready?" Jake nudged his cock against the entrance to her core.

Desire spiraled through her again and just having him there, ready to enter her and be completely with her, brought her back to reality and chased every bit of fear away. She didn't care about anything but Jake, and being with him completely, fully.

She nodded and widened her thighs so that he was seated more firmly between them.

His erection moved in an inch and she gasped. The thickness of him sent more waves of need through her. No longer enhanced by magic. Just the power of pure desire of a woman for a man.

Jake slid himself further inside her and she cried out at the brief burst of pain that followed his entry.

"Am I hurting you?" he said, immediately halting, concern in his voice.

"No." She shook her head and managed to speak. "It's beautiful. It's wonderful. You're wonderful."

He smiled, his skin glowing with so much magic she felt it radiating from him.

Moans of pleasure rose up within her as he sank inside her inch by inch.

The moment he was buried fully inside her core she felt her own power radiating from him. He began moving in and out of her. With every slow thrust he released small waves of magic that she absorbed.

It was so perfect having him there. Having him inside. Having him be the one to take her magic and return it to her. Letting her harness it so that it no longer escaped in wild bursts of power. She could already feel the control she was gaining over her magic.

The glow of his skin lessened with every thrust as he released her magic back into her body. She moved her hands down to his muscled ass and dug her fingers into his skin as she fought to bring him tighter against her, deeper inside her. Every time he drove himself so that his groin met hers, she moaned and squirmed beneath him.

His biceps bulged and trembled as he held his weight off of her, his hands braced on the robe on either side of her body. Despite the cool air, sweat rolled down the sides of his face, and his hair was soaked with it. Whenever he thrust, she felt him so deep, as if his cock reached her navel.

"God, it's so hard to keep it slow." Jake's voice came out even lower and hoarser than before.

"I want it faster." Cassia brought her hips up to meet his, trying to encourage him. "My body is burning with magic and heat, and need for you. Please, Jake."

"Can't." It sounded like he said the word through clenched teeth. "Not yet."

She wanted to ask why not, but more magic surged through her, and she whimpered and moaned. Burning, tightening sensations coiled in her belly. She began to feel light-headed, and sounds faded until all she heard was his voice.

"It's time, honey." His voice shook. "Time to take the rest of it, but take it slow."

Cassia nodded. She closed her eyes and concentrated on the feel of his cock sliding in and out of her, her magic heating her through as it came back into her body.

Sparks began snapping again in the air around them. Not out of control like before, but still a part of the climax she was heading for.

"I can't wait any longer." Cassia's entire body shook and she whimpered. "I've got to come."

"Hold." Jake sounded like he could barely speak. "Just a few seconds."

She fought to keep her climax from ripping her apart. She gritted her teeth, her whole body continuing to shake uncontrollably.

Just as the last ribbon of control began to slide through her fingers, Jake shouted, "Now, Cassia. Come *now*!"

Her scream carried out over the pounding of the surf against the shore. Heat and power pulsated through her as Jake's seed spurted inside her, giving her the rest of the magic he'd been holding.

His mouth took hers in a fierce kiss that cut off the rest of her cry.

The magic inside her wanted to escape again, wanted to spin around them and burn everything to the ground. But she now had the strength to rein it in, even as she was falling apart from her orgasm.

His cock continued to throb as more of his essence spilled into her. She met his gaze as she realized he was staring at her. His eyes seemed unfocused and he looked like he was going to lose consciousness.

"Cassia," he said in a rough whisper, just as he slumped on top of her.

"AND WHATEVER HAPPENS," Daire's voice rang through Jake's mind, "do not lose consciousness."

Easy for him to say.

Jake did his best to keep his full weight off of Cassia while struggling not to black out. His entire world shrank to Cassia and a pinpoint of light. The crash of waves against the shore sounded muffled, like his ears had been crammed with the sand they were lying on.

Stay here, Macgregor, he told himself, even as he fought to breathe.

Distantly, as if dozens of blankets had been piled on his head, he heard, *"Jake!"* over and over. Something was shaking him. Hard.

No, someone.

Cassia.

It was like he was swimming from the bottom of the ocean floor as he struggled to come up. He couldn't breathe. Could barely see. An image wavered above him, as if he was seeing something through dark water, but surrounded by light.

His chest hurt from the pressure of the ocean against his chest as he pushed himself upward toward the figure and the light. He had to get, had to get . . .

Jake broke the surface of the water, sucking in a deep breath and his vision returning. He hadn't been underwater. No, he was lying on his back now, still inside Cassia, only she was on top. His cock hadn't stopped pulsing in her core.

The cold ocean air blasted his body. Her magic no longer circled them, buffering them from the chill wind.

Her voice sounded strained and filled with fear as she spoke. "Are you back? You're shivering. You must be freezing."

Cassia rose up so that she straddled his hips. She ran her hand just above his skin and warmth entered his chest.

At the same time, her magic wove a cocoon around both of them, and it gave off enough light that he could see her features. Soft heat radiated inside and out of his body and he felt nothing but the satisfaction of an orgasm that had just about blown his mind.

So there *was* such a thing as a mind-blowing orgasm.

Energy returned to Jake in a rush, and he felt like he could swim out into the icy Pacific and take on a great white shark single-handedly.

No better aphrodisiac than surviving deadly sex.

He grinned at Cassia, and she laughed as he rolled them both over so that she was on her back again and he was between her thighs. She was so wet and ready as she wrapped her legs around his hips.

The same energy surged back into his cock, making it so rigid he thought he'd explode. Magic had nothing to do with the way he felt at this moment.

"You're mine, Cassia." Jake drove his erection inside her, hard and fierce, and she cried out in surprise at his sudden thrust. "I think I've known that forever."

Her lips parted but he didn't give her a chance to say anything as he took her mouth with his. This time he fucked her fast and hard. They'd made love slow the first time. Now it felt like he needed to brand her as his own. To show her and whatever god, goddess, Guardian—any being who thought he or she had a say in the matter—that Cassia was his forever, no matter what anyone else thought.

Cassia held on to him as she thrashed and moaned beneath him. "More, Jake. More!"

He drove his tongue into her mouth and she tightened her legs around his waist as he took her, almost mercilessly. When she climaxed he raised his head, parting from her so that he could hear her scream.

The sound of Cassia's voice and the way she cried out his name was almost more than he could take without coming himself.

Maintain, Macgregor.

Her body trembled and the inside walls of her core clamped down on his cock with spasm after spasm. He ground his teeth, holding back his own orgasm, not ready to end her pleasure as he dragged out her climax by not slowing his thrusts.

She cried out again as the walls of her core continued to pulsate and grip his cock. "It feels almost too good to take anymore."

Jake gave a grunt of satisfaction before he let out a shout when his own orgasm slammed into him. He pumped his hips a few more times as his come spurted inside her, and he thought he might be close to blacking out with no hope of return.

He finally stopped and stared down into Cassia's turquoise blue eyes and at her brilliant smile. They both breathed harder than the first time they'd climaxed, and he realized she'd dug her nails deep into his biceps again.

Sweat covered him in the warmth of the magical cocoon around them, and he smelled the scent of their sex and the salt in the sand. And Cassia's skin. God how he loved her scent. Pure. Sweet. Womanly.

She parted her lips, but again he didn't give her a chance to say anything. He kissed her hard and long, and his cock stiffened inside her a third time.

Damn, maybe it *was* magic.

No. The only magic now was the love that wove them both together.

This time he took her slowly, and they held each other's gazes, unable to look away.

CHAPTER THIRTY-FOUR

A SUDDEN SHIFT IN THE ENERGY of the Otherworlds told Daire it had happened.

Jake had taken Cassia through the transition.

Daire had thought he would feel pain and sorrow at the loss of the one who had been promised to him centuries ago. He had enjoyed many women through the years as he waited for her, always knowing one day she would be his.

But as he sat alone in the front room of what Kat had called her apartment, he found that an even stranger emotion touched his consciousness.

He shifted on the chair. He wasn't sure "pleased" was the right word, or even "happy," but Daire was perhaps glad that Cassia had found someone who meant so much to her. A man willing to sacrifice his life to be with her.

He sighed. *Humans.*

But when Kat walked from a hallway into the room, his cock went instantly rigid at the erotic sight of her.

Goddess bless humans.

No, erotic did not begin to express the way she looked. Her hips swayed gently as she moved toward him. Her short hair gleamed beneath the lights, and her lips were glossy and red.

But that wasn't what had his full attention. It was what she was wearing. Something black, silky, and lacy, like nothing he had ever seen on any Elvin woman.

She was bared from her shoulders down to the material that barely covered her breasts. His mouth watered at the hint of a rosy areola, and even more as his gaze traveled from her breasts, drinking in how the fabric clung to her waist, only went as far as the top of her thighs, and barely covered her sex.

"It's a merry widow," she said as she reached the chair he sat upon. "Do you like it?"

Daire swallowed and nodded, unable to talk because his tongue was now too big for his mouth.

She smiled, a glint in her dark eyes. "Cat got your tongue?"

A Kat, yes. She had stolen his words.

Her smile was seductive as she straddled his lap and eased herself down so that her barely covered folds rested on the enormous ridge of his cock.

He had wanted her from the moment he met her, and now she presented herself, wrapped like a gift.

Kat tipped her head back and rocked her hips against his, her sex grinding against his erection.

Daire groaned and decided to unwrap his gift—immediately.

She made a sound between a gasp and a moan as he tugged the top of her "merry widow" down and released her small, firm, beautiful breasts. He immediately brought his lips to her nipple and covered it with his mouth.

Kat uttered little mewling sounds as he sucked each nipple and grabbed her ass. He thrust his hips up, willing to bet his cock was hard enough to punch through his breeches and the fabric covering the place he wanted most to be at this very moment.

"Come on, Daire." She reached between them, untied his breeches, and had his cock in her small, warm hand before he had a chance to breathe. He had not known a human could be that fast. "I refuse to wait."

"Far be it from me to argue," he said in a voice so deep he hardly recognized it as his own.

She laughed and rose up just enough to pull the thin material covering her folds and reveal what he wanted so very much at that moment.

And she gifted it to him.

Kat gave a throaty cry of pleasure as she sank on his cock. She began riding him, her hands in his hair while her fingers traced the ridges and points of his ears.

Daire thrust up in time with the movements of her hips.

The way she touched the tips of his ears sent another thrill of lust through him.

They moved at a steady rhythm, Kat's breasts bouncing enticingly above the black-lace-and-silk creation. He had to suck them again and again, and then kiss her over and over. She was no innocent, and he loved the way she knew how to give pleasure at the same time she took pleasure.

An odd roaring grew in his ears and he charged toward his orgasm.

Kat climaxed before he did, and she let out sharp cries as she squirmed on his lap.

Daire gave a fierce smile, for some reason feeling a sense of triumph at making her wriggle and moan as he continued to thrust in and out of her.

When he allowed himself to climax, a storm of sensations blasted through him. His vision darkened, like traveling through the veil from Otherworld at blinding speed. Darkness, then light. But incredible energy accompanied his orgasm and he did not want to stop.

He wanted to be inside her forever. To move inside her forever.

When Kat sank against him with a long, soft moan, he slowed, then stopped, his seed completely spent.

He nudged her face with his own and took her mouth with his.

Humans. He would never underestimate their power again, magic or no.

CHAPTER THIRTY-FIVE

KILLING HAS A WAY OF MAKING *one feel powerful. Murder even more so.*

I take dried yew leaves and grind them to a fine powder with a pestle in a small stone mortar. This will work perfectly.

Yes, there's a difference between "killing" and "murder."

When no one has been looking, I have killed during the battles with Darkwolf, mostly people on the Alliance's side. But killing during battle isn't the same as murder because it's not personal. It's a part of war.

Actually committing murder, doing it out of passion or anger on a personal level—now that's power.

I smile as I take the finely ground yew powder and carefully tamp it into one of Silver's handmade teabags with her favorite ingredients, including cinnamon sticks and other spices. Silver is so predictable when it comes to her tea. She has a cup or two every morning.

That will make this easy.

When it comes to murder, I felt the difference when I strangled Mackenzie. Now, as I make my plans to kill Silver and her baby, I feel almost giddy.

It's exhilarating. A rush like no other.

I haven't told Darkwolf. Will he be pleased when I tell him of her death? Or does he still have a stupid obsession for her?

The thought that he would feel any regret for her death burns my insides. I am even more determined than ever to make her my next victim.

Oh-so-perfect Silver Ashcroft. The bitch.

I grind my teeth as I close the handmade teabag and tie it off the way Silver always does.

To witness the emotional devastation of her filthy D'Danann husband, Hawk, and her blood sister, Copper, will be the ultimate high.

I had considered hemlock to poison her, but decided on yew. Long ago pregnant women wanting an abortion took yew, and not only aborted their babies, but the women died, too.

At first Silver will feel nauseated. Then she'll start vomiting, go into convulsions, and lose the baby. Within an hour or so she'll begin hallucinating before going into shock and then a coma. Then her poor little heart will give out.

This should be fun to watch.

CHAPTER THIRTY-SIX

INCREDIBLE JOY SWIRLED THROUGH CASSIA as she and Jake finished dressing. She couldn't stop smiling, and he didn't seem to be able to stop either.

After he shook the sand out of his clothing and brushed it off the back of her robe, he kissed her with such sweet languor that he stole her very breath.

When he finished kissing her, she sighed and snuggled against his chest. "I don't suppose we can stay here and pretend it's just the two of us on some Otherworld."

"I wish." Jake pressed his lips to her hair. "How long have we been gone?"

Concern spread through her like cold heat for the Alliance and the city—never mind what could happen on a broader scope if they didn't stop Darkwolf. And soon. "Two days."

He shook his head. "Too long." Then he twisted strands of her hair around his finger. "But every minute of it was precious."

"We'd better get back to headquarters." Cassia took both of Jake's hands. "I'll get us as close to the showers as I can."

Cassia gripped his hands tighter as they moved through the darkness of the transference, and he squeezed her fingers hard. When they arrived, it was on the cool concrete floor in front of the bathroom to the showers.

They nearly bumped into Rhiannon and the PSF officer she'd been teamed with. Rhiannon kept her gaze averted, and some of the happiness that had been inside Cassia faded. It felt like her heart was being shredded to see her Coven sisters come to this.

She swallowed back the pain as Rhiannon and the officer

brushed past. Rhiannon's Shadows reached for Cassia as they parted, their ghostly hands sliding over her skin.

Her heart thundered, and she watched until Rhiannon and the officer rounded a corner and vanished.

Cassia shuddered. Could Rhiannon . . . ?

"What's wrong?" Jake asked as they entered the bathroom and shut the door behind them.

"You mean beyond Darkwolf trying to wipe out the Alliance, as well as destroy and take over our city? And one of my Coven sisters being a murderer?" Cassia shook out more sand from her robe. "Nothing."

"Hey." Jake caught her by the chin and brushed his lips over hers. "I have more confidence than ever that we'll make it. Together."

She let herself forget about reality again as she and Jake shared a long, luxurious shower, where they washed each other's bodies before he took her yet another time under the warm water pounding down on them.

Cassia sighed with pure happiness as she felt the cool tile against her back and his cock throbbing inside her core. He was firmly between her thighs, her legs hooked around his hips.

She'd never been so happy in all her centuries of living.

A smile lit her mouth as he slid out of her and settled her onto her feet.

Jake turned off the water and they both stepped out of the shower. Cassia dried them both with her magic before she spoke the Elvin word for "clean" and vanished all the sand from their Elvin clothing.

When they were dressed, Jake started to kiss her.

She ripped herself away from Jake's embrace and doubled over from sheer agony cramping her belly.

Her sight blurred and she saw the kitchen around her.

Silver's teacup—her favorite porcelain one with the colorful sprigs of wildflowers—crashed to the floor, the sound ringing through the room. Shards scattered across the concrete and tea splattered everywhere.

Cassia screamed and flung herself through the transference.

At once she arrived in the kitchen, and terror nearly suffocated her as she saw Silver on her knees. Silver threw up before she dropped onto her back on the floor. She writhed and screamed, clutching her hands to her belly.

Cassia dove to her knees beside Silver. Porcelain shards sliced into her skin through the robe, but she barely noticed.

Tears flowed down Cassia's cheeks as she focused entirely on Silver. Cassia raised her hands above Silver and sent all the magic she could into her friend, to ease her pain and to find out what was happening.

The scent of yew came to Cassia over the powerful acidic smell of Silver's vomit.

Yew. She had been poisoned with yew.

Dear goddess.

Silver's face paled to deathly white and sweat covered her forehead. She screamed and clutched her belly as she began crying out things that didn't make sense. She was already hallucinating.

Vaguely Cassia was aware that Silver's husband, Hawk, was now on the floor holding her head and upper shoulders in his lap. The big warrior cried, tears rolling down his harsh face as he begged Cassia to save his wife and his baby.

The baby. Dear Anu, please be with Silver and her baby, and guide me through what I must do.

Cassia called forth all the power she now controlled as a fully ascended Guardian. The transition had given her so much power she vibrated with it. Even glowed with it.

"Hold her feet." Cassia's own voice sounded far away as she spoke to someone close by. "Keep her still."

She had to get the poison out of Silver and the baby's bodies.

Cassia held one hand over Silver's chest and another over her abdomen.

She closed her eyes and let silence envelop her. Cries and shouts in the kitchen vanished. She began drawing the poison from Silver's body, siphoning it out of her. Cassia captured the poison into herself, caging it in a magical vial with her powers.

Silver fell silent. Pain like knives stabbing Cassia's heart nearly sent her reeling as she felt Silver's lifeforce slipping away.

"No!" Cassia screamed, and opened her eyes. Silver barely moved any longer, her eyes glazing over.

With all the power Cassia had, with one tremendous swell of energy, she sucked every bit of the remaining yew poison out of Silver and into her own body.

Cassia didn't bother to contain the poison with magic. No time. She drew every last taint of yew into herself.

Not a single drop of the poison remained in Silver.

Nothing.

But was it too late?

Cassia struggled against the pain of the poison now in her own system as she sent healing energy into Silver. Cassia grasped Silver's fading lifeforce and thrust it back into her. The same for the baby. The unborn infant's tiny lifeforce had also almost been depleted, but Cassia captured it and returned it to the baby.

Cassia's gaze wavered and she clutched her own abdomen as she tried to focus on Silver's face. Silver's color was slowly returning to her cheeks and her eyes no longer looked glazed. She now held her hands to her belly, over her baby, as if protecting the infant, not like she was in pain.

Hawk stroked Silver's face with his large hands, saying something and still crying. Whatever it was sounded garbled as Cassia's world started to tip.

The urge to throw up became overwhelming, and Cassia turned her head to the side and retched.

Pain, unbelievable pain, wrenched Cassia's body in two and she dropped to her side. Somewhere in the distance she heard herself scream and Jake's frantic voice calling her name.

Images started appearing behind Cassia's eyelids, but she barely saw them through the haze of pain.

A mortar and a pestle. Dried yew leaves being ground into fine powder.

Pale, delicate fingers wrapped around the pestle, and the

thoughts in her head shifted from angry to amused and back again.

Rage. Hatred. Blackness.

Painful thoughts of a past haunted her every act. Drove her to prove she wasn't weak.

That she had power.

Cassia saw her tortured memories and flinched. Memories of a young girl with her skirt up, her panties down, and someone with a rough stick beating her buttocks as the girl screamed for forgiveness.

Thoughts flashed back to the present.

The delicate hands in Cassia's vision tamped the yew powder into a handmade teabag and Cassia heard a familiar laugh.

Then she saw the traitor's face.

Shock numbed Cassia's entire body, paralyzing her.

No. No!

Cassia had known that witch was as suspect as any, but to see it for herself . . .

She threw up again. The acidic smell and taste somehow eased her back to the kitchen.

Perspiration coated her beneath her robe as well as her face, and her whole body shook.

All of the witches except Silver surrounded Cassia. Their combined healing energy vanquished the remnants of the yew poisoning.

Except one of the witches. The traitor. She wasn't trying at all. Just pretending.

Cassia opened her eyes and realized Jake was holding her, murmuring to her.

But Cassia could only focus on one thing. One person.

Her name came out in a choked gasp.

"Alyssa."

Everyone turned to look at Alyssa, who paled.

"It's Alyssa." Cassia coughed again before saying as loudly as she could, "Alyssa murdered Mackenzie and just tried to kill Silver. She's the traitor."

For a moment stunned silence filled the room, as if no one could digest Cassia's words.

Cassia raised one of her hands and tried to use her power to capture Alyssa.

Too weak.

Alyssa scowled and said, "Bitch," as Cassia threw out another burst of power, this time stronger.

But the murdering traitor vanished.

"Alyssa?" Copper whispered as she turned to the other witches. She shook her head as if she was hallucinating.

No one seemed to be able to find any words for a long, almost endless moment.

"I thought it had to be a mistake." Copper spoke again. "I kept telling myself Darkwolf really did find his way in here and killed Mackenzie." Tears filled her eyes and started trickling down her face when she blinked. "I never did believe it could be any one of us."

Copper hugged Sydney and, to Cassia's surprise, Rhiannon hugged Hannah, whom she'd barely tolerated until recently. Then everyone hugged and cried, including the very weak Silver and Cassia.

"I don't think I'll ever get over this." Sydney took off her glasses and wiped her eyes with the backs of her hands.

"I know I won't." Copper looked at her blood sister, Silver. "And I'll never forgive Alyssa."

"She must be possessed or something." Rhiannon dabbed at her nose with a tissue from a box that was now being passed around the kitchen. "How else can it be explained?"

Jake helped Cassia to a sitting position and she leaned her back against him. She had a hard time focusing on anything but Alyssa, but noticed someone had used magic to clean all the vomit off the floor.

"I saw into her mind." Cassia took a tissue from the box and clenched it in her fist. Alyssa's feelings whirled through Cassia, making her want to vomit again.

"Hatred, jealousy, darkness." Cassia tried not to cry as she continued. "It's all been balled up inside Alyssa for a long time. Maybe forever. The blackness in her soul has grown and grown until it finally peaked."

"She must be destroyed," Hawk said in a fierce voice,

causing Cassia to cut her gaze to him. For a moment she'd forgotten anyone but the witches and Jake were in the room, but Keir, Tiernan, and Conlan had joined them.

Hawk still held Silver's head in his lap, and he stroked her hair from her face as his tears dried. "That witch cannot be allowed to live after what she has done."

The absolute quiet in the room pressed down on Cassia.

"Kill her?" Silver shook her head as she looked up at her husband. "We're not like her, Hawk. We can't forgive Alyssa, at least I can't. But I won't see her killed."

"What would you see done with her?" Keir said in a growl as his wife, Rhiannon, stood and embraced him.

"I don't know. Jail?" Silver stared at Cassia with a beseeching expression. "Or can she be moved to some Otherworld as a punishment? Not anything inhumane, but something that would suit her crimes?"

Cassia closed her eyes for a moment, trying to picture the many places Alyssa could be sent to. She opened her eyes and sighed. "I'll come up with something."

Everyone seemed too wrung out to talk about it anymore. Sydney, Copper, Silver, and Rhiannon left the kitchen with their D'Danann husbands. Hannah departed for the Drow realm to be with Garran, her own spouse.

Jake and Cassia were left alone in the kitchen for a few moments. Neither of them spoke as he helped her to her feet. She still felt weak, but her growing powers lent her more strength by the minute.

She gave a shuddering sigh as she slipped her arm around Jake's waist and he brought her closer with his arm hugging her shoulders. They walked from the kitchen and continued to hold each other until they reached his room. Without a word, he brought her down to his mattress and held her tight.

And she cried.

THE NEXT DAY, REGARDLESS of how their lives had just been ripped into even more shreds, the witches knew they had to go on. Cassia mentally leaned on Jake, needing him for comfort and for his love.

Hawk and the other D'Anu declared that Silver had to rest, and she agreed. Cassia knew the thought of losing her child was more than Silver could bear.

Everyone had wanted Cassia to rest, too, but she managed to overcome their objections. What she'd gone through wasn't as serious as Silver's experience because Cassia hadn't actually ingested the poison. She didn't go into detail, but told them that her powers had increased and she would explain at another time.

Cassia and the remaining five D'Anu witches began communicating, needing to be with one another, and without their PSF officer teammates. The witches planned to scry together after Silver had a chance to rest a little more.

Now it wasn't uncommon for them to hug one another in passing. It was as if they were assuring themselves that each one of them was still alive, and that what was left of the Coven was whole.

Cassia wasn't sure the Coven would ever be whole again. When the war was over, would they go their separate ways?

She didn't want to think about her own choices, what the future held for her and Jake. That was one of those so-called bridges they would have to cross when they came to it.

CHAPTER THIRTY-SEVEN

DARKWOLF TREMBLED WITH THE POWER of his anger as he clenched his fists and looked down at his traitor, Alyssa, formerly of the D'Anu. She had dropped to her knees and bowed her head, visibly shaking after he'd threatened to behead her when she appeared with her news.

Thoughts of Silver dying sent waves of pain through Darkwolf's chest. From the first time he'd invaded Silver's mind, he'd been fascinated with her. He'd thought he'd finally pushed that obsession aside—but his anger now . . .

He glanced at Elizabeth, who stood across the presidential suite they now occupied at one of the finest hotels.

She crossed her arms over her chest and studied him with a chill in her blue eyes, her features an icy mask. She'd known about his fascination and desire for Silver Ashcroft.

Darkwolf took a deep breath as he held Elizabeth's gaze. It was then he knew he was no longer obsessed with the D'Anu witch.

But he didn't want to see her die.

"Did I instruct you to kill Silver Ashcroft?" Darkwolf flung his words with a harsh bite as he stared down at Alyssa.

"No," she whispered without looking up. "I thought—I thought you'd be pleased to have another witch eliminated."

Darkwolf growled, intensely aware that Elizabeth was judging his reactions to the news of Silver's near murder. He chose his words carefully. "It was far too risky to try to kill *any* of the witches. You've just proven that. So now you've destroyed my one link into the Alliance because of your idiotic attempt and failure."

The tension in the air between Darkwolf and Elizabeth

lessened, and from the corner of his eye he saw her features relax.

"What am I supposed to do with you now?" Darkwolf grabbed Alyssa by her hair and jerked her to her feet. Pain flashed across her face, which was blotchy from crying. His hand still fisted in her hair, he yanked her head back so that she could meet his gaze and see the fury in his expression. "You're useless."

"I can still fight." Panic edged her words, and her eyes were wide and glassy. "You've given me a lot of power," she said in a rush. "During the next battle I can use that power to fight." She looked like she was struggling to find something to say. "I could cloak myself with a hooded robe. Find my way through the battlefield, and attack them from behind."

Darkwolf almost laughed. "You think you could do better than my Stormcutters?"

Alyssa tried to nod, but his grip on her hair kept her from moving more than a fraction. "I can bind them with my magic too fast for them to react. The Stormcutters will take care of the rest."

He released his grip on her hair and she dropped to her knees again, this time staring up at him. "Maybe you can be an 'ace in the hole.'" He gestured to one of the doors. "Stay in that room until I call for you."

She scrambled to her feet and headed for the door, but he held out his hand and caught her around her neck with an invisible rope of his magic. He jerked her and she clawed at her throat.

"Can't have you using the transference to escape if you change your mind." He raised his other hand and with ease used his power to suck her magic completely out of her. Alyssa's entire body went slack and terror crossed her face. "I'll give you back your magic, and then some, when I'm ready for you."

When he released her from his rope of magic, she dropped to her ass on the carpet. For a moment he saw what looked like rage in her eyes before she hurried to her feet and then to the door.

She came up short as he added, "It will remain locked, so don't bother trying to get out."

Alyssa gave a jerky nod before opening the door and slamming it shut behind her.

Darkwolf locked it with a thought. Since he'd taken all of her magic, she had none to even attempt to escape. He tossed thoughts of her aside. She wasn't worth thinking about until he needed her.

He turned his attention to Elizabeth, and her smile turned sultry as she unfolded her arms and walked to him. His body vibrated with need—and more. Much, much more. He watched her with hunger that burned deep inside. Not only in his cock, but in his soul. And that other place he'd been fighting against admitting for so long.

The way her perfect breasts pressed against her T-shirt made his palms ache to hold them, his mouth watering to suck her nipples. Her curves begged him to touch her, hold her, as her hips swayed while she moved toward him.

When she reached him, he couldn't wait. He had to fuck her. He grasped her hips and jerked her to him, digging his enormous erection into her belly. She moaned as he took her mouth, and then she wrapped her arms around his neck, pulled herself up, and hooked her thighs on his hips.

Darkwolf groaned as Elizabeth's pussy settled against his cock through the tough material of their jeans. He missed having her wear dresses with no underwear. He would be inside her already.

Still kissing her, he carried her out of the suite's sitting room and through the door to their bedroom. He brought her down to the bed, broke their kiss, and tugged her shirt over her head in an easy movement.

Her breasts were so perfect that he had to kneel between her thighs and take each one into his mouth with soft licks of his tongue and gentle pulls with his teeth.

In the past, Elizabeth had always liked it rough, fast, hard. But he knew she'd enjoyed it the last few times, when he'd taken it slow and kissed her body everywhere he could. He'd lick her pussy and make her scream and throb and cry.

Eventually she would beg him to take her. After teasing her a little more he would thrust deep, taking it slow and drawing it out until they both came and he shot every bit of his come.

This time, though, he felt an urgency, a need to bury himself inside her. Now.

He pulled off her shoes and yanked down the jeans that she'd unbuttoned. As usual, she didn't have on any kind of underwear and her beautiful body was completely naked.

Almost blind with carnal need, Darkwolf unfastened his jeans and let out his god-enhanced cock. Elizabeth looked as hungry as he was and she reached her arms out to him.

"Now, Darkwolf." She spread her thighs wide and the scent of her musk was so strong it almost made him dizzy with more lust. "Leave your clothes on and hurry."

He let out a growl of ownership as he got onto the bed and settled between her thighs. She was wet and slick, and he closed his eyes as he rubbed his cock up and down her folds, wetting the length of it.

She let out a whimper and clawed his ass through his jeans.

Darkwolf couldn't take it anymore. He didn't know why, but he had to take her now. He'd taken her in any number of positions, barely pulling her pants down or throwing her skirt up before burying his cock inside her.

He let all thoughts slide away as he opened his eyes and grabbed his erection. He held it at the entrance to her pussy and slammed into her.

Elizabeth screamed her pleasure and shouted for him to take her faster than he ever had before.

Darkwolf thrust in and out of her while his gaze locked with hers. They'd never done that before—watched each other while fucking.

Somehow they couldn't tear their gazes apart, as if doing that would break a spell that wrapped around them.

Elizabeth made loud cries and moans and urged him on. Darkwolf intensified his thrusts, shouting back at her.

"You belong to *me*," he said over and over again.

"Yes, yes, *yes*!" she answered every one of his demands.

And then the words escaped that he never thought he'd say. "I love you, Elizabeth," he said softly while his gaze continued to hold hers.

Her lips parted and her eyes widened, but with one more powerful thrust he sent her over the edge, and she screamed and writhed beneath him.

She begged to the gods for him to stop as he took her relentlessly, that she couldn't take any more of her massive orgasm that wouldn't stop.

With a final thrust, Darkwolf came. He shouted and pressed his hips tight between her thighs. Her pussy continued to convulse around his cock and he pulsed inside her.

He groaned and slid partially off her so that his weight wasn't on her, but he still had her pinned down. She stared at him with wonder and even confusion in her eyes.

Darkwolf kissed her, long and slow, putting everything he felt into that kiss. When he drew away, he smiled. "I love you," he repeated.

She looked at him with something like wonder in her gaze. "I've never felt that emotion—love. At least, I don't think so." Her throat worked as she swallowed. "I'm not sure what it is. Even this human's body and soul that I own never understood that word."

Darkwolf sighed and held her close. "Trust me on this one."

Elizabeth snuggled into him. "Okay."

CHAPTER THIRTY-EIGHT

DARKWOLF AND ELIZABETH-JUNGA *shout and scream as they fuck. Mind-boggling. He's screwing a demon! A fucking demon! I can't stop shaking. Each sound digs. Tortures.*

I'll kill him.

I'll kill them. *If Darkwolf hadn't taken all of my magic, I would escape this room and head straight to where he's in bed with that Fomorii queen.*

And slaughter them both before they even knew I was there.

Strangulation like Mackenzie?

No, better to just blast their heads from their bodies. The demon will turn to ash. With the power of two gods, who knows what would happen to Darkwolf. Maybe that bitch Cassia is right and it would upset the balance of all Otherworlds.

Now wouldn't that be rich after all the Alliance has fought for?

It makes me ill to know that Darkwolf is with one of those beasts from Underworld. How could I have imagined myself with him inside of me? That filthy prick.

Before he took my magic I noticed the look he gave her and sensed his feelings for her. How sweet. He cares about her. Deeply.

Sickening, but interesting.

Light stabs my eyes through the windows as I pace. Without my magic, I'm helpless. Ruined. I can't even scry.

Darkwolf will pay for treating me like this. After all I've done for him. Murdering the witch who thought I was her best friend, betraying my Coven . . . Not that either was any big loss or sacrifice.

The bed creaks as I throw myself across it. My jaw hurts from clenching. A plan. I've got to come up with some kind of plan to get my revenge on him.

Hurt him in ways he's never been hurt before.

But wait.

Ah, yes.

So simple it's laughable.

I reach down and feel for the Mystwalker blade that is strapped to my ankle. I've hidden it there rather than using it as a collar.

I'm going to get Darkwolf where it hurts.

Yes. A way that will tear him to shreds.

CHAPTER THIRTY-NINE

IN THE ELVIN WAY, CASSIA DREW thirteen rune stones from the soft bag. The stones clattered across the tabletop as she cast them, the click-clacking sounds loud in the empty kitchen.

The star birthmark burned beneath her belly button as she studied the runes on the stones that landed faceup.

A visitor.

Discovery. Pain. Suffering.

An end.

The end to everything.

She held her hand to her pitching stomach. Everything would end soon, but the stones gave no clue as to the outcome—who would triumph and who would suffer the loss.

Her thoughts turned to Alyssa and more pain ate at her core.

Echo, Alyssa's former owl familiar, had stayed around the warehouse for a few days, looking mournful. When Echo disappeared, Kael told Cassia the owl had left to find a new path and a new D'Anu witch to serve. Cassia hoped with all her heart he found someone good and pure.

A strong magical presence startled Cassia from her concentration on her rune stones.

When she realized who it was, Cassia gathered her stones into the bag and shoved them into her jeans pocket for the time being.

The visitor her stones had told her of was almost on the Alliance's doorstep.

Cassia reached the front entrance and opened the door before Janis Arrowsmith of the white magic D'Anu had a chance to knock.

The austere high priestess stood in the misty rain, her robe clinging to her bony frame. The normally overbearing, judgmental Janis Arrowsmith was wild-haired and wild-eyed, her expression frantic. She appeared to have thrown on a white robe after just having woken from sleep.

Seeing the thin, now almost emaciated, woman so distraught caused Cassia's stomach to pitch even more than it had when she had cast her rune stones. The high priestess had *never* looked like this—eyes wide and haunted, her lined face as pale and gray as fog, and her gray hair long, wet, and tangled about her face instead of being in its usual severe bun.

Even Mortimer, Janis's mouse familiar, squeaked and ran up and down one of Janis's arms, obviously agitated.

The high priestess seemed even worse now than when Sara, her favorite apprentice, had been taken over by the dark goddess. Janis had thought she could save Sara by protecting the goddess. And Janis succeeded, once, with beyond disastrous results. Even at the end of the dark goddess's life, Janis had thought she could save the part of the goddess that was Sara.

But the gray magic D'Anu knew that only Sara's body had survived during the dark goddess's possession, not the soul that had once been inside Sara.

"What has happened, Janis?" Cassia said to her former high priestess, trying to keep her tone calm. "Would you like to come inside, out of the rain?"

"Is it true? What my visions tell me?" Janis snapped her gaze over Cassia's shoulder to stare into the warehouse before looking at Cassia again. "Is Mackenzie dead? And Alyssa . . . she murdered Mackenzie?"

Cassia's chest hurt and she brought her hand up and clenched her T-shirt over her heart. "It's true," she whispered. "Alyssa is gone now. She left to join Darkwolf."

Janis sagged, and Cassia thought the older woman might collapse. Cassia reached out to catch Janis by the shoulders, but the high priestess went rigid and raised her chin as her eyes turned icy. Cassia dropped her hands to her sides.

"You were completely aware of the fact that gray magic leads to black when you left our Coven." Janis practically spat out the words. "This never would have happened if you and the rest hadn't turned to using gray magic."

Cassia kept her gaze steady and gathered her calm. "I saw inside Alyssa before she left to join Darkwolf. She was black within her soul even when she was part of the white magic Coven. It had nothing to do with any of us practicing gray magic."

Janis's eyes had become hard, flinty. "I do *not* believe that."

"She was tortured as a child in an orphanage by corrupt religious figures," Cassia said quietly, "and she learned anger and hate and revenge. It's not an excuse for the horrible acts she has committed, but it does give a reason as to why she chose the path she did."

"If she hadn't been allowed to practice gray magic, she would never have used that hatred to go to dark magic," Janis snapped.

"We are all mourning the loss of Mackenzie and the woman we thought of as a Coven sister," Cassia said with a heavy sigh she felt straight to her toes. "What brings you here?"

The light rain soaking Janis's robe had relaxed more of the wildness of her hair. "Darkwolf and his—his *monsters*." She remained rigid and ignored water dripping from her hair, down her face, and into her eyes. "I know where they are. I know where they hide."

Hair on Cassia's arms rose. "Where? Do you want to come in and tell the others?"

Distaste crossed Janis's expression as she glanced into the warehouse again. Despite the fact she had come to warn the gray magic witches in the past, she still held her prejudices over anyone who would *kill*, demons or no, or aid those who did.

She was a study in contradictions. It was obvious it tore her apart to have to give information such as this to Cassia and the others, yet she was smart enough to know the salvation of the city depended on it.

"The Presidio." Janis shuddered as if something slimy had crawled down her spine. "The northern end is where Dark-wolf has shielded them from sight with his magic. Around Crissy Field."

Cassia felt the urge to turn and run to tell the others. "You're sure?"

Janis managed to look haughty even as she wilted from head to toe in the gentle rain. "My visions are never wrong."

The high priestess turned, but Cassia caught her by the arm and felt an almost skeletal forearm.

Janis froze as her eyes met Cassia's. "You are not human, are you," Janis stated.

"I am fully Elvin." Cassia squeezed Janis's arm as Mortimer scampered into one of Janis's pockets. "Thank you, Janis. The Alliance is fighting for countless lives. You are doing the right thing."

"There are at least twenty-five thousand of those—things," Janis said in a strained whisper.

As Cassia stood there in shock, Janis drew free of Cassia's hold. The high priestess walked away in the softly falling rain.

"GOT GOOD NEWS AND BAD NEWS." Jake ground his teeth as he braced his palms on the lighted map table and glanced at those around him. "Good news is we know he's got his Stormcutters at the Presidio."

Murmurs circulated the command center. With Alyssa gone, everything had returned to "business as usual," as much as it could, and the planning sessions were no longer limited to one being per race. Three beings once again represented each faction of the Alliance. Now their numbers included Mystwalkers as well as Light Elves.

"Because of its size," Jake continued, "it's been suspect as a potential hangout for Darkwolf's Stormcutters. We've been doing our best to use what manpower we have to patrol that area since this whole mess with him began.

"No sign of activity registered anywhere around there." Jake glanced at Cassia. "But thanks to a vision by the old

D'Anu high priestess, we're fairly certain he's got his Storm-cutters there."

"I don't know why I'm surprised every time Janis has shown up to give us information." Copper shook her head. "She's against us killing, but she gives us crucial information when we need it."

Cassia was seated next to where Jake stood, and she leaned forward as she said, "It's Janis's only way of doing what's right without crossing her own boundaries."

Copper gave a slow nod. "You're correct, of course."

"The Presidio is massive." Rhiannon walked closer to the map table. "What, around fifteen hundred acres? Did she narrow it down to a location?"

"Crissy Field." Jake cued up an aerial view of the area that stretched along the tip of the San Francisco peninsula. "Which is to our advantage." He pointed to the former airstrip on the northern end of the Presidio. "With our US Marine friends, we can come at Darkwolf from the bay and the land."

Jake's gaze met Cassia's when she tilted her head up, and she said, "It's so open there—so few trees. If he was closer to a wooded spot, likely the Stormcutters would have a harder time forming."

"Probably why he chose that particular area—so he's not limited." Jake propped one foot on the seat of a folding metal chair and rested his forearm on his thigh. "Unfortunately for us, that's one of the trade-offs. An ideal location for our forces to come at from all sides, but puts us out there bare-assed."

Bourne shifted his stance on the other side of the map table. "We've got an MEB of seventeen thousand Marines on our doorstep now." He gave a cocky grin. "They got here faster than we expected. As far as I'm concerned, now that we know where the bastard and his Stormcutters are hiding out, they're history."

"Here's the bad news that I mentioned." Jake's whole body tensed as if he was hearing the news for the first time himself. "Apparently the sonofabitch has at least twenty-five thousand Stormcutters now."

One of Jake's lieutenants whistled through his teeth. More

murmurs came from those in the room, along with shocked expressions.

Cassia glanced at Lieutenant Fredrickson, whose demeanor had changed significantly in the past few days. He didn't react to Jake's announcement, and she sensed extreme emotional pain within him. He was not exhibiting his usual in-your-face personality. Cassia started to wonder why when it hit her.

The magic within her caught the current of his feelings. Fredrickson had been having sexual relations with Alyssa. Guilt and anger at being used rolled from him in waves. Alyssa had apparently been using him for sex, and to get information out of him.

Cassia looked away. What was done was done, and she wasn't going to add to his pain by bringing it up—to anyone.

"With Darkwolf's god-powers and the Stormcutter abilities," Jake was saying as his eyes met Bourne's, "they might just be a match for the next wave of Marines you're bringing in."

Bourne shook his head. "We're talking twenty thousand of us, including the Alliance, against a possibility of twenty-five thousand Stormcutters. Not to mention the incredible amount of firepower we've got at our disposal." He looked far from convinced at Jake's assessment. "We're down a few thousand, but with our superior training, I don't see how we can possibly not have the upper hand here."

"Your Marines are very likely not trained for this magnitude of powerful magic," said Alaia, the dark-haired, green-eyed leader of the Mystwalkers. "Even with the Mystwalker ability to transform into mist, along with the use of our daggers, the Stormcutter numbers were too much for us to truly make a difference in the last battle."

"Your people and your weapons helped save many lives," Cassia said as she looked at the Mystwalker leader. "The deaths and injuries our Alliance suffered could have been far worse."

"This is true." King Garran's long silvery-blue hair shone beneath the room's lighting, and the gems on the leather straps crisscrossing his chest glittered. "We have much to thank you for."

The other leaders of the Alliance voiced their agreements.

"We are pleased to do what we can to assist." Alaia gave a low nod and glanced at Daire. "However, were it not for the Light Elves we might all have been destroyed."

Jake's gaze met Daire's. No matter his personal feelings about Daire, Jake respected the hell out of the man. "I don't know that we'll ever be able to repay you and your people."

Daire gave a low nod like Alaia had. "We would do anything for Princess Cassiandra and those she cares for."

"Princess Cassiandra?" Copper shot Cassia a grin. It was the first smile Jake had seen out of any of the witches in days. "To think, all this time we've been mingling with royalty."

"Well, that's interesting." Rhiannon cocked her head as she studied Cassia. "Yet another mystery of our Cassia to come to light."

Cassia's cheeks turned pink as she shot a glare toward the Elvin man. "It's not something I like to announce."

Daire gave a light shrug and an unrepentant grin.

Jake could barely hold back a grin of amusement of his own. Instead, he braced his hands on the map table and looked each of at the Alliance leaders. "We do have more good news."

"And that is?" Bourne asked.

Satisfaction rolled through Jake as he told the group. "The god-containment weapon is ready."

"Goddess, that *is* great news," Rhiannon said with a note of hope in her voice.

David Bourne eyed Jake head-on. "Have you tested it?"

"Only in simulations." Jake pushed away from the map table. "We put in all the specs on the metal, and in the simulations the weapon works perfectly." Jake shoved his hand through his hair. "The only problem we see with the whole thing is that I need to be damned close to Darkwolf to use it. We're going to have to play it by ear, but I've got to find him, and fast."

"I don't like the idea of you using something as powerful

as that weapon," Fredrickson said, lacking his usual vigor, "without testing it first."

"I agree." Cassia gave Jake a pleading look. "It could kill you."

"It'll work." He met and held her gaze. "The containment array will hold him. Then you can send him wherever you're planning on ditching the bastard." He paused as his heart wrenched. "Problem is that, to do your thing, you're going to have to be close, too."

"I can protect myself with my magic." Cassia closed her eyes for a moment before opening them. "I'm afraid that I can't protect you when you use your weapon."

"Don't worry about me," he said, unable to take his gaze from hers. "You don't know for sure his magic won't blow away your shields."

"I'll be fine." Cassia focused on the rest of the group. "Yes," she added quietly. "Jake will hold Darkwolf and I'll take care of the rest."

Expressions in the room ranged from concerned to thoughtful to unreadable.

Cassia cleared her throat. "Magic is what started this. Magic is what will finish it."

CHAPTER FORTY

TONIGHT WOULD DETERMINE WHETHER the Alliance won or lost. Of that, Cassia was certain.

As a black PSF Humvee powered through the night and neared the Presidio, a storm of magic roiled in Cassia's belly. The sensation was like the havoc her magic had created before Jake had helped her complete her transition.

She had full control over her magic now, but as they headed toward their destination she still squirmed in her seat, and she clenched and unclenched her hands.

Goose bumps rose on her arms and she rubbed them from her shoulders to her elbows. The dusty smell of the well-used vehicle obscured any other scents and caused her to sneeze.

Kael sat in the back, but close enough that he was almost sitting between Jake and Cassia.

Cassia flexed her hands again in her lap and looked out into the darkness and the glittering city. The city should be teaming with life, not empty and . . . dead. She caught sight of National Guardsmen patrolling the streets, now sadly quiet due to martial law. Everything that had happened to San Francisco over the last several weeks had ground the city to a halt, and she wondered how long it would take these people to rebuild their lives once Darkwolf was destroyed.

The Alliance *would* destroy him. They had no choice.

And the resilient people of this city would recover and rebuild.

Jake reached over the console and squeezed Cassia's fingers as he drove, drawing her attention to him. Lights from the vehicle's control panel glowed, casting shadows and green light onto his features.

She tried to stop trembling from the nervous anticipation

coursing through her body. He gave her a smile, but his expression was concerned rather than reassuring.

Yes, Cassia had the power of a Guardian now, but she was far from invincible. Unlike the Great Guardian.

She wished more than anything that her mother could be here to defeat Darkwolf, but the Great Guardian never interfered, only guided.

Well, unless she was interfering with her daughter's love life.

Cassia sighed as she thought about her and Jake facing Darkwolf on their own. She knew she wasn't close to being a match for Darkwolf, with his warlock's dark magic and the power of two gods at his disposal.

She was positive the Alliance hadn't begun to see the full measure of Darkwolf's abilities.

And Jake—dear goddess, would his god-trapping gun destroy him instead of performing like he'd planned? Like they all hoped?

To send Darkwolf to a place where he could never do them harm again, Jake's weapon would have to work. Darkwolf needed to be incredibly vulnerable, unable to defend himself, for Cassia to hold as much power over him as she needed to.

A shiver caused her to tremble to her toes for just a moment. Jake was going to have to get close to Darkwolf to use the array gun.

Darkness crowded the vehicle as they continued through the night toward the Presidio. From land and from the bay, thousands of Marines and Alliance warriors were descending on the location Darkwolf had taken over.

One of the biggest questions had been whether or not they could break through the warlock-god's magical barriers. Everyone was counting on Cassia and her newly gained Guardian powers to bring the shield down—at least long enough to let the Alliance regiments flow into the Presidio.

The sheer number of Alliance warriors and Marines who would soon pour onto Crissy Field should keep Darkwolf from reestablishing his barriers. Once breached by so many beings, it should be nearly impossible for Darkwolf to do anything but go on the defensive.

Everything depended on what happened tonight.

The Alliance hoped to take out as many of Darkwolf's men as possible before the warlock-god unleashed the storm that would turn his puppets into deadly water funnels.

The Humvee rounded a corner. Almost there.

Cassia and Jake drove one of the lead vehicles since she had to take care of that barrier.

Her heart beat faster and faster. Magic spread throughout her body, like bolts of electricity shooting inside her. Sparks flickered at her fingertips, lighting the interior of the truck and causing Jake to glance at her.

She ran her fingers over her Kevlar vest, over her beating heart, as if she could feel it through the body armor.

But she had full control over her magic now.

Yeah, she'd just keep telling herself that.

"Do not worry, Princess," came Kael's comforting thought in her mind. *"We will succeed in defeating Darkwolf."*

"I hope you're right," Cassia said out loud and Jake looked at her, but she didn't explain.

When they neared Crissy Field, Cassia could see Alcatraz to the northeast and the Golden Gate Bridge to the northwest. Lights glittered from cities surrounding the bay on opposite shores. Newspaper and television reports made it clear that people in every city around the San Francisco Bay lived in constant terror that the madness in San Francisco— whatever it was—would soon spread to them.

They finally parked in one of Crissy Field's ghostly, empty, tourist lots. Rocks that were scattered across the paving crunched beneath the Humvee's tires, and the engines of their entourage tore up what had once been near silence.

The other Alliance and Marine vehicles pulled in around the Humvee. Through the darkness, massive ships waited— silent death anchored just off the shore. Like the stealth of night itself, Cassia knew countless Marines were positioned and ready for the signal.

Before Cassia could climb out, Jake caught her by the

back of her head and drew her face close to his. "I love you," he said softly.

For just that one moment it was the two of them. Only them.

Oops. And Kael in the backseat.

But she pushed the wolf from her thoughts. So much emotion welled up inside that her throat grew tight. "I love you, Jake."

He brushed his lips over hers in a light kiss before drawing back. "Let's kick some ass, Princess."

Cassia would have laughed if she hadn't started shaking so much at the stark realization that this was it.

"I love you, too," Cassia said to Kael.

"As I do you, Cassiandra."

"Don't let me out of your sight." Jake drew back, sliding his fingers across the nape of her neck as he moved away. "We need to get to Darkwolf together."

"I shall not lose you, either," Kael said.

Cassia glanced up at the sky to see that storm clouds had started swirling, and her heart pounded faster. "He knows we're here. We'd better hurry."

Jake gave her a look that only lasted a moment, but could have been minutes. They both climbed out of the vehicle, Kael following with a lithe jump onto the paving.

Cassia's body positively vibrated with magic as she walked toward the trees at the east end of the marsh, beyond the fenced-off wildlife protection area. A hint of a sweet scent, like honeysuckle mixed with the salt of the bay. She scanned the darkness, searching for some sign of Darkwolf's barriers.

Nothing.

She continued forward, cresting a grassy knoll, Jake at her side, his Glock in his hand, and Kael just feet away. Behind them, Marines and Alliance members spread out and took position.

Thunder rumbled overhead.

Jagged lightning cut the sky, illuminating the empty shore ahead.

Goddess! Darkwolf was preparing to attack.

Maybe his barriers were already down.

But when lightning lit the sky again, it reflected off a clear shield, like a soap bubble with an iridescent glimmer.

Icy wind kicked up, whipping her hair around her face and stinging her cheeks as she neared the barrier. If she touched the shield, Darkwolf might recognize her through the magic and come straight for her, before she even had a chance to take the barrier down.

Instead, she held up both of her palms, several inches away from the shield, and explored it with her magic.

Fat drops of rain began pelting her hair and face, landing on her eyelids and rolling down to blur her vision. She blinked away the water and ignored the rain. She concentrated on feeling the dark god-powers Darkwolf had used to create the barrier.

Her skin crawled and she shuddered from the feel of dark magic oozing from the shield. She pressed her own magic against it and fought not to recoil.

Smells of sour laundry replaced the scents of grass, verbena, and that honeysuckle-like scent. Rain pounded harder on her.

Time was running out.

Even though her mental exploration of the dark magic barrier made her stomach queasy, it also told her something that she'd suspected. Darkwolf had been far too cocky. He'd only put enough of his dark power into the shield to fend off normal magic from any one of the races of beings in the Alliance, including the D'Anu witches.

What he hadn't counted on was her. An Elvin Guardian who had attained her full powers.

"Now, Cassia!" Jake shouted above the growing sounds of thunder and wind.

Cassia focused her magic. Held it tight while letting it build inside her as fast and as intense as the storm that now raged.

She imagined herself a tidal wave, her magic rearing so high and powerfully that it would slam into the barrier and shatter the black force keeping the barrier in place.

With a burst of raw, intense, but focused magic, Cassia released her powers.

Golden magic rammed the shield. She stumbled back from the force of the rebound that hit her straight in the chest. At first she couldn't catch her breath, and almost fell. Vaguely she was aware of Jake steadying her from behind.

The power of her magic illuminated what had been an invisible barrier, her magic making it sparkle with gold.

Jagged lines zipped along the shield, shooting like spears from the location where she had blasted it.

Thousands of fractures appeared in the barrier until it looked like a dome of cracked, golden safety glass.

Heart thundering even more, Cassia pushed herself from Jake. She flung out another blast of magic.

The barrier exploded.

The cracking sound was almost deafening and Cassia clapped her ears.

Sparks lit up the night and the falling rain. The sparks twinkled as they fell back to earth, then faded as the shield dissolved and the noise vanished.

Cassia moved her hands from her ears, her palms facing up.

At her command, gold light shot into the sky like a gigantic sparkler.

Kael released a loud, haunting howl.

The signals.

Shouts, cries, and roars carried above driving wind, rain, and thunder.

The battle had begun.

With the aid of lightning and her Guardian-enhanced vision, Cassia saw everything more clearly than if she'd been wearing military night-vision goggles.

Thousands of funnels erupted on the sand, over the marshes, and on the field.

From their hidden locations, Marine snipers and sharpshooters picked off Stormcutters that appeared when their funnels stopped.

PSF officers used their heart-seeking bullets, and many

used the Mystwalker collars, transforming them into daggers to slice through the water funnels, gutting the men before the funnels even stopped moving. The Stormcutter bodies would appear and flop on the ground.

Elvin and Drow arrows pierced Stormcutter flesh when the men appeared.

Silver had been "allowed," or rather had agreed, to stay on the fringes of the battle. She'd readily taken on the mission to go after the Blades with Hawk at her side.

The Alliance had noticed that Blades tended to stay on the edges, as if protecting themselves from being in the thick of the battle. The Blades turned into more powerful funnels, but they seemed to have a harder time maintaining their forms.

Cassia glanced at Silver long enough to see her whip out two magic ropes that sizzled in the rain. She slung them around the throats of two Blades at the same time, snapping their necks instantly.

Hawk used a familiar move Cassia had seen him use with demons when he carved the heart out of one of the Blades. Polaris, the python familiar, was slinking behind the men, wrapping his long, powerful body around a Blade and crushing the man's body while sinking his fangs into the man's throat.

On the outskirts of the battle, the D'Anu white magic witches cast white magic spells. They erected barriers between Alliance fighters and Stormcutters when the funnelmen got too close to a member of the Alliance.

Janis Arrowsmith's hair was back in a bun, but wet strands escaped as she flung seeds on the rain-soaked ground in strategic spots. Her magical seeds sprang up into plants with thick trunks and hundreds of vines that wrapped around Stormcutters and bound them tight.

The plants' tendrils wound their way around the captured Stormcutters completely. The bound men were protected from magic, as well as human and magical beings' weapons. Cassia had to respect Janis. The high priestess was doing her share, but she wasn't about to contribute to the death of any person or being.

Lightning illuminated the sky so brilliantly that Cassia blinked. She wanted to scream from what she saw. Funnels sprouted everywhere. It looked like they covered every square foot of sand, marsh, grass, concrete, and asphalt.

Stormcutters—from the bay at the north to the stacked freeway behind the field to the south. From the Golden Gate Bridge east to the Marina.

Everywhere. The Stormcutters developed everywhere.

Water slammed into Cassia's face as a funnel stopped and a Stormcutter appeared in its place and jabbed an ice dagger toward Cassia's chest.

Before Cassia had a chance to react, Jake plugged the man in the head with a bullet from his Glock.

Cassia gave Jake a look of gratitude right before she released a surge of magic that blasted every Stormcutter close to them. The funnels evaporated, but more funnels replaced them almost faster than Cassia could blink.

Kael fought with savagery as he sliced the abdomen of one Stormcutter with his sharp claws while he ripped the throat from another funnel-man. Blood sprayed the wolf's fine white coat and Stormcutter guts splattered the dark ground.

Magic sizzled through Cassia's veins as she destroyed Stormcutter after Stormcutter with fire. Jake stayed close, watching her back and shooting every Stormcutter nearby that she didn't get with her magic.

The roar of the storm, along with the shrieks, screams, shouts, and gunshots from the battle were nearly deafening.

Lightning struck so close the thunder boomed like cannons.

Or maybe the Marines were using weapons that sounded like cannons.

Whatever was happening, it was complete, maddening chaos.

As Cassia and Jake fought off their attackers and worked their way through the Stormcutters, different-colored magic sparks erupted in the darkness, coming from each of the other five D'Anu witches. From the colors of their magic, Cassia could tell where each witch was in the battle. So far it looked like they were all alive and fighting like crazy.

The thought of them made Cassia's mind flash briefly to Alyssa. Was she fighting at Darkwolf's side? Would the Alliance, Cassia even, be facing her tonight?

Somehow, Cassia knew Alyssa was here. Somewhere.

Cassia wondered where poor Echo was. She hoped the owl familiar had found a new D'Anu witch to serve. Or would, soon.

The blackness that now filled Alyssa carried over the battlefield, and Cassia's heart broke even more.

Strange sensations crept up Cassia's spine. Little shivers that weren't unpleasant, but odd in the middle of a bloody battle. The feeling was like a sparkling blanket floating above Cassia, shrouding the madness, and made Cassia feel separated from the battle.

"Ahhhh." Kael said in her mind, sounding pleased as he battled, and she cut her gaze to him. *"They have come."*

"What? Who—?"

A brilliant explosion cut off Cassia's question. Colorful fireworks in every color imaginable exploded just above the chaos. Glittering purples, pinks, greens, oranges, yellows, blues. Beauty among horrors.

The explosion of light nearly startled Cassia into dropping her flames. Several fighters on the field, including Stormcutters, jerked their attention to the sky briefly before returning to fighting.

Cassia's jaw dropped as hundreds of Fae beings appeared with the flash.

Tiny Faeries, who normally remained naked, wore fighting leathers. An explosion of flowery perfume swept over the field for a moment, a bizarre contrast to the stench of battle. The scents flowed from every Faerie as their wings glittered and different shades of Faerie dust drifted from their colorful wings.

Usually mischievous, fat but small-winged Pixies carried bows the length of their bodies and had quivers on their backs. Cassia had the absurd thought that they would start braiding Stormcutters' hair—braiding an unsuspecting victim's hair was one of their favorite pastimes.

But no, this was war.

A Brownie dropped just outside Cassia's fire and immediately attacked the knees of a Stormcutter, then went for his belly with long fingernails and gutted the funnel-man. More Brownies dove into the fight from where they had appeared in the air.

Cassia blinked. Did the trees nearby just move? No . . . *Yes!*

Faces of beautiful Dryads appeared in the trunks of the trees as they guided eucalyptus, Monterey cypress, coast live oak trees, and others around the battlefield. The trees came alive and used their great branches to swipe Stormcutters from the ground and toss them into the air. The trees with more flexible branches wrapped them around Stormcutters and squeezed them to death.

Two Faeries Cassia knew well zipped up to her. Queen Riona, with her long dark hair and sparkling lavender wings, along with little, blond, pink-winged Galia, who'd proven herself in battles against the dark goddess.

"We've come to fight!" Galia said with a zealous expression. "No time to talk," she added as she zipped away and threw tiny pink lightning bolts, exploding Stormcutter heads or hearts.

Queen Riona gave a regal nod. "We will help you win this war, Princess Cassiandra."

"Thank you," Cassia said as the Queen whirled and began to battle.

CHAPTER FORTY-ONE

CASSIA SHOOK HER HEAD IN WONDER as she maintained the ring of fire around herself. The Fae had come to the Earth Otherworld to fight beside humans and Otherworldly beings alike.

"I was certain they would come," Kael said in a smug voice as Cassia flung out more fire. Unlike any person yelling through the night, Cassia could hear Kael's voice clearly in her mind. *"Once I discussed it with Queen Riona, she said she would call a summit with all the Fae to make their determination."*

"Amazing." Cassia took one last look at the battling Fae before concentrating solely on the war. *"You are truly amazing, Kael."*

"Stay close, Cassiandra," Kael said in a warning tone. *"I feel something on the air. I believe Darkwolf can sense you."*

"Don't worry." Cassia glanced at Kael, who stayed out of range of her fire as usual so that he could go after Stormcutters her fire couldn't reach. *"I don't have any intention of going anywhere without you."*

"Intention or no"—Kael paused in midsentence as he growled and ripped out another funnel-man's guts—*"be cautious."*

With her magic, Cassia continued to wipe out every Stormcutter in her path with her fire, while Jake took out each one she missed. As always, she was forced to be careful to release her magic only as far as she could see the Stormcutters, to make sure she didn't hurt anyone in the Alliance.

She nearly bumped into Breacán before he shifted into mist at the same time Alaia did. They reappeared almost immediately several feet away, taking down three water funnels each as soon as they rose from the ground.

Many of the D'Danann flew overhead, beheading Stormcutters with their long swords when the funnels stopped and the men inhabiting them appeared. There were so few D'Danann in comparison to the other races of beings, but they were incredibly effective.

Kael howled, a sound that seemed to make the Stormcutters shudder.

Cassia let loose another burst of fire, barely keeping it from toasting Fredrickson's ass. The PSF cop fought with intensity and rage on his features.

Her heart ached for Fredrickson. She didn't know if he had cared about Alyssa, but the shock of having had any kind of relationship with a traitor and a murderer had to have been brutal.

Cassia held her hands out in two directions, firing magic between a group of PSF officers on one side, Marines on the other, clearing their paths briefly of Stormcutters.

The powerfully built Marine, Bourne, took on four Stormcutters at once. He was amazing as he used his martial arts moves along with his skills with gun and dagger.

Cassia gritted her teeth as more of her magic rolled out of her and more Stormcutters vanished into steam, or burned to cinders if they had taken human form.

Many of the Dark Elves shot their diamond-headed arrows from a distance, while others fought with swords and daggers in the middle of the chaos.

She spotted King Garran with his gleaming silvery-blue hair and gems sparkling on his chest straps. He plunged his sword into one Stormcutter's gut, jerked the blade back while ramming his elbow behind him into a Stormcutter's chest. Garran whirled and decapitated a third Stormcutter on his way to finish off the one he'd just elbowed.

Hannah fought nearby, her fireballs blowing up the heads of Stormcutter after Stormcutter. Her long dark hair flowed over her shoulders while the shock of blond hair fell across one of her cheeks. The intensity in her gaze reflected the feelings in

Cassia's heart. They fought not only to save the city but for their lost friends, and for those they would die for.

Hannah's falcon, Banshee, was just as spectacular as Hannah was. Like he had at the baseball stadium, Banshee ripped and pecked out eyes, blinding the Stormcutters and allowing others in the Alliance to take the funnel-men all the way down.

Kael and Jake both stayed as close to Cassia as they could in the madness as the three of them tried to keep one another in sight.

More mist invaded the melee, and Mystwalkers rose up to slice through funnels with their daggers before falling to mist again. They stayed clear of the marshy areas that were filled with saltwater. If saltwater touched Mystwalkers, they could lose their mist forms until cleansed completely with freshwater. However, with all the rain from Darkwolf's storm slamming down on them, that might not be a problem.

The incredible intensity and skill with which the Marines fought was such that they could have been Otherworldly beings. They rivaled the best of any race's fighting legions—minus the magic. Yet, the Marines had a magic all their own.

Anger fueled Cassia's magic fire as she saw Marines and Alliance members go down from Stormcutter blades. Just as many Stormcutter bodies littered the ground, but not enough. The Alliance needed to take out more, with fewer casualties on their side.

As she released more fire, burning away several Stormcutters, she caught Daire's eye through the tearing rain. He'd slung his bow over his shoulder and now fought Stormcutters with his sword. Daire was brilliant, his every move smooth and lithe, as if choreographed. Stormcutter blood spattered his arms and clothing as he sliced into each man's flesh, but Daire still managed to look magnificent. Other Light Elves fought with almost as much grace and style as Daire.

But Jake—he was nothing short of amazing. He saved Cassia's butt more than once when she missed a Stormcutter that came at her almost faster than she could blink. With calmness and professionalism Jake systematically shot every Stormcutter that came too close to him and Cassia.

The times Jake was forced to battle Stormcutters hand to hand, the power and intensity with which he fought were fascinating. The muscles in his biceps and thighs flexed and his jaw tightened in his single-minded determination. His blue eyes seemed to glow with controlled ferocity with each opponent he took on. A few marks marred his Kevlar and his arms bled from several slashes, but he fought as if it was a mere training exercise.

Jake equaled Daire's magnificence with ease.

Magic sizzled through Cassia's veins and out of her body every time she released her fire. Even though the magic she released protected her and Jake from most of the rain, she couldn't keep up a constant flare—every now and then it was like taking a slight breath between each burst of sustained flame.

It was during those breaths that she was vulnerable. She was thankful for her centuries of training with Daire that made fighting Stormcutters by hand relatively easy. Stormcutter blood soon soaked her clothing and splattered her skin. The rain didn't reach her as much because of her magic, so it didn't wash off the worst of the blood.

Cassia wasn't positive where Darkwolf was, but something told her that she and Jake needed to work their way west through the tidal marsh. The warlock-god was somewhere in that direction.

As she continued that way, she brushed elbows with Rhiannon. The redheaded witch's chin-length hair flew around her face as she directed her Shadows to eliminate Stormcutters. At the same time she flung spellfire balls at other Stormcutters. Her D'Danann husband, Keir, looked like the fierce, rugged, bad-boy warrior he was. Blood dripped down the scar on his cheek—it looked like it had been flayed open again.

Spirit, Rhiannon's cat familiar, sprang onto the naked men who appeared out of the funnels, startling them and somehow keeping them from changing back to funnels. Cassia thought she saw Jake wince when Spirit clung to the genitals of one of the funnel-men.

Cassia tunneled her way through a horde of Stormcutters with her magic fire, Jake backing her. Goddess! She had to get to Darkwolf. He was west—somewhere over there.

Copper caught Cassia's eye when she jumped on the hood of a car in the street running through Crissy Field. Good girl! The athletic Copper had found a place where Stormcutters had to fully reveal themselves to go after her. It made it easier for Copper to down most Stormcutters as they came near the car.

Tiernan cleaned up every Stormcutter that Copper missed. The former lord of the elite D'Danann aristocracy fought like he was born to slay these horrible beings.

Cassia saw a couple of Stormcutters flailing their arms and screaming, and Cassia imagined Zephyr, the bee familiar, stinging the funnel-men from head to toe. From the way the naked men looked, Zephyr might be going for their balls like Spirit had.

Mud squished beneath Cassia's jogging shoes, and she glanced down fast enough to see blood flowing from Lieutenant Lander's chest, despite the officer's body armor. Landers, who had survived the very first Stormcutter attack despite almost having her throat slit, was now among the dead or dying.

A wave of sadness and anger rose up in Cassia and she had an incredible urge to drop to the woman's side to see if she could use her Guardian's powers to save the officer. But Cassia knew Landers's lifeforce was almost gone. She had to move on or she might be next.

Cassia had to throw herself out of the way of a Stormcutter's blade when her magic stuttered. She hit her shoulder hard on the ground and pain jarred her so badly her teeth clacked together.

She rolled to a sitting position and flung her fire out in as wide a circle as she could. Covered in mud, Cassia scrambled to her feet. The smell of charred flesh and the sour Stormcutter stench followed her deadly, fiery wake.

Jake never left her side. With skill and precision he took out more funnel-men trying to kill them. He was cut up and bleeding, but despite Cassia's concern, she knew Jake wasn't seriously injured.

Cassia's heart felt like it was going to explode through her Kevlar vest when she saw a horde of Stormcutters going at Sydney, Conlan, and Chaos. So many were nearly on top of them that some were able to slide between Sydney's spellfire balls, past Conlan's blade, and missed the Doberman's jaws.

With a war cry of her own, Cassia released a blast of fire at the Stormcutters. She found she had more control than she had truly realized, and was able to fry most of the Stormcutters surrounding Sydney, Conlan and Chaos, and the trio took care of the others.

Sydney mouthed "thank you," but immediately went back to fighting. Her glasses were askew, her sleeves were tattered, and her upper arm was sliced near her Kevlar vest. The Doberman familiar clamped his jaws around the throat of the next Stormcutter, and Conlan took out another with his sword.

The swarm of Stormcutters around Cassia increased in a massive rush and Cassia found herself entirely surrounded by a horde of them.

"Kael!" she cried in her mind. *"I can't see you."*

Jake! Where was Jake? Dear Anu, she'd been completely cut off from him. They were supposed to stay together to get to Darkwolf, but now—

"I can scent and sense you, Princess," Kael said. *"I will find you."*

Cassia spun in a circle. She released another blast of fire, eliminating all of the Stormcutters within range.

More Stormcutters closed in on her.

No sign of Jake.

Her throat ached with the desire to scream for him. But with the noise of thunder, the shrieks, cries, and roar of battle, she knew she'd never be heard.

As the next throng of Stormcutters rushed her, she flung out more fire. The flames blazed in the night as they evaporated funnels and caught men on fire, destroying them. The Stormcutters' sour-laundry smell changed to hissing steam and incinerated flesh.

Firm ground gave way to wet sand that still shifted beneath her feet. She'd been driven down to the beach.

The sudden change in footing caused Cassia to stumble and wrench her knee. She cried out as she landed hard on her back. The impact jarred her teeth again, and the body armor chafed her back.

Stormcutters dove for her with their ice daggers. Their expressions held nothing but death.

"Take this!" she shouted, still on her back. She managed to let off enough fire to eliminate most of the Stormcutters. They popped and sizzled into nothingness.

Two Stormcutters remained as Cassia took a breath to summon more magic.

The pale, tattooed men aimed their daggers at her belly and chest.

Cassia screamed and flung herself to the side, barely missing being stabbed. She rammed her shoulder into one of the men's shins and drove him to the ground. Even though her wrenched knee sent pain shooting up her leg, her magic came easily to her as she rolled onto her back again, and she blasted the next two men into ash.

Another Stormcutter came at her, but a white blur hurtled through the air and Kael took down the Stormcutter.

Before Cassia could scramble to her feet, a wave slammed over her head in a crushing blow. Seawater covered her entire body. Her eyes blurred, and she coughed and spit out saltwater as she resurfaced. The iciness of the water caused her to shiver before she used her magic to warm herself.

As she came up for air, she spit more water and shoved her sopping hair out of her face. Her clothing clung to her body with the kind of stickiness she always felt in seawater. Her body armor felt even heavier than it had before, and pain shot through her knee.

Kael had taken a protective stance next to her on the

beach. *"Are you all right, Princess?"* At the same time he bared his teeth and growled at the Stormcutters.

Cassia managed to stand, her knee trembling. She scanned the shoreline as she did her best to block the pain from her knee with her internal magic.

"I'll live," she muttered as she flung her sopping hair out of her face.

A long line of Stormcutters waited on the beach, several feet away from her. Staring at her with determination in their expressions.

Another wave slammed into Cassia from behind and she stumbled forward. She almost lost her footing again, but kept her ground.

Cassia glanced at Kael. *"Why aren't the men coming after me?"*

"My wicked bite?" the wolf responded in a wry tone.

She would have rolled her eyes if it wasn't for the madness, the horror going on seemingly everywhere.

Then it occurred to her. Like Mystwalkers, Stormcutters probably had to stay away from seawater. Maybe for different reasons, but they couldn't get any closer to her.

Cassia backed a little more into the water, bracing herself for the next wave as she let her magic build inside her.

She flung out one of the most powerful streams of fire yet and incinerated the long line of Stormcutters. She only had a moment to feel any kind of triumph because, right behind them, was another line of Stormcutters.

What in Anu's name?

"Of course." Cassia stared at the men as Kael moved close enough that his coat brushed her jean-clad thigh. *"I am certain Darkwolf ordered them to gang up on me."*

"It is as I sensed earlier." Kael continued baring his teeth at the men. *"Darkwolf is targeting you. I believe he fears you."*

"Yeah, right." Cassia spit out more saltwater as she looked up and down the beach to assess the situation. *"He's the duo-god."*

"Do not underestimate your abilities, Princess."

"Let's hope *he* does," Cassia added out loud.

"I am sorry to say," Kael growled in her thoughts, *"that Alyssa likely informed Darkwolf of what you explained to the witches of your increased powers."*

"Bless it. You're probably right." Protected by the seawater, Cassia had the opportunity to see the massive battle of what had probably been thirty thousand humans and Otherworldly beings—but now a far smaller number with all the dead and injured.

Behind the battle rose the glittering San Francisco skyline.

Everything suddenly felt so surreal she was almost lightheaded from it.

Such an odd contrast, the city and the battle.

Like "Postcard Row," the Victorian homes on Alamo Square with the modern city of San Francisco rising up behind them. Only this was fire and rain and lightning and ice daggers and swords and blood and death. Along with a few streetlights and moving trees.

She looked toward the expansive bay. The lighthouse on Alcatraz Island flashed its glow eerily over the water, barely visible in the brilliance of the lightning from Darkwolf's storm.

Cassia tried to shake off the distracting feeling that none of this was real. The last several months could have been a nightmare, starting with Darkwolf as a powerful warlock, summoning demons and gods beyond his understanding or his control.

Every bit of this had been a nightmare come to life. A nightmare the Alliance, the city, the world wanted to wake up from.

As she stared at the line of Stormcutters again, and the battle going on behind them, Cassia grew more light-headed, dizzy. Was the strange way she was feeling due to the sense of absurdity of it all?

A magical pull snarled in her mind and she widened her eyes.

Power so dark it made her shudder.

Dark magic.

It drew her attention in the direction of the Golden Gate Bridge. It was like something forced her to turn her head to look west.

Darkwolf.

He was calling to her.

He wanted her. Or something from her. More likely to destroy her.

Well, one warlock-duo-god was about to get something he wanted.

Only what he wanted was going to be delivered with a big surprise.

CHAPTER FORTY-TWO

TORPEDO WHARF JUTTED OUT into the San Francisco Bay in an L shape on the northern shore, near the westernmost side of Crissy Field. Darkwolf's muscles were so tight he thought he might split his T-shirt. He stood on the wharf at the very end of the L as he controlled the storm and watched the battle.

Using his enhanced god-vision, he easily saw through the darkness without aid from the storm's lightning. The clash of swords against ice daggers was loud in his ears, not to mention the sounds of gunfire, the cries and shouts that made up the barrage of noises coming from the field that he could hear even over the rolling thunder.

He smelled blood and the stench of death along with the smell of his Stormcutters. Unfortunately, he had not been able to produce Stormcutters that did not have that sickening sour smell, but that was inconsequential.

His gaze roved over the scene where his bubble of protection had been. The Elvin witch might have shattered the barrier that had shielded his men from sight, but the power of his defenses around himself, Elizabeth, and Alyssa could not be breached.

Darkwolf had only set up a circular wall of protection over himself and the two women, rather than a bubble. He needed to be free of the shield overhead to control the storm. Unfortunately, having the barrier surrounding them kept him from using his other powers, but he preferred not to be noticed by the Marines flowing from the ships to the shore. He could easily incinerate them with his magic, but he didn't want to let anyone know his location.

Not yet.

He would not reveal himself until he had the bitch, Cassia, close enough to destroy. She was key. According to his scrying and what information he had gained from the little twit, Alyssa, he had a good idea of how powerful the Elvin witch was. Rid himself of her, and the battle would be won more easily.

"I think it's time you joined the fray." Darkwolf turned to Alyssa. "You can take care of the witches like you've been promising."

Alyssa faced him. Her wet hair stuck to her neck and raindrops rolled down her pale face like tears. "It might be better to wait and see if they survive the Stormcutters." She trembled beneath his stare. "With so many cutters, I could be in danger. In the past they haven't always known I'm on your side, and I've had to kill a few to protect myself."

Darkwolf studied her for a moment. "I'll let you remain here. For now. Then it'll be time for you to make good on the rest of your promises."

Alyssa nodded. "Absolutely, my lord."

Darkwolf smiled and faced the battle again. When Alyssa and his Blades called him "my lord," it turned him on, making his cock hard and his blood stir.

He glanced at Elizabeth, and wanted to take her back to the penthouse and fuck her half a dozen more times.

Or was it making love now?

Yes. He'd given her his love.

His gut twisted and he swallowed.

The storm lessened, the rain becoming lighter and the lightning less frequent.

Darkwolf shook his head, pushing all thoughts but those of battle from his head. Gritting his teeth, he sent a tremendous surge of power into the skies. He had to keep his focus on strengthening the storm. No distractions now. The storm and Stormcutters were the easiest way to eliminate the humans and the Alliance.

But the energy it took to create a storm and manipulate the Stormcutters demanded a great portion of his magic, keeping him from using most of his other powers against their enemies.

Darkwolf analyzed the battle. Many of his men were down, but his other Stormcutters had slaughtered just as many, if not more, Alliance members and Marines.

What pissed him off, though, was how many of his Blades were down. Worst of all, he sensed Silver Ashcroft had done the most damage to his Blades. He really, deep in his soul, hadn't wanted to kill her. But he'd have to, shortly.

Despite the rain, the sand turned pink in areas along the beach where numerous men and women went down. Countless skirmishes erupted almost the length of Crissy Field, from the East Beach to the West Bluff. The battle was moving west, coming a little too close for comfort, but still Darkwolf had no doubt he and Elizabeth were safe.

He glanced at Alyssa again and saw her eyes dart from Elizabeth to him. Was she afraid of the demon that Elizabeth could become?

Good. Fear in his "employees" was what he liked to see.

When Darkwolf thought most of the Marines that had been on the closest ship had passed him, he dropped the shield around himself and the two women. He concentrated the fierceness of the storm over the battle, doing his best to keep the lightning from illuminating himself, Elizabeth, and Alyssa.

Their jeans and T-shirts clung to them from the rain, water running down their faces. Darkwolf's cock hardened even more when he looked down at Elizabeth, who could have been in a wet T-shirt contest with her large breasts bare beneath her shirt, her nipples hard and prominent.

While keeping a great portion of his power on the storm, Darkwolf searched the battle with his gaze.

Fire. There. Tremendous magical fire and a presence so strong it was nearly staggering.

Unless another being had joined the Alliance, that magical signature could be the Elvin witch, according to Alyssa. But he would search all of the battle to make sure there were no presences more powerful than the one he felt coming from the area where magical fire continually burst from the being.

Darkwolf reached out with his senses, searching for the Elvin witch. Of course, her presence would be different than those of the other witches and any of the Elves. He'd always sensed something unusual about her, but after what Alyssa had told him, he expected an even greater signature—like the one where the magical fire was shooting. Although he hadn't expected *that* much power from any being.

Tendrils of his own powers snaked through the battle. He touched the essences of humans, D'Danann, Dark Elves, Light Elves, Fae, witches, even familiars—and something odd, beings similar to Elves that blinked in and out like fireflies.

Ah, probably the Mystwalkers Alyssa had told him about.

Darkwolf wished he could separate Jake Macgregor's essence from the rest of the humans, but human lifeforces were too similar to one another. He couldn't identify any separate being from any race, for that matter, except for the one in the ring of fire. He knew in his gut that particular being was the Elvin witch.

Who else could it be, if she was as magically strong as Alyssa said she was now?

"Definitely there," he murmured, his eyes still closed. "She's too far right now, but I'll reel the bitch in."

"Cassia?" Alyssa said from where she stood behind him, and he scowled as she interrupted his concentration.

"Shut the fuck up." His deep, godlike voice rumbled along with the storm. He opened his eyes and glared at her over his shoulder. "Don't say a damned thing unless I speak to you."

For a flash he thought he saw defiance in her gaze, but she immediately lowered her head and said, "Yes, my lord."

He turned back to the battle and closed his eyes again, reaching for the Elvin witch with his senses.

Gods, she was powerful. He smiled. All the better.

Despite the number of humans, Darkwolf thought he might be sensing an extraordinarily strong human essence beside Cassia. Could that be Macgregor?

If so, he had to separate the cop from Cassia.

Darkwolf concentrated and sent a greater number of Stormcutters to the Elvin witch's location. He opened his eyes and smiled again.

Her fire blazed brighter and brighter as his Stormcutters formed a circle around her, and she alone stood in the center. By his mental order, the Stormcutters pressed her closer toward the shore, away from the worst of the battle.

In that moment, he decided he didn't want the Stormcutters to kill her. Perhaps maim her and bring her his way. Otherwise, his Stormcutters would herd her toward him.

Or better yet, he'd call to her.

If what Alyssa said was true, and the Elvin witch had ascended, becoming some powerful being, he could use her. When he killed Cassia, he would absorb her magical essence.

Then he would be so powerful he could transform elite military men into Blades even easier. His Blades would be able to produce Stormcutters faster. With the larger numbers they would eventually increase to an army of millions, and spread as far and wide as Darkwolf decided he wanted to go.

The thought of wielding such power was heady.

He focused on the Elvin witch and touched her mind. He teased her by calling to her.

Darkwolf almost grinned when he sensed her acceptance of his call and she started toward him.

CHAPTER FORTY-THREE

My stomach burns constantly and heat flushes my body so much I'm surprised steam doesn't rise from my skin. Darkwolf treats me like I'm a piece of crap. Even after all I've done for the bastard.

All of his promises, his implying that he would reward me in special ways—it was all lies. I suppose that I've been naive, at best. What more could I have expected from someone as evil as Darkwolf?

Damn him. Damn me!

I'm so hot. My skin's burning. I hate him. I hate everything about him and around him, and most of all I hate myself.

But no more. It's time for me to take what's mine. It's time for me to do what I have to do.

Beneath my lashes I glance from Darkwolf to Elizabeth-Junga and back to Darkwolf. I know exactly how he'll react, and his devastation will fill my soul with greater magic. Perhaps when I take my full revenge, his powers will become mine.

Wouldn't that be the ultimate payback to everyone who's ever crossed me or treated me like I'm less?

"Poor little Alyssa. We have to watch out for her because she's so frail. Too weak to defend herself."

A smile curves my lips and I want to laugh, even as I lower my head again. Barely holding back a grin, I feel the blade strapped to my ankle and I stare at the splintered wooden wharf beneath my shoes. I don't really see the worn planks, though.

I see blood.

I feel power.

I feel victory.

CHAPTER FORTY-FOUR

CASSIA! HER NAME ROARED through Jake's mind, and fear for her raged in his heart like the storm as he fought off Stormcutter after Stormcutter. Yeah, Cassia could take care of herself, but she wasn't immortal, and if too many Stormcutters pressed in on her . . .

No, not happening. Not again. Never again. I won't lose the people important to me another time.

Jake realized then what it meant to fight like a man possessed. Long ago he had abandoned shooting his Glock in a two-handed grip. Instead, with his right hand he used his weapon to plug Stormcutters with bullets while using his left hand to slice others with his dagger. He utilized his martial arts skills like he never had before to fend off some of the Stormcutters so he had time to take down others with his Glock and his knife.

The god-containing array gun bounced against his thigh, giving him renewed determination. It was *not* going to blow up in his face. It would do what they needed to capture Darkwolf. The gun was dark as brass, made so that it couldn't easily be seen.

Jake turned his attention from the Fae who had, miraculously, just appeared.

Blood pounded in his heart and veins like liquid fire. His arms burned from slashes.

He slipped in the mud and winced when he rammed his elbow into one of the park's huge metal trash cans.

Water continuously splashed his face whenever a Stormcutter materialized from a funnel. He'd learned to ignore the surge of water in his eyes, nose, and mouth when a Stormcutter came to a stop. He went for the being just as the thing fully formed, before it had a chance to attack.

Jake tried to work his way back toward where he and Cassia had been fighting together, but the Stormcutters pressed him farther away. Almost as if intentionally separating them.

Maybe that's what Darkwolf was doing.

Without Cassia's blazing fire to turn the rain to steam above him, rain drenched him, leaking beneath his Kevlar vest and T-shirt, and into his boots. The sour smell of the Stormcutters would have nauseated him if he wasn't so filled with rage that he wanted to tear each and every one of the bastards apart. Personally.

Where was Cassia? He couldn't see her magical fire due to the height of the funnels flowing around the Alliance and the Marines.

The back of Jake's upper thighs hit the low fence of one of the marsh's wildlife protection areas. He almost flipped over the chain-link fence and into the bushes. He recovered by throwing himself forward and burying his dagger in one Stormcutter's heart while shooting another Stormcutter in the head with his Glock.

On the edge of the battle, Jake spotted Silver as she used her spellfire to take down Stormcutters and Blades.

Jake was thankful to see Silver's husband, the D'Danann warrior Hawk, pumping his powerful wings as he hovered beside her. He beheaded Stormcutters one after another with smooth strokes of his sword. Silver was an incredibly strong witch, and it had been declared she had fully recovered from being poisoned, but the fact that she was pregnant made it difficult for anyone to want to let her fight.

There'd been no holding Silver back, though. Like she'd said more than once, "I was there at the beginning. I will be there at the end."

Jake's thoughts about Silver were brief since he had to focus on keeping his own head on his shoulders, and his heart beating without an ice dagger sticking out of it.

Fire shot up ahead and to Jake's right, the flames lapping

the storm-filled sky. Magical, glittering flames. The fire came from the northwest and, judging by how far out the flames were, they were approximately in the vicinity of the shoreline.

Cassia. It had to be her sending him a message.

Kael howled from the same direction.

Messages received.

He was so certain it was both of them that relief gave him renewed strength to fight off Stormcutters and work his way in the direction of the signals. His arms burned from countless lacerations and he realized his thigh hurt like a sonofabitch. He glanced down briefly to see a Stormcutter ice dagger protruding from his thigh. With one hand still on his Glock, he snapped the blade of the ice dagger, leaving the tip in to keep from losing too much blood. He immediately let the rest of the ice dagger drop to the sodden grass while bringing his weapon up to shoot another Stormcutter.

Jake gritted his teeth as he blocked another Stormcutter blade with his own. He shot a second Stormcutter even faster than he thought he was capable of.

A couple of explosions rocked the night to his left, and huge black clouds roiled above red and yellow flames. Even though his heart jumped, he knew at once the explosions likely came from nearby vehicles. He'd seen cars parked along the road and across from the field in front of one of the many buildings that lined the southern side of Crissy Field.

It was tough going, but determination drove Jake to get to Cassia. His heart thundered like he was running a marathon, racing against a clock. Something inside Jake told him that her life and his depended on reaching her.

Hell, this whole battle rested on the two of them getting to Darkwolf. He knew it in his gut.

Just when his spine tingled with concern that he wouldn't reach Cassia in time, more magical flames punctured the sky, followed by Kael's howl. Again the fire came from the shoreline, only farther north.

He'd worked his way far enough northwest that he was closer now than he'd been when he'd first seen the flames.

Not much farther and he'd reach the shore.

The pain in his thigh was merely an irritation as Jake jabbed, shot, kicked, and hit his way through the battle. He spotted fellow officers doing the same.

Jake almost stumbled over Lieutenant Fredrickson's body. His friend's sightless eyes stared up at the stormy sky while rain pummeled his body.

Such rage seared Jake, it was like boiling oil in his veins. He let out a shout of fury that rivaled any Elvin or Fae warrior battle cry.

Goddamn. Not Fredrickson.

Jake ground his teeth. Yes, he would kill Darkwolf himself.

If it wasn't for that "fucking up the balance of all Otherworlds" bull, that was.

Goddamnit. He'd have to settle for Cassia sending the duo-god away. Hopefully to Underworld.

Jake tore into more of Darkwolf's army, battling through rain, funnel water, and Stormcutter flesh.

He finally made it over the promenade and fought his way closer and closer to the shore.

Another burst of flames speared the darkness at the same time lightning spread like veins beneath the clouds, and he glimpsed Cassia with Kael at her side. They were a lot farther ahead of him now. At least he was almost to the shoreline.

He ground his teeth as he fought with all his might to get to Cassia. He passed Hannah, who battled beside her husband, Garran. With spellfire, she obliterated the heads of some of the Stormcutters while Garran used his sword to decapitate others.

The remaining gray witches didn't hold back from killing evil beings either. It was obvious they knew that to end this war they were going to have to go beyond their beliefs and do what was necessary to save millions of lives.

When Jake's boots hit sand he found a break in the Stormcutters, and saw a clear view of the shoreline and the waves slamming the beach.

He slashed through the two closest Stormcutters and made a break for the shore where it was clear of the bastards.

Funnels whirled after him but he kept running. His boots pounded the sand as he bolted westward, in the direction the fire had come from.

Jake searched the darkness with his gaze as he ran. Flames whooshed up and he caught a glimpse of Cassia and Kael ahead, Cassia jogging in the water while Kael loped beside her. Stormcutters whirled just out of reach of the waves.

It dawned on him that the Stormcutters must not be able to cross into saltwater. Immediately, he ran the several steps that took him into the waves.

A glance over his shoulder confirmed it—the Stormcutters that had been following him stayed on the shore, their funnels whirling along the sand beside him like an escort instead of beings intent on killing him.

Saltwater caused the slashes on his arms to burn and the wound in his thigh to throb enough that he ground his teeth to bite back some of the pain.

A wave slammed into him so hard it almost drove him to the sand. He kept to his feet and continued running after Cassia, trying not to limp as he pressed on.

Damn, she was limping too. But she was still so far ahead of him. How would he catch her attention?

Jake glanced at the Glock in his right hand. He looked out at the water as he continued to run and waited for lightning to give him a clear view. As soon as he was certain there would be nothing in the bullets' path, he shot his Glock over the water three times in rapid succession.

Cassia flung up more flames, illuminating her slim form as she glanced over her shoulder. Even at a distance he caught her relieved expression, and she came to a stop to wait for him.

Jake's own relief lessened the burn in his wounds, as well as the deep, aching throb in his thigh. Water sloshed his feet. The waves, plus the fact he was running in water, made it hard to maintain a steady pace.

When he finally reached Cassia, she cried out, "Jake!" and flung her arms around his neck.

He hugged her close and kissed the top of her wet head.

"I was so damn worried. Even thought I know you can kick anyone's ass."

She gave an exhausted and humorless laugh as she looked out at the wharf. "We'll see about that."

Jake glanced at her leg. She was favoring her knee. "What happened?"

"Oh." Cassia slid her arms away from his neck and braced her now glowing palms on her knee. "That should help. I can't fully heal it—that would use too much of my power."

Jake hugged her again. "You'll be okay?"

She nodded.

"I know you can kick as much ass as Cassia," Jake said over her shoulder to Kael, who had a glint, like a spark of approval, in his eyes.

The pause only lasted the briefest of moments, urgency pulling them in the westward direction. Jake shoved his dagger into its sheath, but clenched his other fist around the Glock's grip.

Still favoring her knee, Cassia took him by his free hand and they started running again. Stormcutter funnels spun, ever present on the sand several feet away. Kael bounded ahead of Cassia and Jake.

As much as he tried, he couldn't help limping a little, too, from the pain in his thigh. The wound was deep, but the rain darkening his clothing and the fact that it was night made it difficult to tell if he was bleeding.

Not that it really mattered, unless the blade had melted and he lost too much blood. As long as he had enough strength to remain conscious, get the job done, and take care of Darkwolf, it all would be worth it.

They ran so long and hard, Jake was amazed they managed it with both of them injured. The array gun bounced at his side and he hoped to hell it was rainproof. The men who'd taken his design and made it come to life had worked their asses off. One of their goals had been to make it resistant to the rain.

When more lightning illuminated the sky, he spotted the long L-shaped wharf ahead. "Are we headed for Torpedo Wharf?"

"I think so." Cassia didn't slow her pace. "He's calling to me."

Dread hit Jake's gut like a lead ball. "What do you mean?"

"He senses me." Her wet hair slapped her face when she shook her head. "Maybe Alyssa told him about me. That I'm fully Elvin, and the other things I shared with my Coven sisters."

For a moment Jake remained quiet as rain barraged them and he and Cassia splashed through waves. Their funnel guard kept up with them on their left.

Jake slowed. "He's set a trap."

"I'm certain, and Kael agrees." Cassia eased her pace, too, because they were still holding hands. "But it's the only way I can think of to get close to him."

Jake glanced at the wolf and looked back at Cassia. "What do you mean, Kael agrees?"

"We have a mental connection." Cassia looked up at him, rain rolling down her face. "I really haven't had time to tell you. Kael and I have been able to speak to each other in our minds since the moment I could form a thought."

"No kidding?" Jake said.

Cassia smiled, and he swore Kael rolled his eyes.

They all came to a walk as they neared the pier. Thunder seemed louder here, the lightning more intense.

In the next burst of lightning, Jake spotted three figures at the very end of the L-shaped wharf that jutted out pretty far into the bay.

His heart pounded harder at the realization that the culmination of everything could come down to whatever happened now.

"There are three people on the wharf." He narrowed his eyes. "Darkwolf, Elizabeth-Junga . . ."

"And Alyssa," Cassia added in a voice so low he barely heard it in the midst of the battle roar and the rampaging storm.

Cassia, Jake, and Kael stopped at the foot of the pier and stared at the three people—beings—who stared back at them.

"This is it." Cassia squeezed Jake's hand as they stepped onto the wharf and Kael loped behind them.

In silence they walked farther down the pier.

"What's our plan again?" Jake muttered over the din they were leaving behind, and Cassia laughed.

The pleasant sound of her laughter, no matter how strained and nervous, brought warmth to his insides. He stopped her and pulled her close, not caring for that moment what was waiting for them at the end of the wharf.

"I love you, Cassia." He pressed his lips to hers and kissed her softly. "We're going to get out of this. You, me, and everyone else."

She nodded and kissed him back. "I know."

But were either of them really certain they would bring this all to an end tonight? That San Francisco and its people would be safe, and Darkwolf would be history?

That she and Jake would make it out alive?

More than anything, other than stopping this war, he wanted to spend a long, happy life with Cassia. But he'd die for her. He'd die for the people in his city.

Every hair on Jake's body stood on end.

Kael gave a warning howl.

A bolt of lightning cracked the air.

The blast rocked the wharf.

Wood, water, and sand exploded into the air.

Purple lightning hit the pier close to the shore.

The impact was so massive Jake and Cassia each lost their balance.

Cassia screamed as she swung off the edge of the pier.

Jake lunged for her and caught her fingertips even as his head spun and sound dulled.

The wharf rocked as if the entire thing might crumble and collapse into the bay. His fingertips were numb and he wondered if he still had a grip on her.

"Hold on," he shouted and could hardly hear himself due to the near deafness caused by the lightning. "Don't let go!"

The smell of burning ozone, crude oil, wood, and burned hair barely registered through the haze in his mind.

Shit. It was oral sex with Cassia all over again.

Without the fun.

A whoosh of flames erupted not far from them.

Purple lightning. Purple fire. Darkwolf's magic.

They had to get away from the purple fire that scrabbled along the pier in their direction from behind.

Darkwolf was herding them in.

Jake hadn't realized Kael was beside him. The wolf clamped Cassia's T-shirt in his jaws and pulled at the same time Jake fought to draw her up by her hands.

When they got Cassia onto the wharf, she and Jake were coughing from the smoke. Jake had a strange desire to lie down and sleep, but he jerked Cassia up with him. With Kael behind, they ran from the advancing flames.

He glanced over his shoulder. The wharf now burned and smoldered with purple fire where they'd been standing only moments before. The pier was now completely separated from the shore by at least twenty feet.

Blood thrumming in his ears and heart, Jake snapped his gaze in the direction Darkwolf was standing. In a quick flicker of lightning, Jake clearly saw the warlock-god, along with the two women standing next to him.

Darkwolf wasn't moving and he had his arms crossed over his chest. It was a little too far, and the lightning had flashed too quickly to tell for sure, but Jake swore Darkwolf was smirking.

Why wouldn't he be? He was a duo-god, for Christ's sake.

Jake shook his head as if he might hear better just by doing that. His legs and arms trembled from the lightning hitting so close, and he saw that Cassia trembled, too.

"So, he's cut off our way out of here, if we wanted to make a quick change of plans," Jake said as he glanced at the purple fire eating the wood behind them. He looked back to Cassia. "Not that we had any intention of doing that."

She stared at where Darkwolf stood. "He could have done it to keep anyone from helping us."

"He can blast us with his magic any time he wants to." Jake gripped his Glock tighter, wishing they were within range so he'd have a clear shot at Darkwolf. Yeah, he'd like to plug Darkwolf in the head with a bullet instead of worrying about containing him.

As if she read his mind, Cassia looked up at him. "Remember, we can't kill him because—"

"It'll upset the goddamned balance between Otherworlds," Jake said in a low growl.

Cassia gave a deep sigh. "If he hadn't sucked up the power of two Underworld gods, it wouldn't be a problem."

Jake grunted but kept his grip on his weapon. "That doesn't mean I can't shoot him in the kneecaps. That'll make it easier to use the array gun."

She gave a weak smile as she glanced back at the warlock-god, who remained motionless at the end of the wharf. "Unless Alyssa told him, Darkwolf doesn't know we have a means of easy escape with my ability to transport us. And we're going to get to him faster than he expects."

Jake's stomach churned. "Let's do it."

Cassia grabbed his free hand at the same time she clutched Kael's fur and they entered total blackness.

USING THE TRANSFERENCE, Cassia brought them within a few feet of Darkwolf, who jerked his head toward them with a shocked expression. Thank Anu Jake recovered from the transference immediately.

Cassia threw a spell toward Darkwolf and the two women in a desperate attempt to capture them, but his duo-god powers allowed him to react with unbelievable speed. He flung up a glittering shield.

Her magic rebounded and belted her, Jake, and Kael. Jake and Cassia stumbled back, but she instantly surrounded them in a cocoon that caught them from behind and protected the three of them from all sides. She counted on the shielding to block Darkwolf's powers no matter what magic he used.

She hoped.

"This needs to end now, Darkwolf." Cassia kept her voice steady. She refused to look at Alyssa as she spoke to Darkwolf.

Just the briefest thought of what Alyssa was and what she had done made Cassia's heart hurt. "Don't do this."

"Sure, babe." The warlock-god's laugh was mirthless. "I'll just pack up my things and leave."

"That would be a damned good idea," Jake said in a harsh tone.

Darkwolf glared at Jake and the warlock-god's expression turned so furious that Cassia could practically see dark magic rolling off him like a thick fog.

"You almost killed Elizabeth when you fought the goddess, you fucking bastard." Darkwolf raised one of his hands and pointed his finger at Jake. "You're history, Macgregor."

Jake held up his gun, gripping it with both hands. He moved his feet shoulder width apart and aimed his weapon at Darkwolf. "Not if I take you down first."

"Don't shoot!" Cassia shouted and shoved one of Jake's arms down with her hand. "The bullet will rebound within this shield and kill one of us instead."

Jake scowled.

Darkwolf smiled.

The wharf started shaking.

Hard jerks tossed Cassia and Jake from side to side within her bubble of protection. Kael managed to brace himself as he growled at Darkwolf.

Cassia hit her back against her shield so hard the breath was knocked out of her. As she slid down the barrier and landed on her ass, she had a hard time bringing air into her lungs.

Only the place where they stood rocked from Darkwolf's magic. He smirked as his end of the wharf remained still and solid. If it wasn't for her bubble shield around the three of them, they would have easily been tossed into the bay.

He was toying with them. The cat-playing-with-his-mice game—before he ate the mice.

"You have the power, Cassiandra." Kael stared at Darkwolf, his eyes practically glowing as he curled his lips back from his teeth and snarled at the warlock-god. *"Do not let him make you doubt your powers."*

Cassia didn't respond, other than giving a sharp nod.

She called on her Guardian's powers, letting them expand within her like liquid heat.

The power burning through her veins became almost heady. Intoxicating.

But she had complete control over it—and that made her feel even more powerful.

She sent out a flow of magic that radiated from her body in golden waves. The wharf stopped shaking as she fought against Darkwolf's powers and stabilized the pier.

It didn't even surprise her how easy the magic she'd used had been, and that she didn't have to concentrate to keep the wharf from shaking.

"So Alyssa was right. You have come into some pretty impressive magic." Darkwolf tossed a look over his shoulder at Alyssa.

Cassia's former Coven sister held her hand up, her fingers splayed over her heart in a nervous gesture.

"Of course, my lord." The witch turned her gaze on Cassia and the darkness in Alyssa's eyes churned Cassia's stomach.

No, not witch anymore. *Alyssa was a warlock.*

Alyssa looked from Cassia to Darkwolf and smiled, a dark, chilling smile. "Everything I've told you has come to pass, hasn't it?"

Elizabeth-Junga stood a step back from the two, her arms crossed over her chest as she studied each person who spoke. She was just as sopping wet as the rest of them, but she was still incredibly beautiful. It was hard to believe she was a former demon queen.

"Quit screwing around," Elizabeth-Junga said to Darkwolf. "Let's be done with this."

Darkwolf looked at Elizabeth-Junga and the expression on his face for just that moment was—tender? Loving?

Cassia shuddered. *Yeah, right.*

"I have plans for the Elvin witch's death." Darkwolf smiled at Elizabeth-Junga, but it turned cold when he focused on Jake next. "But like I said, you're history, Macgregor."

"Bite me." Jake's jaw tensed and his knuckles whitened from how hard he gripped his Glock.

"Sure." Darkwolf laughed. He glanced at Elizabeth-Junga again. "Or better yet, Elizabeth can do the honors since you almost killed her."

It occurred to Cassia the storm had lessened. Rain came in a steady drizzle that rolled down their shields, but the lightning and thunder had abated.

Cassia's heart raced. He was gathering more of his magic, drawing it away from the storm.

What was he going to do?

She had no idea, but she put more power into their cocoon shield, so much so that it glittered and sparked with gold.

Could the shield of an untried Guardian hold against an onslaught from a warlock-god?

Tingles raced up and down Cassia's spine and she grew suddenly cold. *"Watch out, Kael."*

She glanced at Jake, only briefly, before she stared at Darkwolf again. "Be ready for anything," she said in a low voice as she thrust more magic into her shield.

Without looking at her, he gave a sharp nod and shoved his Glock into its holster. He drew out the god-containing weapon and stood, his feet shoulder width apart. He held the gun with both hands, the weapon pointed directly at Darkwolf.

The warlock-god didn't look concerned one bit.

A burst of massive purple energy shot from him, full force, at Cassia's shield.

It felt like every molecule in her body was going to explode.

She cried out as her shield evaporated.

Pain ripped through Cassia from the force of him tearing apart her magic.

The impact flung her and Jake away from Darkwolf.

Kael yelped.

Cassia's knee wrenched again, sending pain through her entire leg. The back of her head struck the hard wood of the wharf and stars sparked in her mind.

An electrical sensation prickled her skin as she rolled to her feet and formed another shield. This time not a cocoon, but a flat barrier that she forced more power into.

In that moment she realized Jake and Kael weren't anywhere around her.

They were gone.

CHAPTER FORTY-FIVE

I would laugh at how easily Darkwolf knocks away Cassia's barriers if I didn't have my own agenda.

I don't see Jake and that stupid wolf. They aren't on the wharf any longer.

What happened to them?

Interesting.

Did Darkwolf blow Jake to pieces? Incinerate him? And all because Jake had hurt Darkwolf's precious Elizabeth.

I take a step back so I can stare at the bitch without her noticing. The brilliance from Cassia's destroyed shield still sparkles in the air, making it easier to see Elizabeth. Her attention is completely on Darkwolf and what he's been doing to Cassia, Jake, and the wolf.

Well, just Cassia now.

It's the perfect moment.

My belly tingles with excitement as I reach down and pull up my pant leg just enough to draw out the gold Mystwalker dagger I have strapped to my ankle.

So nice of the Mystwalkers to give me the tool I need.

The moment my fingers come in contact with it, the hilt of the jagged-edged dagger warms in my palm. The weapon feels good, solid in my hand, like it belongs there.

When I glance at the wharf I see that Cassia looks terrified as she throws up a shield so weak it's laughable. Some powerful Elvin witch she is.

Not.

I clutch the grip of the dagger hard enough that my hand hurts. My heart beats faster and faster.

Now, before Darkwolf looks this way. I must do it now.

Then I'll get the warlock-god from behind.

I take a step forward, my body trembling slightly. My legs are even a little shaky.

The only way to kill a Fomorii demon is to behead them or take out their heart—except if they're in human form. Then they're as weak as a mere human.

Which will make Elizabeth's death all the easier.

When I'm standing even with Elizabeth, I tense my muscles. This is it. This will be easy.

I smile.

With every bit of strength I possess, I whirl to face her—

And I drive the dagger into her heart.

The satisfying feel of metal on bone and the blade tearing through flesh travels through my arm.

She screams Darkwolf's name, but I barely hear her over the sound of my pulse, which rockets from the glee soaring through me.

What a rush, a high, even more than I felt when I murdered Mackenzie.

Elizabeth's hands shift into blue demon claws as she reaches for my hand. Her eyes are filled with terror and the knowledge that she is going to die. She doesn't have the strength now to shift into a demon and repair the damage I have done.

She starts to go slack. Blood bubbles from her mouth and pours from her chest, so much that it's visible even in the rain.

Elizabeth calls to Darkwolf, softer this time, saying something I can't hear.

So fast. It all happened so fast.

From the time I stab her until she's on her back on the wharf it's been less than seconds.

I feel a moment's exhilaration and triumph.

Powerful, black hatred slams into me and knocks me to the wharf.

Darkwolf . . .

He'll get me before I can get him.

Where will my soul go when I die?

Do I have a soul left?

I'm aware just long enough to feel my body explode.

Chapter Forty-six

Anguish punched Darkwolf's chest like a wrecking ball had slammed into him. Tears flooded his cheeks as he dropped to his knees beside Elizabeth.

"Shift!" He shouted as he slipped one hand under her head and placed his other hand over her heart. "Goddamnit, shift, Elizabeth!"

Blood gurgled up from her throat. He dropped every bit of magic from the sky, the Stormcutters—everything but a light shield, to protect him and Elizabeth so that he could care for her.

Darkwolf poured the rest of his power into healing Elizabeth.

Tears mixed with remnants of rain on his cheeks, hot against cold.

Darkwolf's entire body shook as he ground his teeth and struggled to heal her failing heart. He could repair the damage. He could.

"I'm not going to let you die," he managed to get out as his whole body seemed to expand from the amount of power he was channeling and forcing into her body. "I'm repairing you. Mending your heart." His voice trembled. "Shift, Elizabeth! Shift!"

Her mouth opened and closed, and she started to say something. More blood poured from her mouth as she tried again to speak

He didn't stop what he was doing, but he leaned closer to hear her.

"I think"—she swallowed as her words came out in a gurgling gasp—"I know what love is now."

"No!" Darkwolf shouted as he felt the whole world

crumble to pieces around him. A hundred daggers stabbed his own heart. "You're not leaving me!"

But Elizabeth's eyes became wide and glassy. Her body completely still.

In the next moment the body of the blue demon Junga appeared.

A brief flash of what Elizabeth had been.

She crumbled to silt, and a light rain began washing what was left of her into the bay.

CHAPTER FORTY-SEVEN

JAKE'S LUNGS BURNED AS HE HELD his breath beneath the surface of the bay's icy depths. The water chilled him to the bone, dangerously cold and causing his muscles to spasm and cramp. It was so dark he couldn't make anything out.

Thank God he still held the containment gun in a death grip. He hoped like hell it was waterproof.

His boots, Kevlar vest, and duty belt weighed him down. He had to get out of them.

With one hand gripping his array weapon, he struggled with his vest as he tried to unfasten it. No go.

He was going to die from lack of oxygen.

No. He was *not* going to let down countless people like he'd let down his team in Afghanistan.

After fumbling a few precious moments, Jake holstered the containment gun to free his hands and hurried as fast as he could to unfasten his body armor and kick off his boots.

As they floated away, he didn't have time to feel relief. His chest was on fire from his dwindling air supply. He had to get air.

A brief flash of light showed him the surface and he put every bit of effort into pushing himself toward it. His muscles didn't want to work as they cramped from the iciness of the water. Goddamn, but his whole body hurt from the cramping.

Jake started to see spots, as what little air in his lungs was almost gone.

Images of the explosion outside that cave, Pacer's body being ripped apart, seared his mind.

With one more massive effort, Jake broke the surface.

He took a great gulp of air, his lungs aching so much his chest hurt. He sputtered and spit out the salty, fishy taste of the water as he fought his cramping muscles to keep afloat. His duty belt was heavy, but he needed it.

He reached for the hip where his containment weapon was still holstered. Thank God he hadn't lost it while ditching his vest. He'd lost his Glock, though. Now the problem was whether or not the array weapon worked after being completely submerged underwater.

No time to think about that now.

Not only was he feeling the aftereffects of what he'd just gone through, but he was fuzzy-minded and his skull hurt like a sonofabitch. He must have taken a blow to his head on the wharf before ending up in the drink. And then there was the magic lightning that had created havoc in his mind. No wonder his brains felt scrambled.

More images from that night when dark magic had torn apart the lives of his men and their families sparked in his thoughts.

And all those captives, those dark magic slaves.

Jake ground his teeth.

I'm not losing these people. I'm not letting Cassia down.

Jake took another welcome, deep breath of brine-scented air. For a moment he was disoriented. Where the hell was he?

The lighthouse on top of Alcatraz Island strobed across the water and he gained his bearings at once. That had probably been the flash of light he'd seen while underwater, too.

The huge water swells didn't help his fight to keep afloat.

Even with his boots and body armor off, he constantly had to struggle to keep his head above water. His teeth chattered. His muscles cramped. His mind felt cloudy.

When he had a chance to catch his breath, he analyzed the situation as he treaded, his back to the wharf. He turned to his right. As he stretched out his arms and kicked his feet, he did his best to ignore the pain—the fierce burn from freezing saltwater in his wounds along with the cramps in his muscles.

Rain now fell in light drops, like tears, and the lightning and thunder had stopped. He glanced at Crissy Field as he was turning toward the wharf.

Light coming from the field showed him only what he was sure were Marines and the Alliance—no water funnels.

They'd done it! They'd kicked those bastards' asses.

Was Darkwolf dead or sent on his way?

Jake swallowed.

Cassia?

When he finally worked his cramping body around to face the wharf, the first thing he saw was Cassia behind a glittering gold shield that gave off enough light to see her by. Relief that she was alive warmed some of the chill inside him.

He realized he'd been thrown a good thirty feet from her and the wharf.

She was staring at something with her mouth open. Jake's stomach cramped as much as his muscles when he saw the expression of horror on her beautiful features. Heart pounding, he adjusted his position as he continued to tread water, moving in the direction she was looking.

Jake barely had a chance to see it happen.

One second Darkwolf was bent over the supine form of Elizabeth-Junga. The other woman was no longer there.

For only a flash, Elizabeth-Junga transformed into a huge blue Fomorii demon.

The demon crumbled into a pile of silt.

Jake's blood had been pumping at a sluggish pace in his frozen body, but his pulse moved a little faster when the realization hit him.

The demon-bitch is dead. The demon that had ordered legions of other Fomorii demons to murder thousands of humans. Junga, whose own claws and wickedly sharp teeth had killed countless people and members of the Alliance. The same demon that had scarred Rhiannon's face.

Jake stared at Darkwolf.

The warlock-god looked like he was sobbing. His entire body shook as he bent over the place where Elizabeth-Junga had been.

Jake slowly started for the wharf, needing to keep moving and needing to take care of the warlock-god. To help Cassia send him away while he was vulnerable.

Darkwolf really had felt something for the demon-woman. *How twisted is that?*

If Darkwolf hadn't murdered thousands, hadn't been responsible for bringing the Fomorii demons and the dark god and goddess to San Francisco to begin with, Jake might have felt sorry for the warlock-god.

Nope. Not even close to feeling bad for the sonofabitch.

Like the dark magic bastards who had caused the event that hung over him for years, he held no compassion for Darkwolf.

They had caused it.

Jake had fallen for it.

That wasn't happening again.

He sized up his alternatives. The cramps in his body lessened as he numbed even more from the iciness of the water.

Rather than going to Cassia, he'd head to the other side of the wharf to come at Darkwolf from behind. The purple shield around Darkwolf glittered, even though it didn't seem as strong as it had before. Jake didn't know how he and Cassia were going to take on the warlock-god, but somehow they would.

Jake could barely move his arms and legs. One of the reasons the prison had been built on Alcatraz was because the water was so cold a person wasn't likely to survive swimming from the island to shore.

Thank God he didn't have to go that far. He wasn't sure he was going to survive the thirty or so feet to the wharf if he didn't get out of the water.

Water crushed his chest, and it became harder and harder to breathe. The wharf seemed so far away. He prayed that Darkwolf would drop his shield once Jake got there. And that he'd have the strength to go after the warlock-god.

The rule about not killing Darkwolf sucked big-time.

Great Guardian and her "balance in Otherworlds" bull.

It seemed like ages before Jake finally reached the wharf. He clung to one of the pilings—one of the pier's enormous legs—grateful to have something help bear his weight. Smells of pitch, water-battered wood, and brine were strong.

The tide was high enough that it wasn't a long shot to climb from the water onto the wharf.

First, he had to find the strength to climb.

Second, he had to do it without Darkwolf noticing him.

No problem.

Jake grabbed the edge of the planks with his numb fingers, finding it hard to even hold on. Every muscle in his arms shook and cramped as he pulled himself up—thank God for his extensive military training. Not to mention the strength he had from rock climbing, and his intensive regular workouts in the gym at the warehouse and when he'd worked out of the precinct's PSF office.

He rose just high enough to peek at Darkwolf and to see if he could spot Cassia.

Immediately to his right, Cassia stood behind her golden shield—it was a much deeper gold now. She'd obviously enhanced the barrier during the time Jake swam from where he'd been tossed into the bay. This time she didn't surround herself in a bubble—she only had a wall of protection between her and Darkwolf. It looked stronger than her bubble had, even though the bubble had seemed unbreakable—until Darkwolf proved them wrong.

Kael was nowhere in sight.

Cassia spotted Jake as he raised his head just enough that his eyes met hers. In the glow of her shield he saw her shoulders slacken as if with relief to see him. She didn't give any other sign of acknowledgment and focused completely on Darkwolf.

Jake turned his head slightly to the left and saw a pair of black running shoes and soaked jeans. His gaze traveled up to see the warlock-god, now standing. Pain and rage twisted Darkwolf's features.

He let out a howl filled with anguish and fury—

And vengeance.

Darkwolf faced the shoreline, his back to Jake. The warlock-god spread out his arms, tilted his face to the sky, and howled again.

Oh, shit.

Dark storm clouds swirled so furiously over the bay that it looked like a cyclone would rise from the water.

Lightning strikes lit up the night, one after another, so close that the crack of thunder caused the wharf to shake. The almost continuous sound was nearly deafening and Jake's ears rang.

Rain poured from the sky in a rush, as if some great being had tipped over an enormous bucket with a never-ending supply of water. The rain was warmer than the bay, and partially thawed out the half of Jake that was out of the water.

The power of the storm increased, loud and furious, matching Darkwolf's next roar of pain-filled rage.

In what light there was from the lightning strikes, Jake could make out funnels on the expanse of Crissy Field, again tearing into the Alliance and Marines.

Jake's own rage rose up in him, boosting his strength. He was behind the seven-foot-tall warlock-god. The storm was so loud Darkwolf wasn't likely to hear him, so Jake didn't bother to be quiet.

He hoisted himself onto the pier. It hurt like a sonofabitch. His muscles trembled and screamed. His body shook from cold and pain. The wood dug into his flesh as he scraped his body across it.

Jake staggered to his feet.

He jerked his containment weapon out of its holster and pushed himself to go on.

As he gripped the gun with both hands, Jake paused for a moment and sucked in a deep breath of air.

That brief moment cost him.

Darkwolf turned.

Faced Jake.

Not only did Darkwolf's eyes gleam a furious red in the night, but a bright orange-red glow came through his T-shirt where his heart should be.

With both hands, Jake brought the gun up and aimed it at Darkwolf.

The warlock-god flicked his fingers.

A force jerked the weapon from Jake's hands so hard it felt like his own fingers would be ripped off.

Still, he tried to hold onto the array gun, but it slipped from his hands and skittered across the landing.

Fuck.

Jake had the urge to take a step back. But a thought whirled through his mind. If he could keep Darkwolf busy—

Praying Darkwolf would want to fight hand to hand, and not use his magic to blow Jake to pieces, he held his stance.

It was this or nothing. "Why don't you stop hiding behind your magic?" Jake said in a taunting voice. "Why don't you take me on like a man?"

Darkwolf clenched his fists at his sides as he took a step closer to Jake. The warlock-god seemed to grow even taller than his seven feet. Jake was six-six, but he found himself looking up at least a foot at Darkwolf. Bastard was as big as a horse. Probably bigger than one of those underground Otherworld giants he'd heard of.

Jake gave a dry smile. *Guess I'll just have to go for his kneecaps after all.*

"Sure. Why don't we take each other on like heathens?" Darkwolf raised one of his fists. "I'd love to slam my fist into your face and smash your nose clean into your brain, Macgregor."

"Think you could lay off your god-powers, Kevin Richards?" Jake asked, going for the surprise as Darkwolf took a step closer to him.

Darkwolf came up short, shock on his face. "How the—"

"What happened to Richards?" Jake didn't let his defenses down as he taunted Darkwolf. "Is there even a piece of the man inside you? Or did Balor and Ceithlenn turn Richards into their servant, their slave? Dirt beneath their fucking feet."

Darkwolf's eyes glowed a brighter red, his expression turning even more vicious. He started toward Jake again.

Shit.

Jake ground his teeth. *Should have stopped while you were ahead, Macgregor.*

No use waiting. Jake threw himself at the warlock-god. Dead-leg front kick to the gut—and a reverse punch, too.

Jake's teeth slammed together as his foot and fist bashed into what felt like solid steel.

Double-shit.

Darkwolf laughed, a dark, ominous laugh, and he picked his rear leg up high to deliver a front kick as he stepped closer to Jake.

He turned his body to avoid Darkwolf's kick. The warlock-god used his forward momentum and took Jake down with a roundhouse kick to his chest.

Jake couldn't help a loud grunt of pain as at least one of his ribs cracked and air whooshed out of his lungs.

"What's this about fighting like a man?" Darkwolf said as he rammed Jake with another powerful kick to the side while Jake was still on his hands and knees.

A sickening crack that Jake felt to his toes.

There went another rib.

"Doesn't look like there's much man in you, Macgregor." Darkwolf tossed a look at Cassia as Jake pushed himself to his feet. "After you die, she's next."

Rage boiled inside Jake. No way in hell was Darkwolf going to get to Cassia.

Jake barely leaned out of the way—or maybe he just staggered out of the way—closer to the array gun as Darkwolf aimed his fist at Jake's head.

Ignoring all the screaming pain and numbness throughout his body, Jake charged Darkwolf, who came up short at the unexpected move. It gave Jake the chance to deliver a reverse punch to Darkwolf's jaw.

Jake felt Darkwolf's jaws snap together as the bastard's head jerked back.

Good. Damn you. I hope that *hurt like fuck.*

Snarling louder than a pissed-off grizzly, Jake jammed his foot behind Darkwolf's closest leg, tripped the warlock, and rammed his elbow into Darkwolf's throat.

Darkwolf was so big that when he hit the wharf it actually shook. Jake knew he hadn't done any real damage. Darkwolf was a god now, for Christ's sake.

But it had gotten Jake closer to the array gun.

He fumbled as he reached for it, his fingers brushing the weapon's grip as Darkwolf sprang to his feet.

The faces of his men who had died that night from dark magic flashed through his mind, one after another.

Jake dug the heel of his foot into the wooden planks of the pier and shoved himself close enough to the gun to grab it by its grip.

He fought back the pain in his chest from the broken ribs. Blood flowed into his mouth as he tried to take a deep breath. One rib no doubt had punctured his lung, and who knew what else.

Darkwolf stalked toward Jake, a malicious, murderous expression on his face.

Jake snatched the gun and raised himself just enough that he could grip it in both hands. He aimed it at Darkwolf.

The warlock-god dove for him.

Jake pulled the trigger.

A laser beam shot from the gun.

The weapon exploded in Jake's hands.

Brilliant red glow.

Shrapnel piercing his skin.

Lights out.

CASSIA SCREAMED WHEN SHE SAW JAKE go down. Blood flowed from his nose and mouth. Pieces of metal from the gun had pierced his body.

Jake didn't move.

Cassia's love for Jake almost tore her apart at the thought that he could be dead.

But Darkwolf was surrounded in red light.

The warlock-god touched it and jerked his hand back, crying out as if in pain.

The containment array had worked!

But Jake . . .

You've got to take your mind off of him.
It's time to deal with Darkwolf.

Cassia readied herself for what she'd been working on while Jake fought Darkwolf.

She dropped her golden shield.

Cassia called forth untapped powers she'd known resided deep within her magical core. She filled her lungs with air.

She started to take the step that would finish it all. End this insanity—

Darkwolf punched a gap through the containment with focused dark magic.

The red containment fell away.

His power slammed into her.

Cassia screamed at the agony. It felt like a hole burned through the Kevlar and inside her chest, straight to her spine.

As she struggled to focus her eyes and even to breathe, she looked down to see there wasn't a gaping hole in the body armor.

But she still felt the burn, the fire. She wanted to roll over and curl into a ball until it stopped hurting. She swore she could smell burning flesh along with Darkwolf's wolfsbane scent.

Memories of her ascension day returned, the agony she had endured without revealing her pain.

She'd do the same thing now, and not give Darkwolf the satisfaction of knowing how badly he'd hurt her.

Barely able to focus at first, she got to her knees, her wrenched knee screaming with pain. She moved to her feet. With effort, her magic filled her, cooling the burn in her chest and easing the ache in her knee.

"You've got to stop this, Darkwolf." She extended her arm to encompass the city as she took several shallow breaths. "What good is all of this going to do you?"

Darkwolf stared at her for a long moment. "Without Elizabeth, it means nothing now. All I have left is the pain in my heart and the stains of thousands of deaths on my souls."

"Then stop," she whispered. Even as she spoke, she built

her power inside her again. More intense, more fierce. No matter Darkwolf's choice, she had to do this.

He shook his head. "I've come too far." He smirked, but it was sad. "Besides, what is there left for me but domination of cities, states—the whole fucking country for that matter."

"There are other choices." Cassia felt the glow of her magic wanting to burst from her skin, but she now easily managed it. "You can go to Otherworld, and live someplace—"

"Where I can be controlled, caged?" he said as he crossed his arms over his chest. "I don't think so."

"Darkwolf—" she started.

She stumbled over her words as she saw Jake pushing himself up. *He's alive! Jake's alive!*

Darkwolf was oblivious to Jake, who got to his knees behind the warlock-god.

Cassia quickly tried to keep Darkwolf's attention on her. "Kevin," she added softly, "you can start over. You don't have to be this anymore."

"I don't have to be this *what*?" he shouted, and his face grew red as purple lightning cracked the sky. "This freak?"

She tried to keep her poise as she saw Jake, still behind Darkwolf, bring his hands together. Confusion raced through her as she saw Jake lace his fingers into a doubled fist. He swayed a bit but then seemed to gain control of himself.

"I didn't say you're a freak." Cassia's magic built higher and higher as Jake raised his arms.

Then Kael crawled onto the wharf.

Cassia's relief was sharp, immediate.

Kael stood beside Jake, behind Darkwolf, and bared his teeth.

Even as relief that Kael was all right flowed through Cassia, she focused completely on Darkwolf.

She knew exactly what she had to do—and the timing had to be perfect with his action. "I—I think you'll be happier there."

This time Darkwolf's laughter sounded like a bark. "Give me a fucking break—"

Jake slammed his fists and arms at the back of Darkwolf's knees.

Kael snatched Darkwolf's shirt in his jaws, helping to jerk the warlock-god down.

A look of surprise shot across Darkwolf's face.

Cassia's hair prickled and an electrical sensation traveled beneath her skin as she put every bit of force that she had into her power.

Gold magic shot from her body, straight to Darkwolf.

As he fell she engulfed him with her power.

It surrounded him like a mummy's wrappings, binding his arms to his sides and forcing his legs together.

The moment Darkwolf's body hit the wharf, her magic snatched him.

She focused with all her might and sent him to the first place that came to her mind.

The warlock-god vanished.

Her gold magic fell away.

Darkwolf was gone.

Kevin Richards was gone.

The nightmare was finally over.

CHAPTER FORTY-EIGHT

JAKE REMAINED ON HIS KNEES, shivering from the cold, still unable to believe Darkwolf was gone. Finished.

For a long moment Jake, Cassia, and Kael stared at the spot Darkwolf had been. Kael sniffed the area with his big nose, as if making sure no sign of the warlock-god remained.

Jake's breathing came hard and fast. *I didn't let them down. I didn't let them down.*

It had stopped raining, and the storm had cleared so completely that stars sparkled in the sky. Bright and clear, as if the heavens were sharing in the Alliance's victory.

Jake's gaze finally met Cassia's. He drank in every beautiful inch of her, from her wet, matted hair to her bloody, mud-smeared face and clothing.

Despite every ache, every pain in his body and face, he pushed himself from his knees to his feet and stumbled toward Cassia. He had to hold her, feel her, make sure she was real, that she was okay.

She rushed to him and he grabbed her, crushing his broken ribs, digging shrapnel into his skin. But he didn't care.

Her voice shook from the force of her sobs. "It's over. It's really over."

"It feels so good to hold you." He squeezed her tight and shut his eyes. The thought that something could have happened to her seized his chest as if giant Mystwalker collars banded him.

"I was so worried . . ." He choked up and his eyes burned as she drew away. She had scratches and cuts on her face and arms. "You're bleeding—" he started.

"Superficial." But her eyes looked wide with fright. "But

you—I sense the extent of your injuries. All this blood—
your mouth, your nose—everywhere."

Adrenaline that had kept him running all night started to
fade.

He blinked as his vision wavered. His body burned from
every single cut down to the stab wound in his thigh. He
ached from his fight with Darkwolf, his broken ribs, the toll
his trek in the bay had taken on his muscles, and the iciness
that had frozen the blood in his veins.

Jake's body suddenly felt as cold as if he was back in the
bay, and he started to shake. He couldn't stand any longer,
and dropped to his knees. The impact was hard enough to jar
his now chattering teeth and his broken ribs, and he almost
cried out.

Cassia's surprisingly strong grip kept him from falling on
his side.

Jake heard her calling his name from somewhere far
away, yet he was looking right at her. Her mouth was moving. What was she saying?

The faces of his men no longer passed through his mind
like an endless loop.

Darkwolf was gone. Cassia was okay.

And right now he wanted to sleep. He wanted the comforting warmth the darkness would bring.

And it came.

"YOU ARE SO NOT GOING TO DIE ON ME," Cassia shouted, still
gripping him, before she eased his unconscious form down
to the wet planks. "You've heard of haunting? Well I know
where to come after you if you pass from this Otherworld,
and you'll wish you hadn't died once I get through with you."

At the same time she settled him on the wharf, she let
her healing magic pour into him. Not only was he going into
shock, but his body temperature had dropped dangerously
low.

"I will attempt to warm him, too." Kael nuzzled the side
of Jake's neck. *"He is much too cold."*

Kael's wet coat shimmered, then dried, as if he had never

been in the bay. He lay beside Jake, lending him his tremendous body heat.

"Thank you." Cassia whispered in his mind.

She infused Jake with gentle warmth, bringing him slowly back to a normal temperature and drying his clothing at the same time. Color returned to fingers that had been nearly blue with cold, and the rest of his skin gained its normal hue.

His face went from pale to tan again, and the bruises on his face vanished. Shrapnel that had been stuck in his skin fell away, and the cuts healed along with other wounds.

Cassia relaxed as Jake settled into a light, healing sleep rather than shock-induced unconsciousness. Just by allowing her magic to surface along her skin, she dried her own clothing and healed what scratches she had on her body.

The gentle wind caressing her face as she concentrated on Jake seemed warm compared to the cold of Darkwolf's storms.

A lump rose in her throat as she thought about Darkwolf.

Yes, he'd committed horrors and brought about the forces that sought to destroy San Francisco and whatever stood in their way . . . But Darkwolf had been possessed from the beginning of every atrocity he'd been associated with.

Cassia stared down at Jake as she let more healing magic flow into him, and a second lump in her crowded the first. She could have lost Jake tonight.

Like Darkwolf had lost Elizabeth-Junga. How ironic that the warlock would fall in love with one of the demons that had been sent to control him all those months ago.

Memories of the pain in Darkwolf's eyes, in his cries to the heavens after Elizabeth's death, caused the backs of her eyes to burn.

The pain, the suffering brought to thousands and thousands and thousands of people—

All due to the wills of two ancient gods who had sought to return to the Earth Otherworld and gain control over what they once ruled—the Old World.

But Alyssa. Where had she gone wrong? What happened to make her choose darkness and death over light and life?

Cassia's gaze strayed to the spot where Darkwolf had killed Alyssa, had caused her body to evaporate.

Can the lump in my throat get any bigger? she thought as her eyes watered and burned more.

Cassia finished repairing and knitting up Jake's injuries with her magic. The worst of what he'd been through had been the hypothermia, his broken ribs, his punctured lung, and where he'd been stabbed in his thigh. Fortunately the stab wound hadn't been a little more to the left or it would have severed the femoral artery.

But now he was completely healed.

When she was finished with Jake, she focused her magic internally and healed her own wounds, including her wrenched knee. Before, she'd had to make sure she had enough power to fight Darkwolf, contain him, and send him away.

Jake stirred, coughed, and let out a low groan. Cassia stroked one of his stubbled jaws as he opened his eyes. "Took your time, Jake Macgregor," she said with a smile as she moved her face close to his.

"Hi, Princess." He returned her smile as he reached for her and drew her into his embrace.

He gave her the sweetest kiss of her life.

A MIXTURE OF RELIEF, anger, pain, and concern anchored itself in Jake's chest. The feeling grew heavier and heavier as he squeezed Cassia's hand.

The power of her transference took them to the beach. Now they trudged through the sand, back toward Crissy Field where men and women were picking up the pieces of their lives.

Countless others' lives.

Kael strode alongside, his head high and proud as always.

Now that the storm was over, helicopters could safely monitor the skies and carry in volunteers and medical personnel. Many people would be working hard to save the lives of the injured, and many others would start the process of caring for the bodies of those people they hadn't been able to save.

Massive spotlights flooded the grim and grisly scene. Emergency vehicles' red and blue strobes flashed on pale, dead faces.

So much death.

Jake's stomach churned.

The fact that Darkwolf was gone—the demons and the dark god and goddess were gone—that didn't mean things were going to be fine and dandy. The city and its people would take a long time to heal. What had happened over a period of weeks had taken its toll on the entire country.

One thing about Americans, though. As a people they persevered. They never gave up.

Jake knew in his heart that even if the Alliance had lost tonight, Americans would eventually have found a way to bring about Darkwolf's downfall. That was how the United States was built. Millions of men and women had given and continued to give their lives to gain and protect America's freedom, for over two centuries.

A Nation indivisible.

Liberty and justice for all.

No matter what the toll, no matter how long it took, America would have persevered.

Jake swallowed and kept a firm, grounding grip on Cassia's hand as they walked.

After dealing with gods and goddesses and beings from Otherworlds and Underworlds, Jake didn't know what to think. He'd never been totally sure he believed in a God, much less multiple gods.

And now?

Jake looked up at the heavens, at the stars that so clearly sparkled like they never had before.

If there was just one God watching over Earth, Jake hoped He heard Jake's prayer of thanks.

Thanks that this Otherworldly war had finally ended tonight.

Thanks that the life of the woman he loved had been spared.

CHAPTER FORTY-NINE

DAIRE WALKED AMONG THE LIVING and dead, searching, searching. Blood dried on his sword as he gripped it while he looked for Cassia and Kat. He'd have known if either one of them had died.

He gripped his sword tighter. Yes, he would have.

Wouldn't he?

But Kat was human.

And Cassia . . .

He glanced again toward the dark pier that had been lit up with Cassia's magic, what seemed like an Otherworld lifetime ago. The rain had stopped, the warlock-god's funnel men had vanished—but everything now remained dark and quiet at the end of that wharf. For too long, far too long.

The ache in his side where he'd taken a Stormcutter dagger increased, but he simply pushed the pain away. It was a mere irritation. He would deal with the injury later, once he found Cassia and Kat.

Flashing blue and red lights from human emergency vehicles were somewhat bothersome. Hundreds of humans were working to save the lives of injured Marines and Alliance members. Some humans carried wounded persons from the battlefield to waiting vehicles with more flashing lights.

Daire frowned. Magic would save lives faster than human means. However, it was true that not enough magical beings were present to save everyone.

Most of the magical beings couldn't stay, though. The Fae had left, all but the D'Danann warriors.

The Drow had vanished—probably because the battle had raged so long that it neared dawn.

Mystwalkers hovered around trees in their mist form. Probably waiting to be sent back to Otherworld. They needed to get to freshwater, no doubt.

Daire strode toward the mist and Alaia rose. "Your people fought with such bravery," he said.

"As did yours." Alaia glanced down to the mist. "We must return home, and soon."

"The Great Guardian granted me the temporary power to move large numbers of peoples through the veil." Daire held out his hand, and he and Alaia clasped each other's arms in the traditional warrior's hand-to-elbow grip. "Travel well."

Alaia gave a deep nod as she released him and he bowed in return. She faded into the mist swirling around the trees. The Dryads had moved the trees, marching them across the field while fighting Stormcutters.

Daire closed his eyes and reached out to every Mystwalker who remained alive. Thank Anu most of them had survived.

With little effort, thanks to the Guardian, Daire sent them to their home with a mental command. When he opened his eyes he no longer saw mist, only mud, grass, and trees where the Mystwalkers had been.

Daire straightened his shoulders and continued looking for Cassia and Kat.

He had been introduced to the Coven of white magic D'Anu witches after the last battle. Those witches now rushed alongside Light Elves and D'Danann, moving from one downed person to another. Sparks and glowing healing magic mingled with the annoying red and blue flashes of the human emergency transports.

Daire had come to greatly respect the five D'Anu gray magic witches and was pleased to see all of them alive. Silver, Copper, Hannah, Sydney, and Rhiannon had their mates at their sides as they healed and saved lives.

On the hint of a breeze, Daire caught the same exotic perfume that had captured his attention in the last battle.

Kat.

He snapped his attention to the left, and started jogging

away from the shore and toward Kat. His heart beat a little faster. Smells of blood, death, and the Stormcutters' stench almost obscured the scent of Kat's perfume. But she was there. Somewhere.

Daire slowed his steps as he saw her. Kat's dark head was lowered as she bent over an injured woman. Blood covered Kat's fingers as she applied pressure to a wound in the woman's side.

Something akin to a boulder formed in his chest, and another one in his throat. He hadn't realized just how much he had come to care for the human woman.

Kat had agreed to stay with the emergency vehicles until the fighting was over as she had no fighting skills. Although she had stated she could bring a man down with a kick to his bollocks, and Daire believed her. But he was pleased she had the sense not to fool herself into thinking she would have had a chance against the Stormcutters.

Daire slipped around humans and Otherworld warriors until he finally reached Kat. He knelt next to her and wanted to wrap his arms around her, hold her tight, and kiss her countless times to know that she was alive. But at this moment she was far too busy saving others' lives.

She looked at him, and her relief to see him was as obvious as his was to see her. "Thank God you're okay, Daire," Kat said in a whisper as she continued to press a large bandage to the woman's side.

"Thank the gods and goddesses you are as well," he replied in return, with the hint of a smile.

"Can you help her?" Kat glanced from him to the woman, who moaned, her breath rattling in her chest.

He raised his hands over the woman and fed her some of his healing magic while touching her essence. "Yes, this one can be saved."

When he was certain the woman would live, Daire brought Kat to her feet and kissed her, tender and slow. But not as long as he wished to. They had work to accomplish.

Kat and Daire moved away from each other, then held hands for a moment until they reached the next person who needed to be saved. They continued on and on through the masses to find and heal injured human and Alliance warriors.

Before they reached their third injured warrior, Daire's breath stuck in his chest for the second time that night.

At the foot of the wharf, with Kael beside them, Cassia stood with Jake Macgregor. The pair looked well despite their ragged clothing and battle-worn appearances.

Daire smiled and worked with Kat to tend to the next person they came to.

Preordained destinies were highly overrated.

CHAPTER FIFTY

THE THUMP OF CASSIA'S HEART grew louder in her ears. She and Jake waited in the palace in the trees for an audience with the Great Guardian.

Oh, and how her mother was making them wait.

"It'll be okay, Princess." Jake draped his strong arm around her shoulders and squeezed her to him.

She hoped like crazy he was right.

Cassia sighed. He smelled so good, all spicy and masculine and delicious. She laid her head against his muscular chest and settled into his embrace. After all they'd been through, he was like a cove sheltering her from a storm. He'd become her world and she couldn't imagine one without him.

She had completely dropped her glamour for the first time since she was twenty-five, and her ears were again pointed. Jake had enjoyed tracing them with his tongue when they made love that morning. It felt different completely revealing every part of her that was Elvin.

Kael had remained in the San Francisco Otherworld with the witches while Cassia and Jake made the journey to meet with the Great Guardian.

Cassia and Jake both wore clean jeans, T-shirts, and jogging shoes—funny how she'd come to be used to them since the war began. She had wondered if her mother would disapprove of her not wearing a dress or robe, but Cassia had decided she didn't care. She was tired of doing everything in her power to please her mother. It was time to do something for herself.

With all her heart, she hoped there wasn't a condition that would destroy all of the Otherworlds if she chose Jake. If she was even given the opportunity to choose him. The Great

Guardian had the power to wipe her memory of Jake, and his of her.

The idea was too painful to bear and her body went numb. She did her best to push the thought away.

She let her gaze drift from window to window in the great, magnificent, and incredibly bare chamber where they had last met with her mother. Despite her best efforts to not dwell on the future at this moment, a heaviness settled inside Cassia's chest.

How lonely it must be for her mother. To be an all-powerful being who had lived so long. Who had seen peoples, places, and things come and go, grow and evolve. Change. And die.

While she stayed the same. All-knowing, all-powerful.

Guarding.

Guiding.

Living.

Forever.

Alone.

Cassia swallowed. She didn't want that. Goddess, but she didn't.

Please, there has to be some other way.

Yellow butterflies floated in and out of the arched windows of the orchid-scented room. The ivy climbing around the columns between windows gleamed deep green in the golden light. The brilliant reddish-orange fire orchid petals flickered in a light breeze, causing them to look like the flames that had given the orchids their name.

Her mother had probably named them. She'd been around so long she'd probably named everything. Even dirt.

Cassia looked up into Jake's eyes and found him studying her. "I keep worrying about those 'consequences,' " she said.

"And well you should, Daughter." The Guardian's voice came at the same time brilliant white light flashed in the room and the sweet smell of wildflowers flowed around them.

She always had to make an entrance lately with Cassia and Jake.

Cassia closed her eyes only briefly before turning to her mother, dread cramping her belly.

As usual, the Great Guardian radiated beauty and power. Somewhere along the way, her mother had lost her ready, mysterious smile—at least for Cassia and Jake.

Again, Cassia pulled him down with her and they each lowered onto one knee as they bowed before her.

Hair at Cassia's nape prickled as the Guardian made them wait. Seconds slipped by and Cassia darted her gaze to Jake, who was looking directly at the Guardian. She wanted to smile at this man who knew who he was and his place in the world.

"Rise," the Great Guardian said after an interminable amount of time that Cassia thought came close to unacceptable.

Cassia and Jake eased up, and stood straight and tall before the Guardian. Cassia couldn't help tilting her chin up, perhaps with a hint of defiance. Yes. Defiance.

Her mother's expression was cool and appraising. "Daire requested an audience with me earlier," she said, and Cassia's belly fluttered, wondering what he had come for. She saw Jake's frown from the corner of her eye. "Daire asked for leniency, and asked that I accept the human into our fold."

Jake's surprised expression mirrored the wonder within Cassia. Could Daire's intervention somehow make this all work out?

"However," the Guardian said, dashing Cassia's hopes as she continued, "I have been lenient in our past encounters, but in this I cannot and will not be."

Jake slipped his hand into Cassia's and she clung to him, grateful for his support and for the love flowing through their connection.

The Guardian didn't acknowledge their show of unity. She looked from Cassia to Jake, letting her gaze rest on him long enough that Cassia would have had a hard time meeting her mother's eyes for that length of time. Jake didn't so much as blink.

Finally the Guardian returned her gaze to Cassia. "You have three choices, and only three."

Jake squeezed Cassia's hand tighter. Her heart beat faster.

"Your first choice, Cassiandra," the Guardian said, "is to remain in Otherworld and take your permanent place as one of the Guardians. As you have been destined, you will become the next Great Guardian after six more centuries of training. Your powers will continue to grow far beyond your imagination." Her gaze turned on Jake. "The human must return to the Earth Otherworld, and I will wipe your memories of each other."

Jake went completely still and his grip on her hand was so tight it was painful.

Cassia wanted to shake her head. *No, no, no.* Instead, her body trembled as she waited for her other choices.

The Guardian looked at Jake, whose jaw was tight, probably from holding back the urge to shout at the Guardian.

"The second option is that your human stays in the realm of the Light Elves," the Great Guardian said. "He will forsake *everything* in his San Francisco Otherworld. If he wishes I can bestow upon him magic and immortality. He will never return to his own Otherworld."

"What?" Cassia's gut twisted. No, she couldn't do that to Jake. "No. You can't do that to him."

Jake looked stunned, like he was unable to process what the Guardian had just said. Cassia swore she heard his heartbeat slow to a crawl and the hairs rise on his skin. For once he remained speechless, like he couldn't get a word out.

Before either Cassia or Jake could speak, the Great Guardian continued with the conditions. "The third and final option is that you return to the Earth Otherworld with your human."

Cassia went limp with relief, and she leaned against Jake's arm. This was an easy choice.

"However," her mother said, then paused as her gaze hardened. Cassia immediately tensed again. "Should you choose this option, the consequence is that you shall be stripped of your magic and you shall not serve as a Guardian in any capacity."

Dear Anu.

Intense heat burned in Cassia's ears as she heard the words but didn't want to accept them.

No magic?

Over four centuries of magic and then to have her powers taken away from her would be like losing a limb. A part of her that she couldn't imagine living without.

Just being without her magic for that brief time when she went through her transition with Jake had been beyond frightening.

"What the *hell*?" Jake was saying, his face flushed dark. Cassia could barely keep up with his words the way her mind was whirling, and from the heat expanding through her. "You can't do that to her."

The Guardian gave a dry laugh. "Not only can I do so, I do not have a choice should I want it."

Jake's face was still flushed with anger. "What do you mean?"

Her mother looked as if she was only indulging his questions because she was in the mood. Maybe in the mood to torture them both.

"Once again we're talking about the balance in Otherworlds," the Guardian said with an expression Cassia couldn't identify. "Her powers are becoming, and will be, so magnificent that they must be bestowed upon a replacement."

The weight of possibly losing her powers was so great, and her responsibility to her mother was strong, too.

"If I choose Jake"—Cassia could barely speak, but forced out the words—"what does this mean to you? I—I don't want you to suffer because of my decision."

"Another millennium to train my replacement is but a brief flash of time." The Guardian's expression was the equivalent of a shrug. "I will bear another female child immediately who will go through the same rigors of training that you have." The Guardian's gaze hardened as she fixed it on Jake. "Only I will ensure her training is not compromised."

"What a bunch of bull." Jake took a step forward, releasing

Cassia's hand and clenching both fists. "You don't have to take away her magic."

"I accept the third option." Cassia let her voice cut across Jake's even as her head spun and her heart ached over the knowledge she would lose her magic.

"I will give up my powers to live on the Earth Otherworld," she continued, "to spend my life as a mortal and live the rest of my years with Jake. My love is too great for him to choose otherwise. And I *will not* take from him his human life and make him subject to the prejudices of the Light Elves. Never."

His jaw dropped and he snapped his gaze to hers. "Cassia—"

"Jake." Cassia hardened her tone as she cut in. "This is *my* decision. I believe my mother truly has no choice but to give my powers to a replacement." When he tried to interrupt again, she put her fingers over his lips and said softly, "The fact that I've been given choices at all is a gift."

His throat worked and he looked as if so much emotion was welling up within him that he was having a hard time speaking. "I can't ask you to do this."

"You're right." Cassia smiled. "You can't. It's my decision."

"I love you so much." Jake grabbed her in a hold so tight he knocked the breath from her. "I don't know what the hell to say."

Cassia gave him an impish grin. "Just say the hell you'll marry me."

Jake grinned back. "Are you proposing?"

"Absolutely," she said, and Jake brought his mouth to hers, hard and urgent.

His kiss held the depth of his love for her. She gave everything of herself into their kiss in return.

"Cassia Macgregor." She drew away and couldn't help her smile. "I've never had a last name. It sounds great."

Jake brushed his thumb across her cheek as he looked down at her. "Yeah. It does. Really great."

"Now that you have made your decision," came the Guardian's dry voice, "I will return you to Otherworld."

Cassia felt too giddy with love for Jake to think of anything else, and she'd all but forgotten the Great Guardian. She pulled away from Jake and stared at her mother, who had always been an untouchable being. A being who had borne Cassia, then stayed at a distance as she grew up.

Cassia walked away from Jake to stand inches from her mother.

"What the heck," she said before she took one more step, wrapped her arms around her mother's waist, and embraced her. "I love you, Mother."

It was like hugging sunlight, warm and bright, only something substantial enough to hold onto.

At first her mother seemed shocked into immobility, but then her mother embraced her in return and whispered, "I do love you, Cassiandra."

"I know." Tears formed at the corners of Cassia's eyes, one tear rolling down her cheek as she drew away and met her mother's gaze. Cassia didn't let her mother go. "You've only done what you've thought is right."

Her mother's expression turned softer than it had been in the time since Jake and Cassia had challenged her on Cassia's destiny.

"I truly am sorry I cannot leave your magic intact." Her mother cupped her cheek and warmth radiated from her mother's palm. "But you understand."

Cassia nodded as a tear rolled down her cheek. They completely parted and Cassia managed a smile. "Thank you for what you have been able to give me."

The Guardian gave a low nod.

"I have just one question," Cassia said, wondering what her mother's response would be. "What is your true name?"

Her mother gave one of her mysterious smiles. "Eternity." She paused and added, "And you, my daughter . . . Your true name is Destiny." Then the Guardian vanished like a bright light blinking out.

"Maybe I do believe in destiny after all," Jake murmured.

But as her mother disappeared, Cassia didn't have time to explore her emotions.

A force tugged her magic, jerking her forward a step.

Harsh, hot tears flooded Cassia's cheeks as her magic drained from her.

It was slow, painful, agonizing. Almost as bad as her ascension ceremony.

Like her very breath, her heart, her soul were all torn from her.

She wasn't sure it was the pain of loss, or the pain of her magic being taken. Maybe both.

Her powers slipped completely away, the sparkles and warmth at her core were gone. A vessel that had been full and rising for centuries now depleted. Empty.

More and more hot tears burned her eyes as she shut them tight and sobbed in harsh jerks.

Her star birthmark—somehow she knew it was gone, too. As well as her pointed ears.

With never-ending tears, she pulled her T-shirt out of her jeans just to see her belly button—

Yes. No birthmark.

Another blow. Almost every part of what had been her had been stripped from her.

At least she had her memories.

She prayed her mother wouldn't take those, too.

Jake wrapped her in his large embrace, against the solid, comforting warmth of his chest.

"It hurts so badly." Cassia's body shook as she cried and slipped her arms around his waist. "I didn't know it would be so painful."

"You can change your mind," Jake said, and it sounded like the words brought him close to tears, too. "I never wanted this for you."

"No." Cassia struggled to get herself under control. "I choose *you*." She tilted her head back to look at him. "I have no regrets. None." She buried her face against his chest again. "This pain will lessen with time. Losing you—that's something I could never get over."

Jake rocked her as he held her, and she thought she felt a hot tear land on her head.

Her body weakened and grew heavier as the last of her magic vanished.

Then everything went dark and the Guardian sent them through the veil.

Chapter Fifty-one

The moment their feet touched something solid, Cassia thought she was going to vomit. Her stomach clenched as nausea rolled through her.

Cassia gave a combination laugh and sob as she stepped back, but gripped Jake's biceps. "I see what you mean." She sniffled and smiled as they looked at each other. "Going through the veil without my Guardian powers is a 'real bitch.'"

Jake answered her smile with one of his own, but it looked strained. "Are you sure about all of this?"

She smacked him on the arm. "If you ask me that one more time, I'm going to—to tackle you."

At that he laughed. "I'm ready when you are."

Cassia looked away from Jake to see that they were standing in a foyer in a house she didn't recognize. It was narrow. On the left, wooden slatted steps ran from the foyer onto a landing above. To the right, a couple of steps went down that would take them into a living room. A hallway disappeared behind the stairs, probably to a bedroom.

The house was older, but well kept. Taupe carpeting covered the floor, and the walls were a lighter taupe that went well with the flooring. The trim was all off-white, including the crown moldings on the ceiling.

Jake's place. It must be.

The house looked like an average-sized San Francisco home that had been modernized inside. She had no idea what the outside looked like. Yet.

Comfortable-looking leather couches filled the living room, and beyond that she could see a kitchen through a doorway. A huge wall unit held a large-screened TV, stereo, and other electronic devices. There weren't decorations, knickknacks on anything else of the surfaces, or pictures on the walls.

It looked like a bachelor pad, with magazines and newspapers scattered on a coffee table, jogging shoes kicked off in a corner, and a pair of white socks next to them. A Styrofoam cup sat on one end table with an energy bar wrapper next to it. Both sat beside a remote control that probably went with all the high-tech equipment in that wall unit.

In one corner sat a pile of rappelling equipment, including nylon cord and harnesses, along with boots. A large framed backpack was braced against the wall next to the equipment, with a sleeping bag bound tight beneath it. Jake no doubt used all of that for his rock-climbing and hiking hobbies.

A medium-sized, yellow, well-used kayak was propped against another wall and Cassia imagined herself going down the rapids with Jake.

She couldn't wait until he took her with him. Everywhere.

The place had a familiar scent, but also that certain smell homes got when no one had lived there for a while. Dust on the coffee table and other surfaces confirmed it.

"Your place?" she asked as she moved her gaze from the room to him.

He shrugged. "First time I've been here since we moved headquarters into that warehouse."

Cassia gave him a sly grin. "Why don't you show me what your bedroom looks like—so I can tackle you?"

Even drained of her powers, Cassia felt an empowerment of a different kind. A woman filled with love for her man.

Jake held her hand, leading her upstairs, and sparkles tingled in her belly as if she still had magic. But she knew it was the magic of the moment, which somehow made it even more special.

At the top of the landing, Jake drew her into a large bedroom on the right. She smiled at the sight of rumpled white bed sheets and a denim-colored comforter tossed to the foot of the bed. Scattered by an oak bureau were a couple of pairs of jeans and T-shirts, along with more balled-up socks.

Through the closet door she spotted shelves with extra cop things, including another Kevlar vest and what Jake had called a "duty belt." A jacket with POLICE on the back of it hung next to a few shirts, a karate tunic and pants, and his police officer's dress uniform.

Honey-colored oak blinds were open, showing a drizzly San Francisco day. The good kind of drizzle. Familiar and real, not magical and terrible like Darkwolf's.

No more demons. No more dark god and goddess. No more warlock.

It all had a dreamlike quality to it. Well nightmare, really. Months after the Fomorii had first been called to this city, starting it all, it was finally over.

Cassia didn't have time to take in anymore of Jake's room or for thoughts of any kind, because he brought her around to face him and brought his mouth close to hers.

"I can't believe you did this for me," he murmured as he kissed the side of her mouth.

"You're awfully cocky." She smiled as he looked at her with raised eyebrows. "I did it for more selfish reasons. I did it for me." She placed her palms on his chest and gripped his soft blue T-shirt in her hands. "Because I can't imagine being without you."

"Princess, I intend to indulge your every whim." Jake moved his lips over hers, and she moaned with every soft brush. "So you just go on being as selfish as you want."

"I guess I'm not a Princess anymore," she said as he trailed his lips to her ear.

"You're still your mother's daughter." He nipped her earlobe. "But no matter what, you'll always be *my* Princess."

Cassia moved her lips to find his. The feelings bound so tightly within her for him started to unravel and flow from her body to his, so that she felt as if they were one.

The hard ridge of his erection pressed against her and she realized how wet she was, anticipating having him inside her. How she loved it when they were joined so intimately.

There were no words in all the Otherworlds that could describe his taste. Warmth and male. And Jake's scent—there was nothing like it.

His firm lips moved across hers and he dipped his tongue into her mouth, gently exploring her as she explored him. She understood the expression "never able to get enough." She felt that way with Jake. Like she could kiss him forever and ever.

He brought his large hands to her breasts, his big palms covering them as her nipples grew harder. She made soft little moans as she explored the expanse of his chest to his broad shoulders. She skimmed her fingers over the hard curves of his biceps, which flexed as he cupped her breasts that were covered only by her T-shirt.

Jake pinched her nipples and tugged at them. She made little cries into his mouth and he gave a soft laugh that tickled her lips.

"I like the way you sound," he said in between kisses. "Innocent and passionate."

"One can sound innocent?" Cassia asked as he tugged her shirt out of her jeans.

"You do." He skimmed his fingers up her rib cage to rest his hands beneath her breasts, then flicked his thumbs over her nipples. She laced her fingers together behind his neck and tipped her head back as she let out another low moan. "And I really love the way you don't wear anything beneath your clothing."

"All the better to seduce you with," she said as she looked into his eyes.

"Princess, all you have to do is be in the same room with me and I want you."

"That's a sentiment I can definitely echo." She raised her arms to help him draw her T-shirt up and over her head.

He tossed it aside and groaned as he looked down at her bare breasts. "Damn," was all he said before he bent down and slowly licked one of her nipples.

Cassia had never felt anything more exquisite. Without her magic, she was experiencing his touch in an entirely different way.

She fell into the sensations of Jake taking his time licking and sucking her nipples, and she brought her hands to his waistband. After she jerked his T-shirt out of the way, she slipped her fingers in between his jeans and his taut abs and immediately reached his erection.

THE WAY CASSIA WRAPPED HER FINGERS around his cock sent searing desire through Jake. His breath stuck in his chest and he was unable to move, despite the fact that he wanted to sink to his knees. He let out a low groan.

Cassia stroked his erection and her fingers found the drop of wetness. She rubbed the semen around the head of his erection in a slow, erotic torture.

He captured her mouth again and moved his hips so that his cock slid back and forth in her grasp. When she withdrew her hand he almost groaned again, but she brought her fingers to the button of his jeans and he was more than glad when it came apart easily.

After she drew his zipper down, she hooked her fingers in the sides of his jeans and briefs and pushed them over his ass. She tugged his jeans a little farther. "Shoes. Off."

"Yes, your majesty," he said with a grin as he kicked them off.

Cassia playfully slapped his arm. "We've got to work on something with you."

"What's that?" he said, feeling out of breath as she knelt in front of his erection.

She snapped the edge of his briefs. "*You* need to get used to going without these things."

"Your wish is my command." His teasing response turned into a hiss of pleasure as she wrapped her fingers around his cock and slid her mouth over the head. "Oh, Christ."

He cupped her head with his hands while he pumped his hips, slipping his erection in and out of her mouth, in motion with her as she moved her mouth up and down his shaft. He'd never felt anything so good. Never.

The little moans she made brought him closer to climax.

He felt every sound vibrate through his cock to his balls, which were drawing up tight to his body.

"Can I come in your mouth again, Princess?" he asked in a harsh voice as he looked down at her and watched his erection slide through her lips.

She looked up and smiled around his cock, but barely slowed in her movements.

He slipped his hands into her hair and he was actually shaking, his skin moist with sweat.

His balls were tight in one of her palms as he neared a total explosion. Cassia sucked a little harder while keeping her gaze on him.

"Jesus." He clenched his hands tighter in her hair as he thrust faster through her soft lips.

Her permission was all he needed because, a few moments after her smile, his orgasm rocketed through him like dynamite.

Semen shot from his cock into her mouth. It came in spurts that she swallowed, her mouth working around his cock, drawing out the intensity of his climax. She kept sucking as she swallowed until his cock softened and he had the presence of mind to release his hold on her hair.

He could barely breathe as his body stayed heated with sensation from his orgasm. When Cassia rose and pushed his T-shirt up and over his chest, he managed to help her tug it over his head and he flung it onto one of the nightstands.

A crash reminded him briefly of how she'd destroyed furnishings with her magic and he smiled.

She pointed to his socks. "Off."

"Damn, Cassia." He braced one hand on a bedpost as he removed his socks. His jeans went next. "After that, I barely have enough strength to move."

She kicked off her own shoes and shimmied out of her jeans. Dear God, she was beautiful. "It'll make it easier to tackle you," she said just before she placed her hands on his chest and shoved him away from her. She caught him off balance and his legs hit the bed.

She brought him down so that he was on the bed, flat on his back, the springs squeaking from how hard he'd dropped.

He laughed as she climbed onto him so that she was straddling him. But his laugh caught in his throat as her naked, wet folds brushed his chest.

"Told you I'd take you down." She leaned down and kissed him. "Don't mess with this former Princess."

He caught her lower lip in his teeth before releasing it and held her head in his palms. "I told you that you'll always be a Princess to me."

"If you insist." She nipped his lower lip in return. "Of course, that means I'll expect ceremonies and a handmaiden."

His heart thumped as he moved his hands from her face, skimming her arms and waist until his palms reached her buttocks. "I'll have to ask for a raise. I don't think a handmaiden is in the budget."

Cassia scooted down until her folds were over his cock. "I guess I'll have to make do." She rose up so that he could nudge her entrance with the head of his cock. "All this great sex would make it hard to find time for ceremonies, anyway. And if I'm not wearing clothes most of the time, there's no need for a handmaiden."

Talk about a perfect woman. Jake groaned as she slid slowly down his length.

Cassia gasped as his thick erection entered her core. Why did it surprise her every time just how long and big his cock was? It matched the rest of him. Like Silver had always said, Jake was built like a linebacker, and Cassia knew he had the equipment to go along with it.

With a gasp she lowered herself so that he was fully inside her. Everything fled her mind. She had a hard time even focusing, much less thinking.

She rode him, rising up and down in slow strokes, wanting to enjoy the experience for all she could. He palmed her breasts and pinched her nipples. She tilted her head back in sheer ecstasy at the combined sensations of his touch and his cock so deep inside of her.

Her climax was building, growing. She needed more of him, now.

Just as she picked up her pace, Jake grabbed her by the waist and stilled her. Cassia thought her eyes might be as wild as she felt, because if he didn't let her come soon she was going to kill him.

"Hey." He looked as pained as she felt, but concerned at the same time. "I know when you were a Guardian you could choose if you wanted to get pregnant. But now . . ."

The thought of raising a child or children with Jake warmed her from head to toe. "If I can have your baby," she said as she looked at him, "I want to."

A huge smile spread across his face. "Yeah, I'd like that, too."

Jake rolled her onto her back, suddenly fierce and intent.

He kissed her hard as he thrust in and out of her. The sounds rising in her throat became louder and her breathing heavier.

So close, so close—

And then she was there.

Spasms gripped her body, and heat and tingles spread throughout her and she moaned loud and long. Her orgasm was so intense and wonderful.

Jake followed her and she felt his semen pump inside her as his cock pulsed while her core throbbed.

A sensation of weightlessness took over Cassia's body. She scooted into the crook of his arm as he rolled to his side and brought her close to him.

She sighed as they snuggled together, feeling more happy and more content than she had ever felt in her very long life.

CHAPTER FIFTY-TWO

IT SURPRISED CASSIA AT HOW CALM she was throughout the ceremony. The monumental moment had come and she was ready, so ready.

Cassia faced Jake on the landing of the sweeping staircase of the marble rotunda in beautiful San Francisco City Hall. Now that she would be living with Jake in her adopted city, they had decided on a simple ceremony by a Justice of the Peace.

Jake looked sexy and handsome in his official police dress uniform. His muscular form filled out his shirt and pants so well they hugged every hard inch of him. His gorgeous blue eyes never strayed from hers and sent butterflies racing through her belly.

Cassia wore a backless turquoise dress, and Kellyn had woven blue-green diamonds in her hair again. The dress reached just above Cassia's knees.

Kellyn had been allowed to transfer through the veil from the City of the Light Elves to be Cassia's maid of honor. Kellyn had been Cassia's best friend over the centuries, other than Kael, and Cassia hadn't wanted to choose from among the five remaining gray magic D'Anu witches. She loved each of them too much to select just one.

Kael rested on his haunches on the other side of Kellyn, and Cassia sensed that he was pleased for her.

David Bourne stood at Jake's side as his best man, looking incredibly handsome in his Marine dress uniform. He had a thick scar from a deep cut on his forehead, thanks to one of the Stormcutters in the final battle. A D'Anu witch had treated it, so it had almost completely healed.

Perfume of roses, lilies, and orchids scented the air from

all of the vases filled with bouquets their friends had surrounded them with. The air was cool and not stifling in the gorgeous open rotunda.

Before they had walked into City Hall, glittering San Francisco lights relieved the darkness. Somehow that had been comforting, knowing that the world would gradually return to normal. The officials had consented to allowing the ceremony in City Hall at night, and a few Drow were able to attend, including the King. Inside, the lighting spilled over everything in a soft, warm, golden glow

Jake and Cassia had joined hands and held onto each other tightly as they exchanged vows.

And now . . .

After promising their hearts and souls to each other, the Justice of the Peace pronounced them "spouses for life."

Jake grinned and claimed Cassia in his embrace before taking her mouth in a fierce, loving kiss. Applause broke out, along with excited chatter, but Cassia enjoyed the kiss far too much to pay attention.

When she didn't think she could breathe any longer, Jake raised his head, only to take her mouth hard again, as if he couldn't get enough of her. Love and need for Jake filled her heart and soul like warm honey. It replaced every bit of the emptiness that had been inside her since the moment her magic had been taken.

Eventually Jake seemed willing to part long enough to let their friends congratulate them. After Kellyn gave Cassia her tearful well-wishes, Cassia was immediately swallowed by groups of their friends and drawn away from Jake. He was tall enough that she saw his dark head over the crowd, but no one gave her a chance to miss his closeness.

PSF Officers Marsten and Hopper were the first to get to Cassia. She knew Jake missed his friends, Lieutenants Fredrickson and Landers, along with the other officers who had died during the many battles over the past weeks and months. Cassia's heart ached for every loss of life.

David Bourne gave Cassia such a crushing hug that she lost her breath. "Welcome to being a Marine wife."

"Jake's not a Marine anymore," Cassia said with a smile as she tipped her head back.

"Bull sure is." He winked. "Once a Marine, always a Marine," he said, before letting a few more of Jake's old Marine buddies shake her hand and congratulate her and "Bull" on their marriage.

Bull? Cassia thought, a little bewildered. Interesting. She'd have to ask Jake about that one.

They'd only invited twenty-six people to their small ceremony, but it seemed like a hundred, as crazy as everything had gone since she and Jake were officially joined. Every well-wisher had to raise his or her voice to be heard over the excited din.

Part of Cassia wished they could also have an Elvin ceremony in Otherworld, but still she was content, and happy to be with Jake any way she could.

Cassia's smile broadened when Daire stepped forward with Kat DeLuca close beside him. Like Kellyn, Daire had arranged his hair so that his pointed ears didn't peek through.

Daire hugged her and pressed his lips to her cheek before drawing away. "I am happy for you, Princess Cassiandra." He gave a formal bow and rose with a smile.

"Cassia." Her cheeks heated a little. "No more of this Princess stuff."

Kat hugged Cassia, her exotic scent matching her dark beauty. "Jake's a great guy." She separated herself from Cassia and took Daire's hand. "A real keeper." She looked up at Daire, who met her gaze. "Almost as much as the one I found."

"Are you two . . . ?" Cassia let her question drift away.

"Yes." Daire gave Kat such a look of love that it made more joy rise in Cassia's heart. "The Great Guardian has consented to let us travel through the veil to live part of the time in Otherworld, and the other part here in San Francisco."

Cassia smiled for them, even when she felt a sense of loss for herself at not being given the same gift. She could cross occasionally, but had to have someone who was at least part Elvin help her.

"I'm very, very pleased for you," she said, and meant it.

Daire kissed her cheek again, and Kat gave a regal nod of her head before they moved away.

"Finally!" Silver caught Cassia by the hand and dragged her to where the other D'Anu witches stood with their husbands. "We've been waiting forever to get you away from that mob."

Silver's snake bracelet gleamed in the soft lighting, and her silvery-blond hair flowed around her shoulders. Cassia was pleased to see her friend wearing a short, thigh-high skirt, silk blouse, and three-inch heels, just like she had before the madness began. Another touch of normality. Only Silver had apparently obtained a size bigger than normal for her to accommodate her growing belly from her pregnancy.

Cassia hugged Silver tight, breathing in her sweet scent of lilies and enjoying her friend's comforting embrace.

When they parted, Cassia glanced up at Silver's D'Danann husband, Hawk. "You two are going back to live in Otherworld, yes?"

"Pretty much." Silver looked up at her husband. "Hawk's been away from his daughter far too long, and he misses her so much," Silver said as she returned her gaze to Cassia. "I don't blame him for never wanting to leave Shayla again for such a lengthy time." She squeezed Cassia's fingers. "But I am coming whenever I can to help the Covens rebuild."

"I'm so, so glad." Cassia couldn't help her broad smile. "And we'll get to see the baby in just months."

Silver rested her palm on the small pooch. "You'll all have to come to Otherworld as soon as he's here."

"I'll be there faster than you can blink." Her smile turned wry.

Hawk grinned with fierce pride. Cassia gave him a quick hug. If it wasn't for Hawk breaking D'Danann rules, and Silver breaking D'Anu rules, San Francisco would have been overtaken long ago. He was also the first one to suspect Cassia of being *other*, and that she wasn't merely a D'Anu witch.

"I'll miss being around you both when you're away," Cassia said to him.

With a slight nod, Hawk said, "As we shall miss you."

The corner of his mouth curved even more. "And I shall miss your chocolate chip cookies."

Cassia had to laugh at that. "I promise to bring a batch when the baby is born. A *huge* batch."

Jake came up behind Cassia and she had that warm, delicious feeling she got whenever he was with her.

After Jake shook hands with Hawk and Silver, Cassia embraced Copper next. The witch was wearing one of her short skirts with her thigh-high boots. Another return to normality.

"Otherworld for the two of you?" Cassia asked Copper after she had also hugged Copper's mate, Tiernan of the D'Danann.

"Are you kidding?" Copper's laugh echoed in the hall. She glanced up at Tiernan with an impish expression. "I'll be around. It'll take some juggling, but I don't intend to leave the Coven high and dry. But we have to get our men more used to Earth clothing. They stick out like giant sore thumbs here."

Tiernan shook his head. "Human jeans and T-shirts are most confining."

"Isn't that the truth," Jake said in a wry tone as he looked down at Cassia, "in certain situations where I wish they'd have a little give."

Tiernan laughed and heat rose in Cassia's cheeks yet again.

"It'll be so good for all of us to be together and rebuild." Copper's mouth quirked as she looked at Hannah, who was having a civil conversation with Rhiannon. "Never thought those two would *ever* see eye to eye."

Now they had something in common—Rhiannon's father was the Drow King, and Hannah had married him—they were actually talking. Frequently, even.

After another quick hug with Copper, Cassia found herself engulfed in Sydney's embrace. Sydney usually wore fitted suits, but today she had on an elegant purple dress that brought out the lavender of her eyes.

"You've been our glue," Sydney said, and tears glistened at the corners of her eyes behind her chic glasses. "You've held us together and guided us through the worst of times."

"We were equals and always will be." Cassia took Sydney's hands in hers. "We couldn't have done any of it without each other."

Cassia didn't know Conlan, Sydney's D'Danann husband, very well, but Cassia had instantly liked the green-eyed blond man with the playboy smile when she first met him.

"We're taking a couple of weeks in Otherworld, and then we'll be back," Sydney said. "Can't get rid of us."

"You don't know how happy this makes me." Strong feelings rose up in Cassia, making her feel almost as giddy and light-headed as she felt now that she was married to Jake.

After Jake shook hands with Conlan, Cassia found herself in front of Rhiannon, whose chin-length auburn hair had swung forward and covered the Fomorii scars Junga had given her. Rhiannon wore a vivid fuchsia shirt with a lemon yellow skirt and high-heeled fuchsia sandals, brilliant colors like she had always worn and surrounded herself with "before."

Cassia and Rhiannon studied each other for a moment. Their relationship had always been a bit strained, but when Rhiannon had learned of Cassia's involvement with her upbringing—after Rhiannon's mother was killed in an accident—she had been a little stiffer in Cassia's presence.

"I understand now," Rhiannon said, her voice softer than normal. "I wanted you to know that."

Cassia fought back tears. Even though Rhiannon hadn't had any idea about it, Cassia had watched over Rhiannon from a distance from the time she was an infant. Cassia's choice to not tell Rhiannon of her Drow King father had been a difficult one, but Rhiannon had been and still was a child of the light, like her human mother had been. If Rhiannon had been raised underground with the Drow, her life would have been far more difficult than she would probably ever realize.

"Thank you for understanding," Cassia said.

Even though Rhiannon wasn't a huggy-type person, she gave Cassia a fierce embrace. "There's nothing to thank me for." She pulled back and smiled. "Whenever we cross into San Francisco, you have to *promise* to make loads of your cinnamon rolls."

"All of your cooking," added the gruff warrior, Rhiannon's husband Keir. "The Cauldron of Dagda has never produced anything so fine as your creations. Especially your sweets."

"Every now and then I'll be sure to take packages of scones and several cakes and cinnamon rolls through the veil to you," Cassia said with a grin as Keir squeezed her hands in his version of affection.

Lastly, Cassia stood in front of the sophisticated Hannah Wentworth, who had built a multimillion-dollar software corporation from the ground up. Now she was married to a King. Being a Queen suited Hannah.

If Cassia wasn't mistaken, Hannah was wearing a pair of her Jimmy Choo black sandals, with three-inch heels and straps that wrapped around her ankles. The shoes were fabulous with her black Versace sheathe dress. Hannah's gold armband gleamed in the hall's lights. Hannah had always dressed to slay, and by the look in her husband, Garran's, eyes, she had him on his knees.

"What are your plans?" Cassia asked Hannah, having a hard time believing she'd consider living totally underground, and give up her social and business life, to be solely a Drow Queen.

Hannah glanced up at Garran and confirmed it when she said, "We had already agreed to live between worlds. He needs to be in the Drow realm most of the time, and I'll join him at night. But weekdays I have a company to rebuild and run."

"Then I'll see you now and again?" Cassia said.

"Of course. I'll be here to help the Coven when I can." Hannah smiled and brushed her thick blond lock against the darkness of the rest of her hair. Hannah had never been much for hugs, either, but she gave Cassia a quick embrace. "When you and Jake get back from your honeymoon, I'll expect someone to arrange a time for all of us to get together."

"Honeymoon?" Cassia said, and looked up at Jake.

Before he could answer, Alaia of the Mystwalkers appeared, as if she had risen from the mist to stand beside them. Behind her stood Breacán, and she noticed Jake giving him a wary look.

Alaia wore a floor-length gown of dove gray, so beautiful and soft that it looked as insubstantial as mist. Her dark hair was braided as usual, a thin braid banded with gold to either side of her face, and a long braid down her back.

Her green eyes were a vivid contrast to her unusually dark hair. "I come to give you most sincere wishes for a future of joy and happiness." Alaia smiled. "And to tell you your mother wishes she could join you, but as you know, she cannot."

Pleasant warmth swept through Cassia that her mother had sent such a special message. Of course the Great Guardian couldn't leave Otherworld, but the fact that she *wanted* to meant so much to Cassia that her heart lifted even more.

"Tell Mother I love her," Cassia said softly.

"I will." Alaia cocked her head to the side. "She said she sends you two gifts for your joining."

Cassia looked at Alaia in surprise. "What are they?"

Alaia shrugged. "She would not say what they are."

What could the Great Guardian have sent? Cassia glanced around but saw nothing unusual.

Cassia kissed both of Alaia's cheeks. Alaia as always smelled pure, like the unusual scent of lyria blossoms that reminded Cassia of orchids, roses, and carnations. "Thank you for coming, Alaia. Jake and I both are pleased to have you here."

Alaia bowed, and Cassia did the same. To Cassia's surprise, Jake bowed, too.

"I will leave you now to enjoy your festivities." Alaia and Breacán vanished into the crowd before Cassia had the opportunity to ask them to stay.

She looked up at Jake as she remembered what Bourne and the other Marines had called Jake. "So why do those guys refer to you as Bull?"

One corner of his mouth quirked. "For some reason Bourne thought I was bullheaded when we were in training together, and the nick stuck."

"*You*, bullheaded?" Cassia held back an unladylike snort as she laughed. "Wonder where he got that idea?"

Jake grinned and kissed her hard before she gently pushed him away.

"Next question," Cassia said, her mouth still moist from his kiss. "What's this about a honeymoon?"

He brushed the top of her head with his lips. "I thought we could use a little break before we start helping San Francisco rebuild. I'm hoping New Zealand is one place you haven't been in all of your travels."

Cassia smiled and wrapped her arms around his neck. "Perfect! It's always sounded so beautiful, and I've never had a chance to go there."

"I've already booked a hang gliding expedition and a helicopter ride over the mountains," he said. "We're going to satisfy your thrill-seeking heart."

Cassia laughed and kissed him. "I'm so ready."

"Bungee jumping, too?" he added with a cocked eyebrow and a broader smile.

Cassia pursed her lips. "I'll have to get back to you on that one."

Jake didn't seem to be able to stop grinning, and neither could she. "Two weeks I'll have you all to myself." He took her by her arms and brought her around to face him. "Just you, me, sunshine, sand, a few thrills, and an extraordinarily nice hotel room." He glanced down at Kael, who happened to be nearby. "Sorry bud."

"Humph," Kael said in Cassia's mind, but she could tell he was teasing. *"Enjoy your human, Cassiandra."*

"I am," she said out loud, and smiled at Jake as she added, "very much in love with you, Jake Macgregor."

"Always, Princess." Jake caught Cassia's mouth in a sweet, wonderful kiss.

She closed her eyes, reveling in the kiss. The soft touch of his tongue, the firmness of his lips. So much happiness whirled through and poured out of Cassia's heart and soul that she was nearly overwhelmed with it.

The sensations were so incredible she thought she saw gold sparks through her closed eyelids.

That, of course, was impossible.

For a second, it felt like something brushed Cassia's mind, and tingles filled her from head to toe.

Jake groaned. Her whole body throbbed with such need for him that she held onto him tighter and pressed her belly against his erection. A moan rose up in her throat. She needed him inside her now—

A series of sharp cracks echoed throughout the rotunda as one flower vase after another shattered.

Jake and Cassia paused in their kiss and she met his gaze, her eyes wide and his surprised.

The skin around her navel burned and tingled.

Her star birthmark had been returned to her. She knew it without even having to look. Excitement sent a thrill tingling throughout her body. Was that her mother's second gift?

And the exploding vases . . .

A soft voice within told her to close her eyes. As soon as Cassia did, a vision of the Great Guardian flowed into her mind like sunshine glistening on a crystal-clear pond.

"My darling Cassiandra . . . I have been able to 'pull some strings,' as your human—as Jake—would say." Her mother's smile was radiant, and it sent warmth through Cassia as the Guardian used Jake's name for the first time. "You are a full D'Anu witch now, my wonderful daughter. I cannot return to you your Guardian powers, but you have the magic of the D'Anu, the magic you have known and used your entire life. You are whole once again."

Joy rose inside Cassia as the vision of her mother faded. The happiness bubbled up as her soul swelled with D'Anu magic. And it swelled even more with love for Jake, and for every other person she had been gifted to know in her long life.

Cassia opened her eyes and tilted her head back. "Thank you, Mother," she whispered to the domed ceiling before she kissed Jake again.

CHAPTER FIFTY-THREE

WARMTH BRUSHED KEVIN'S SKIN as he stirred from the nightmare.

Talk about fucking intense.

He scrubbed his hand over his face and opened his eyes. He had to blink several times because sunshine hit him like a spotlight.

The light started to fade and he found himself staring up at a gap in soft gray clouds where the sun had shone so brightly. Within a breath, the gap closed and all of the sky was gray.

Cool breezes brushed his skin and goose bumps rose on his arms. Sounds, like the push and pull of the sea, rushed in his ears. The things poking his back must be rocks and pebbles.

He frowned. What was he doing outside? Where was he? How long had he been here?

As he pushed himself to a sitting position, he felt hard, water-smoothed stones beneath his palms. Several feet from him, waves rolled in against a rocky shore where bowling-ball-and football-sized rocks lay scattered with strips of sand anchoring them in place. When a wave hit one of the enormous boulders near the shoreline, the water shot up and glittered like hundreds of crystals in the sky.

Or like sparks of magic.

Images started rushing through his mind. They came so fast, so hard, so painfully that he gripped his head in both hands and fought back a shout.

He clenched his eyes shut, praying the barrage would stop. One thing after another hit him—

Like memories.

Blood sacrifices, demons, a flame-haired goddess, a one-eyed god—

A glowing red stone eye.

His entire body went still and, for a moment, all he could see was that eye.

Glowing redder and redder, brighter and brighter, until his head wanted to explode.

His chest heated over his heart.

Everything clinked together, like rune stones spilling onto a wooden tabletop.

Darkwolf.

His name wasn't Kevin anymore. He was Darkwolf.

The memories swept over him, and he opened his eyes and held his hand to his heart. Yes, his flesh felt warm. Balor's eye still resided in his chest.

The last thing he remembered was the Elvin witch, Cassia, capturing him with her magic—

Then nothing.

For a moment he rested his arms on his bent knees, stared out at his surroundings, and tried to control his heart rate and his breathing. It was cool here near the rocky shore where the sea surged and drew away. Surged and drew away.

Familiar—he'd been here before. But it wasn't San Francisco.

He rubbed his palms on his jeans, then realized where he was.

She'd sent him to hell.

The bitch.

A humorless laugh rolled out of Darkwolf. The Elvin witch had sent him to the same shore in Ireland where he'd found Balor's eye.

Or at least a damned good imitation of the place. The coast along Dingle Peninsula near Cathair Con Rí. The breeze even carried the same scents he remembered—the clean, light, salty ocean air mixed with sea-battered stone.

No telling what date in time she'd sent him to, or if he was anywhere that actually existed on Earth.

Hell, he could be in a white padded cell after his sanity had gone bye-bye.

Then every other thought left his mind and pain squeezed his chest as his memories turned to Elizabeth.

His eyes burned and the pain in his chest became so bad that he began to wonder if life was even worth living with Elizabeth gone.

He didn't care who or what she had been to anyone else. What mattered was who she was to him. With him.

Darkwolf stared out at the gray sea and the lines of low-hanging gray clouds. The hurt he felt so deep inside from her loss would never leave him.

Nor would the memories of all the things he had done since finding Balor's eye.

He held one of his palms over his stone heart again, remembering the time Elizabeth had shown him how vulnerable he could be. But even then, he'd had no idea how much more vulnerable it was possible to become.

Until he'd lost her.

A voice came as soft and as distant as the low-hanging mist off the shores of Ireland. "Darkwolf," the voice whispered.

He froze, frantic tingles running up and down his spine. "Elizabeth?"

Epilogue

Six years later

WARMTH SIZZLED THROUGH CASSIA as she looked at Jake over the dark-haired five-year-old Ryan, and she grinned. Their son bounced up and down in his seat. Popcorn would have been flying out of the bag in his lap if Cassia wasn't using her magic to keep every kernel where it belonged.

"Yay, Giants!" Ryan yelled at the top of his lungs as the San Francisco Giants scored another run.

As he leaned closer to Ryan's ear, Jake pointed to the next player up to bat. "One more home run and Mike Jones will break the record for the most home runs in San Francisco Giants history."

"Yay, Mike!" Ryan shouted, and bounced up and down even more. This time Cassia barely saved her son's soda with her magic.

Ryan's name meant "little king" in Gaelic, and Cassia was beginning to think he was living up to that label.

Like his father, even at five, Ryan was a diehard Giants fan. He'd also inherited his dad's gorgeous blue eyes and dark hair.

Recently it had become apparent the five-year-old had inherited at least some of his mother's talents.

They now had to keep an extra eye on their son because he'd been showing some odd tendencies. Such as the cat often jumping about ten feet in the air when Ryan was playing with her—as if the cat been zapped with a small bolt of magic. And sometimes he'd twirl his finger in the air when he would make himself a glass of chocolate milk, and the spoon would mix the drink without him touching it.

Kael could speak to Ryan in his thoughts, just as he did

with Cassia. Something only one with strong magic could do, Kael maintained.

Ryan would also "disappear" for awhile, making Jake frantic with worry if Cassia wasn't in the house. When she was home, Cassia could easily see through her son's glamour.

And Jake swore he could "smell" what he thought of as the scent of magic around Ryan. The same as other magical beings Jake had been around.

Their son might or might not grow up to be a practicing D'Anu witch, but whatever the case, Cassia intended to make sure he didn't get his little self into trouble.

Smells of buttery popcorn, hotdogs, and the sweet scent of cotton candy circulated throughout the huge stadium. Fans cheering and the shouts of vendors hawking food and drinks kept up a steady rumble.

It had been six years, and Cassia no longer got a chill when she looked at the pitcher's mound and remembered when the dark goddess took the lives of thousands in the stadium.

As always throughout the centuries, Cassia's memory remained perfect, but sometimes she wished she didn't have full recall of Darkwolf and his Stormcutters when they'd invaded the park.

She glanced at Jake, who was so incredibly virile and handsome he made her heart thrum every time she looked at him. He'd stopped crying out in his sleep, his nightmares of losing his Special Ops team to dark magic having left him when the battle with Darkwolf had ended.

Jake had talked with her about what happened in Afghanistan, and she knew it was still painful to him. But some of the blame he had placed on himself had faded and he accepted the fact that there was nothing he could have done to stop it all from happening.

The crowd bellowed so loud all of a sudden that Cassia winced.

"Mommy, Mommy, Mommy!" Ryan tugged her arm and she focused solely on her son. "Did you see it? Mike Jones

broke the home run record." His blue eyes sparkled with excitement as he looked up at her. "Daddy says I just witnessed
a piece of his-story." He frowned. "What's his-story?"

Jake laughed, but Cassia managed to maintain a serious
expression. "Ask your dad."

When Ryan turned to Jake, he swallowed his laughter and
winked at Cassia before explaining the definition of history
to their son.

Cassia, Jake, and the entire Alliance had been a huge part
of San Francisco's history. Thankfully those horrible, horrible events were fading from people's minds. It was like what
had happened was a distant dream, a nightmare that was too
bizarre to believe had really happened.

As she'd always known they would, San Francisco's residents had picked up the pieces of their own lives as well as
helping others. It had taken a few years of rebuilding, but the
city was now as beautiful as it had been "before."

Although several reminders of the "war" still existed.
Like all of the trees in Crissy Field that had uprooted themselves and moved from the east end of the field to the west,
where they had replanted themselves. No one had been able
to figure that one out.

Cassia and the rest of the D'Anu witches hadn't been inclined to enlighten anyone by explaining that Dryads had
crossed over from Otherworld and used the trees to battle
the Stormcutters. Not that anyone would begin to believe
them, anyway.

Ryan held onto his baseball mitt as he stood. He clapped
with the mitt on his hand while Mike Jones received a standing ovation for his record-breaking home run.

After the game, Cassia and her small family were meeting Silver, Hawk, Copper, and Tiernan at the new ice cream
parlor on the Embarcadero. The parlor was not too far from
the warehouse that was once the Alliance HQ.

What seemed like a lifetime ago. Thank the goddess.

Silver and Hawk were bringing Hawk's eleven-year-old
daughter Shayla and their almost six-year-old son Duncan.
Copper and Tiernan had twin sons, Keegan and Lachlan.

Hannah and Garran, and Sydney and Conlan, didn't have kids—yet. Hannah had never believed she would have children, but she'd been reconsidering it since her marriage to Garran. Over the years she'd grown a little softer, her hard edges rounding a bit.

Rhiannon was pregnant with her first child, and Cassia had never seen Rhiannon's big, gruff, warrior husband so proud. He was even more protective of his wife than Cassia had thought possible.

Ryan let out a loud whooping noise, and this time his soda splattered on the concrete and on Cassia's jeans because her thoughts had strayed. When she was certain no one to either side of them was looking, she used her magic to clean the mess on the concrete and her jeans.

The D'Anu Covens had, thankfully, healed over the past six years, too. Janis Arrowsmith's white magic Coven and the rest of the original D'Anu Covens across the nation, and even the world, were functioning like they always had.

Now when they sought new apprentices, the D'Anu focused on training and bonding to prevent another "Kevin" or "Darkwolf" situation. They couldn't allow the schism between white and gray magic, and the blindness that allowed Kevin to become Darkwolf in the first place.

Darkwolf . . . Sometimes Cassia wondered how he fared, and she felt a little sorry for him, too. She sincerely hoped he had found a better life despite the fact she'd sent him to Ireland, almost four thousand years in the past. It was a time before the rise and fall of all the old gods and goddesses, including Balor and Ceithlenn.

Darkwolf—or Kevin—would have been forced to design a whole new life during a period in time when he wouldn't have the technology or the power to do what he'd done here in this place and time.

Being a duo-god, Darkwolf would likely live forever. It would no doubt be a real bitch to fight any number of the old gods and goddesses once they came into power.

"We won!" Ryan shouted over the cheers in the stadium as

he grabbed Cassia's arm and she jumped back to the moment. She looked at him and smiled, then noticed his popcorn was all over the place. "The Giants kicked butt, Mommy."

Cassia widened her eyes and looked at Jake, who winced and mouthed, "Sorry."

She held back a laugh, and stood with her husband and son and the thousands of fans who now began flowing out of the stadium.

As she was jostled while she walked at Jake's side and Ryan rode on his father's shoulders, Cassia gave one last thought to Janis and the part she'd played when they first tried to defeat the dark goddess.

All of the world's white magic Covens had given grudging acknowledgment of the gray magic Covens as a separate but equal, and equally desirable, group and path. It was an option for half-Elvin witches across this Otherworld, as well as D'Anu witches who wanted to follow the gray magic path.

The gray magic Covens practiced between all of the Otherworlds, as life and need called them to do. Gray witches were happy to train others like them, those called to the gray.

If any threat as horrible as what they'd been through with Balor, Ceithlenn, the demons, and Darkwolf ever arose again, there *would* be strength to meet it.

In the meantime, gray magic witches did what they could to aid the Paranormal Special Forces in any number of paranormal situations that arose.

Thankfully, those had been relatively small situations that required little from the witches.

As for herself, Cassia figured she had all she needed, and all she would ever need, to be happy and fulfilled and whole. She thought about her Coven, the original gray witches of this world, and all the new apprentices in training.

Victory. Duty. Purpose. Hope.

She had all of that, yes, and two worlds to call home, and a good relationship with her ever-enigmatic mother.

Most importantly, though, she had herself, her true self, and she had her true love.

Cassia reached up and squeezed her son's hand as he rode on Jake's shoulders, and gave her husband and son each a smile.

A witch couldn't get any luckier than this.

AUTHOR NOTE

Dear fellow miscreants,

We've reached the end of one exhilarating journey, and we're now at the beginning of new, thrilling, and provocative adventures.

I've enjoyed traveling with you to San Francisco along with the D'Anu, D'Danann, and the rest of the "Magic" world. It's been a wicked, fascinating trip.

Now I'm charged-up to guide you onto unknown roads with three exciting, deviously new series.

Hot, tempting, and dangerous, *Zack* leads the blood-pounding, seductive "Armed and Dangerous" series in December 2008.

In early 2009, *The First Sin*—the beginning of a sexy new suspense series—will sweep you deep undercover with take-no-prisoners Lexi Steele. Special Agent Steele battles underworld crime in a covert NSA division: code-name RED. A division that officially doesn't exist. This explosive series pushes the boundaries, a thrill ride that will leave you breathless.

Also coming in 2009 is *Demons not Included,* the first book in an urban fantasy series. You wouldn't want to cross paths with Nyx, who's half-human and half-Drow. Nyx solves one paranormal crime after another and she's going to make sure every bad thing that goes bump in the night goes down.

Together we'll blast into the New Year and conquer what's at the end of every dark path on our way.

Deviously yours,

Cheyenne

FOR CHEYENNE'S READERS

Be sure to go to http://cheyennemccray.com to sign up for her PRIVATE book announcement list and get FREE EXCLUSIVE Cheyenne McCray goodies. Please feel free to e-mail her at chey@cheyennemccray.com. She would love to hear from you.

*Keep reading for a sneak peek at
Cheyenne McCray's next novel*

ZACK:
ARMED AND DANGEROUS

*Coming December 2008 in trade paperback
from St. Martin's Griffin*

Sky danced with Gary for another song, laughing and flirting with the man the entire time—just to distract herself from Zack's dominating presence. She wasn't very successful, since she could feel his gaze like a weight on her. And she knew he wasn't happy.

Sky cleared her throat as she looked up at Gary. "Any more information pop up about those rustlers?"

"Sorry, Skylar." Gary shrugged. "Unfortunately, we're nowhere near finding the bastards."

She gave a frustrated sigh. "I feel like I'm banging my head against a wall."

"You and me both," he said with a half smile.

The next thing she knew, Luke cut in and she found herself in the arms of her foreman. She looked up at him and he gave a sexy grin. "Hunter looks ready to pull me apart."

Sky shook her head. "The history between Zack and me is so ancient there's a foot-high layer of dust on top of it."

At that, Luke laughed. Sky caught Zack's eye as Luke turned her on the floor and she bit the inside of her cheek. Zack's scowl was positively thunderous. Where did he get off looking so possessively at her?

"Did you find anything?" Sky asked Luke as she glanced up at him.

Luke's expression changed, his smile fading. "Nothing more than what I told you earlier."

"That sucks."

"No kidding."

Tingles prickled Sky's arms as the song ended and Luke escorted her across the dance floor to Zack.

She'd barely had a chance to thank Luke for the dance when Zack took her by the elbow and propelled her from the edge of the other people dancing.

"This isn't part of the deal," she said when they reached a corner where they were somewhat alone and the music wasn't as loud.

Sheer possessiveness rolled off him. "We have a lot of catching up to do." He leaned one shoulder against the wall, boxing her into the corner, the look in his eyes showing only too clearly how worked up he was.

"What about your job? Your calls? You seem to be in demand." Sky tried to sound annoyed.

"I turned my phone off for now." Zack gave her a dark, sexy look that made her shiver. "Unavailable." He leaned close and murmured in her ear, "To anyone but you."

Sky swallowed as her stomach pitched as he drew back and she could see his eyes again. The wall felt cool to her bare back, and for a second she considered stomping her three-inch heel into his boot to get him to back off. But every sane thought fled her mind as she studied him.

Lord, he looks good.

Tremors rippled through her at Zack's nearness, and she wondered how she would begin to walk away from him when that one dance was over. Her body hummed as he stood close—not quite touching, yet not far enough away.

"How'd you end up running your dad's cattle ranch?" he asked, that smoky gaze fixed on her.

"I love ranching." Sky swallowed, wishing for a drink of water to soothe her dry throat. "I guess you could say it's in the blood." She flattened her palms against the wall behind her. "Your turn. Tell me what you've been up to."

"Had a nice spread in Texas, enjoyed my work as a fed, and did all right." Zack bent closer, invading her space. No, more like conquering it. "But I was lonely as hell."

She kept her tone light. "What? No friends?"

"I had friends." He reached up and traced the line of her jaw, his eyes intent. "But something was missing."

At the same moment, the lights dimmed and a slow tune started.

A shiver skittered through her as Zack trailed his finger down her neck. "How 'bout that dance now, Sky?"

Sky hesitated, then nodded. The sooner they got this over with, the better. She'd give Zack one dance and then get away from him before she jumped right into bed with the man.

His hand burned the bare skin at the small of her back as he guided her. He stopped at the edge of the dance floor on the fringe of the other couples, where it was darker.

As Zack brought her into his arms, her nipples tightened. He swept his gaze over her breasts and gave her a slow, sensual smile that caused her mouth to go even drier. His hands settled on her waist and he moved his hips against hers until she felt his erect cock through her thin dress, pressing against her own softness.

A thrill blossomed inside her abdomen despite herself. Damn. It felt so good to have him pressed up against her.

He bent his head next to hers, and Sky automatically moved her hands to his shoulders, letting her body sway with his in time to the music. After the way he'd left her all those years ago, she shouldn't feel so turned on, but was she ever.

"Remember the first time we made love?" he murmured in her ear, and she caught the scent of mint on his breath. She could imagine how good he'd taste and almost moaned at the thought.

Sky shivered at the feel of his mouth so close to her ear, and nearly melted when his lips brushed her earlobe.

"It was our hideaway." He pressed her closer along his solid length, all but making love to her on the dance floor. "It was a clear October day and we went horseback riding in the mountains with a picnic basket, a blanket, and a bottle of wine." His voice was raw, filled with desire. "The sun was shining, and it was still warm enough that you were wearing a pair of tight jeans with a T-shirt. No bra."

Her fingers tightened on his shoulders. God, yes, she remembered.

"I could even see your nipples through the shirt, it was so skimpy." Zack trailed one finger up Sky's bare spine and she shivered as he continued, "We went to our secluded spot, our own little hideaway, and it was like we were the only two people left in the world. Then you begged me to make love to you."

Sky pulled away and looked up at him with a frown. "I begged you?"

He brought her back into his arms. "Maybe we both did a little begging."

How Zack's kisses had unraveled her and how badly she had wanted him. *Needed him.* And it was true, she had begged him not to stop.

He had smiled, handling her so gently, as if he cherished every part of her. His mouth had teased her nipples, slowly working his way down to her folds. She couldn't believe he put his mouth on her clit, tasting her until she was writhing, and dying for him to be inside her.

Before he entered her, he had caressed her clit until he brought her to orgasm. And then he slid into her, taking her slow and easy. She'd cried out from the incredible pleasure rippling through her body once she got past the brief burst of pain as he took her virginity.

He had stopped, afraid he'd hurt her, but she had ordered him to keep driving into her, clenching his hips between her thighs. Harder and faster he moved within her, filling her, until he reached his own climax.

Zack's warm breath on her neck and his low voice brought her out of her memories. "I never thought I could want you more than I did that day. But every day after that, I couldn't get enough of you."

His hands moved from her waist, caressing her through the dress, down her hips, and back again to her waist, and she couldn't stop the shivers trailing along her spine.

His voice rumbled as he spoke close to her ear. "And somehow I want you now even more than I did then."

Damn the man. How could he do this to her?

Sudden anger flowed through her. "Hear me loud and clear, Zack," she said. "Nothing's going to happen between us. I agreed to be friends with you. Not fuck you."

Zack tried not to smile, but whether she realized it or not, her words were as effective as a dare. Like waving a red flag in front of a primed bull. Without a doubt, Zack knew she wanted him with the same fierceness he felt for her. Their one dance had already melded into a second, and if he had his way, he'd be dancing with her all night.

And then he'd get her home and in his bed.

Just the thought of what she was wearing under that scrap of a dress was enough to make him want to throw back his head and let loose a primal chest-beating howl, throw her over his shoulder, and take her home and bury himself inside of her.

When he'd arrived at the fairgrounds, Sky had pulled in and parked her Rover directly in the row in front of him. After a moment she'd slid out of her SUV and her tiny dress had climbed up her thighs to reveal garters holding up sheer stockings. Pure lust had bolted through him at the sight. All thoughts of work, smuggling, and rustlers blew away with the breeze.

Now she was in his arms, her scent of orange blossoms flowing over him, and it felt so completely right. He knew he'd been an idiot to leave her and he wasn't going to make that mistake a second time. And he'd be damned if he'd let her go any time tonight.

He lifted his head to look down at Sky, taking in her generous curves underneath that barely-there outfit. Through the netting at the top of her dress, Zack could see the mole above her left breast. He yearned to peel away the material and run his tongue over that beauty mark, and every inch of her body.

Sky's green eyes met his, challenging him. "Your one dance is over."

He wrapped a loose strand of hair around one of his fingers. "Dance with me all night."

"I—no." Her voice was firm as she shook her head, tugging at the strand.

He brought his lips to her hair, traveling along her temple and down to her ear. His voice was a rumbling growl and his words came out as a demand. "Dance with me."

Sky gasped as Zack nipped at her lobe, hard, and when he raised his head he saw her eyes had turned a deeper green with sensuality and her lips had parted. He needed to kiss those lips again.

His mouth neared hers. She lowered her lashes and tilted her head back. Her scent was warm and inviting, arousing him even more.

"Zack." Their lips came closer as she spoke in a husky whisper that made his cock grow harder. "I—"

He didn't let her finish whatever it was she was going to say.

Her soft lips were his to take, her mouth his to taste. His hunger for her was so strong, so deep, that he took control of her body by dragging her close and pressing her tight against his erection. He cupped the back of her head, holding her so that she couldn't draw away, even if she wanted to.

And by the way she was kissing him that was the last thing on her mind.

She returned his kiss with the fervor he remembered from long ago. Much too long ago. Her mouth, lips, and tongue were the sweetest, softest things he'd ever felt or tasted.

Her moans and desperate whimpers grew loud enough for him to hear over the music and his body grew hot with such incredible need that he knew if he didn't have her right now, he would die.

Coming soon...

New York Times bestselling author

CHEYENNE McCRAY

ignites a new, high-velocity series whose heroine
pushes danger—and desire—past the limits with

THE FIRST SIN
A Lexi Steele Novel

ISBN: 0-312-94644-9

Available in February 2009
from St. Martin's Paperbacks